Ivory Temptress

"You are so beautiful, Cathy," Jesse said huskily.

Trembling under his admiring gaze and the touch of his hand, Cathy felt a rush of pleasure at his words. Her hands shook slightly as she reached up to help undo the laces of her chemise, but Jesse stopped her.

"Let me."

Slowly, surely, Jesse untied the laces, pushing the soft material aside, holding back the urge to rush, to take her in his arms and crush her against him. It took all his resolve not to hurry what should be slow.

And then he stood there, silent, in deep appreciation of the beauty of Cathy's body, soft lamplight giving her exquisite form a pearly, ethereal glow . . .

Books in the **Americans Abroad** *Series*
from St. Martin's Press

CRYSTAL RAPTURE by Sarah Edwards
PASSION'S TEMPEST by Emma Harrington
DESERT ENCHANTRESS by Laurel Collins
SAPPHIRE MOON by Peggy Cross
PASSION'S SONG by Carolyn Jewel
IVORY TEMPTRESS by Emma Harrington

IVORY TEMPTRESS

EMMA HARRINGTON

ST. MARTIN'S PRESS / NEW YORK

IVORY TEMPTRESS

Copyright © 1988 by Virginia Brown and Jane Harrison.

ISBN: 0-312-91298-6   Can. ISBN: 0-312-91299-4

Printed in the United States of America

First St. Martin's Press mass market edition / December 1988

10 9 8 7 6 5 4 3 2 1

Chapter 1

A thousand candles sparkled in the ballroom the night Cathy Weston first saw him. She stood beneath the glittering brilliance of crystal chandeliers and flickering candles suspended above the ballroom floor, unaware that life was about to bestow upon her a great adventure.

In spite of the cool fall temperatures outside the sprawling mansion it was hot inside, and Cathy stepped over to a cooler spot near an open set of double doors leading onto the veranda. This was a charity ball to benefit those less-fortunate London souls, and the ballroom was packed with people she did know and people she didn't know. Even her elderly great-aunt and rather ebullient cousins had attended the affair, and she'd taken as early a leave from their company as possible. Cathy found her aunt and cousins entirely too energetic for her tastes. It was also the reason she had moved to a fashionable hotel four months before, with only her longtime companion, Miss Mooney.

Fanning herself lightly, she smiled as she listened to the famous woman who held hundreds enthralled as she spoke. It was Florence Nightingale, and she was speaking about her efforts to nurse wounded soldiers.

War. Talk of the Prussian War had dominated every social occasion since March. Queen Victoria had declared war with Russia—officially on March 28—and twenty-seven thousand men had been shipped to the Black Sea with weapons used by Wellington's soldiers two decades earlier. Britain hoped for France's cooperation, but despite the emphasis of unity in struggle, collaboration between the two countries was difficult. England was constantly trying to persuade France to lend support and send her troops.

Cathy edged closer to the doors, craning her neck to see over the hundreds of heads in front of her. She was fascinated by the cultured woman who spoke so eloquently about the needs of the wounded, and so did not see the two women nearby. But they saw her, and their conversation seized eagerly on the fresh ammunition now presented to them.

Lorgnettes on slender black ribbons lifted as the women perused the girl standing not far from them.

The taller, stout woman standing near a potted palm by the doors leaned over to ask her companion, "Do you know her name?" It was a rather difficult task for her fleshy frame to manage beneath the grim restriction of the whalebone hoops of her cage-crinoline, but she completed the gesture with only a small wheeze of effort. Pudgy, beringed fingers smoothed the olive brocade and guipure lace of the wide skirts spreading out in the shape of a pyramid, and she gave a satisfied sigh as her companion nodded.

"Yes. Her name is Weston . . . an American, I do believe," was the low, sharp reply.

An imperious smile that spread catlike over the broad face turned toward the American. "Ah, Miss Weston! I understand she always wears ivory lace—is this true, Amelia?"

"Oh, yes, quite true. And can you imagine? She is wearing that ivory silk without a crinoline tonight! Why, it's almost indecent the way it clings to her . . . her *limbs* in that fashion . . . and her hair—a most improper style, I'd say. All twisted in that long braid at her neck instead of caught up as it should be, but there you have it. She is, after all, an *American.*"

"Quite. I have heard the most delicious on–dits about her, you know, Amelia. They say she is quite daring in other aspects as well as her choice of costume. *I* heard that she almost accepted Lord Compton's proposal! Can you imagine such a thing? A peer of the realm offering for an *American?* And she *refused* him! Absolutely shocking, is what it is, refusing one of the most eligible gentlemen in all of polite society! And to be refused by a *merchant's daughter* must have been quite distressing for Compton. But I always did wonder if he was a bit sound in his judgment, you know."

There was a brief, rich pause as both women digested the perfidy of the English gentleman and the American girl. Then the taller matron observed, "Just look at the rapturous expression on her face as she listens to Miss Nightingale speak! *I* find all this talk about wounded men and war *most* upsetting, but there you have it. Young women today have no conception of the more genteel side of life, but must run about willy-nilly, pursuing such vile subjects instead of the more proper pursuit of a husband. Not that some of today's young women could attract a man, mind you. No, they are far too bold and masculine, instead of being proper and well mannered. I don't think I like the young women of today, Amelia, they know *nothing* about the art of being a female!"

"Perhaps not," Amelia agreed with a thoughtful gaze at the American, not far from them, "but I cannot help but think she is rather attractive for all of that. What do you think?"

"Striking," came a deep voice from behind them, startling the matrons into turning around to seek the source.

Nervous, deprecating smiles flickered briefly on their faces for a moment. The tall gentleman who had intruded upon their conversation was smiling, a bored, frosty smile that held more cynicism than humor.

"Mr. Lamont!" Amelia exclaimed softly, and was rewarded with a slight bow of acknowledgment.

"At your service, madam," Jesse Lamont said, but his attention had already shifted back to the young woman garbed in ivory silk and lace.

The two matrons exchanged significant glances as Jesse Lamont's gaze lingered upon the American; glances that said "I told you so." After all, her attire *would* attract attention, even if the wrong kind, it seemed!

And Jesse Lamont, if he had cared to guess their thoughts, would have most obligingly agreed. Cathy Weston's attire did, indeed, attract his attention. The off-the-shoulder bodice of her ivory silk gown dipped low, revealing a creamy expanse of skin that gleamed in the soft candlelight with a most appealing glow. It was a fitted gown that only a woman with a tiny waist could have worn, and the skirts fell in graceful folds to brush along the floor when she walked.

Lamont's smile deepened with genuine appreciation, softening the features of his face from their customary hardness. Miss Weston moved with unconscious grace instead of the more stilted, affected walk cultivated by the women he was accustomed to seeing. And instead of being round and petite—the current fashion—she was tall and slender. Her single concession to fashion was an exquisite porcelain complexion usually attributed only to English beauties. This was set off by the lustrous, rich color of her thick brown hair.

Privately confessing to being intrigued, Jesse Lamont took a step closer to observe this unusual woman who was moving through the ballroom. There was an air of innocent sensuality about her that he found most tempting—and contradictory. Dark eyes narrowed thoughtfully as he regarded her.

An ivory temptress . . . an American temptress by the name of Miss Weston . . .

Jesse gave a distracted nod to the two matrons who were attempting to draw him into further conversation, and moved away, drawn to the pale figure who was now standing quite near Miss Nightingale. His black eyes glittered with appreciation as they fastened on the American girl's delicate profile, and he was faintly surprised by his surge of anticipation.

Maybe she would turn around.

But she didn't. Cathy was far too absorbed in the fiery speech by Miss Florence Nightingale. Her thoughts lingered on England's war with Russia, and the thousands of wounded men who often died for lack of proper care. There was no adequate medical system for caring for the wounded. Sir Robert Peel was endeavoring to raise twenty-five thousand pounds for medicine, but there was little money for military chaplains or nurses. That was the purpose of this evening—Florence Nightingale was not only enlisting nurses, but was now recruiting funds for the journey. Cathy fervently longed to join those going to care for those poor wounded soldiers.

Miss Nightingale's speech was so stirring that Cathy did not notice Jesse Lamont, nor did she notice the woman forcing her way through the press of people in the ballroom. Fiery red hair shimmered beneath the flicker of candlelight as the strange woman pressed closer. Her green eyes glittered with fear and anxiety, and her body was as taut as a bowstring, tense with anger and forced courage. Those emerald eyes were fastened upon Jesse Lamont with bright intensity, seeing nothing and no one else in the entire room.

A spattering of applause that swelled to a thundering crescendo signaled the end of Miss Nightingale's speech, and the nurse turned to smile at Cathy Weston. She was obviously pleased with the results.

"You were marvelous . . . so moving," Cathy said impulsively, her hands outstretched.

"Thank you, my dear." Florence Nightingale took Cathy's hands in her own and gave them a slight squeeze. "Success?" she questioned with a teasing smile.

Laughing, Cathy quickly nodded. "Of course! It is most successful! How can you doubt it? These people love you—soon we shall all be off to Scutari."

Miss Nightingale gave Cathy a sharp, searching glance. *"We,* Cathy?"

"Yes—*we.* I have decided to join you."

Shaking her head, the older woman smiled gently. "Dear, dear Cathy. This is not your war. You've been in England only a little more than a year. I cannot expect you to go chasing off to Scutari. There is great danger, and much misery there."

Dropping her hands, Cathy clenched them into tight fists, bunching the gloves she wore into lacy wrinkles. What would it take for anyone to believe that she would not return to the United States—ever? There was nothing in New York for her, nothing. Hadn't she made that plain enough in the past year? England was her home now. Here in England she had found the incentive to make life worth living, to give her some purpose—nursing. Cathy passionately desired to devote her life to nursing and caring for others, just as Miss Nightingale did. Nursing made her feel needed and loved; it gave her a sense of self-esteem, which had always been lacking in her life prior to her arrival in England.

"I'm sorry, Cathy," Miss Nightingale said. "I can see that I've distressed you. I didn't mean to do so." She put her hands on Cathy's shoulders. "I know that you are sincere about traveling with me, but there is so much to consider. Your training isn't finished, and your father . . ." The last word rose questioningly, and Cathy forced a thin smile.

"Yes, *Father,*" she repeated in a sighing tone. Cathy's father desperately wanted his daughter to come home to New York. But New York was still synonymous with pain in Cathy's mind, and returning to her father would mean the loss of her hard-won independence.

Then Miss Nightingale was smiling at her young protégée

and telling her not to worry. She gave her an affectionate pat on one shoulder. "Let's not spoil our evening. We shall talk of it tomorrow."

Nodding, Cathy was about to ask Miss Nightingale if she still wanted her to report for duty at her hospital the next day, but her attention was distracted. There was a man staring at her, a most handsome man, and he was staring at her so *rudely* that it quite took Cathy by surprise. Who on earth could he be gazing at in that positively wicked way? she wondered, squelching the urge to glance behind her. But he had to be gazing at her, for there was a blatant appraisal in the man's eyes as his gaze quickly skimmed from her toes back to her face, and Cathy flushed.

When she would normally have favored the boor with her most severe stare, one that would have put any man quite out of countenance, she found herself once more surprised by his sudden smile. It abruptly altered the harsh planes and angles of his face, lending an appealing humanity to features remote and cold. Unexpectedly—and distantly shocked by her reaction—Cathy found herself smiling back at him.

The gentleman was exceedingly good-looking, not that looks mattered that much in this world, Cathy silently admonished herself, for they didn't. Yet there was a subtle, worldly appeal in the lean lines of his face, a face that indicated maturity and experience. This was no callow youth, but a full-grown man. Shades of silver frosted the thick mahogany curls at his temples, and his broad shoulders looked as if they were accustomed to the burden of responsibilities. But neither, she told herself, could this man be a gentleman, for gentlemen did not stare so conspicuously at decent women. No, that dark, soulful gaze was more suited to lust and greed than admiration and respect, she decided.

Cathy knew she should look away and pretend he did not exist, but somehow she couldn't. There was a magnetic pull that kept her eyes from shifting and her chin from jutting indignantly into the air, and she was powerless to avoid it. The man's utter brass was too fascinating to ignore.

And because she was staring back at him, Cathy saw the pistol.

Scarlet hair flashed briefly at the outer limits of her vision, and Cathy glimpsed the quick lifting of a small weapon. The pistol took deliberate aim, and the moment took on an unrealistic quality as Cathy watched in fear and horror. There was a scream—hers?—and she was vaguely aware of the handsome man's pivoting to stare at the unknown assailant.

Jesse Lamont swirled, cursing himself for being caught off guard. Jade eyes glared back at him with feral hatred and satisfaction. As he started in recognition, the pistol exploded. There was an orange burst of flame and the sharp, acrid odor of gunpowder, and the noise of the single shot seemed to ricochet from the walls and ceiling, reverberating through the crowded room in waves of sound.

Staggering, Jesse clutched his hands to the burning pain in his left side. His dusky eyes flared in disbelief, then focused upon his assailant. Slowly, unbelievably, a caustic smile curved his mouth. Blood bubbled between his splayed fingers, and he lifted one hand to gaze with detached interest at his crimson palm.

Cathy stifled a gasping cry of horror at the blood-smeared hand, and Lamont slanted her a glance of mild inquiry. Instinctively, she rushed forward the few steps between them. Jesse Lamont's smile faded slightly, and he knew a moment's regret that the expression in the lovely young face gazing at him was one of anxiety instead of the attraction he had hoped to find earlier. This emotion passed swiftly into the vague thought that he had certainly not anticipated this type of introduction. Then his vision blurred and he staggered again.

Oddly enough, Cathy had the same thought as Mr. Jesse Lamont pitched forward to fall on the floor at her feet.

* * *

As Lamont crumpled to the floor there was a blended rush of reactions. Screams and long-held sighs sliced into the air, and feet thundered across the highly polished tiles of the ballroom floor as people scattered in every direction.

Slowly regaining her senses, Cathy knelt beside the wounded man, vaguely aware that Florence Nightingale had arrived at her side. Several men had leaped at the unlikely assailant, and one of them had snatched the still-smoking pistol from her shaking hand, while another tugged at her arms. Chaos reigned supreme.

Cathy assisted as Miss Nightingale gently turned the man from his side to his back. His face was pale, long eyelashes lying upon cheeks that were rapidly growing gray beneath the tan. His breathing was shallow and uneven, and his lips were tinged a bluish color.

"A physician, please!" some anonymous person shouted, and the word *physician* rippled through the crowd like waves on the seashore. The surrounding murmurs were now a constant roar in Cathy's ears.

"It's Lamont . . ."

"A spy . . ."

"The Russians!" someone guessed in a loud gasp.

"One of his scorned lovers shot him," commented still another faceless voice as a hundred curious eyes peered down on the fallen man.

Florence Nightingale had little patience with the wild guesses being hazarded. "Move back at once!" she commanded loudly. "The man must be allowed to breathe."

"Oh, where's the physician?" Cathy fretted as she lifted Lamont's head onto her lap, heedless of her silk dress.

"On his way, I am certain." Miss Nightingale pushed aside the lapels of Jesse's coat in an attempt to determine the extent of his injury. It was serious, she noted, as her fingers probed gently at his bloodstained shirt, feeling the fleshy pucker beneath. "We must stop the bleeding."

Cathy cleared her throat in an effort to keep her voice steady, but inside she was trembling like a new leaf. "Who is he?"

Swiftly pressing the heel of her palm against Lamont's chest, Miss Nightingale absently replied, "Mr. Jesse Lamont," as she attempted to staunch the free flow of blood from his wound. "He is one of Lord Clarendon's men . . . in the foreign ministry. Here, Cathy—take your hand and press here. . . ."

While Miss Nightingale guided her hand, Cathy let her fingers slide over the warm, slick skin to the gaping little crater of raw flesh. She swallowed hard, feeling suddenly light-headed and sternly reprimanded herself for doing so. How could she be a nurse if she fainted at the sight of blood?

"Get back . . . get back!" a male voice said impatiently, followed by the burly figure of a man Cathy instantly recognized as Dr. Alexander. Looking from Cathy to Miss Nightingale, the man's gaze then slid to the man lying upon the floor. His voice was gruffly cheery as he observed, "It seems that you two are always in the midst of trouble, ladies! It appears you need my assistance again, what?"

Managing a smile, Cathy murmured some answer to his remark, keeping her fingers pressed tightly to the wound. As Miss Nightingale apprised Dr. Alexander of the wound and how it had been inflicted, Cathy let her thoughts wander to the man beneath her hand. Her other hand unconsciously stroked the damp hair from his sweat-beaded forehead.

That red-haired woman intended to kill him. She wanted to murder him in front of all these people.

It was a desperate act, an act of passion.

Focusing her gaze upon the slack features, Cathy wondered why. What had possessed that woman to commit such a terrible act in full view of so many witnesses? Perhaps he was what she'd first thought him—a boor, and no gentleman, to boot. But was that sufficient reason to kill a man? Hardly. The man must have enemies.

Then she stifled a smile at her own obvious conclusion. Of course the man had enemies! No *friend* would shoot him!

"I still say it was one of his many scorned lovers," a voice insinuated, the whisper sliding stealthily through the crowd to Cathy's ears. She looked up and saw only the avid stare of eyes, curious stares, that morbidly ghoulish interest that people ofttimes show in the face of calamity. Blinking, Cathy reflected that the whisper was probably valid. Hadn't he smiled at his assailant? It had been quite apparent that Lamont knew the woman. And from her brief encounter with him, she also knew that he was a man who liked women.

"We need to remove him from this area immediately," Dr. Alexander was saying firmly, dragging Cathy's attention back to the business at hand. "Call for a litter, please," he instructed, snapping shut his medical bag. Cathy's gaze shifted from the physician's face to the bandages he had wrapped around his patient. While Miss Nightingale made arrangements for a litter and a coach to transport the wounded man, Dr. Alexander made a much closer examination.

When Miss Nightingale returned, he looked up and met her frowning gaze. "We must operate quickly, or this man may bleed to death," he said.

"Is there . . . time . . . to transport him to your office or the hospital?" she asked with swift intuition, glancing from Cathy Weston's dazed face back to the man on the floor.

"No, no . . . I think he needs somewhere *closer*, another facility, perhaps," Dr. Alexander murmured. "Yes, that is it. . . ." There was a pregnant pause, during which time both of them exchanged meaningful glances.

"Then so it shall be," Miss Nightingale interjected in a firm tone. Her hand closed on Cathy's arm, and she gave it a comforting squeeze. "You've had quite an introduction to danger," she said, and the girl blinked as she seemed to snap out of a deep haze. Her gaze focused on the older woman, then shifted to the unconscious man on the floor.

"Oh, yes, quite. But then . . . he appears to be a dangerous kind of man."

Miss Nightingale's lips twitched. "I daresay."

Several men arrived with a litter, and when they had cradled the unconscious Lamont within its folds, they moved him to the waiting coach. Florence Nightingale accompanied the physician and patient, but Cathy willingly remained behind. She would be of little help now. Jesse Lamont was in the best possible hands.

She stood awkwardly, feeling suddenly useless and ill-at-ease. It now occurred to her that she had come to the ballroom with Miss Nightingale, and she had no transportation home. The crowd began to disperse, drifting away as music began to play.

The woman—Lamont's assailant—had been removed by the local authorities, and servants were already busily mopping up the smears of blood from the tile floor. All traces of violence were being wiped away, and Cathy felt as if she were enmeshed in a strange dream. Slowly, as if she were indeed a sleepwalker, she began to cross the ballroom.

Several people stared curiously at her, and there were more whispers behind cupped hands, glances, and avid stares. Confused, Cathy wondered as to the cause. Perhaps they thought she knew the man who had been shot, or . . .

"Can I get you a carriage, Miss Weston?"

Startled, Cathy stumbled to a halt and glanced up. A tall, elegant gentleman barred her progress, but the expression on his rather austere features was polite and kind. As she hesitated, he smiled.

"Excuse me, but . . . what did you say?" she asked, pushing

at the damp mop of dark curls that tumbled onto her forehead in wild disarray.

"I thought that perhaps you would care to leave and exchange your . . . attire . . . for more proper clothing," he suggested, confusing her even more.

"Exchange my . . . but whatever can you mean?" she asked in a dazed voice. Her brow wrinkled as she glanced down at her gown. Ruffles and layers of rich ivory silk were spattered with gouts of blood. Her fingers grazed the ruined material in dismay. "Oh, my!" she gasped. "I didn't know."

"Yes, I rather thought you didn't. Shall I escort you to the exit?" the gentleman persisted.

At Cathy's continued hesitation, he offered, "Let me introduce myself, Miss Weston, since there seems to be no proper person here to perform the introductions. I am Lord John Bothmourne, the—"

"Duke of Bothwell!" Cathy finished for him.

He smiled. "Yes, that is so."

Belatedly recalling proper protocol upon being introduced to a member of the realm, Cathy bobbed a dazed curtsy that only made the duke's smile grow wider. "I . . . I am so pleased to meet Your Grace," she said. Then she blurted, "You know my name!"

"Ah, yes," he said with a significant lift of his brow. "There are many who know your name, Miss Weston." There was a brief, thick silence before he added in a rush of words, "I also know Mr. Lamont, and I wish to extend my appreciation for your kindness to him just now."

"Then he is a friend of yours?"

"In a manner of speaking, yes, Miss Weston. We worked together."

"Then you will be visiting him at the hospital, I assume?"

"Of course, but first I intend to see that you have a coach and proper escort," Lord Bothmourne replied.

"Oh, but . . . if you please, Your Grace, I should much prefer—if it's not too presumptuous of me—that you would let me ride in your coach. It shouldn't delay you too very much, as I live quite near the hospital." There was the seed of an idea in the back of her mind that perhaps this duke would satisfy her curiosity about Mr. Jesse Lamont.

After a brief start of surprise at such an unconventional suggestion, the duke agreed to escort Cathy home. "Do you still live with your great-aunt and cousins?" he inquired as he fetched her cloak.

Shaking her head in a numb fashion, Cathy said that no, she had recently moved to a most genteel hotel with her constant companion. "Miss Mooney will not be expecting me home this early," she mused aloud.

"I daresay not, after some of the late evenings we've all kept with your cousins' set," the duke remarked with a laugh. "It's no wonder you've moved from their home to a more *quiet* residence!"

The duke draped her cloak around her shoulders as they paused at the front entrance. Lord Bothmourne then posted his footmen and outriders alongside the coach in order to allay any hint of impropriety, and handed Cathy into an extremely well-appointed carriage. It was well sprung and luxurious, and she settled back against the plush velvet squabs with a sigh of relief. Her fingers knotted the splotched material of her gown in tiny wrinkles as she pushed the memory of the pistol and shot to the back of her mind. There was time enough to think of that later. Now she felt an overpowering desire to extract any information that she could from Lord Bothmourne.

But Lord Bothmourne proved to be a veritable clam. He gave her no hints as to Jesse Lamont's occupation or habits, but merely reasserted the earlier information that they had both worked for Lord Clarendon. This Cathy already knew, but she did not allow her frustration to show. And it occurred to her after the duke had graciously and politely seen her to the door of her home, that it was rather peculiar that a man should go to so much trouble to avoid talking about a friend who had just been shot.

Chapter 2

*A*rriving back at her lodgings earlier than originally planned, Cathy was met at the door by Miss Mooney, her aged companion. The woman's usually stiff expression did not alter as she eyed her charge's strained face.

"Is there anything amiss?"

Peeling off the cape that covered her bloodstained gown, Cathy slumped into a chair by the window. Her gaze was drawn to the darkened streets outside the window, and it took her several moments to answer. She stared distantly at the flicker of gaslamps lining the street, the odd shapes and shadows that danced along the cobbled stones and walkways. It was so hard to think about, so hard to say anything, yet the memory of the night's events were still burned into her mind. When Ida Mooney drew closer, Cathy managed to glance up and force a thin smile of reassurance.

"There was an . . . incident . . . at the ball."

"An incident?"

Cathy's eyes involuntarily returned to the smears of blood on her gown. It was *his* blood, blood that had flowed from the mysterious Jesse Lamont.

Miss Mooney crossed the room, her eyes following the direction of Cathy's gaze. They widened slightly at the bright, unmistakable stains. "My word! Whatever happened?"

"There was a shooting at the ball . . . a man was shot . . . and he fell at my feet," Cathy explained. Her mind flicked back to the event, reliving it, seeing it happen again—the shot, the slow crumpling of the man to the floor, his cynical smile and dark burning eyes. . . .

Her head jerked up. In spite of the outcome, she could vividly recall the manner in which Mr. Lamont had been staring at her before he was shot. His gaze had been so intent, so . . . *knowing,* as if he had pierced the shell so carefully erected around her to see inside her soul. Cathy shook her head. Fanciful notions. She was romanticizing every tiny detail in her mind, attributing reactions and thoughts that were not there. Perhaps she'd only imagined his attraction to her. And perhaps not.

Yes, he was a rogue, a devilish heartbreaker. The woman who had shot him had probably been driven to it. . . .

"Is he dead?" Miss Mooney was asking.

Cathy was puzzled by the question. Of course he wasn't dead. Or was he? "I . . . I don't know," she answered softly, suddenly aware that he very well may have died by this time. The thought was insupportable for some obscure reason. Cathy straightened with sudden conviction and looked at her companion. "He was gravely wounded, but no—a man like *that* does not die so easily."

"Miss Cathy!" Ida Mooney exclaimed, faintly shocked by the girl's vehemence. "You should not say such things. It is always ill to speak of another person's misfortune in a light manner." Her thin lips pursed when Cathy said nothing, but she continued to gaze at the young woman. "And he might have already perished, too," she added.

Rising from the chair, Cathy shook her head in a grim fashion. "Nonsense."

Miss Mooney's lips tautened with disapproval. She had known her charge far too long to expect immediate agreement, yet that had never deterred her from giving her opinion whenever she felt it necessary. Miss Cathy needed a strong hand to guide her, and Ida Mooney did her best to oblige.

A long sigh slipped from between her lips as she moved to pick up Cathy's cloak. From long experience, she knew the best way to deal with the headstrong young woman.

Cathy also knew Miss Mooney's ploy, and she gave a sigh of her own as she recognized the familiar tactic of silence that the woman frequently employed. It would be an icy quiet with no reply for any question ventured, nor would there be any hope for peace until Cathy broke the reign of silence with an apology. She might as well get it over with, Cathy thought with sudden capitulation. The day had been wearing enough.

"My apologies if I have offended you," she offered. Then, when Miss Mooney only nodded, she added, "Is there something else wrong?"

After hanging up Cathy's cape, the older woman turned to look at her. Round gray eyes gazed pensively at her charge, and she hesitated before saying bluntly, "There is another missive from your father, Miss Cathy. It arrived here directly from the dock while you were out this evening."

When Cathy remained silent, Miss Mooney stepped to the walnut vanity and lifted a thin, crackling sheet of folded paper. She held it out, and Cathy reluctantly took it.

"Slip out of that ruined gown and I will see what can be done to save it," she instructed, and Cathy silently obeyed.

This was worse than a shroud of silence, she reflected as she turned the paper over in her hands, dreading opening it and reading the controlled script that would be inside. It would be the same words, couched differently, perhaps, but the same, terse demands. Her dark eyes glowed as she gazed down at the folded sheaf. The words were all the same.

"Damn," Cathy muttered when she finally relented and tore open the letter. Her expletive rang in the room with all the force of a hammer on stone, and Ida Mooney flinched.

"Miss Cathy, *please,*" she protested. "You should not speak so vulgarly. It's so common, and I just cannot bear to—"

Waving an impatient hand, Cathy cut her off. "All right, enough! I know my faults."

But Miss Mooney was not to be deprived of her opportunity to instruct. Her face took on the expression that Cathy could only term *mulish,* and she lowered her head in the same manner as a tenacious terrier as she continued. "I have often told you that I cannot abide that wicked tongue, Miss Cathy. If I did not already know you to be the fine young lady that you are, I would depart your employ in an instant! It is only because I know how very badly that you need me that I stay, and that your father—dear Mr. Weston—depends upon my assistance. Being the Christian woman that I am, I am absolutely determined to see this struggle through to the end, until you are once more reunited in the bosom of your loving family. . . ."

"Pray, cease your lecture!" Cathy begged. "Besides, you may get your desire more quickly than either you or I had imagined." She handed the letter to Miss Mooney, her spirits flagging badly. It wasn't that Miss Mooney's lecture affected her, for it didn't, but it was the grim news contained in the letter that left her preoccupied. Her father, Nathaniel Weston, had expressed his intention of coming to England—was, in fact, already on his way. The ship bearing her father had departed New York several days before. And when Nathaniel Weston left Britain's shores for America again, he fully intended that his daughter would accompany him.

"But this is wonderful!" Miss Mooney exclaimed as she skimmed the letter, her thin lips curving in a rare smile.

"Oh, yes, I was quite undone myself," Cathy said with a mocking grimace. She wandered to her vanity and plopped down on the embroidered petit-point stool. Leaning over, she propped her chin in the cup of her palms and gazed dolefully into the round mirror. Large chestnut eyes stared back, and she suddenly recalled the dark burning eyes of earlier. They had lingered on her in a most disturbing fashion, and she had not been able to look away.

In a detached sort of way, Cathy assessed her features, trying to find some reason for Jesse Lamont's earlier attention. Her eyes —though some said they were large and lovely, with long, sweeping lashes and a color that altered from brown to a molten gold—seemed quite ordinary to her. Her hair was thick enough, perhaps her nicest feature, she decided, for it *was* a rich, coffee color, but it was her complexion that elicited the most compliments. She knew she was pretty enough in a common sort of way, but she had never quite understood the fascination some people had with her unusual coloring. Her skin had a clear, almost translucent sheen, as if powdered with cornstarch, and there was a most becoming natural pink tinge flushing her cheeks. Yes, she supposed she was pretty, but thought it rather silly to dwell upon such things. Vanity was definitely not one of her vices.

Pride and impatience were another matter. She frowned at her reflection, her thoughts shifting back to her father. There must be a way of persuading him to allow her to remain in London. She did not want to be entombed in the musty society of New York again, listening to the same old gossip that circled about, suffering the empty vanity of the debutantes and the vain posturings of their mothers. And most of all, she could not face Darcy Sheridan and his newly married *wealthy* wife.

A shudder skipped up her spine and lodged at the base of her neck. Cathy still found it difficult to accept the fact that Darcy had broken his engagement to her and planned a subsequent marriage to his third cousin, Patsy Sheridan of Charleston. His excuse was that his family wanted him to breed with his own kind—his *wealthy* kind. Cathy had been wealthy, but she was not a widow with land and business properties that would further the Sheridan estates. And she was not a Sheridan.

"I know what you're thinking," said Miss Mooney, interrupting Cathy's brooding. "You're thinking that you can wheedle your father into letting you stay." She crossed to lay the letter on the vanity, and her voice softened. "Well, it won't do this time, Miss Cathy. Read it again. Mr. Weston is most determined that you are going home this time."

"Is he?" Cathy asked listlessly. She stared at Ida's reflection in the mirror. Ida Mooney was a feisty woman who gave Cathy a fair measure of her own in return. Who else could put up with Cathy's own idiosyncrasies? Not many. And in spite of an occasional difference of opinion, Cathy had long admired Ida Mooney for her strict adherence to her own code of behavior. The older woman may have been temperamental and a bit self-righteous, but she did speak her mind. She was a valuable person to have as a friend—loyal, dependable, and sharp as the proverbial tack. Cathy greatly admired women who were not only intelligent, but not too shy to show it. That quality had attracted her to Florence Nightingale.

"Don't be sullen," Miss Mooney was saying. "You'll find that going back to New York isn't as painful as you've feared, I'm certain. Haven't you ever heard the old saying that today's tidings are soon old tidings?"

Cathy shot a severe glance at her companion, her raw nerves flayed by the reminder of her broken engagement. "You always slice right to the point, don't you?" she asked, with only the slightest trace of sarcasm.

"Yes," Miss Mooney replied modestly, "I do try to be blunt. It's the only way to handle you, Miss Cathy, and I have been handling you since you were a child."

"You make me sound like a slab of beef," Cathy muttered with a grimace.

Miss Mooney merely smiled mirthlessly as she lifted the chenille hair net from Cathy's hair and began unbraiding the heavy braid on her nape. Her nimble fingers unraveled the thick ribbon of dark hair, untwisting the strands to let them hang in graceful coils.

Relaxing, Cathy smiled at the familiar touch of her hands. It was comforting to have Ida Mooney care for her. The older woman had been her nurse and companion since that terrible month following the death of Cathy's mother from tuberculosis. Cathy had been ten that year. Now she was twenty-three, and still enjoyed this nightly ritual, which was filled with comfort and unspoken affection.

"Your father often remarked that your late mother loved your hair down like this," Miss Mooney murmured as she raked a tortoiseshell brush through the luxuriant mane.

"Yes, she did."

"I know the fashion is shorter hair with those bouncy ringlets on each side, but I prefer the soft braid coiled at your neck, or even hanging down your back," Ida continued. "Wasn't that your mother's favorite style for her own hair?"

"I think so, but there are times it's hard for me to recall those things," Cathy admitted sadly, summoning up the image of her mother. "Time has a way of destroying some memories, or at least distorting them. I try to see Mother's face and hair in my mind, or her smile. . . ." Cathy's voice grew soft. "Sometimes I just stare at her portrait, trying to imagine what her smile looked like, the curving of those painted lips into laughter, or even the sound of her voice and laughter." She lapsed into pensive silence.

"I understand that your mother had a very lovely smile."

"Like mine?" Cathy couldn't resist teasing in an attempt to lighten the mood.

Miss Mooney jerked sharply on the hairbrush. "Nonsense. Your smile is very like your father's! Your mother was a gentle lady, from what I know of her, and she never raised her voice. You, Miss Cathy, are just like your father—quite opinionated and stubborn. When you laugh, everyone knows you're happy, but that is also true when you're miserable. Then the world must grieve with you!"

Chuckling, Cathy nodded. "You are too hard on me, Miss Mooney. I like to think that I am a bit like my mother, at any rate."

"Oh, you are. You very much resemble her, Miss Cathy. Everyone says that."

Turning to look back into the mirror, Cathy once more stared at her reflection. *How often Father has said those very words.* Perhaps that was part of the problem with their relationship. Cathy had replaced her beloved mother in his eyes. He was smothering her with his love and attention, just as he would have done with her mother had she lived. It had been Nathaniel Weston's forceful will that had maneuvered Cathy into the arms of dashing Darcy Sheridan, his hopes and struggle for an alliance with the powerful Sheridan family.

Only it was Cathy who had suffered the broken heart, not her father.

A deep frown creased her brow. "Father is expected in a few weeks," she observed aloud. "He's certain to cut off my allowance this time, and I will be forced to return to New York with him."

"New York is your home," Ida pointed out. "It's where you belong, Miss Cathy. You don't belong here in London at all these parties and operas with people who look down their noses at Americans—it's such a waste of time."

"But that's not entirely true now," Cathy interjected quickly. "I've been helping Miss Nightingale at her hospital, and soon I intend to accompany her to Scutari."

The hairbrush froze in midair, and Miss Mooney's horrified gaze met Cathy's in the mirror. An appalled expression was etched into her features. "How can you even consider going off to that place! It's unheard of. You will be in the midst of a *war*, Miss Cathy! Why, that is no place for a well-bred young woman such as yourself. Oh, my, there is so much filth, disease, and death, and . . ."

Death. The word rolled slowly in Cathy's mind. She wasn't afraid of death, really. It happened all the time. *In the midst of life we are in death.* . . . It was life that was hard, life she was beginning to fear, life that she was trying desperately to cling to. . . . She turned to look up at Ida.

"I am determined, Miss Mooney. With Miss Nightingale's approval, I fully intend to travel with the nurses to Scutari. I must make a life separate from Father."

Miss Mooney's mouth tightened in disapproval. "It is a mistake," she said flatly. "Your father only wants what is best for you, Miss Cathy."

"He wants what is best for *him,*" Cathy contradicted.

"Miss Cathy, please do not speak so badly of your father to me."

"I apologize, Miss Mooney. I understand how you feel." Her eyes crinkled with frustration as she added, "But I must have my freedom."

"Freedom! Pah! What a thing for a woman to think about!" Miss Mooney countered. "Freedom is being securely wed to a man who is kind and responsible. Do you call my life free, Miss Cathy? Do you? Well, this is what you have to look forward to if you do not make a good match . . . being on the fringe of a family, always an outsider and never quite an insider—expendable. You will be resigned to a life of *companionship.*"

Shocked by the vehemence of the older woman's words, Cathy became aware of emotions that she'd never dreamed existed inside the prim, proper little woman who had been her companion for so many years. How had she not guessed? How had she not known that Ida Mooney would feel so unfulfilled, would long so for her own husband and children?

"Oh, Ida!" she said impulsively. "Are you so dreadfully unhappy?"

"No, child, I didn't say that. I'm quite content with you. You've come to mean as much to me as any child of my own. My meaning is simply that you will have no husband, no children of your own to love and care for, no children to look after you when you are too old and feeble to make your way in the world."

Now Cathy sensed the fear behind her companion's eyes and words, and she reached out to put a hand on her arm. "I will always take care of you, Miss Mooney. Surely you must know that."

The older woman's mouth curved the tiniest bit in a smile. "Yes, I do know that, Miss Cathy. But if something should happen to you—"

"Oh, nothing will, but I do see what you mean," Cathy said, turning back to face her own reflection again. Of course, Ida Mooney had already been provided for in the will filed with Cathy's solicitor, but perhaps she should make further provisions for her. Yes, that was what she would do just as soon as she came into her mother's money. There would be a much more ample provision made for Miss Mooney.

"Miss Cathy, I can see what you're thinking. It's not me I'm concerned about now, it's you. As generous as your father may be at times, he will not leave a *penny* to a daughter who has scorned his wishes. You know how difficult it was for him to allow you to travel even to London. And now he is coming after you. He will not leave without you."

"I refuse to go back," Cathy warned stubbornly.

"Oh, dear! What's to become of all this?" Miss Mooney shook her head and pulled the brush through the gleaming strands of Cathy's hair. "I never saw two people with such stubborn tendencies! You and your father are too much alike for your own good—that's what I say!"

Cathy remained silent. For once, she and Miss Mooney were in complete agreement. Mr. Weston could be so single-minded at times, and when his mind was set on something there was no deterring him from that course.

"There—all finished." Miss Mooney set the tortoiseshell hair-brush on the vanity and moved to the armoire for a nightgown of white muslin. Delicate lace trimmed the cuffs and collar, falling across her arm as she carried it back to Cathy. "Slip into your nightdress and get some sleep," she said.

Cathy found it quite easy to oblige. She slipped the gown over her head and slid under the freshly scented sheets. Stretching out, she tightened the muscles in her legs, curling her toes, then relaxing. It was an excellent manner in which to relieve tension, she'd found, and it worked now. A fat feather-stuffed pillow cradled her head and she closed her eyes, letting her mind drift.

Flaming hair, the cold blue metallic gleam of a pistol, that small deadly eye spitting orange fire, and emerald eyes filled with hate and satisfaction . . .

Though Cathy had seen her for only a moment, the image of the beautiful assailant glowed in her memory as vividly as it had in reality. Who was she? And *why* had she shot Mr. Jesse Lamont?

Pushing the memories determinedly aside, Cathy rolled onto her side and bunched the pillow beneath her head. But then her eyes opened slowly and her mouth curved in a frown. Jesse Lamont. The name burned into her brain, pricking her awake. Was he still alive? Had he—as Miss Mooney had suggested— died? She had to know. First thing in the morning, she would go straight to Miss Nightingale at the institution to discover the truth for herself.

Chapter 3

*H*er footsteps echoed down the empty tiled corridors as Cathy approached Miss Nightingale's office door. The halls were swept clean, and gleamed from a recent mopping. Fresh paint covered the walls, and the atmosphere was one of cleanliness—quite an innovation in hospitals.

"Good morning, Miss Nightingale," Cathy said cheerfully as she stuck her head around the corner. "How are you this fine day?"

Looking up from the stack of papers she was reading, Florence Nightingale's expression shifted from weariness to pleasure. "Cathy, it's so good to see you."

"I thought you might need me today," Cathy said as she stepped into Miss Nightingale's Spartan office. "I didn't have an opportunity last night to ask you if you'd need me, so I just took the liberty of coming in to the hospital and seeing if there was something I could do to help."

"You know quite well there's always work to be done," Miss Nightingale replied with a smile as she rose to her feet. "I shall talk to Miss Bracebridge about a suitable post for you. Just give me a few moments to find her."

Selina Bracebridge was Miss Nightingale's right hand. She was the one who tidied up all the loose ends and took care of the most minute details that otherwise cluttered up the normal routine of daily hospital tasks. Cathy seated herself in a chair near the door while Miss Nightingale went in search of the redoubtable Selina Bracebridge. She sat with her hands primly folded in her lap, clutching the lace reticule that carried only a few shillings, a linen handkerchief, and a small comb. Her gaze wandered about Miss Nightingale's office, studying the portraits of dour-faced men of medicine and the insignia of their profession. A few framed documents also hung on the walls, as well as a painting of Socrates and his fatal dose of hemlock. A rather melodramatic painting, Cathy thought, but appropriate in its way.

Within a few minutes Florence Nightingale had returned, and her face was wreathed in smiles and satisfaction.

"I have a special assignment for you, my dear," she began as she seated herself behind her desk again. "It's an assignment that may require your complete attention for the next two or three weeks. Do you think you can arrange to be here every day for the next fortnight?"

Pleased with this unexpected opportunity, Cathy didn't hesitate to reply. "Yes, of course I can."

"You're not even going to weigh your decision?"

"No, I don't need to think about it. You know how much nursing means to me, Miss Nightingale. It's been my greatest pleasure for the past few months. What else should I want to do?"

"Well, there are always the parties, operas, routs, and such. You were quite sought after when you first arrived in London last year. Haven't you missed that gay, carefree life at all?"

Though she waited politely for an answer, Florence Nightingale already knew what Cathy would say, and she was wondering what Miss Weston would do when the other nurses had departed for Scutari. Her decision concerning Cathy Weston's future had already been made, and she felt very strongly that Cathy belonged in London.

"Pooh!" Cathy said, just as Miss Nightingale expected. "I am sick to death of that sort of thing! Parties hold no more attraction for me. Nursing does." Sending Florence Nightingale an inquisitive glance, Cathy could not resist asking, "Do you miss that type of life? I find it hard to think that you might."

Miss Nightingale's indulgent smile was answer enough as she shook her head, and Cathy leaned forward to add fervently, "Give me the position! I shall do it to the utmost of my abilities!"

"It won't be easy," was the warning. "The patient has been seriously wounded and needs a great deal of care."

"Seriously wounded?" Cathy echoed, her large eyes growing even larger and darker. Her first thought was of Jesse Lamont, but she quickly dismissed that notion. No, this was a hospital for the care of gentle*women*.

"Yes, a tragedy, as I'm certain you agree. Mr. Lamont is doing as well as—"

"Mr. Lamont! But . . . but this is a hospital for *women*," Cathy repeated, as if that would deny the fact. She could not hide her shock that a man such as Lamont would be a patient at the Institution for the Care of Sick Gentlewomen. "How can he be here?"

Frowning thoughtfully, Miss Nightingale tapped the point of her pen against the desktop for a moment, gazing at Cathy in deep reflection. Her instincts told her that Cathy could be trusted, but her voice was soft, as if the walls had ears.

"There are people who fear it may have been an attempt at assassination."

Hazel eyes darkened to a smoky brown as Cathy stared at her in surprise. *So—it was not passion, but politics.*

Miss Nightingale continued in the same low tone. "Mr. Lamont is a very important man just now. The government wishes to assure his recovery. It much prefers that he be taken care of here until he is able to go home. You will find that he is not an easy man under the best of circumstances, I'm afraid, and you may also discover yourself wishing you had not accepted the position. I understand that he can be quite demanding."

"But he is so badly injured that I am certain he will be manageable under those conditions," Cathy observed. "I doubt that I shall have any problem with tending to his needs. They should be simple enough, due to the dire circumstances of his injury."

"Quite true, Cathy. I just wished to apprise you of the entire situation so there would be no unexpected surprises in the near future," Miss Nightingale replied. "Mr. Lamont can be very trying. Because of his . . . vocation . . . there are people who must do business with him no matter the time or situation. You may find those occasions trying."

"You seem quite concerned with my feelings about this," Cathy commented. "Is there a reason for this—other than my affection for you and yours for me?"

"You are very perceptive as usual, Cathy." Miss Nightingale paused and gazed at her for a moment. She could not tell Cathy Weston everything, but she had to tell her enough to ensure her safety and satisfy her curiosity. And besides all that, she had grown very fond of the American girl.

"Well?" Cathy prompted, sensing that Miss Nightingale was holding back important information.

"I am not at liberty to tell you too much, my dear. I can only say this—it is very important that Mr. Lamont have the best of care. He is an important person to England right now. There is a war going on, you know. Just this morning, I received a message from Lord Clarendon inquiring as to Mr. Lamont's care while under my supervision. It was made quite plain that Mr. Lamont is to have the very *best* of care while here, and we are to ensure his safety and security. Lord Clarendon quoted even Queen Victoria as expressing concern over Mr. Lamont's recovery in a public institution instead of a private hideaway."

"I see. Then I will be under close scrutiny."

"Yes, that sums it up quite well. Do you still care to take on the position? I only offered it to you because I know that you are qualified and trustworthy. And I am also positive of your discretion."

"Of course." Pausing for a moment, Cathy reflected on the situation. Nursing was agreeable to her, of course. She needed an occupation that would divert her thoughts from her father's imminent arrival in London. And Jesse Lamont was certainly an intriguing person. Somehow Cathy had the unshakable feeling that this position might take more of her energies and emotions than she'd first thought when she'd asked Miss Nightingale for a nursing post. Those fears had nothing to do with Jesse Lamont's association with the government.

"Are you reconsidering the position?"

Cathy looked up, then shook her head. "No. I can start now if you like."

"Excellent! This certainly relieves me of a lot of worry, Cathy. I wasn't at all certain who to ask to take on such a strenuous job, so your arrival this morning seems godsent."

Cathy rose from her chair. "You can depend on me."

"I know," Florence Nightingale replied as she stood. "I know."

"Good morning, Your Grace," Cathy said softly.

Startled by the voice, Lord John Bothmourne turned from Lamont's bedside. His expression was even more startled when he saw the visitor framed in the open doorway.

"My dear Miss Weston!" he exclaimed, striding forward and taking her delicate hand. He permitted a ghost of a smile to pass across his lips, but no sign of condescension was evident on his face, nor did he feel any. For some reason, this fresh-faced young beauty appealed to his gentlemanly instincts. The redoubtable duke—who had been known to wither many a po-

tential debutante with his quick wit and barbed set-downs—
brushed his lips lightly across Cathy's knuckles. "What a pleasant surprise," he said smoothly.

Unaware that she had elicited any interest from the duke, Cathy blithely vowed that she, too, was delighted to see His Grace again.

"How is he?" she asked then, nodding her head toward Mr. Lamont, who lay in a deep sleep on a clean hospital bed in a long row of other beds. Draped sheets and blankets bisected the large, airy room, forming a tiny cubicle for Lamont.

"It appears that he is sleeping extremely well," was the duke's reply.

"That's to be expected, considering the severity of his wound. I imagine he will be up and around soon enough," Cathy said, gently disengaging her hand from the duke's lingering grasp.

Sharp blue eyes skimmed approvingly over Cathy's slender frame. In spite of the bulky domestic apron worn by most of the women who worked at the hospital, her curves were easily recognizable, and the net she wore over her thick chestnut hair did nothing to disguise its lustrous beauty. She stood and self-consciously pleated the crisp folds of her apron between her fingers, obviously a novice nurse and obviously anxious to prove herself. Lord Bothmourne bit back a smile.

"Are you the fortunate soul who has the burden of caring for Mr. Lamont?" the duke asked in a faintly amused tone.

"Yes, I am." Cathy's chin lifted defensively, as if she recognized the amusement in the duke's tone. "I was chosen by Miss Nightingale for the position."

"Were you, now? A most admirable reference, I should say. Miss Nightingale would not allow any but the best to care for Mr. Lamont, I am sure. She is a most remarkable woman."

"Indeed she is, and I am honored to know her. As a matter of fact," Cathy added, "I hope to be traveling with her to Scutari."

" 'Pon my word! Do you really?" The duke lifted his brow in surprise.

"Surely you don't think me unfit for such a task?" Cathy asked with a smile that masked the prick of sudden anxiety that someone might find her unworthy.

"Of course not, Miss Weston! I never meant such a thing at all," the duke assured her. "It's just that I find it dashed difficult to imagine you . . . being a young lady of such, such . . . oh, dear, I believe I have muffed it, indeed, haven't I?"

Suppressing the laughter rising in her throat, Cathy said, "I know what you are trying to say. A young lady from my background does not involve herself in such common tasks as caring for wounded soldiers in foreign lands. I should be at the opera, or, at the very most, out collecting funds for orphans. Anything else would be less worrisome, more *genteel*, and certainly less dangerous. Am I correct, Your Grace?"

A smile curved his mouth as Lord Bothmourne nodded. "You remind me very much of your mentor, Miss Nightingale. She is also a woman who says what she thinks. I apologize for my lack of faith. I am certain you would admirably grace any battlefield you chose to honor with your presence. England is fortunate to have you on her side."

"My thoughts exactly," Cathy replied with a mischievous twinkle in her eyes. "Thank you." Her gaze shifted from the duke to Jesse Lamont, who still lay on his back in the same position. His face appeared much more relaxed than when she'd last seen him, and his breathing was steady and regular. "Mr. Lamont seems to be quite at peace," she could not help observing.

Without turning to look, Lord Bothmourne agreed. "Yes, which is quite a remarkable feat for Jesse."

Noticing the familiarity of his tone and words, Cathy made a mental note that they must be close companions. She stepped to the bedside, and in her best professional manner proceeded to check Mr. Lamont's pulse rate.

"Steady," she stated for Lord Bothmourne's benefit. Which was more than she could say for *her* pulse, which had accelerated rapidly for some reason. Cathy replaced Jesse Lamont's arm on the snug-fitting sheets of the hospital bed.

Watching her closely, Lord Bothmourne said, "I am very pleased that you are to be Jesse's nurse, Miss Weston. I've a feeling that you will be good for him." The suggestion of a smile lurked about the corners of his mouth as he leaned over to lift his felt hat from a chair. "I am afraid that I must bid you farewell for now, though I am certain we shall meet again soon."

"Leaving so early, Your Grace?"

"Yes. I find that I am already late for a pressing appointment, but I had wished to visit Jesse this morning." He gave a small bow, adding, "I anticipate our next meeting, Miss Weston."

"I also, Your Grace."

Cathy waited until the duke left the hospital ward, then turned back to her patient. Jesse Lamont slept heavily; it was a medicine-induced slumber that was much heavier than normal sleep. His chest was bare and brown, and he was swathed in white bandages around his stomach. Her brow furrowed as she saw the telltale signs of heavy bleeding, the slight crimson spots barely visible on the strips of linen.

Pulling back the sheet a bit to show the bandages, Cathy examined them more closely, and satisfied herself that it was no more than the normal amount of blood after a surgical procedure. She let the sheet fall back into place, thinking how painful the wound must be. She'd seen so much pain and affliction during her hours spent at the institute under Miss Nightingale's tutelage.

Cathy's thoughts shifted to the nurse's words of the night

before. *There is much filth and misery in Scutari.* Could she deal with the hardships of Scutari? Cathy wondered. It had been difficult enough several times in the hospital. Surgical procedures were crude, medications few, and ofttimes the agonized screams of a patient would leave her feeling squeamish. Her imagination created a vivid image of hundreds and hundreds of men dying on a blood-soaked battlefield where there were few doctors and even fewer medical supplies.

Slumping down in the narrow bedside chair, Cathy stared at her sleeping patient. Jesse Lamont may very well be her final effort at nursing if she did not go to Scutari with Miss Nightingale. If there was nothing suitable to justify her remaining in England, Cathy knew she would be forced to return to America with her father. Even as strong as her will was, Nathaniel Weston's resolve had always been more forceful, more determined. He would have his way in the end, as he always did. A smothering emotion choked her at the thought. . . .

Hours ticked slowly past. Cathy changed the bandages as Dr. Alexander had instructed her, smiling in triumph when she managed to move Mr. Lamont's inert body by herself. She gently washed Jesse's arms, shoulders, and his neck with a soft cloth and mild, soapy water. He stirred slightly under the wash of tepid water over his flushed skin, and when Cathy turned back from wringing out the cloth over the small china washbowl, he was awake. She paused with her hands in midair, staring back at him.

Dark, dusky eyes were fixed on her face, his pupils large and dilated beneath the heavy lashes. Cathy attempted a friendly smile, but emotion evaded her grasp. Instead, she found herself just staring silently at him.

"You," he rasped thickly, blinking in slow surprise.

"So you do remember me," she said softly.

"Yes . . . the ball . . . ivory and lace . . . a temptress . . ." His voice slowed to a halt, trailing away on the last word, and he licked his dry lips.

Uncertain if she had heard him correctly, Cathy stifled the temptation to ask him to repeat his remark. When his tongue flicked out to moisten his cracked lips again, Cathy was mobilized into action.

"Would you like some water? I've been told that you can drink as much water as you like."

Lamont's head bobbed in a barely perceptible nod, and Cathy laid down the washcloth and reached for the pewter pitcher on the tiny bedside table. Lifting it, she poured a half glass of water. Crooking one arm behind his head, she lifted him slightly so that he could sip from the glass.

Making a slight slurping noise, Jesse managed to drink without dribbling. "More," he rasped when she took the cup away.

Obliging, Cathy put the glass to his mouth again. Jesse gulped thirstily, then relaxed back into the crook of her arm. The thick sweep of his lashes fluttered shut, and finally Cathy smiled. For a man reputed to be so dangerous, Mr. Jesse Lamont certainly appeared tame at the moment. "Better?" she asked after a moment.

Long eyelashes lifted again, revealing dark eyes rife with curiosity. They focused on Cathy. "Much better," he answered in a low murmur. Then he added, "What day is it?"

"Saturday—only the day after the ball."

"It seems like it's been forever since then."

"Oh, yes, I can well imagine that for you it certainly does seem that way, Mr. Lamont," Cathy said as she lowered his head back to the pillow and removed her aching arm. "But a man of your good health shouldn't miss those lost hours at all."

Her cheerful, nonchalant tone irritated him, and his eyes narrowed. "You're a cold fish," he muttered hoarsely.

An amused smile curved Cathy's lips at his observation. Mr. Jesse Lamont certainly didn't seem prone to wasting his compliments, it seemed! At least he wasn't one of those tiresome individuals who seemed to find it necessary to lavish unwarranted and undeserved flattery upon a woman until she felt like the veriest wretch for being absolutely none of the things he said. A cold fish, indeed!

"I'm going to take that remark as a compliment, Mr. Lamont," she returned lightly, turning to pull clean linen from beneath the bedside table.

Lamont lapsed into brooding silence, watching as Cathy went about her duties. Fully aware of his dark gaze, she did so a bit self-consciously, wondering why he was so easily able to ruffle her composure.

And her throat tightened with dismay when she removed the soiled bedsheet from atop her patient to discover that he wore shockingly little beneath. But what had she expected from a man so recently out of surgery? she scolded herself. She was being ridiculous, and unworthy of her profession. Masking her discomfiture, Cathy went about removing the sheet and shaking out clean linen, then tucking it about his long, lean frame. Nothing was said as she performed this task, and finally she was through and putting the soiled sheet into a straw hamper.

"Tell me your name," came the unexpected whisper.

"You may call me Miss Weston."

Her icy reply prompted a ghost of a smile. "No, tell me your Christian name. I already know your surname."

After a brief hesitation, she complied. "Catherine."

"Ah, it suits. A fiery Kate . . ."

"No, not at all—a sweet-tempered *Cathy*," she corrected in a sugary tone.

Another weak smile and the suggestion of a chuckle, and he repeated, "Cathy, then."

"Miss Weston to you," she reminded him tartly, and this time Jesse smiled broadly.

"Miss Weston."

She swiftly changed the subject, stepping around the foot of the bed as she tucked the corners into neat hospital folds. "You seem to have made quite an impression last night, Mr. Lamont."

"On you, I hope," he muttered with a trace of his familiar mockery.

Cathy's gaze flicked to his face. That was the exact tone she had expected from the man with the dark, burning eyes, that faint hint of cynicism and worldly indifference, as if he were weary with all of the human race. Bending her head, she went back to pulling the sheets taut.

"Most certainly on me, Mr. Lamont," she said smoothly, determined to counter his mockery with her own. "I have never met a man like you before, nor have I ever been witness to an assassination attempt."

"*Assassination?*" The word stung, and Jesse grimaced. Then he demanded, "What are you talking about?"

Surprised by his sudden change of tone, Cathy looked up at him. "I have heard it said that your injury might have been the result of an assassination attempt."

"Ridiculous!" Jesse snapped, struggling to sit up. He didn't yet have the strength, and sagged back against his pillows, glaring at Cathy in pain and frustration.

She rushed to his side. "You mustn't try to move, Mr. Lamont," she cautioned. "You may open up the stitches." Her small hands pressed against the upper portion of his chest, gently urging him back down. "Relax, and lie flat on your back. It's too soon for you to try to move."

Black eyes pierced her sharply. "Get Bothmourne—now!" he grated between clenched teeth. Jesse's gaze darted between the draped folds of blanket and sheet around his bed, widening at the sight of another patient, then darting back to Cathy. "Where in the hell am I?" he demanded.

"Please, Mr. Lamont. You must remain calm. I shall see that Lord Bothmourne is summoned for you—"

"Now!"

Jarred by his rudeness and surprisingly strong demand, Cathy strove to remain calm herself. It would not do to upset a gravely wounded patient. "Lie still and be quiet, and I shall have a message sent to him immediately. If you do not, however," she warned, taking him aback, "I shall remain here at your bedside until you are calm."

Jesse stared at her, nonplussed and too weak to argue. He was left with little choice in the matter, and though his brow drew down in a black frown, he did as she commanded and relaxed against the pillows. His eyes closed, more in frustration and irritation than a desire to please, but they closed nonetheless. When his breathing slowed to a more steady pace, Cathy relented.

"I will be gone for only a few moments, Mr. Lamont. If you should need anything, please ring the bell tied above the head of your bed. It will summon a nurse at once."

He gave a terse, blind nod of his head, and she tucked the sheet in more tightly and left. Perhaps he needed the duke for an urgent matter of state, she thought as she scurried down the long hallways. It was certainly unusual for a wounded man to be more interested in business than the extent of his injury.

Yet when she returned to his bedside, Jesse Lamont was asleep. Cathy smiled, briefly checked his wound, then sat in the rickety bedside chair to wait. Miss Nightingale had given her some books to read about the proper care for patients with consumption, and Cathy deemed this the appropriate time to read them. Almost a third of the women in the institution were suffering from the dreaded disease, and there was little that seemed to slow its inexorable progress. Death was always the end result. Removing the books from the cloth bag she'd brought back with her, Cathy flipped one open and was soon immersed within the pages.

She was made aware of the time that must have passed only when Lord Bothmourne cleared his throat behind her. Turning in surprise, she saw him standing a few feet away.

"We meet again, Miss Weston," he said with a practiced smile. Bothmourne shifted his hat to his other hand and reached out for Cathy's hand. Feeling rather awkward at observing the proprieties in such a situation, Cathy stood and allowed him to kiss it lightly. "I didn't expect another visit so soon," the duke commented as he released her hand.

"Mr. Lamont was quite adamant about seeing you at once," Cathy replied softly.

"So the message stated."

"I may be partly responsible for his apprehension," she confessed.

The duke's brow lifted in inquiry. "Whatever can you mean?"

"When he first awoke I mentioned—unwisely, I now fear—that it may have been an assassination attempt."

"Ah, I see the whole of it now." Lord Bothmourne's lips pursed, and he placed his hat on the foot of Jesse's bed as he moved around the end. "Wake up, Jesse, old man," the duke said, gently nudging the patient.

Stirring, Jesse opened his eyes with an effort. "John . . ."

"I'm here, though it's a dreadful nuisance," Lord Bothmourne responded with a smile.

An answering smile pressed at the corners of Jesse's mouth. Then his gaze shifted to Cathy. "Get rid of her," he rasped hoarsely to the duke, and Cathy stiffened.

When Lord Bothmourne turned toward her, Cathy spoke quickly. "I shall take a brief rest and leave you two to your privacy."

"Quite good of you, Miss Weston," the duke returned.

"Could I prevail upon you to bring me back a cup of tea? I find that I am quite in need of refreshment."

Cathy nodded with a grateful smile, then flashed Jesse Lamont a quick glance. And he had referred to *her* as a cold fish? she thought as she walked away.

Chapter 4

Cathy did not return again while the duke was with Lamont. Instead, she waited until she saw Lord Bothmourne pass down the hallway. Stepping from the alcove where she had been reading with one eye on the book and the other on the corridor, she halted the duke.

"Would you care for your tea now, Your Grace?"

He shook his head. "No, there's no time. But I should like to offer you an apology for Jesse's rather abrupt tone earlier. I'm certain you understand."

"Of course I do."

Smiling, he gave a quick nod of his head and a murmured farewell, then quickly left the hospital. Cathy stared after him reflectively. Lord Bothmourne was a gentleman, but intensely loyal to Mr. Lamont, it seemed.

When she returned to Lamont, the patient was testy and cold by turn. One moment he would berate her fiercely for talking to him; the next he would ask cajolingly if she liked the seaside, or what books she preferred reading. Cathy was not provoked to show anger, but there were several moments when she had to remain silent before answering so that she would not blurt out the hot words on the tip of her tongue. Jesse Lamont was—as Florence Nightingale had predicted—a trying patient. And over the next several weeks, his behavior grew no better.

As his strength returned, so did his restive spirit. He grew cranky and belligerent at having to remain in bed, and his hostility toward Cathy grew in direct proportion to his recovery. Cathy found it increasingly difficult to study the books Miss Nightingale had given her, but in spite of Lamont's grumblings she managed.

Ofttimes she would look up from her book to find Jesse's dark eyes resting on her, glittering with some unknown emotion. Each day she found him more intriguing and more difficult. She wavered between utter dislike and a grudging amicability, but underneath it all lay a thin layer of some other, nagging emotion that defied her best attempts to define it. It lurked, waiting to be brought out into the light of day and examined, then dismissed. Was it admiration that she felt for him, perhaps? A sense of pity? Or perhaps it was . . . something else.

Lord Bothmourne's frequent visits were guaranteed either to enliven the day or leave Lamont so frustrated as to be almost unmanageable. And then there were the others, the mysterious men who entered the institution by the back doors to converse with Jesse Lamont, conversation that was conducted in sly whispers and great secrecy. At those times Cathy felt the greatest strain, the greatest sense of displacement and anxiety. It was as if she had entered another world, a world of intrigue and danger and clandestine meetings among dangerous men, and it always left her feeling uneasy.

By the end of Jesse's second week at the institution, he was able to sit up for longer periods of time, and his eyes were brighter now, and more fully aware. Cathy felt his gaze on her as she went about her morning duties. It had been a particularly bad day already, as it was raining and the carriage that took her from her hotel to the institution had broken an axle and forced her to walk three blocks in a fine drizzle that left her wet almost to the bone. October had arrived with a howl of winds and bleak skies, and Cathy felt almost as bleak as the weather.

"That's quite a lovely gown," Jesse commented abruptly, startling her as she placed the clean linen beneath his bedside table. She almost leaped from her shoes at the pleasant sound of his voice.

"I . . . I beg your pardon?"

"I gave you a compliment on your gown. You always wear those ivory lace collars at your throat . . . quite lovely."

Uncertain whether he meant her lace collars or her throat, Cathy gave him a blank stare. "Thank you," she had the presence of mind to say, and finished putting away the clean linen. Nothing else was said until she had completed her few tasks, picked up her book, and sat down in the chair beside his bed again.

"I'm afraid I've been rather a bad patient," Jesse said then, his tone easy and friendly.

Cathy did not look up, but merely nodded her head in agreement. It was a vast understatement as far as she was concerned. Then she heard him laugh; it was a slow rumbling that began deep in his throat, swelled, and burst from his lips in resonant mirth. She looked up. Jesse Lamont was gazing at her in the same wicked fashion as he had at the charity ball, his black eyes glittering with amusement and mocking curiosity. When his eyes lowered to rake over her slender frame, Cathy felt a hot flush creep up her neck at her face and stain her cheeks.

Speaking around the sudden knot in her throat, she said, "I am quite happy to see that you are feeling so much better, Mr. Lamont. It won't be long before you will be going home."

His dark brow rose. "No? It sounds like you will be happy to see me go, Miss Weston."

Noting his wide, mocking grin, Cathy couldn't resist a taunt of her own. There was something about Jesse Lamont that fairly demanded a rebuttal.

"Of course I shall! And so will everyone else, from what I have heard!" She smiled sweetly. "You have been aptly dubbed 'the terror,' Mr. Lamont." Putting her book aside, Cathy rose and moved to the bedside.

Whatever else he had expected, Jesse had certainly not expected the quiet, demure Miss Weston to respond as she had. "What are you doing?" he demanded suspiciously when she reached for the sheet covering him.

"I am only examining your dressing, Mr. Lamont, just as I do every day."

He relaxed only slightly, his muscles tensed and ready for any pain that she might inflict by removing his bandages. Satisfied that the wound was healing nicely, Cathy rewrapped the linen strips, noting his grimace.

"I'd swear that you chose this profession because you enjoy the pain of others," he muttered between clenched teeth, and she smiled.

"You will soon be well, never fear."

Her fingertips lightly grazed his chest, and Jesse reached out in a reflex action and grabbed her hand. "And you are very lovely, Miss Weston."

"Thank you, Mr. Lamont," she answered primly, and tried to extricate her hand. But Jesse snared her arm, his fingers curling around her with surprising strength as he pulled her to him.

"You're so remote and distant . . . I think I would like to kiss you, Miss Weston. What do you think of that?"

Cathy's heart lurched and her throat tightened. Jesse was smiling at her, that devastatingly potent smile that she had first seen at the ball, and his eyes glittered with mischief. Their faces were so close that she felt as if she could not breathe without inhaling part of him. His eyes burned into her, hot and searing.

He's really going to kiss me. . . .

Swallowing her first surge of apprehension, Cathy wavered between surrendering to that emotion or playing his obvious game. She was still trying to decide which course to follow when Jesse jerked her close, kissing her hard and long on the mouth. It took her so by surprise—though it shouldn't have—that Cathy did not struggle.

I'm going to let him kiss me. . . .

His mouth was warm and seductive, moving against her lips in a tantalizing slow fashion. It had been a long time since Cathy had been kissed, and Jesse Lamont was a very handsome, very persuasive man. His lips were firm and inviting, subtly luring her into a deeper embrace that she tried to resist. A hot fire burned deep in the pit of her stomach, coiling upward, engulfing her entire body and making it ache for relief. *Shameful!*

I shouldn't be kissing this man, here, in this place, or anywhere else. . . .

Gasping, Cathy pulled away from the lulling security of his embrace, her cheeks flaming with rage and confusion. "Stop that!" she flared.

Jesse Lamont had the temerity to laugh. "I think you liked it," he suggested.

Pinching her lips firmly together, Cathy's brown eyes narrowed as she retorted, "That, sir, is entirely beside the point."

"Ah . . . then you don't intend to deny it. What a pleasure to meet a woman who does not hide behind subterfuge and pretense. I detest those simpering females who plead *no* the entire time they are really meaning *yes*."

Stiffening, Cathy clenched her hands at her sides. "You are incorrigible, Mr. Lamont! And presumptuous, as well! I find it ludicrous that you have the utter gall to think that I should *want* to kiss you—then to *compliment* me on being so wise as to do so. Why, it seems that your ego has not been at all deflated by your recent injury!" Throwing back her head, she faced him with defiant, righteous anger. "I can well understand your assailant's anxiety. The poor creature probably said *no* and meant *no!*"

Tossing that last acid rebuke in his face, she watched in great satisfaction as Jesse Lamont's smile quickly faded. Cathy knew at once that she had struck to the core with her words, but she wasn't quite certain how. And she wasn't sure if she should have been so hasty and bold. Lamont was silent—too silent. She stood there not knowing whether to apologize or feel triumphant. Though Lamont needed a proper set-down, there was something in the way he was looking at her that made her regret her hot, careless words.

Then he surprised her by saying, "You are quite a woman, Miss Weston."

Cathy stared at him, nonplussed. "I . . . I probably shouldn't have said what I did," she began. "It was very unkind, and very unprofessional of me."

"No, I am at fault. I should not have teased you so. I can see right now that you are not the playful kind."

"No," she said gently, "I am not."

"Please accept my apology. I am far older than you, and should not be kidding young ladies who are almost young enough to be my daughter."

"Oh, it wasn't that," Cathy assured him quickly. "You may certainly kiss whomever you wish, Mr. Lamont, but not under such circumstances as these. After all, if one of the other nurses had seen us, I could very well have been relieved of my post. And just now, Mr. Lamont, I need this position very badly."

"I thought you were traveling to Scutari with Miss Nightingale and the others."

"Yes, I certainly intend to do so."

"I'm surprised you're not already packing for the journey, then."

Confused, Cathy stared at him. "What do you mean?"

Lamont's brow rose, and he pushed at a stray fall of dark hair on his forehead. "You do not know? I had thought John said you were traveling with the others, and would soon be leaving."

"I don't know how soon . . . I mean, I haven't heard."

"But Miss Nightingale and her nurses will soon be departing," Lamont said.

Struck dumb by this information, Cathy frowned. But how could that be? Miss Nightingale had said nothing to her about it. Hadn't she just seen her the day before yesterday? It would be most unlike Miss Nightingale not to inform Cathy in plenty of time to make arrangements, so that must mean that she would be asked to stay behind. Disappointment welled in her throat, but Cathy pushed it firmly down. She would not leap to conclusions. She would ask first.

"I was hoping to go with them," she finally murmured aloud.

"I'm certain that if Miss Nightingale does not wish you to go, she will have a good reason," Lamont said kindly. "She is intelligent, and has an excellent sense of justice."

"That's true, of course. I know she may have her reasons, but I do not know them yet. I will have to ask her. I do so wish to help with the war effort."

"I understand your feelings, Miss Weston. But think on this —Scutari is a harsh place, and war is a nasty business, with no sense of fair play. As I understand it, you are not a full-fledged nurse. Perhaps Miss Nightingale is thinking of your need to complete your training. And besides all that, you are an American, a guest in our land. We should not send you off to risk life and limb."

"I appreciate your concern and comfort," Cathy began stiffly, "but this is really none of your concern. Do you know when the others are to leave?"

Realizing his error, Jesse said, "I'm afraid I have already said too much. I can see how troubled you are. Perhaps you should ask Miss Nightingale for more information."

"Yes . . ."

"Take comfort. There are a great many things a lovely young woman like yourself can do to fill your time. There is a great war relief effort going on right here in London."

Cathy gave him a severe glance. "I am not one to knit mittens for the soldiers like a lady of the peerage, Mr. Lamont!"

"True, but you are far too innocent and naïve to be running halfway around the world to a bloody battlefield!"

She stiffened. "I may not be as innocent as you think."

Laughing softly, Lamont said, "You are—a man always recognizes that kind of thing."

"And what *kind* of *thing* are you referring to, may I ask?"

"Surely you wouldn't want me to have to spell it out for you, Miss Weston."

Glaring at his cocked brow and mocking grin, Cathy put one hand on her hip. "I think that I prefer for you to do so, Mr. Lamont. Statements such as that one should not go unexplained."

"You see? You've just clarified my point. A woman of the world would have understood my meaning." His tone grew harsher. "You, Miss Weston, are only a child—and a rather spoiled one at that."

"But you didn't kiss a *child* a few minutes ago."

He smiled knowingly. "True enough . . ."

Cathy jerked to a halt, stilling her tongue before any more impetuous words escaped. How had the conversation degenerated to this so quickly? She took a deep breath.

"I will see to your noontime meal now," was all she said as she turned to leave. Her footsteps quickened as she strode away from his bed.

"You're running away, Miss Weston," Lamont's voice called after her, mockingly, derisively.

That halted Cathy where she stood. She swung around to glare at him. "I may be a *child,* but I still have sense enough to know when I'm in dangerous waters with a shark, Mr. Jesse Lamont. As far as I am concerned, our conversation is ended."

The drapes fluttered wildly as she pushed toward the exit. Cathy was so angry at hearing Lamont's deep, mocking laughter that she did not see the three little girls who were just entering the room. She stumbled over the smallest child, and paused to offer an apology.

"Oh! I'm dreadfully sorry," she murmured as she reached out to adjust the bonnet that had been knocked askew by their collision. As she straightened, Cathy caught the eye of Miss Nightingale, who was obviously shepherding the children, and her cheeks flushed in embarrassment. "I . . . I . . . I was in such a hurry . . . it's noontime and . . . well, I was distracted. I apologize for not watching more carefully," she ended lamely.

Miss Nightingale smiled. "That's quite all right, Cathy. There's been no harm done. Were you going after Mr. Lamont's noon meal?"

Cathy nodded. "Yes. He seems to have acquired a voracious appetite for something besides his nurse."

As Miss Nightingale's brow rose in amusement, one of the children giggled, and Cathy looked down. They were lovely children, garbed in pretty, frilly dresses and pinafores. The three girls were obviously sisters, though their coloring was not similar. The child who giggled had dark hair and velvety black eyes, while the other two girls had gleaming red hair. The unusual combination was arresting, and Cathy found herself smiling back at them.

"Miss Weston," Miss Nightingale was saying, "these young ladies are here to visit Mr. Lamont." When Cathy's head jerked up and her eyes widened in mortification, Miss Nightingale continued: "These are his children, so do you suppose it would be too much trouble to delay his meal for a half hour? They may not get the opportunity to visit again for some time."

Somehow Cathy found the presence of mind to nod and say, "Yes, of course." She hadn't known—even considered the fact—that Mr. Lamont was married, nor had she entertained any notion of his having children. But of course he would. The man was probably in his late thirties or early forties, though it was difficult to tell because he appeared so youthful. She should have thought of that, but somehow she never had.

"Thank you, Miss Weston," Miss Nightingale said as she ushered the children forward, and Cathy nodded numbly.

Cathy kicked her heels against the rungs of the kitchen stool as she ate her lunch and talked with the cook. They discussed Mr. Lamont's dinner menus at great length, and she discovered to her surprise that he was in the habit of taking his evening meal with Lord Bothmourne. The cook also took great pleasure —exhibiting her disdain—in the fact that on two separate occasions, Mr. Lamont had sent for his and the duke's meals to be brought in from one of the private clubs that specialized in French cuisine. Cathy now felt that there was no limit to the surprises in store where Jesse Lamont was involved.

After waiting for two hours, Cathy deemed it time to take up a tray of food to her recalcitrant patient. She hefted the well-laden tray and retraced her steps down the long corridors to the ward, taking a deep breath before she stepped inside. Lamont was alone, perusing the daily papers with great attention. There was no sign of the three girls, and Cathy allowed herself only a moment's curiosity about them as she entered the draped cubicle and set down his tray.

"Your lunch," she said tersely.

Lamont looked up for a brief moment, then returned his attention to one of the papers.

Feeling slightly rebuffed, Cathy shrugged and held out his napkin. "You need to eat, Mr. Lamont. Your work can wait until afterward."

"I don't need a nanny, thank you, Miss Weston!"

Cathy replaced the ignored napkin on his tray, folded her arms across her chest, and said coolly, "I can see that you don't think so, Mr. Lamont."

Turning her back to him, she retrieved one of her own papers from the bedside table, pulled up her chair, and sat down to read. She did not give Jesse another glance but stared with rapt attention at the flimsy pages of the periodical. It was the latest installment in *Household Words,* the beginning of chapter four of *Hard Times* by Charles Dickens. In her present mood, Cathy did not dare even attempt to read her other material, *Paradise Lost* by John Milton, though she especially liked the part about Satan, Azazel, and Beelzebub in their revolt against God. Not that she was cheering the devil on, of course, for she wasn't. No, she just found it easy to identify with their rebellion against the fatherly figure. Milton had realistically portrayed the revolting angels, and Cathy could well understand their defiance. Wasn't it the same with her? And poor Miss Mooney had been exceedingly shocked by Cathy's professed opinion of the same, and strongly cautioned her young charge against harboring such wicked feelings.

"Read Dickens instead," Miss Mooney had advised. And so Cathy had smilingly laid aside Lucifer and his angels in exchange for the trials of Bitzer and poor Sissy Jupe. Of course, she enjoyed Dickens, having read one of his novels and being eager to read more, and at this time—with Lamont proving to be such a *temperamental* patient—she could not have read the more absorbing Milton, or even her nursing texts. Dickens provided her with a satisfactory escape.

After several minutes of silence, except for the mutual turning of newspaper sheets, Jesse said, "Miss Nightingale is leaving next week."

Cathy looked up from the periodical. "Is she? How have you become aware of this?"

"She told me just a short time ago, when she was here."

Cathy was silent for a moment, then murmured, "Would you please excuse me for a time? I must speak with Miss Nightingale as soon as possible."

There was a brief hesitation and a rattle of news sheets. Then Jesse said, "I'll miss you, Miss Weston."

"I *said* I would be gone only for a few moments," she began in exasperation, but he smiled and shook his head.

"Never mind. That's not what I meant."

There was a peculiar gleam in his eyes when she stared at him uncertainly, and Cathy might have stayed had he not returned to his former, crabby self and insisted that she go away at once.

"I'll be just fine, Miss Weston. You go. And . . . and take care of yourself," he said, lifting his news sheets again as if they were a shield between them.

Irritated, but with a nagging sense of words left unsaid, Cathy still hesitated before she pivoted and walked from the hospital ward. Jesse Lamont was, indeed, a very odd man, but in spite of his occasional rudeness, he was also a very intriguing man. She shrugged away her feeling of impending disaster as she walked down the long, tiled corridors of the hospital in search of Miss Nightingale.

Chapter 5

"$\mathcal{D}$o not take on so, Miss Cathy," Ida Mooney said with a fair amount of exasperation mixed with her concern. Cathy's head lifted, revealing an unhappy face, and Miss Mooney's tone grew kinder. "There's no need to grieve," she said softly.

"I'm not grieving," Cathy said. "It's . . . it's just that . . ." That what? she asked herself silently. That Jesse Lamont had gone without saying good-bye? That she had returned from Miss Nightingale's office to find his bed empty, and no trace of him? Or maybe it was that everything seemed to be happening at once. It was now October 21, the day Miss Nightingale was leaving for Scutari with her nurses. Selina Bracebridge had seen to the making of the uniforms, money had been raised for supplies, and arrangements had been made to purchase some of what the contingent would need on its way to Turkey. Maybe that was it. Maybe Cathy felt left out, abandoned by all. She had nothing to look forward to now. After all, many of her friends would be leaving, and her special duty as nurse to Jesse Lamont had ended with his strange disappearance. Nothing had been heard from him.

Where could he have gone?

Miss Mooney's hands gently cupped Cathy's shoulders. "Hold your head up, child. You must. Remember—your father will arrive soon."

Pulling away, Cathy turned to stare out the window at the busy street below, idly watching passing carriages and pedestrians. How could she forget? How could she forget for a single instant that Nathaniel Weston would soon be arriving in London expecting his daughter to curtsy submissively and say "Yes, Papa" to his demands to return to America with him?

I can't! I just can't go back to New York with him!

Cathy pressed her face against the glass windowpane, solemnly watching a man try in vain to keep hold of his umbrella as the winds howled and tugged mercilessly at it. Brown leaves curled and skittered along the sidewalks, racing ahead of the wind, catching on pedestrians' outer garments and against brick walls. October. What a dreary month, with cold, wet rain and bare-limbed trees in the park. The entire world seemed cheerless at the moment.

Twisting away from the gray day outside the window, Cathy looked at Miss Mooney. "There's something I must know," she murmured as she gazed into those familiar gray eyes.

"What is it, Miss Cathy?"

Suppressing a smile at Ida Mooney's carefully cool tone, Cathy resisted the urge to tell her that her secret had been found out, that she knew "Ironclad Ida" wasn't nearly as cold and emotionless as she pretended to be.

"If I decide to stay on in London—alone—would you be adverse to staying with me?"

Miss Mooney's glacial eyes thawed to alarmed concern as she gasped, "Stay here? How can you even consider it? Miss Nightingale is gone, and your duties at the institution are over until she returns. How can you even consider it?" she repeated.

When Cathy didn't answer immediately, Miss Mooney stalked over to the bentwood rocker by the fire and snatched up her knitting. She sat down, working her needles with a furious clackety-clack. The rocking chair swooped back and forth like an angry bird of prey, and Cathy had to smile. She moved close to the fire and looked down at Miss Mooney.

"Won't you consider the notion that I may be old enough to make my own way in the world? I'm no longer in the nursery, Miss Mooney. Father is smothering me, choking the very life and joy of living from my entire soul! If I don't leave him, I'll *die!*"

Small, birdlike hands deftly twisted a length of ivory thread around a gleaming needle. It darted in silvery flashes through the lace of the collar she was fashioning. *Oh, no—the silent reign again,* Cathy thought with a groan. Her hands rested on her slim hips as she faced Ida Mooney with a defiant grimace.

"I will not return with him!" she said loudly, and Miss Mooney laid down her knitting and looked up.

After gazing searchingly at her for a moment, Miss Mooney said, "I think I believe you. Just how do you propose deploying this irrevocable resolution of independence? Mr. Weston is certain to cut you off without a penny! Yes, without a penny! And he will most certainly have an attack of apoplexy if poverty does not dissuade you! What then, Miss Cathy?"

"I have no ready answers, Miss Mooney. I am confident that time will provide them." There was a lengthy pause during which Cathy's gaze remained fastened on Miss Mooney's face. "You did not answer my question—will you stay with me?"

The answer was simple. "Of course I will stay with you, Miss Cathy."

Cathy's relief was evident, and she threw her arms around Miss Mooney's neck, and the older woman lost her composure. "Oh, thank you, Miss Mooney! I would have hated it without you, you know, and been so lost without your guiding force beside me."

"I'm well aware of that," was the prim answer, but the pat on Cathy's back was gentle and comforting. "Someone has to look after you, you know," Miss Mooney said. Cathy sat back, while

Ida rearranged her spectacles and mussed hair. "I would never forgive myself for leaving such an impressionable young woman like yourself alone in a city like London! Why, there's no end to the trouble you could find if left to your own devices." A severe frown creased her face as she asked, "Have you considered the fact that there will quite probably be no funds for our living expenses when you inform your father of your decision?"

Taken aback, Cathy paused to think of the consequences that might occur. Being financially deprived herself was one thing, but that Miss Mooney might have to suffer along with her was an entirely different matter.

"Perhaps I could take in some sewing," Miss Mooney suggested quietly, "or even—"

"No!" Cathy was quick to say. "This is my problem, and I intend to solve it alone. You will not be required to hire out your talents, Miss Mooney!"

"But whatever can *you* do without training, child?"

"I can teach," Cathy said doggedly. "Father gave me a wonderful education. I have certain connections here in London. After all, there's Aunt Ophelia and—"

Miss Mooney shuddered delicately. "I can imagine your aunt's reaction should you broach the subject of common employment!"

Cathy's mouth pursed into a determined frown. "Then I shall enlist the aid of Francis Compton!"

"Oh, Miss Cathy! The man is deeply in love with you! If you desire independence, Compton is decidedly *not* the sort of man you should ask for help. Have you considered that he may expect some sort of *obligation* on your part?"

Plopping onto the hearth rug at Miss Mooney's feet, Cathy sank her chin into the cup of her palms and stared morosely into the fire flickering in the grate. "You're quite right, of course."

Miss Mooney's hand rested briefly on Cathy's gleaming hair as she said, "Let's not worry more about it now. First things must come first, and your father has not yet arrived. Perhaps we should give him the benefit of the doubt, and hope that he will understand your desire for independence. If he does not, then we shall know what must be done."

Picking her knitting back up, Miss Mooney clicked her needles for several minutes as Cathy brooded silently. The fire popped and crackled, and the French clock on the mantel ticked rhythmically, marking the passage of time. Time was often her enemy, often her friend, and for once Cathy could not decide which it was.

"Are you going to wish Miss Nightingale farewell?" Miss Mooney asked several minutes and dropped stitches later. Her nimble fingers made a looped stitch as she waited for Cathy's reply.

Cathy's chin sank lower into her cupped hands. She had avoided such a scene, uncertain of her ability to remain cheerful while they departed. After all, she had grown so close to Miss Nightingale over the past few months that it would be hard seeing her off. Both Miss Nightingale and Miss Bracebridge had urged her to go with them to the docks, but she had been hesitant. She hadn't wanted to see them off—she had wanted to go with them. Joining the nurses would have been an excellent method of escaping Nathaniel Weston, and Miss Nightingale had sensed the reason behind Cathy's strong desire to go.

"Fleeing one's responsibility is not the correct motive for taking on an even larger burden, Cathy," she'd said. "You must face your father if you are ever to be free of him. True independence is gained by standing up for your beliefs, then trying to live them."

Cathy's chin lifted, and she looked up at Miss Mooney. "I think I shall wear my rose wool gown to the docks," she said. "After all, it's cold and blustery, and . . . and I may never see her again," she ended.

Miss Mooney put down her knitting. "I'll arrange for a carriage."

Miss Mooney waited in the warm carriage with a heated brick at her feet while Cathy braved the cold winds and occasional drizzle on the dock. A passenger steamer was crowded with people, all of whom seemed to wave and yell at once. Craning her neck, Cathy searched the sea of nameless faces, hoping for a glimpse of Miss Nightingale or one of the nurses. Finally she saw Selina, and pushed her way through the throng to greet her.

"Miss Bracebridge!" Cathy had to shout over the noise of the others. "Miss Bracebridge!"

Glancing up with her slight, perpetual frown, Selina Bracebridge's expression lightened when she recognized Cathy. "Miss Weston! Miss Weston—over here!" she shouted back, signaling that Cathy should try to press closer. It was a struggle, but finally Cathy stood beside her.

The wind blew over their heads, spitting droplets of rain and adding to the pandemonium, and when Florence Nightingale managed to push her way through to them, she was out of breath and laughing in amazement.

"Shocking, isn't it?" she said cheerfully, lifting her voice to be heard. Cathy laughed and nodded.

"Dreadfully so," she agreed, giving the woman a hug of welcome.

Swathed in wool and furs, Cathy did not feel the cold wind, and she felt slightly ashamed as Miss Nightingale stood there garbed in only a cotton gown and cloth coat. But the older woman did not seem to feel the cold. She was too exhilarated, too filled with purpose to notice. Her mind was filled with a thousand tiny details, all scurrying about as usual, like mice in a cage, and she now directed her thoughts toward Cathy.

"I wasn't certain you would come," she began without preamble.

"Oh, I could not let you leave without coming to bid you farewell and safe passage!" Cathy cried. "And I am going to miss you so. . . ."

When hot tears spurted in Cathy's eyes, Miss Nightingale drew her close. "Keep up with your studies while I'm gone, dear. When I get back we will finish them. Until then, you must be patient."

"I know," Cathy murmured, wiping at her tears with her little fur muff. She forced a wan smile. "I'm just behaving as a child afraid of what's ahead, that's all."

"We're all afraid," Selina Bracebridge put in briskly. "But we have little choice except to be courageous! You are a strong person, Miss Weston. You will manage well."

Florence Nightingale gave Cathy a reassuring squeeze. "You are much stronger than you realize," she said, lifting a black ledger she carried. She flipped it open to reveal four letters loosely tied with a white ribbon. These were her most important letters, letters she felt were vital. One of them was from her mother, one from Father Manning, who had assisted the younger Florence Nightingale with her early training in Paris, another from Richard Monckton Milnes, and the last letter from Jesse Lamont. "Ah, this is for you, Cathy," she murmured, withdrawing it from the packet. She held it out to Cathy, gripping it tightly so the wind would not carry it away.

"For . . . me?" Cathy inquired in surprise, reaching out for it. "Why, whatever . . . whoever is it from?"

"It contains a request for an undertaking that I wish you to perform for me, Cathy," was the answer, shouted above the rising wind and clamor of voices. "It's not only for me, but for you. No, don't open it now," she added when Cathy would have done so. "It's too rainy and there's so little time to explain." Nodding, Cathy tucked the letter into the reticule hanging from her arm.

There was no time for questions or answers then, for the last passenger call was bellowed out from the bridge of the steamer. Final farewells were taken as those leaving began to kiss friends and relatives. Baggage was swung aboard and last-minute hugs were given and received. A shriek of steam emanated from one of the slender stacks atop the steamer, signaling that it was about to depart.

"Good-bye, Cathy! Take care!" Miss Nightingale shouted into her ear, giving her a last tight hug. "I will write to you," she added.

"I'll write back!" Cathy called as Miss Nightingale was pulled away by the press of the crowd. It moved forward like an inexorable tide, pulling along all in its path as Cathy struggled to avoid being dragged aboard the steamer. She watched from the safe vantage point of a stack of cargo bound for another port as Miss Nightingale, Miss Bracebridge, and the fourteen nurses were swept aboard. She stood on tiptoes waving good-bye, though she wasn't certain any of them could see her, watching until the gangplank was pulled up. They were on their way to Scutari.

Hunching her shoulders against the brisk wind blowing across the harbor and along the rotting quays, holding her breath against the foul odor of decaying fish and vegetation, Cathy made her way back to the carriage in total misery. It was only when she had clambered into the waiting vehicle and slumped onto the velvet squabs beside Miss Mooney that she recalled the letter in her reticule.

"What's that?" Miss Mooney asked curiously as Cathy removed it and broke the seal.

There was no answer for several long moments. The carriage lurched forward, horse hooves clattering over the cobblestones as they went along at a moderate pace, and Miss Mooney watched Cathy's face with a growing frown. Her fingers twitched impatiently as she saw Cathy's expression go from surprise to pleasure to dismay.

"Well?" she demanded again.

He's alive—he's alive and in England and wishes me to live in his house. . . .

Cathy recovered from her daze and looked up at her companion. "It's from Mr. Jesse Lamont. I . . . I can hardly think why he would write to Miss Nightingale concerning me, but it seems—"

"Lamont? The gentleman who was shot?" Miss Mooney asked sharply. When Cathy nodded, the older woman muttered something about true gentlemen never being in a position to have themselves shot before she asked, "What does he say?"

Half laughing, Cathy held up the letter and said in a faintly incredulous tone, "He wishes to offer me a *position* in his home!"

"A position? I daresay! I can well imagine what sort of position a man who gets himself shot by a mysterious woman would offer! Humph! Let me see that. . . ."

The letter was duly handed over, and Ida Mooney's brows rose as she read aloud, ". . . offer you a room, meals, and eight pounds a month as governess to three young girls." The paper was crumpled in her hands as she exclaimed, "Can you imagine such a thing! *Eight pounds!* Why, that is almost a hundred pounds a year."

"Unheard of, I'd say," Cathy said doubtfully.

After a moment of silent consideration, Ida Mooney said, "Mr. Lamont has been very explicit in his offer, Miss Cathy. Perhaps this post may be a solution to your problem. Only think—he *was* recommended by none other than Miss Nightingale, whom I trust implicitly. She would not have given you this letter to consider had she not believed you would be quite safe." Miss Mooney tugged thoughtfully at her lower lip for a moment, then added, "Perhaps you should write to him and say that you are considering the position. Your father can hardly force you to return with him to New York if you are earning nearly a hundred pounds a year, can he?"

"No, but I am not entirely certain Mr. Lamont's motives are —shall we say?—selfless." Cathy did not care to mention the kiss, and instead offered the argument that fifteen shillings a week was the normal payment for such a post. "He has more than doubled the salary," she pointed out.

"Could it be because of the invalid child he mentioned in the letter? You are to act as nurse to one of the girls, if I understand correctly, and he is paying you in both capacities."

Shaking her dark head, Cathy stared curiously at Miss Mooney. "Just a few hours ago you were berating me even for considering remaining in London. Now you are practically pleading with me to accept a post with a man who was shot under quite curious circumstances. I find this departure from your earlier protestations most confusing."

Miss Mooney threw up her hands in exasperation. "Think what you must! I was only attempting to secure a decent post for you, and I *do* trust Miss Nightingale's judgment in those matters. I can be as contented in New York as I can in London, Cathy, but only as long as you are."

Recognizing the wisdom of the older woman's sentiments, Cathy lapsed into pensive silence, staring out the windows of the carriage. Jesse Lamont. How could she explain her reticence to Miss Mooney without scandalizing that good woman's finer sensibilities? How could she tell her of his kiss, that warm, lingering touching of the lips that had stirred her far more than she'd thought possible? She couldn't. She could not admit to anyone that she had lain awake many nights thinking of Jesse Lamont, recalling the feel of his firm mouth on hers and the texture of his skin beneath her hands. No, it would be best to say nothing.

Tightening her mouth, Miss Mooney sniffed indignantly and said, "Well, I shall not say another word about it, Miss Cathy, not another word! But mark my words—when your father arrives in London you had best have something in mind!"

This proved to be the case much sooner than either of them expected. When they arrived at their hotel a letter was waiting. It was from Nathaniel Weston.

"Directly from the dock, I suppose?" Miss Mooney inquired as she removed her cloak and shook it free of rain.

"Of course," was the weary reply.

Paper rustled ominously as Cathy opened the letter and spread it out on the lamp table to read:

> *My dearest Cathy,*
>
> *This letter has been sent the day before my departure upon the fastest clipper ship available. I am pleased to inform you that by the time you read this missive, I shall be almost docking in a London port. Too much time has separated us, my darling daughter. No more. I long for your company and your presence at my side. We will soon be reunited as a family. My only regret is that we are not surrounded by the serenity of our own home. But with spring, we shall celebrate the birth of a new relationship in New York.*
>
> > *Fondest wishes and all my love,*
> > *Father*
>
> P.S. *I am bringing you the most wonderful surprise!*

Despairing, Cathy crushed the letter into her balled fist. Love? What did her father know of love? Nathaniel Weston was far too possessive and domineering to understand about the tenderness of real love. He'd never once thought of Cathy's feelings; he'd considered only his own selfish needs. And even with just the threat of his arrival she was already beginning to feel the suffocating confines he would bring.

I won't go with him! I will be free!

"Miss Cathy? What is it?"

Ida Mooney paused in the act of brushing out her damp cloak to stare closely at the young woman. "Are you ill?"

"Yes," was the wry answer, "but not physically. My father will arrive at any moment. He speaks," she added in a bitter tone, brandishing the letter, "of love and returning to New York."

"I see."

Drooping, Cathy turned blindly toward the windows along the front of their rooms, pressing her face against the glass. It felt soothing against her flushed, angry cheeks, and she stared out without seeing. There was a lump in her throat, blocking her efforts to swallow her sudden surge of tears so that she had to try several times before succeeding.

Damn! she said silently. *Damn, damn, damn!*

There was a hiss as the fire caught, and Cathy shivered against a sudden chill. Miss Mooney was busily setting about making their rooms comfortable, but for Cathy there was no comfort to be had. Oppression hung heavily over her head, and she saw no way out, no way, but—why not?

Turning with sudden decision, Cathy said, "Miss Mooney, I have reconsidered my earlier decision. I've decided to accept Mr. Lamont's offer, as he seems a great deal more . . . agreeable . . . under these circumstances. I shall pen a reply to his letter at once, while you, Miss Mooney, shall pack our belongings! I wish to be firmly situated in my new post by the time Father arrives."

Chapter 6

With his dark head propped in his hands like a wishful schoolboy, Jesse Lamont perched on the edge of the window seat, gazing out the window at the vast, spreading darkness. He liked the night, particularly nights like this one when the sky was wide and black and sprinkled with the faintest glow of starlight. And it was nights like these, when the city streets were quiet and vacant of life or shrill sounds, that he enjoyed most. There was only the low hum of family activity emanating from the other houses along the row. This was a special time, a time when Jesse could relax and calmly reflect on the day's events.

The little girls were asleep, tucked snugly into their beds in the nursery. Jill, Erin, and Leigh—all sweet-faced angels beneath their covers, dreaming of sugarplums and fairies . . . at least they should be, Jesse thought wryly.

Lately the children had weighed heavily on his mind, especially since the shooting. It had been another unpleasant reminder of his mortality. The girls needed so much more than he'd been giving them the past few weeks, so much. Only recently he'd made a decision that should eliminate any liability of neglect. He had taken pen in hand and written to Miss Nightingale with the request that she entreat Miss Weston to accept the position of governess, and nurse for Jill.

Cathy Weston—a sparkly eyed, spirited woman . . .

A slight smile flickered briefly on his lips. Miss Catherine Weston was, indeed, everything he required in a governess. She was elegant, genteel, and, most important of all—intelligent.

And beautiful, the inner voice reminded.

Jesse's smile returned, and he laughed quietly to himself. Yes, Miss Weston was a headstrong young woman. He had managed to eavesdrop enough to know that Miss Weston was attempting to lead an independent life free of her possessive American father. And, to no one's great surprise, Mr. Lamont had also been able to ascertain that one Lord Francis Compton wished to wed Cathy Weston, but she had refused to have him. He liked that. It meant the woman was not a fortune hunter, as were so many young women these days.

Turning away from the window, Jesse shoved his hands deep into his trousers pockets as he paced the carpeted floor of his room. Commitment. It was a word he understood as few did. Maybe this Miss Weston understood it also. He had been dedicated for most of his adult life to serving his country. England was his true mistress. Could it be possible that Miss Weston was also dedicated to her own principles and ideals, dedicated enough to risk her entire way of life for them? It was a novel notion.

And even without a certain unwilling admiration for her pluck, he had to admire her beauty. There was just something about her that attracted him. Perhaps she wasn't the most beautiful woman he'd ever seen, but if there had been another, he couldn't bring her face to mind. A grin slanted his mouth, and he chuckled. For a temptress, Cathy Weston did not seem to appreciate his attentions at all! In spite of her reluctance, however, he intended to assist her in any manner possible, and, in turn, she could assist him.

Tap . . . tap . . .

The sharp rap on his door startled Jesse, and he turned to face the heavy oak portal as if it would immediately swing open to reveal the intruder. Clearing his throat at the second hesitant rap, he called out, "Yes? Who is it?"

"Pickworth, sir."

Jesse strode across the room, his footsteps noiseless against the carpet, then swung open the door. "Yes, Pickworth?" His brow lifted inquiringly as he gazed down at the man who had been with him for more than fifteen years.

Pickworth's bald head was as pink and shiny as his face, and he seemed somewhat embarrassed and perplexed when he offered the news that there were two ladies waiting downstairs for his employer.

"Two ladies?" Jesse echoed incredulously, glancing at the mantel clock, which had only just chimed nine of the evening.

"Yes, sir. They seem refined, sir, and claim to have business with you. I tried to explain that you had retired for the evening and they should come back in the morning, but they would have none of it—particularly the young one." Pickworth coughed discreetly. "She was . . . er . . . *quite* insistent that I inform you she was here, sir. Her name is Miss Catherine Weston. Being rather at a loss as to what was proper in this unusual circumstance, I showed them into the front parlor while I came to you, sir."

Jesse almost smiled. "That was correct, Pickworth."

"And, Mr. Lamont—they have their *baggage* with them," was the final pronouncement, delivered in a haughty tone.

"Their bags—very good, Pickworth. Tell them I will be down directly, and then ask cook to prepare a light repast for our guests. They will be staying in the blue rooms."

"Staying in the blue rooms?" Pickworth repeated in a bewildered tone. "Very good, sir."

This time Jesse did smile at the elderly servant's obvious confusion. Poor Pickworth. During the entire time Pickworth had been in Lamont's service, the man had never quite gotten accustomed to some of the stranger aspects of Jesse's life in the foreign ministry. He placed a hand on the man's shoulder, and his smile was reassuring.

"Don't fret, Pickworth. Miss Weston is the governess whom I engaged for the girls. One blue room adjoins the nursery, and the other is Father's old room. Those should do quite nicely for them, don't you think?"

"Oh . . . oh, yes, sir. Quite nicely. Do you think they will be comfortable there, sir? I mean, your father's old room is quite a distance from the nursery."

But Jesse had turned and was searching for the coat he'd removed earlier. "Dammit!" he muttered. "Where could my coat have gone to?"

"Here it is, sir," Pickworth said, taking two steps and lifting up the olive-drab frock coat Jesse had earlier laid across the back of a chair.

"Whatever would I do without you, Pickworth?" Shrugging into his coat, Jesse followed his servant from the room.

The front parlor glowed cheerily, the fire in the grate casting long shadows and bright pools of light across the furnishings and guests. Cathy and Miss Mooney were stiffly perched on the edge of a brocade settee as they waited, both of them starting when the parlor doors opened.

"Miss Weston," Jesse said as he entered the parlor, his hands still straightening the rumpled collar of his frock coat.

Standing at once, Cathy let her gaze rake over his tall frame. Inexplicably, her first thought was to wonder if his wound still bothered him; the second was to think that he looked much taller than she remembered him to be. Of course, he had spent his entire time in the hospital stretched upon a bed, but still . . . and he exuded *force* and energy now, when before he had been quite vulnerable.

And he is so wickedly handsome—like Mr. Milton's Azazel, the angel who helped Satan build his new world. Or do I think so because I am still being rebellious?

But nothing of Cathy's private thoughts showed as she lifted her hand to Lamont and said in a steady voice, "I do hope you will forgive our coming on such short notice, and at this disgraceful late hour, but circumstances demanded that we vacate our hotel this evening."

As Lamont took her hand, Cathy ignored the pricking of her conscience that bade her tell him of her father's arrival in London and her subsequent flight. Her narrow escape from Nathaniel Weston could hardly interest Jesse Lamont, could it?

"No need for an apology, Miss Weston," he was saying as his lips grazed the back of her hand. Dark eyes shifted to the elderly woman standing by the settee. "This is your companion, I presume?" Jesse said, stifling a laugh at the woman's narrowed gaze directed at the hand still holding Cathy's.

"Yes, this is Miss Mooney," Cathy offered. When Jesse dropped her hand and turned to her companion, Cathy opened her mouth to warn him not to cozy up to her, but it was too late. Jesse had grasped Miss Mooney's reluctant fingers in his hand and was lifting them to his lips in a formal gesture of greeting.

Well aware of the older woman's reluctance, Jesse took a rather perverse pleasure in this token gesture. Miss Mooney's austere mien reminded him of his own nursery days, and how dear old Miss Thistlegood would have gazed at him with just such an expression of distaste.

Eager to leap into the icy breach yawning before them, Cathy plunged in with, "Miss Mooney is my companion and closest friend. Why, she has been with me since I was only ten years old. I was certain that you would not mind her accompanying me, though nothing was mentioned in your letter, Mr. Lamont. Shall we discuss it?"

"There's no need for discussion right now," Jesse said, dropping Miss Mooney's hand and turning back to Cathy. "Of course she may stay. I did not expect you to abandon your companion out of hand, Miss Weston. I suppose I assumed it would be understood that she would arrive with you. We shall discuss terms later."

Miss Mooney remained silent, her thin lips compressed in a straight line as she assessed Jesse Lamont. This was no callow youth Cathy was dealing with, but a mature man who obviously knew what he wanted. The question foremost in Miss Mooney's mind was: What did he want? A governess for his children, certainly, but was there perhaps another benefit he expected to derive? She had seen the slight gleam in his eyes when he'd looked at Cathy, that telltale flicker of interest that told so much more than his face or words had revealed. And she didn't trust him—not for an instant.

So when Jesse turned to Miss Mooney and suggested that she unpack their things, that Pickworth would show her to their rooms, she gave him a baleful stare and said, "Thank you, Mr. Lamont."

Pickworth chose that moment to arrive with a silver tray well laden with an ornate pot of tea and three china teacups and matching saucers. Tiny cakes and biscuits were arranged on the tray, as well as a pot of honey and a small pitcher of milk.

Jesse indicated that Pickworth should place it on the teakwood table nearby, then turned his attention back to Miss Mooney.

"I'm certain you will wish to get some of your things unpacked now," Jesse said smoothly, beckoning to the hovering Pickworth to come forward. "Pickworth, show Miss Mooney to the blue room beside the nursery. Miss Weston may take Father's old room."

"Very good, sir." Pickworth made a polite bow and stood ready to usher Miss Mooney from the parlor.

"Oh, and see that cook sends a light repast to their rooms, Pickworth. I have some matters to discuss with Miss Weston before she goes up, so we shall remain here for a short time."

"Very good, sir," was the reply.

Miss Mooney leveled a meaningful glance at Cathy before she strode from the parlor with Pickworth, her look saying quite plainly that Cathy should be careful. The double doors closed softly behind them, and Jesse turned to Cathy.

Nervous at being left alone with the man who had dwelled in her thoughts for so many weeks, Cathy stepped to the teakwood table. "Shall I pour our tea?"

"By all means." A thoughtful smile tugged at his lips as he moved away, stepping to the long table positioned at the left side of the fireplace. Several crystal decanters sat on glass trays, and Jesse reached out to lift one. "Do you care for a spot of brandy in your tea, Miss Weston?"

She lifted her head to stare at him, brown eyes growing large. The heavy teapot shook in her hands. "Brandy?" she echoed, struck by the unusual notion. Perhaps it would be a sort of celebration. After all, she had narrowly escaped her father's grasp this evening, and now she was here with a new position, and Mr. Lamont seemed to be in such a fine mood. "Yes, brandy sounds perfect, Mr. Lamont."

"It tastes as good as it sounds," Jesse remarked with a smile.

A healthy splash of brandy was duly added to the tea, and Cathy and Jesse lifted their delicate china cups from the saucers and paused.

"I think this calls for a toast, Miss Weston—a toast to our renewed acquaintance," Jesse said, holding up his cup.

Smiling, Cathy agreed. "Yes, and shall we toast England also, Mr. Lamont?"

"Excellent! To victory!"

"England's victory," Cathy said.

Jesse's teacup was drained in one swallow. Cathy took a small sip, then another, her eyes peering over the rim of the cup at her host. He poured another dram of brandy into his emptied cup, added a splash of tea, and drank it while Cathy was still sipping at her first cup.

"There are things you need to know," he began without preamble.

Cathy sat back down on the edge of the settee, smoothing her skirts and holding her teacup in her lap. "Yes?"

"First, I am not an easy man with whom to live. I keep irregular hours. I detest being bothered by petty household problems. There are many peculiarities attendant to this position, which you will soon discover for yourself." He paused to stare pointedly at her. "One thing in particular that annoys me is being disturbed with routine decisions. One reason I felt you would be so appropriate for this position was my judgment that you are capable of making sound decisions without my assistance. I trust you understand my meaning?"

"Yes. Thank you for your confidence in me."

"Kindness is *not* one of my virtues, Miss Weston!" Jesse retorted sharply. "I have little confidence in anyone. I've discovered it wise to trust no one, so do not make any unfounded assumptions. As for my *confidence* in you, that remains to be proven." Pausing, he allowed a smile to curve his mouth. "You will soon find that I dislike pretense and idle words."

Tensing, Cathy swallowed the hot rush of words that quivered on the tip of her tongue. What a rude man he could be! "I shall not doubt it again," she responded with a raised brow.

"Then we have arrived at an understanding. Good. I need a governess with your particular qualifications, and you need this position. We shall deal well together, as that is the basis of our relationship. I rely upon you to perform the task of caring efficiently for my three nieces—"

"*Nieces!*" Cathy could not keep from blurting out. The china teacup almost fell from her hands. "But I thought they were your daughters."

"Did you? How wrong of you to leap to such a conclusion, Miss Weston."

"Apparently," she said, recognizing from his sudden withdrawal that she had offended him. When he lifted the decanter of brandy and held it out, she shook her head. His black eyes were remote and distant, and he seemed to retreat even more. "Never having been told differently, I suppose I just assumed the girls were your daughters," she said after a moment of awkward silence.

Jesse placed the crystal decanter on the tea tray. "No one should have been presumptuous enough to mention it, Miss Weston. It is no one's business but my own."

Chilled by his cold rebuff, Cathy nodded. After all, she should be accustomed to his verbal abuse by this time. Hadn't she listened to it daily while he was her patient? Mr. Jesse Lamont was probably equally as rude to Queen Victoria, and Cathy wondered with a wry twist of her lips how he had ever been drawn into the diplomatic field.

"I understand, Mr. Lamont," she said quietly, squelching the urge to say more.

"I never discuss my past, Miss Weston. And as I do not sense in you a raging desire to dwell upon your own personal history, I suggest we leave such matters as they are now. The most important matter on my mind—and I'm sure on yours—is the fact that Jill, Erin, and Leigh should be properly cared for. Jill is the eldest, and she has an extremely delicate constitution."

"I see. I must know the nature of her infirmity if I am to be able to help to the best of my abilities, Mr. Lamont."

A baffled expression crossed Jesse's face. It was the look of a man who had dealt with physicians for a great length of time and found no satisfaction. "If I listen to the leeches," he said bluntly, "we are privileged to have had her with us this long. I find them a damnably incompetent lot at best." He took another swallow of brandy and stared moodily into the fire.

Cathy searched his face for a trace of pity or tenderness for the child, and was dismayed to find none. Irritation, yes; exasperation, yes; tenderness, no. Her gaze skimmed his lean features with a distracted admiration for their sculpted perfection, and she felt that annoying, irregular thump of her heart when he turned back to face her. Their eyes met, clashing silently, two strong wills battling. Then Jesse's brow lifted, dispelling her magnetic pull toward him.

"There's no point in being maudlin, you know. People die every day, Miss Weston, and we are powerless to prevent it in most cases. I'm certain you dealt with that on a daily basis in the hospital."

Though she wanted to deny any emotions concerning the sick child or Jesse's reaction and callous remarks, she did not utter a word. And yes, she'd seen enough death in the past few months to know that the Grim Reaper spared no one, and had immunity to all emotions. No, it was not only Jesse's indifference that bothered her, but her own intense reaction to him as a man was what disturbed her the most.

"Maudlin? I should hope not. And yes, of course I saw much death and suffering in my short time at the institution, Mr. Lamont. Is it surprising that I would feel sympathy for the suffering of another human being?" Cathy answered.

"No, not so surprising. Perhaps you misunderstand, Miss Weston," Jesse said, putting down his teacup and stepping close to where she sat on the settee. "Jill is a . . . well, a *special* child, and I will not have her treated as an invalid because of her illness. I do not feel it would serve her well to be constantly reminded of her infirmities, nor do I think it advisable to cater to them. She is one of three children, and shall be treated as such. The only concessions shall be those recommended by Dr. Alexander. Have I made myself quite clear, Miss Weston?"

Bristling with irritation, Cathy did not name him the brute

she thought him, but merely nodded her head and said crisply, "Everything is perfectly clear, Mr. Lamont."

"Splendid. Now, there is just one other obstacle to surmount, and that is the question of your companion. While I had expected her to accompany you, I made no arrangements for her upkeep. That will be up to you. I am prepared, however, to offer her room and board for the sum of five shillings a week. That amount can be deducted from your pay if you wish."

"That is very generous of you, Mr. Lamont," Cathy said, relieved that Miss Mooney would be allowed to stay. And, after all, five shillings a week was a pittance compared to what it would cost to live elsewhere, as she was certain Jesse Lamont must know. Perhaps underneath that crusty exterior beat the heart of a man with *some* generosity!

Chapter 7

Thwack! It echoed down the hallway, a heavy sound that reverberated dully through the house. It sounded again, and again.

Half asleep, Cathy stirred slightly, opening one eye to peer through the dark shadows of her bedchamber. Had she been dreaming? But no, there it was again. Another *thwack*. Both eyes were open now, and she shook her head clear of the lingering wisps of dreams that had haunted her sleep. Father, Darcy, and Jesse Lamont had peopled her dreams in vague fragments and loud words.

Cathy sat up when the noise sounded again. It had adopted a rhythm now, a steady thumping that went on for several minutes. Then it stopped as abruptly as it had begun, and Cathy jerked upright. Snatching her robe from where it lay draped across the foot of the tall canopy bed, she threw it around her shoulders and lifted a lamp from the bedside table. Her fingers shook as she lit it, then crossed to the door. It creaked slightly as she opened it and peered into the dim hallway.

It was empty and silent.

Sighing, Cathy began to swing the door shut again when she heard the door just next to hers creak open. She stepped out and glanced down the hallway as a shaft of light illuminated the gloomy corridor. A tall silhouette was framed in the light, and

Cathy recognized Jesse as he stood in the doorway. So that was it. He was conducting some sort of activity in the room directly behind hers, and that must be the source of the strange noise.

Closing the door behind him, Jesse turned, and seemed surprised to find Cathy in the hallway. She pushed self-consciously at the stray tendrils of dark hair curling over her forehead and into her eyes as she felt his gaze upon her. She held up the lamp to illuminate the hallway.

"Hello, Miss Weston. You're up early."

"Yes, aren't I?" Cathy returned sweetly. "I don't suppose you'd know why." Lamont's hair was damp, and his forehead was beaded with perspiration. Attired in a long silk robe, he looked quite different from the man she was accustomed to seeing. Only his eyes were the same, black and filled with ironic amusement, a sort of constant mockery of the world—and women.

Cathy's gaze dropped to a safer area, his feet. They were bare beneath the striped-silk robe, and she wondered if he had forgotten his slippers as her gaze rose to search for an even more neutral spot at which to look. There was none. Jesse Lamont in a robe was a virile, potent sight. The silky material clung snugly to his broad shoulders and crossed over his chest, revealing a pelt of dark hair that lightly furred his chest. The elegant robe was cinched by a wide sash at his narrow waist, and she felt goose bumps feather up her spine. Cathy took a deep breath, lifted her dark eyes to his fathomless black ones, and forced a smile.

"Mr. Lamont . . ."

Taking the towel he was holding, he wrapped it around his neck. A broad smile slowly replaced the cynical quirk of his lips. "It is a bit too cool to stand here in such a state of undress, Miss Weston, so I shall carry on—that is, if you don't mind?"

"Mind? No, no, I don't mind," she managed to say.

"That's very good of you," he commented dryly, then moved

past her down the hallway. The door directly across from hers shut behind him.

Left to her own thoughts, Cathy retreated to her room and shut her door. She placed the lamp on the small table by the door, then leaned back against it with her hands splayed against the cool wood. How could she have been so silly, like a . . . a *schoolgirl!* She pressed her palms to her flushed cheeks and shook her head, stifling a laugh at her own foolishness. The redoubtable, always correct Mr. Jesse Lamont, and he had been wearing less than she was at this moment! Cathy would have solemnly vowed that he wore absolutely nothing beneath that thin silk robe, though she had not been quite daring enough to stare too closely.

Pushing away from the door, she ran her fingers through her dark tumble of curls. The clock on the fireplace mantel struck half past four, and she gave a start of surprise. Half past four in the morning? What on earth was Jesse Lamont doing up and about at that ungodly hour? He had definitely been doing something, for he had been wet with sweat. What did such a man have to do at such an early hour? It defied logic.

A thoughtful frown creased her brow as Cathy crossed to the high canopy bed and perched on the edge of the thick mattress. A soft hump of blankets was crumpled in a heap, and for the first time since she'd arisen, she felt a shiver of chill shake her. It was cool, much too cool without a fire or proper clothing. The fire in the grate had long since died to just smoldering embers, and soon a housemaid should be arriving to stoke it with fresh coal.

Perhaps she should forget about sleeping any more today. Too much would be going on, and she was already wide awake, wasn't she? It would be best just to get ready early and be ready for her first day with Jesse Lamont's nieces.

Sliding from the high bed, Cathy stepped to the carved-oak armoire and opened the doors. Miss Mooney had already hung up her garments, and they were arrayed on padded and scented hangers, waiting. She chose a subtle brown dress with Italian lace on the collar and cuffs of the basquin jacket. The plain skirt had no flounces, but simply draped softly to the floor.

Cathy performed her morning toilet leisurely, washing her face and hands in the huge china bowl on the washstand. The water was cool because of the room temperature, waking her even more and leaving a pink flush on her cheeks. Rather than wake Miss Mooney, Cathy chose to do her own hair, combing and coiling it into a thick braid at the nape of her neck. She covered it with a chenille net and was satisfied with the result. Miss Mooney could hardly have done better. Pearl earrings were her only adornment, and they matched the tiny buttons of her jacket.

The clock on the mantel struck half past five, and Cathy strode to the windows and opened the drapes. It was not yet light, but a diffused glow pinkened the eastern sky. Perhaps the weather would clear, and instead of gray skies, there would be blue, an auspicious beginning for her new life.

A smile curved her lips at the thought, and Cathy turned away from the windows to gaze with interest about her new quarters. She'd been too weary and absorbed the night before, but now, in the clearer light of day, she could see that it was a nice room. It was tastefully furnished in varying shades of blue, with the bed curtains matching those over the window. The canopy bed was crafted of a deep, rich wood and polished to a bright luster. Several deep-cushioned chairs of the same material as the drapes were placed about the room, and the dressing table had a gilt-edged mirror hung above it. A glass-globe lamp hand-painted with a cabbage rose stood on a lace-draped table before the window, and there were two silver-framed portraits on tiny tabletop easels. It was a comfortable room, a welcoming room, and Cathy was glad it had been chosen for her.

Smoothing her long skirts, she decided to brave the day and

confront the proverbial lion in his den. There was no time like the present to become acquainted with the daily ritual, and also the staff.

Cathy's first encounter was with Pickworth, whom she met in the downstairs hallway.

"Good morning, Mr. Pickworth," she said with determined cheeriness. "What time do the children normally rise?"

"Good day, Miss Weston. The children normally do not rise until they are sent for," he replied in a frosty tone. "Shall I send Beakins up for them?"

"Beakins? Who is . . . never mind. I wish to establish a new routine, but only if it will not upset your staff too much, Mr. Pickworth," Cathy said. "However, I shall not try to do too much too soon. I prefer first to watch and see how things are done before I go about changing things willy-nilly. If it is not asking too much, I shall need your advice on many things. Would you be averse to helping me?" Cathy gave him her most winsome smile, one that had been known to thaw even Nathaniel Weston at times. If she did not win over the staff to her side, she would have great difficulty getting anything done at all. Mr. Lamont had made it quite clear that he had no intention of becoming involved with petty household squabbles and problems.

Though having his own private thoughts about just how long this governess would stay, Pickworth appreciated being asked for his advice and help. Slightly inclining his head, he replied, "I shall do whatever I can, Miss Weston."

"Excellent! As I do not wish to tread upon any toes my first morning here, what do you suggest I do about taking my morning meal?"

"Miss Weatherly—the former governess—always ate in the kitchen instead of with the children. She said they made her nervous and spoiled her appetite."

"Did she, now? Well, I have an iron constitution. I fully

intend to be taking my meals with them for quite some time, Mr. Pickworth."

Again the bald head dipped, and there was a suggestion of approval in the gesture. "Very well, Miss Weston. I do suggest that you take your breakfast in the dining room this morning, however, as Mr. Lamont expressly requested that you do so. I can arrange to have Beakins wake the children as usual."

"Whatever you think is best, Mr. Pickworth," Cathy said, well on her way to winning him over with her tact and fresh beauty.

Pickworth cleared his throat, and the hairless expanse on his head pinked. "Yes. Well . . . ah . . . I do think Mr. Lamont would be highly pleased to know that you had done as he requested."

"Then so it shall be. Is this the way to the dining room, Mr. Pickworth?"

"Oh, no, Miss Weston, I shall be most happy to show you," the elderly man said. "And I shall tell cook you are ready to eat now."

"Thank you." Cathy followed him through the wide hallway to the dining room, asking as they neared the double doors, "Will Mr. Lamont be breakfasting with me this morning?"

"Mr. Lamont never breakfasts, Miss Weston. He eats only his evening meal here."

They had reached the end of the long staircase and Pickworth was pushing open the doors so that Cathy could enter. Swallowing the disappointment in her voice, Cathy murmured, "I regret that I shall not share breakfast with him this morning. I had several questions to ask."

"I shall be happy to inform him upon his return, but Mr. Lamont does not keep regular hours, I'm afraid."

"I see." Seating herself in one of the graceful chairs at the dining table, Cathy glanced around the huge empty room and asked, "Do the children ever come down to dine in this room, Mr. Pickworth?"

"The children? In the *dining room?*" Pickworth queried in such a scandalized tone that Cathy knew the answer immediately.

She laughed. "Are they such wretched little monsters that they cannot be taught proper table manners, Mr. Pickworth?"

"No, it's not that they cannot be trained, it's just that they *have not* been trained," he specified. "I shudder to think what Mr. Lamont's reaction might be at seeing them seated at his table."

"Quite interesting, I should say," Cathy responded with an irrepressible smile. "Nonetheless, I shall not do anything too entirely shocking, Mr. Pickworth. Table manners can also be taught in the schoolroom. It's just that they are better practiced in the dining room."

"Quite so, Miss Weston."

Cathy tapped her silver fork idly against the bone-china plate beside her. She could recall meals with her parents, meals in the elegant dining room of their home. It had been a much happier time before her mother had died, of course, but even afterward, Nathaniel Weston had not sent his daughter to the nursery for her meals. She had taken her mother's place at the end of the table. How pompous she must have looked—a ten-year-old girl puffed up with self-importance and reigning over a long dining room table cluttered with silver dishes and lit by gleaming chandeliers!

Pickworth cleared his throat. "Will there be anything else you require, Miss Weston?"

"Oh . . . oh, no, I'm sorry, Mr. Pickworth. I am quite ready to eat now, I think."

"Very good," he said, affecting a half bow in her direction.

Only a few minutes later a footman arrived with a tray of steaming dishes. Cathy ate silently, hardly noticing what she ate or how little. Her thoughts strayed from memories of herself as a child to the present. She wondered if Jesse Lamont was deliberately avoiding her, and if he would voice any objections with however she decided to train his nieces. It hardly seemed likely, but there were times one could not tell what another's reaction would be.

Miss Mooney was already in the nursery when Cathy arrived upstairs. It was a large, sunny room with long windows. A fire burned cheerily in the open hearth, and not far from it sat three small secretaires that were obviously used as desks. A comfortable settee helped to dissect the study area from the play area, and a large round table dominated the entire room.

Three little girls were seated quietly at the table with bowls of porridge before them, napkins tied neatly beneath their chins and silver spoons clutched in their hands.

"You've done well, Miss Mooney," Cathy said, with a smile. "Thank you."

Gazing up at her were three solemn faces, one dripping a small bit of porridge from her chin. "Are you Mith Wethton?" a voice lisped, and Cathy nodded.

"Yes, I am Miss Weston," she answered, stressing the *s*'s in her name. "And when you have finished your breakfast I would like to know which of you is Jill, which is Leigh, and which is Erin."

"I'm Erin!" the red-haired moppet with the porridge on her chin said at once.

Cathy reached out, lifted a corner of the napkin tied around her neck, and wiped away the porridge congealing on Erin's chin.

"Hello, Erin. We'll become better acquainted after you've eaten." Turning to Miss Mooney, who was watching Cathy with a skeptical expression on her face, she asked, "Have you eaten yet?"

"No. Mr. Pickworth has sent for a tray for me."

Cathy sensed her companion's skepticism at her former charge's chance of success with three young girls in pinafores and short skirts, and her grim expression plainly showed it. Suppressing the bubble of laughter in her throat, Cathy turned her attention back to the girls.

The oldest was Jill, a dark-haired child with a petulant expression and large thick-lashed eyes. She was gazing at Cathy with her lips pinched together and a frown creasing her brow. Her sallow complexion showed no sign of having seen the outdoors. There was no healthy color in her thin cheeks at all, and her constant frown only accented her pallor. Neither was there any sign of welcome or friendliness in the flat black eyes regarding Cathy as if she were an insect on a stick. This was obviously going to be a much more difficult task than Cathy had first envisioned, but she'd never been one to quit.

Leigh had to be the middle child, a bright-eyed girl with the look of perpetual laughter in her eyes and a ready smile on her lips. Her glossy hair was caught back with a red ribbon, and two more ribbons adorned her hair in a rather haphazard fashion. Someone's cast-off bracelets jangled on her little arms, and an old necklace bumped against her stomach as she leaned forward to dip porridge from her bowl. This was obviously a child who loved pretty jewelry and clothes.

And then there was Erin, a bright-haired, impish sprite with glittering eyes and no front teeth. Her gap-toothed smile showed no animosity or preconceived opinions, and Cathy was grateful. Jill's obvious displeasure would be enough to deal with for the moment.

When they had finished their breakfast and washed their faces and hands, Cathy assembled the children in front of her.

"Now, then. Let me guess—you are Erin . . ."

"You already know that!" the child cried with a giggle.

". . . and you are Leigh . . ."

"Yes!"

"So you must be Jill," Cathy finished. The sullen girl only gazed out the window, refusing to be drawn out that easily.

"Jill's got the sulks," Leigh confided. "She always does."

There was no reaction from Jill, and Cathy ignored the comments as she continued. "Beginning tomorrow, girls, I think it would be much nicer if we were to all take our morning meal in the dining room. It will be excellent training for you, and as Mr. Lamont never eats breakfast, we shall not disturb anyone. What do you think of that?"

"It's splendid!" Leigh said, enthusiasm bubbling in her eyes. "We have never eaten there."

"Yes, we have," Erin lisped. "Don't you remember? It was *awful!* I think that's why we never got to eat there again."

"Well, the next time you are invited to eat in the dining room, you will be properly prepared," Cathy said. A glance at Jill showed no reaction, but at least the child had not said anything derogatory.

The negative comments were issued by Pickworth. He drew her to one side of the schoolroom and began to remonstrate.

"You simply cannot do such a thing, Miss Weston!" he said, aghast. "Why, Mr. Lamont would be terribly irate if he were to learn that those children had been in the dining room!"

"Why? Does he intend to keep them in the nursery forever, Mr. Pickworth? I had rather intended it to be a pleasant surprise for him, don't you think? Just imagine what his reaction would be upon discovering how well behaved and well mannered his nieces are at the table!"

"I . . . I had not thought of that," Pickworth muttered in a thoughtful tone.

"Well, I had."

"And what if they are not? They were allowed last Christmas, you understand, and it was a *complete* disaster! Mr. Lamont was livid, and the governess was fired, and the entire staff was threatened if we ever allowed such a thing again."

"Believe me, Mr. Pickworth, I am quite capable of teaching proper manners to these young ladies."

New respect dawned in the elderly servant's eyes, and he nodded slowly. "I believe you are."

She smiled. "I knew you would understand. I take complete responsibility for their training. All that is required is that Mr. Lamont stay away from the breakfast table!"

Her small triumph did not quite outweigh the unsettled feeling that flared inside, however. She still had doubts, still had not been able to discover the source of the strange noises she had heard so early in the morning. It was a mystery she intended to solve if at all possible. All she had to do was spend a few moments alone with Jesse Lamont!

Chapter 8

*T*he day was spent well. Cathy conversed with the girls, who, after their initial shyness, freely discussed their studies and the house rules. At least the two younger girls spoke freely. Jill remained cool and distant, and when she was forced to answer a direct question, she did so in a resentful tone. Mystified by her coldness, Cathy did not press the child too closely. Perhaps a more relaxed attitude would prevail when Jill realized that Cathy meant her only well, and that she would not force her to give more of herself than she wished.

After all, didn't Cathy herself understand how it was to be alone and motherless? She could remember. And Miss Mooney had been a blessing to her. Perhaps Cathy could also be a blessing to these girls. The thought was warming.

It occurred to Cathy during the afternoon tea—when she listened to the girls chatter among themselves about their beloved uncle—to wonder what had happened to their parents. No one had spoken of the matter. She presumed they were both dead, but was reluctant to ask the children. Asking Jesse Lamont would probably only earn her an icy stare, so she made up her mind to ask Pickworth at the first opportunity.

That chance did not arise during the day, and Cathy sat thinking about it that evening while Miss Mooney brushed her long hair until it gleamed. Opportunity had, however, arisen for Miss Mooney, and she proceeded to wield her tongue sharply.

"Whatever would your father say, Miss Cathy? Did you think that because you managed to escape our hotel before his arrival that he will not search for you? I am warning you now that is not so. If I know anything at all about Nathaniel Weston —which I do—I can assure you that he will not leave a stone unturned in his search for you! And furthermore—"

"And furthermore," Cathy cut in wearily, "I will not be coerced into leaving my position here, Father or not!"

Miss Mooney gave a disbelieving sniff. "You may not have a choice!"

"I am old enough to choose my own way of life."

The brush stilled in midair, and Miss Mooney hefted the weight of Cathy's hair in one hand, staring at her in the mirror. "I agree with your feelings, Miss Cathy, but you must consider matters from your father's point of view. He will be first alarmed, then hurt, then angry when he discovers that you fled upon his arrival. Your actions will finally be misconstrued as denial and rebellion—which I am not at all certain is a misconception. At any rate, Mr. Weston will be quite angry."

"I am a grown woman," Cathy reminded her.

"Yes, and you are now making your own way in the world," Miss Mooney agreed. The brush moved through Cathy's hair again, the strokes long and firm.

"Then that means Father will have to reconsider how he feels about this."

Miss Mooney snorted. "That means nothing of the sort!"

"No?"

"No! He will come here and demand that you leave the employ of Mr. Lamont. Have you considered what Mr. Lamont's reaction will be to such theatrics? Your position may go out the window at that time! Only think how unsettling it is to be caught in the midst of familial dissension, especially when one has expressed a ferocious preference for the lack of it in one's own household."

"Oh. I had not thought—but surely Father will not come here to cause a scene?" Cathy said with a beseeching glance at Miss Mooney. When there was no reply, only a lifted brow and knowing stare, Cathy felt her earlier convictions flag. He would. Nathaniel Weston would do whatever he deemed necessary to regain control of his errant daughter. There would be a heated scene, and Lamont would look at her with that faintly mocking, contemptuous gaze, and she would shrivel inside. Lowering her head, she looked down at her hands, clenched in her lap. There was nothing for it but that she must speak with him first. She could not allow her father to come without preparing Lamont for the inevitable scene.

"I must speak with him first," she murmured aloud, lost in thought.

"Who? Your father?"

Cathy looked up. "No, Mr. Lamont."

Another disparaging snort issued from Miss Mooney's thin mouth. "I daresay! However cool and overbearing this Mr. Lamont may be, I do not consider him an equal match for your father, Miss Cathy."

"We shall see." Cathy's fingers drummed against the surface of the dressing table for a moment. Then she asked, "Do you recall that pelisse-robe we purchased last year? The one with the lace bodice and cuffs?"

Miss Mooney's eyes narrowed. "Yes, I do. It is hanging in the wardrobe. Why?"

"I think I shall wear it this evening."

Miss Mooney's lips pinched even more disapprovingly. "Is that so? Any special occasion, Miss Cathy? As I recall, that pelisse-robe is very . . . ornate."

"Ornate?" Cathy repeated with amusement. "Yes, I suppose

you could name it that, though it's rather an unusual term for such a lovely article of clothing."

"You prefer the term *unsuitable*, perhaps?"

"No, no. Ornate is quite adequate. Would you fetch it for me, please?"

"Delighted," Miss Mooney replied with a dour grimace. The hairbrush clattered to the dressing table, and Cathy almost winced at the reproof in the gesture.

Clearing her throat, she said, "I think the pelisse-robe will do nicely for a meeting with Mr. Lamont."

Miss Mooney halted immediately and turned to stare at Cathy. "A meeting with Mr. Lamont in *that* pelisse-robe? Have you gone daft, Miss Cathy?"

"Probably, but that has little to do with this. I must talk with him, and I have no intentions of doing so in my peignoir, yet I do not wish to appear as if I have waited up in my most elegant finery to speak with him. I would like to look casual . . . yet elegant."

"Refined, yet available?" Miss Mooney shot back sourly.

Exasperated, Cathy stomped her foot on the floor. "Do not judge me yet! I must give Mr. Lamont warning of what my father is likely to say or do . . ."

"So you intend to dazzle him with cleavage?"

Throwing her hands in the air, Cathy surrendered. "Have it your way, Miss Mooney! But I *shall* wear that pelisse!"

"By all means! Don't let *my* aversion to immodesty give you pause," was the acid reply as Miss Mooney yanked the offending pelisse-robe from the oak armoire.

"It's not that immodest," Cathy was heard to mutter as she took the garment from Miss Mooney and held it up to her body in front of the mirror. And indeed, it was a lovely creation, combining most charmingly the effect of day dress and pelisse. If the bodice *was* a bit low, scooping to the top of Cathy's breasts and revealing just a *shadow* of cleavage, it was more than com-

pensated for by the froth of lace trimming that descended from
the shoulder points, front and back, to form a blunt point at the
waist. The snug-fitting waist only showed how tiny Cathy was,
and that could not be considered at all immodest. How was she
to smooth out what could be a dreadful coil if she did not look
her best? Cathy wondered. She couldn't. The pelisse-robe would
do nicely, in spite of Miss Mooney's expressed reservations.

"Mr. Lamont may not wish to talk about your father this
evening," Miss Mooney observed as Cathy shrugged into the
lacy garment. "He may prefer discussing your attire—or lack of
it."

"Indeed?" was all that Cathy would say.

"Indeed. Men like Lamont have no scruples, you know."

"And what do you know that I don't, Miss Mooney?"

"I do not have to have a picture drawn to know that he is a
rather wild individual, Miss Cathy. It's in his eyes, and the way
he looks at you . . ."

"At *me?*" Cathy turned to stare at her.

"Don't feel flattered. Men like Lamont look at any female
that way."

"How do you know so much about men?" Cathy shot back,
turning to gaze into the mirror and rearrange the lace.

"One does not have to *play* cricket in order to recognize a
cricket bat, Miss Cathy," was the gentle reply.

"Now you're comparing Mr. Lamont to a game of cricket?"
Cathy inquired with an exasperated shake of her head. "I do
wish you had more confidence in my abilities to care for myself,
Miss Mooney! After all, I traveled in society's circles for over a
year with less remonstration than I have received in the past
fortnight!"

"The circles you frequented did not contain such a dangerous
element, Miss Cathy. Hold still while I fasten this button. . . .
There. You are now ready to do whatever it is you intend to
do."

Turning around to look directly at her grim-faced companion, Cathy asked softly, "Do you not understand me at all?"

"Oh, yes. That is part of the problem. I *do* understand you, Miss Cathy. I understand your need for independence, but I also understand that you have a reckless disregard for caution. You underestimate this Jesse Lamont."

"Do you think so?"

"I *know* so."

"Perhaps you are right. Only time will tell, but I just know that I must talk to him before Father comes to shatter our peace." Pacing the bathroom floor, Cathy said, "Mr. Lamont is seldom at home—*never* in the mornings, and only late in the evenings. That may be my sole opportunity to speak with him." Almost wringing her hands in anticipation of the impending interview, Cathy looked up at Miss Mooney with a pleading expression. "Pray that I can convince Mr. Lamont to ignore Father's tirade, or we may be seeking a new position!"

The clock on the fireplace mantel struck ten before Cathy heard Jesse Lamont's steps on the stairs. Her heart lurched into her throat, and she took a deep, steadying breath as she tiptoed to her partly opened door. He was home and the time had come to talk with him. Why was she so panic-stricken all of a sudden? There was no reason to feel so nervous. But she was.

Cathy girded herself with determination and stepped into the hallway. Dim light flickered from the sconces on the walls, throwing faint shadows as Jesse ascended the wide stairs. He was alone—another point in her favor.

"Miss Weston?" Jesse inquired in mild surprise when he saw her standing in the hallway. "Is anything amiss?"

"No . . . yes. I mean . . . could we speak for a moment?"

Dark brows lifted in amusement at her garbled reply, but he nodded. "Of course. Are the girls well?"

"Oh, yes! They are fine . . . fine."

There was a brief silence. Then Jesse inquired, "Did Pickworth show you everything you may need?"

"Oh, yes! He was quite helpful. I am sure that he and I will deal well together." Cathy stood awkwardly, uncertain whether she should invite him into her room to converse—which would be dreadfully improper—or if he would ask that she step into his room—another improper situation. What did one do when confronted with such circumstances?

Realizing that Cathy did not wish to pose just a short, simple question, Jesse frowned. "I suppose that this cannot wait until morning, Miss Weston?"

His obvious irritation and reluctance made Cathy's temper rise. "When? At four in the morning, when you are busily making all kinds of strange noises? Or at the breakfast you never attend? Or perhaps at the dinner that you are quite likely to miss?"

"Your sharp tongue is showing, Miss Weston."

"So it is."

"Very well. Shall we repair to my study for our little discussion? I have no wish to invite gossip from the servants, nor, do I imagine, do you."

Without waiting for agreement, Jesse Lamont pivoted and started back down the stairs, leaving Cathy to follow like a spaniel brought to heel. She fumed as she trailed down the stairs behind him, throwing dark glances at his straight back as they wound through the darkened hallway to the room at the foot of the stairs. What an absolutely insufferable man!

Her ire increased even further when Jesse pushed into his study without holding open the door for her, and she stood with arms folded across her chest as she waited for him to light a lamp. There was a sharp scratch, a hiss, then a flare of light as the lamp was lit on his desk, and Cathy stepped forward.

Ignoring her, Jesse turned to the small butler's table behind his desk, reaching for a decanter of brandy. He poured a liberal amount into a crystal snifter, then glanced at his shivering guest. A smile curved his mouth at her obvious discomfort. It was cold without a fire in the grate, and Jesse held out the snifter of brandy he had just poured.

"Would you care for a little inner fire, Miss Weston?"

"Do you think I need it?" she shot back, tempted to refuse but too cold to do so. "Yes, thank you."

He gave her the brandy with an amused smile, then turned to pour himself a draft. "Now, do you suppose we can get right to the point? It has been a long day and I am weary."

"No more so than I, Mr. Lamont. I was awakened extremely early, you may recall, and my hours have been spent quite busily, I assure you." Cathy took a deliberate sip of the brandy for courage, then said, "My subject is rather delicate, I'm afraid. A personal matter, you understand. I am not certain how to begin."

Throwing himself into the deep-cushioned leather chair behind his desk with a sigh of resignation, Jesse said, "Try to begin at the beginning. That usually is the best way, and certainly the swiftest, if my guess is correct."

Cathy bridled, her fingers tightening around the stem of the snifter. "Not in this particular case! If I should do that, you will hear the very boring details of my early life: my birth in New York, the stories of my innumerable governesses, my first birthday party, my first pony, my—"

Jesse waved a deprecating hand. "Please! I mark your point, Miss Weston. Pray, go on with only the most *necessary* details!"

Cathy set her brandy snifter on the desk, leaning forward and placing her palms upon the surface as she faced Jesse Lamont. Unfortunately, this also gave the gentleman a more than adequate view of Cathy's fine-textured skin and the tempting cleft barely visible under the layers of lace on her bodice. His brow rose, and he found it difficult to keep his attention from wandering as he listened to her interminable tale. Of course, it was a tale with which he was already acquainted, having left nothing to chance in his investigation of Miss Weston and her credentials. But she didn't know that, so he was forced to give her the surface courtesy of listening unless he wished to let her know how extensively he had researched her background.

"And then, Miss Weston?" he inquired politely, stifling a yawn.

Pausing in her recital of the events leading up to her arrival on his doorstep the previous evening, Cathy glared at Lamont. "You don't care a fig for a thing I've said, do you, Mr. Lamont?"

"No, not really," he admitted, rising from his chair before he yielded to the temptation to place a kiss on that sweet expanse of flesh so visible and taunting. "But I do care that you are content here, and that you remain here. I understand your desire for independence, and I admire you for it. Not many females want or need that. They seem quite content to fawn upon a man, leeching him for every cent until he's quite used up and useless. An independent female is a remarkable thing in these days."

"And whose requirement is that, I'd like to know?" Cathy returned hotly. "It's the men who force us into . . . into bonds of *servitude!* A woman is not a companion, but a possession, like fine horses or a nice carriage . . ."

"But, unfortunately, not as expendable. It's much easier to rid oneself of a fractious mare or shabby curricle than it is to rid oneself of a shrewish female."

Gasping with sheer rage, Cathy would have offered a stinging retort, but Lamont was continuing as calmly as if he had not just offered the most wretched insult. "Yes, Miss Weston, I admire your desire for independence. Freedom is a rare gift, as rare and precious as love."

Having only barely redeemed himself with this last comment,

Jesse looked up at Cathy's furious, flushed face. "Oh, dear, have I upset you?"

"You! You . . . you are the most provincial . . . *beast* I have yet to encounter!"

"I beg your pardon?" Jesse asked, recoiling from the fury in her face.

Fires blazed in Cathy's eyes as she snarled, "I should have realized that you were little better than my father, though you mouth more pleasing platitudes! Females are no more than chattel to you, Mr. Lamont, just another matter to be dealt with when you have the time or inclination! I will *not* be owned, and if you think that just because you pay me a salary to be governess to your nieces you can—"

"Miss Weston!" Jesse interrupted loudly. "Please control yourself! I meant no offense—"

"Oh, yes, you did! Perhaps not to me personally, but to my entire gender! I find it inexcusable that a man of your intelligence and experience would dwell in the medieval mentality in which you obviously bask! Why, there are women of great intellect and expertise, Mr. Lamont, and I—"

Taking her hands as she gestured wildly, Jesse did his best to soothe her. "I apologize most profusely, Miss Weston! I had no idea you would react so impulsively to my admittedly careless comments."

"Impulsively!"

"I meant only to assure you that I will most certainly deal with your father when he arrives at my doorstep," Jesse hastened to add, holding tightly to Cathy's hands. "I have no intention of allowing you to be dragged unwillingly back to America by your overanxious parent."

Cathy's hands stilled in his grasp, and she gazed into Jesse's face. "Truly?"

"Truly. I seem to have botched my reassurance, but I do mean that, Miss Weston. I should not have burdened you with my cynical viewpoints, and I shall endeavor not to do so again."

Fully aware that Jesse Lamont's words were merely an echo of the niceties that social rules demanded of any exchange between male and female, Cathy did not reply. The main point was his expressed intent to allow her to remain in her post in spite of her father's attempted intervention. She managed a smile, then realized that Jesse Lamont was still holding her hands and still standing much too close.

She blinked, and the flutter of her moth-wing lashes drew Jesse's attention. They were long lashes, shuttering such lovely eyes, such rich, dark eyes. His gaze shifted from her eyes to the lips quivering beneath a short, straight nose. He'd dreamed of those lips, imagined them parting under his kiss, warm and moist and sweet as honey. Now they were mere inches away, and they were already parted, quivering with . . . anticipation?

Then Jesse's broad palm was cradling the back of Cathy's head, and he was almost as surprised as she when he kissed her. The kiss was as sweet as he'd dreamed it, the gentle opening of her mouth like a spring flower, welcoming him, drawing him into the moist heat of her. She tasted of brandy, of that special woman essence that had so enchanted him once, when he was a youth and knew no better. Jesse was vaguely astonished to find that it still had the power to enchant him, that sweet lingering of the lips, the touching of souls, and he pulled away slowly.

Cathy blinked, her eyes hazy with confusion and her lips aching for more. She leaned into him, into that broad chest and the comforting circle of his arms. What had happened? One moment they had been talking like civil people did, and the next—an explosion of the senses. Her mouth was throbbing and her chest aching, and deep inside a fire flared upward, burning steadily and strongly as she gazed in silence at Jesse Lamont's dark, handsome face. The world reeled out of bounds, careening through the universe in a blur of motion, leaving Cathy feeling airborne. She was brought to earth with a thud when Jesse released her and stepped back.

"That was an interesting little experiment," he said casually, the familiar tinge of mockery accenting his words. "Much better than the half-drugged attempt at the hospital, wouldn't you say?"

Emerging abruptly from her daze, Cathy could feel her cheeks flush, but her voice was steady and tart as she shot back, "Hardly! I find that both your efforts are a bit . . . dare I say *lacking*, Mr. Lamont?"

"You, Miss Weston, would dare anything," he said with feeling, smothering the laugh that pressed against the back of his throat.

"Remember that," she said coolly, though she was anything but composed inside. How dare he kiss her and then behave as if he had not enjoyed it! *But had he?*

"It shan't happen again," Jesse was saying. "Our kiss, I mean."

"Can you promise me that, Mr. Lamont? I shudder to think that I must creep about avoiding you."

"On the contrary. I do not propose to be in residence for long periods at a time," he replied. "Do not inconvenience yourself on my account."

"Now, Mr. Lamont, we are of the same mind," Cathy said. "I trust the forthcoming interview with my father will not leave us both desirous that I had not accepted this post. In the meantime, I shall devote myself to your nieces. They are quite well behaved in spite of their familial connections. Good night."

"Good night." Jesse barely had time to respond as Cathy swirled and walked regally from his study. A smile lingered on his lips for some time after she had gone.

Chapter 9

*T*he buzz of male voices floated into the hallway outside the dining room early the next morning, stopping Cathy just outside the doors. Guests for breakfast? But Pickworth had said . . . and now the children were with her. Cathy turned to the three girls behind her.

"Girls, it seems that your uncle is already downstairs for breakfast for some reason. We shall postpone our little training session in manners until another day. Will you please go upstairs and have Miss Mooney arrange for your morning meal? I will be up shortly."

Two faces registered disappointment, while Jill merely shrugged indifferently. Her sullen expression didn't alter as she turned to follow her younger sisters back up the staircase to the nursery. It was only when she glanced back at Cathy that any expression showed, and then it was a glare of contempt.

Recoiling as she intercepted that look, Cathy wondered what had happened to cause the child to be so bitter. It may be an excellent idea to find out, she reflected as she smoothed her skirts and turned back to the dining room door.

When the doors swung open Cathy was surprised to see Jesse Lamont seated at the head of the dining table. This surprise was augmented by the gentleman seated at his right side, and her delicate brow arched high.

"Good morning, Miss Weston," Jesse was saying, his tone as cool as if the previous night had never happened. He rose politely, and his guest did also.

"Mr. Edward Mahoney!" Cathy exclaimed with pleasure. "How is London's most famous artist?"

"Glowing with delight at seeing your lovely face again, Cathy," was the prompt reply. "So this is where the prettiest woman in London has disappeared! I'd wondered where you'd got to when you dropped from sight. Thought perhaps you'd married a duke or some such nonsense!"

"I imagined you'd forgotten me until just now, Ned," Cathy teased in return.

Ned Mahoney stepped from the table to take Cathy's hand in his palm, brushing the back lightly with his lips. "It is truly a pleasure to see you again."

"And you also, Ned," Cathy returned sincerely. She then turned to face Jesse, who was gazing at the artist with a frown of surprise. "I've known Ned since my arrival in London," she explained. "He was a member of my cousins' circle, and we became fast friends. We were always at the opera, a rout or ball, and even on outings in the park. Ned does the most fabulous paintings, as I'm sure you know, and I greatly admire his talent."

"Now you embarrass me!" Ned declared stoutly. "But you will recall that Jesse and I are old friends also. He is well aware of the range of my talents."

"I certainly am," Jesse said dryly, indicating with a wave of one hand that they were to be seated. "As is Lord Compton," he reminded Mahoney.

Making a wry face, Ned murmured, "That old fox!" Then he returned his attentions to Cathy. "So tell me, my dear friend, what brings you to the house of such a grim man as Lamont?"

"His nieces," Cathy answered promptly. "I have been charged with their care."

"Splendid!" Ned exclaimed, beaming at her. "The same cause has drawn me here, only I have been commissioned to do their portrait. This means that we shall be thrown into each other's company quite frequently, I suppose."

"Supposition can be quite dangerous, Mahoney," Jesse interrupted, arching his brow.

"Ah, I seem to have heard that before," Ned replied. His eyes twinkled with laughter at Jesse's scowl, and he added, "Fear not, old boy. I shall not keep the lovely Miss Weston from her appointed duties! I shall require only her free time, I assure you."

"How comforting a thought."

Laughing, Cathy let her gaze roam from Ned's fair face and light hair to Jesse's lean features and dark, dark hair. A definite contrast, not only in appearance, but in their natures. Jesse was dark and moody, Ned fair and sunny. Very little seemed to affect Ned Mahoney, and if it did, he never let it show. Even the most trifling event seemed to affect Jesse Lamont, and he had made it quite clear he did not wish to be bothered with anything at all. . . .

"Miss Weston?" Jesse repeated for the second time, startling her from her reverie.

Cathy flushed. "Oh, I'm sorry! My attention was wandering, it seems."

"No wonder, with our fair Ned here to distract you," Jesse said, ignoring Mahoney's subsequent burst of laughter and Cathy's widened eyes. "But as my time is short and I do not wish another midnight tête à tête, I should very much like it if you would ask me any questions you may have now, before I leave for the day."

Flushing at the reminder and avoiding Ned's curious gaze, Cathy shook her head. "There are no questions," she said in a choked voice.

"Excellent!" Standing, Jesse slid back his chair and surveyed

Cathy and Ned for a moment. "Shall we repair to my study, Mr. Mahoney, and leave Miss Weston to her morning meal in peace?"

Ned Mahoney's amused glance slid from Jesse to Cathy, and he stood. "Of course. Good day, Cathy. It was frightfully good to see you again."

"Good-bye, Ned," Cathy murmured, at a loss to explain Jesse Lamont's sudden rudeness. Not that he'd ever needed an excuse to be rude, for he hadn't, but this seemed even to fall outside those bounds. She watched in silent irritation as the men left the dining room and went into the hall. A footman served her meal deftly and quietly, and Cathy listened to the deep baritones in the hallway while she picked idly at her food. She could not hear what they were saying, just the rumble of their voices, and in a few moments she heard the front door open and close, and the door to Jesse's study click shut.

An excellent time to beard the lion in his den . . .

Feeling rather like a Christian martyr, Cathy rose from the table and left the dining room, crossing the hallway to the door of Jesse's study. She took a deep breath, then tapped on the carved-oak door. When Jesse bade her to enter, Cathy turned the brass knob and pushed open the door.

Her gaze fell on Jesse behind his desk, and a flood of inexplicable memories washed over her: Jesse offering her a brandy, Jesse spouting chauvinistic nonsense about women, Jesse taking her into his arms and kissing her.

Cathy gave a mental shake of her head. Utter foolishness to recall those things! Especially as Jesse Lamont was now staring at her with a distinctly unfriendly gaze, and the glass of whisky cupped in his hand did not seem at all the proper thing to be drinking before eight o'clock in the morning!

"What is it, Miss Weston?" he demanded in a crisp voice.

Cathy's brow puckered into a frown. This was not Lamont's normal testiness. She recognized that brittle tone and the grayish pallor of his complexion, and there were deep white grooves bracketing his mouth. He was in pain.

"Your wound is bothering you," she stated firmly. "Let me have a look at it."

"Don't be ridiculous!"

"Shall I send for Dr. Alexander?"

Jesse's scowl deepened. "I have already seen him, Miss Weston. I am imbibing the only remedy he can offer." He held up the glass of whisky in a mocking salute and added, "Now, what may I do for you?"

"It was a small matter. There is no pressing need to speak of it now. I can talk to you another time, when your wound is not giving you trouble."

A faint smile flickered briefly on Jesse's taut mouth. "There may not be such a time for a while. Miss Weston. I promise not to growl quite so harshly if you would like to go ahead with what you wish to say."

"Thank you," Cathy said softly as Jesse stood and walked around the corner of his desk. He was standing much too close again, as he had the night before, and one hand rose unconsciously to her throat as she regarded him in the shaft of sunlight streaming through the opened window. As usual, Jesse was garbed in correct fashion, with a starched high round shirt collar and the slender shoe-tie now in favor. His snug-fitting trousers were of white coutil, and his lounging jacket was bright blue. His half boots were polished to a blinding luster, and Cathy began to feel quite dowdy compared to Jesse. Smoothing her skirts with one hand, she dared a glance at his face.

The bright light picked out little details to leave them imprinted on her mind—the sunburst of lines fanning from the corners of his eyes, the shadow where he had shaved the beard from his strong jaw, and the warmth that could kindle in his eyes. His dark hair was lustrous, with a silver glitter at the temples and long sidewhiskers in front of his ears, then curling into his collar at the back—and how had she never noticed that his mouth was so sensitive and vulnerable. Or had she?

Dragging her attention from his mouth, which was beginning to curl in a knowing smile, Cathy said, "I wanted to inform you that the girls will be taking their morning meals in the dining room. I trust this will not be a problem."

"Why on earth would you want to do that?" Jesse began, then gave an irritated shake of his head. "Never mind. Do what you wish, Miss Weston—as long as it does not interfere with the tranquility of *my* meals."

There was a brief pause, during which Jesse inspected Cathy in very much the same manner as she had just looked at him, his gaze skimming her from head to toe, noting the burnished wealth of curls caught atop her head, then raking over the sensible day dress of brown serge that covered her slender form. It was an assessing stare that brought a pink stain to her cheeks, and Cathy said stiffly, "There is something else, Mr. Lamont."

"Really? And what may that be, Miss Weston?"

"It pertains to Mr. Mahoney . . ."

"Ah, the redoubtable Ned Mahoney! I suspected as much. It was obvious that you know each other well."

"Yes, but not as you infer," Cathy was quick to point out.

"No?"

"No."

"How . . . quaint. Perhaps I should warn you, Miss Weston, that if you wish to see Mr. Mahoney in a social sense I have no intention of objecting—with a single reservation."

"And that is?"

"That is that you do so on your own time, not on mine. I have no intention of paying you to carouse with an artist. Nor do I—"

"*Carouse?*" Cathy cut in with a gasp of anger.

"Nor do I intend that you shall confuse your personal time

with your business obligations," Jesse continued imperturbably. "My time is my time."

"And just when is *your time*, Mr. Lamont?" Cathy snapped.

"Every day except Saturday, Miss Weston."

"I see."

"I'm extremely grateful that you do. Do you have any complaint with it?"

"No, Saturdays will be quite adequate, thank you."

Jesse's expression softened at Cathy's terse answer and stiffly held shoulders, and he stepped even closer. "I must seem a terrible beast to you."

Her brow arched. "Yes. Does that bother you?"

Jesse's lips twitched at her tart reply, and he gave a brief nod. "Yes, I believe it does."

"Then it can always be rectified, Mr. Lamont."

After a short pause, Jesse said, "Perhaps I should explain some things to you, Miss Weston . . ."

"I would be terribly grateful if you would," she shot back. "I know so little about the children, and no one seems willing to supply any information."

"Yes . . . that, too. First let me explain that Jill, Leigh, and Erin are my dead brother's children. He died more than a year ago. They have no one in the world but myself, and I am of very little use to them as a parent most of the time. Their short lives have not been easy, I'm afraid." Jesse paused to gaze at Cathy. "Jill, as you may have noticed, is very bitter, and feels more abandoned than do the other two. I regret that. I want them to feel happy and secure, Miss Weston, and I look to you to provide them with a more stable atmosphere. That is the reason I wrote to Miss Nightingale—I knew you could offer them that security they so desperately need."

Some of Cathy's anger ebbed, and she said, "I shall do my very best, Mr. Lamont."

"Somehow I knew you would," he replied with the warmest

smile she had yet received from him. "And . . . why don't you call me Jesse? It's less formal, and more . . . friendly."

Starting, Cathy said slowly, "Yes . . . I suppose I could do that."

"It is important that the children live in a more relaxed situation than that we've begun with, don't you think?"

"Yes, of course."

"Then shall I call you Cathy?" he asked, startling her again.

An unwilling smile curved her lips, and she looked at him. "Yes. Do call me Cathy—all my *friends* do so."

Taking her point, Jesse laughed. "Very well—I shall do my best to be counted as a friend, Miss . . . Cathy."

"Then perhaps we shall deal a bit better with each other, *Jesse.*"

Jesse—it sounds odd on my lips, though I've said it silently so many times before. Jesse, Jesse—just the sound conjures up images of rainbows and sunshine, warm lips and heated embraces . . .

"Perhaps we shall," he was saying, and she gave him a mechanical smile, snatching her thoughts back from the forbidden realm where they had wandered.

"Well," she said briskly, "I must go to the girls now. They will be wondering what has happened to me."

"Yes, of course," he replied immediately. "And, Cathy . . ."

She turned back. "Yes?"

"I'm glad we had this discussion."

Her smile was soft. "Yes, I am too . . . Jesse."

When the door shut behind her, Jesse drummed his fingers against the surface of his desk. He frowned thoughtfully at the closed door. Cathy . . . her name lingered behind just as her perfume did, the light, delicate scent of lavender that usually surrounded her, a clean fragrance that brought to mind sunshine, warm breezes, green fields studded with tiny flowers, and . . . Cathy. Why ever had he asked to call her by her given name? It had been foolish, entirely too intimate for a woman in the position of his governess, yet he had done so.

Jealousy. That had spurred him into asking, spurred him into banishing mental visions of Cathy with Ned Mahoney. The artist had called her Cathy, denoting friendly familiarity, and that had burned into his brain. *Cathy*, Mahoney had said; *Cathy*, in that soft voice like she had meant something to him.

Jesse's hands curled into fists. He stalked to the tall bookcases lining the rear wall and selected a slim volume of his favorite poetry. There was a verse . . . a reminder, and he flipped quickly to the right page.

> I cannot give what men call love:
> > But wilt thou accept not
> The worship the heart lifts above
> > and the heavens reject not,
> The desire of the moth for the star,
> > Of the night for the morrow,
> The devotion to something afar
> > From the sphere of our sorrow?

Slapping the book closed, Jesse shoved it back into the bookcase. Yes, a definite reminder.

Striding from the study, Jesse took the stairs two at a time. Laughter floated from the nursery and he slowed, lingering in the hallway, listening to the children. The two younger girls were giggling, and he thought he heard even Jill's voice as Cathy played a game with them.

Jesse yielded to temptation and pushed open the door to the nursery. The three girls were seated at the round table in the center of the room with Miss Mooney and Cathy. Beakins had served breakfast, and the girls had already done justice to eggs, muffins, sausages, kidneys, and piles of fresh fruit.

"Quite an assortment of dishes," Jesse remarked as he entered.

Leigh and Erin greeted him with a chorus of glad cries, while Jill's entire face altered completely. The child leaped to her feet, and her familiar sullen expression darkened even more than Cathy had thought possible.

Jill turned her back on her uncle, her small frame as rigid as a board as she deliberately gazed out the schoolroom window.

Cathy was amazed at the transformation in the girl. She had begun to open up slightly, at least to join in with the conversation, even if she wasn't contributing more than a word or two. But this—Jill's large dark eyes that looked so much like her uncle's had grown narrow and spiteful, and her mouth curved down in a sour bow.

At a loss for an explanation, Cathy strove to smooth over the obvious rejection. "You seem to be an excellent tonic for your nieces, Mr. Lamont," she observed, nodding her head toward Leigh and Erin, and he looked at her and smiled.

"Jesse," he reminded.

Miss Mooney's head jerked sharply around and Cathy flushed, wishing he had not said that in front of her. But the damage was done now, and there was nothing to do but go ahead as if matters were all proper and correct. Which they were, she silently scolded herself. There was nothing improper about using given names between two adults!

"Yes, Jesse," she echoed, feeling as if Miss Mooney's eyes were boring into her like two hot pokers. "Would you like to join our little group?"

"No, no, I just thought I would stop in and greet my little ladies," he replied, then teased, "though they may soon burst from eating so much!"

Leigh and Erin giggled, while Jill stared at Jesse in cold rejection. It was apparent that he had offended the child in some way, and Cathy made a mental note of it. It would be useful to remember in her efforts to reach Jill.

"It seems that our Miss Cathy has also changed the menu," Jesse was saying. "Do you prefer this fare over your porridge?"

"Oh, yes!" Leigh and Erin chorused, but Jill refused to utter a word.

"I hope you don't mind," Cathy said. "I thought the girls might like something other than oats and milk for breakfast. Besides, it teaches them the proper order of courses and which eating utensils to use."

"An excellent notion," Jesse approved, and Cathy marvelled at how quickly a leopard could change its spots. Was this the same glowering man with whom she had conversed only a short time before? Did being with his nieces make him into this congenial soul who seemed the very essence of glee and conviviality? Hardly likely, Cathy mused, then scolded herself for being so harsh in her judgment. It was quite possible for three little girls to soften even the hardest heart. Children and animals ofttimes had that effect on a man.

She'd keep that in mind. The next time she expected another unpleasant interview with Jesse Lamont, she would take along a puppy or a child and see if it did not go more smoothly.

"How about you, Jill?" Jesse was asking with a bluff cheeriness that did not fool the child for a moment. She just turned and gazed at him with the same somber stare, her liquid dark eyes boring a hole into him. "Aren't you enjoying the change in your food?" he persisted.

"Yes, Uncle Jesse," she finally answered, looking away from him so that her words floated into the far corner of the nursery. Her tone was prim and proper to the letter, and it was evident that she would abide by the proprieties, but no more.

Jesse's distress was more evident, and the sigh in his voice when he turned away told Cathy more than he would have liked. What could have happened between them? Cathy suddenly wondered then, in a brief flash of illumination like a lightning bolt, about the mother. It occurred to her that Jesse Lamont had not mentioned the fate of the girls' mother. Nowhere in his explanation had he even included a reference to her. Was she also dead? Had it been an accident that claimed both parents? If not, *where was the mother?*

Chapter 10

*T*wo events occurred the following morning, events that sharply affected Cathy. The first was the disconcerting news that Jesse had gone, and that he would be away for a couple of weeks. There had been no parting words, no message—nothing. Though she realized Jesse Lamont was hardly obliged to leave her his farewells or an explanation of his whereabouts, she still found it disturbing that he had not mentioned *something* about it.

The second event was the arrival of Ned Mahoney, almost directly on the heels of the discovery of Jesse's departure. He arrived with a grand flourish of flowers, which he presented to Cathy with a bright grin.

"For you, the fairest flower of all!" he said grandly.

"Oh, Ned, you shouldn't have," Cathy reproved. "How ever did you find such lovely blooms when it is almost November? And they must have cost a pretty penny."

"Nothing is too much for you, Cathy."

"More idle words," she teased, moving from the parlor into the hallway. "I shall find Beakins and ask that the bouquet be placed in a vase of water."

Ned followed behind like an obedient, playful puppy, and when they happened to encounter Miss Mooney in the hallway he rang out cheerily, "Miss Mooney! I declare you are especially lovely today!"

"Ironclad Ida" regarded him with a glacial stare. "Humph! Is that so, Mr. Mahoney?"

"Of course it is so," he returned gaily, not to be forced from his exuberant mood. "And I see your charming temperament has not changed since our last conversation, either."

This last remark elicited a reluctant smile. Then a laugh issued from Miss Mooney, and she murmured, "Impudent, saucy creature!"

"Yes, I am, aren't I?" the irrepressible Ned countered with a wide smile.

"Well," Ida said, "it's absolutely disgraceful of you to tease old maids, Mr. Mahoney."

"Old maid, Miss Mooney? You? Nonsense! You've tread upon half the hearts in London, including mine."

"Now you've descended into utter foolishness," Ida shot back, taking the bouquet of flowers from Cathy. "I shall put these away while you try to teach our impulsive artist the proper parlor rules, Miss Cathy."

"I think it is too late," Cathy mourned, but she took Ned by his arm and steered him firmly from the hallway.

"I say," Ned began, glancing toward Jesse's closed study door, "is the old boy in residence?"

"No, you're safe. Mr. Lamont has left the city for a time, I've been informed."

"How heartening. Then he shan't be about for the next few days while I work on the portrait of his nieces?"

Cathy shook her head as she led the way up the stairs. "No. Pickworth said he would be gone for two weeks or more. How do you want the girls, Ned?"

Ned gave her a blank stare. "I beg your pardon?"

"The girls—his nieces. How do you want them posed?"

"Oh . . . oh that. Yes, Mr. Lamont insisted that they be in

118

their Christmas gowns, and I think the parlor should do nicely for the initial sitting. Or . . . or perhaps the study would be more suitable," he added suddenly. "You know, with the books and things?"

But Cathy was shaking her head. "Won't do, Ned. The study is tightly locked."

"Ah. Well, the parlor is probably much more elegant anyway."

They reached the upstairs landing, and Ned turned to Cathy and said slyly, "Fran would be so jealous that I am here with you, Cathy."

Turning in alarm, Cathy said, "You didn't tell Lord Compton where I am, did you?"

"No. Why? Doesn't he know? I would have thought he would have kept in touch with you, as head over heels in love as he was . . ."

"I have not spoken with him in some time, and though I did receive a note from him the week before I left my hotel I did not leave a forwarding address, just a reply. I . . . I thought it best to tell him I had taken a position and would not see him again."

"And here I am with you instead!" Ned replied happily.

Cathy's eyes narrowed. "Did you know where I was, perchance, Ned?"

"Oh, no, this is pure coincidence, my dear. Lamont was attempting to secure an artist, and happenstance threw us together. I had no idea you were here." Relief was evident in her face, and Ned looked at her curiously. "Why, Cathy? Does no one else know your whereabouts?"

She shook her head. "No, Ned. Just Miss Nightingale and you."

Puzzled, he asked, "But why?"

She flapped her hands at him, laughing to ease the sudden tension as she said, "It's a long, bor-r-ring story, dear Ned! I shall tell you later, when you are not likely to fall asleep with the telling of it. Over dinner, perhaps?"

"Dinner, sweet Cathy, sounds excellent. Starving artists and all that, you know."

"Liar," she said fondly, and turned to open the door to the schoolroom.

The next two weeks found Cathy busily rearranging schedules and juggling math lessons, grammar, elocution, and the rudiments of geography. She hardly had time to miss Jesse Lamont, she told herself, and it was true.

November 1 was heralded by a frosty blanket of white that shrouded trees, bushes, and sidewalks. It added a pure glitter to the world, masking the harsher realities of littered alleys and open gutters. And on the second day after the snowfall, Cathy succumbed to the pleas of the girls to romp in the garden snowbanks. Garbed in their warmest garments, Cathy and her three charges went into the garden and made snowmen, snow angels, and had enthusiastic snowball fights. Upon their retreat into the house, they were immediately wrapped in warm, dry blankets and given hot tea or chocolate to drink. This was a favorite time for the girls, as Cathy would read to them while they sat in blanket cocoons before the nursery fire. The short time spent outdoors brought a healthy blush to their cheeks and put a sparkle in their eyes, a definite improvement if one was to believe Miss Mooney.

"Even Jill seems better for it," Miss Mooney was heard to remark, "And her, such a pasty-faced, wan little thing! I think she's been overprotected."

"Perhaps," Cathy agreed, "and then again, perhaps not. Dr. Alexander is an excellent physician, but he did agree that Jill needed more outdoor exercise."

"Did he also mention that Ned Mahoney was to get more

exercise?" Miss Mooney asked innocently, and Cathy turned with a start to glare at her companion.

"Why ever would you ask such a thing, Miss Mooney?"

"Oh . . . no reason. I just thought that since Mr. Mahoney was *here* so much, and since he played outside in the snow with you and the girls, he had been advised to do so."

"You know very well that Ned comes every day to have the girls sit for their portrait," Cathy said defensively.

"Ah, yes—the famous portrait. I trust it is coming along well enough to satisfy Mr. Lamont when he returns?"

"I'm certain it will. The girls look quite lovely in the new gowns Jesse—Mr. Lamont—had made for them. It had not occurred to me that he could think of such a nice thing to do."

"I understand that he chose the gowns himself," Ida Mooney remarked as she picked up her stitchery and rearranged the blanket draped over her lap. The nursery fire crackled cheerily, warming the area where she sat in a comfortable, overstuffed chair. "I think it unusual for a man to know anything at all about fashion."

"No more than I do," Cathy said in a wry tone. She glanced over at the girls where they were seated for Ned to paint them. Arrayed on chairs before the wide windows, the children looked very pretty in their matching dresses. Blond lace trimmed the bodices of their moiré gowns. Dyed a rich kelly green, the gowns had gabrielle sleeves and multiple flounces on the skirts. Short, tight-fitting gloves and hand-painted fans completed the effect as the children sat stiffly watching Mahoney dab furiously at his canvas.

Cathy watched for a long time that day, thinking of the three little girls and their uncle. Perhaps Jesse was not the bad sort she'd once thought him. Any man who cared as deeply about his nieces as he obviously did could not be the villain she had once painted him. The two younger girls adored Jesse, and wasn't it true that children always seemed to sense who was their friend and who wasn't? All Cathy could conclude was that if Jill did not like her uncle, there must be some other reason for it.

And the girls seemed to be thriving under her care. Three faces glowed with color as they sat patiently in the small chairs, and Cathy watched them with an indulgent smile. It was all going so well, so smoothly.

Yet that night Jill became violently ill.

"What did Dr. Alexander say?" Miss Mooney inquired when Cathy returned from the nursery. It was well past eleven at night, and Cathy had spent the past four hours at the child's bedside.

Sick with anxiety, Cathy wondered fretfully where their uncle could be. He'd been gone for two weeks with no word, and now Jill was ill and Cathy felt she may be at fault.

"It's her heart," Cathy blurted, sinking wearily onto her boudoir chair. "And . . . and I am *sure* that I should not have allowed her to play in the snow, but he said . . . and I thought . . . and now she's ill!" Hysterical laughter bubbled in her throat, and she struggled against it as she said, "Instead of a nice healthy *glow,* as I thought, the poor child had a raging fever! What a marvelous nurse and governess I have turned out to be!"

"Do not blame yourself," Miss Mooney advised, pulling Cathy up and helping her off with her robe. She tossed the robe across a boudoir chair and said, "You listened to Dr. Alexander, after all, and even he thought it a good idea for the child to play in the snow. Here, lie on your bed and I will plump your pillows for you. . . . No, I insist on it. I will sit at her bedside for a time now."

Yielding reluctantly, Cathy allowed Miss Mooney to help her up onto the high bed and rearrange the feather pillows behind her head. The quilted coverlet with the gay cabbage roses seemed too cheerful now, and she closed her eyes. Poor Jill. She seemed so suddenly gaunt, with her large dark eyes sunk into her little face and her complexion so flushed and feverish. The little thing reminded Cathy quite strongly of her uncle, and that made it even worse.

Plumping Cathy's pillows, Ida Mooney clucked her tongue sympathetically. "Such a tragedy about the children's parents, and now Jill's being so chronically ill—almost an invalid."

Cathy's eyes snapped open in surprise and interest. "What are you talking about, Miss Mooney?"

"Why, about the tragedy. I heard little Jill talking to her sisters about it just the other day. She was talking of Italy, and the warm sun and soft winds . . ."

"Italy?"

"Why, yes—didn't you know?"

"No, I didn't know," Cathy said. "Tell me."

Straightening the floral-print coverlet over Cathy's legs, Miss Mooney recited in the tone of a confidant, "It seems that the girls' father was tragically drowned in the bay off Leghorn."

"Drowned?"

"Yes, in a sudden squall. I understand that the boat went down with full sails."

"How dreadful! And I suppose their poor mother was drowned also."

"Oh, no. She is alive and lives here in London, if Jasper is to be believed."

Gaping at her, Cathy let this bit of information sink in while she struggled to understand. "But . . . but if she is still alive, why are the girls not . . . why are they here with their uncle instead of with their mother?"

"I'm sure I don't know, Miss Cathy. No amount of prying would loosen that juicy tidbit of information from Jasper. All he would say is that Mr. Lamont takes good care of the girls. I had the distinct impression the witless fool was afraid to say any more."

"How odd."

"Shall I put more coal on the fire?" Miss Mooney asked. "It's snowing again, and the wind is finding all the tiny chinks in the windows."

"Yes, do," Cathy said absently. "I truly wonder how it is that Mr. Lamont has custody. . . ."

Miss Mooney shrugged. "That's a well-kept secret. I do know that it is a touchy subject with the servants, though they show no reticence in speaking about the father. There is even a portrait of him in my room—you know the one over the mantel? But if the mother is mentioned, everyone closes up as tight as a clam."

While Miss Mooney poured more coal into the grate, Cathy reflected on what she had just learned. The father drowned off the coast of Italy and the mother living somewhere close by. It was definitely odd. Why had she not come to visit her children in the past weeks? And why wasn't she mentioned at all by not only Jesse Lamont, but her own daughters? Quite *definitely* odd!

"No stranger than Mr. Lamont is, I'd say," Miss Mooney remarked, startling Cathy into wondering if she'd spoken aloud. "The man even has a *gymnasium* in the house, Miss Cathy. Can you imagine that?"

"A gymnasium?"

"Yes! What an odd thing for a man to have in his home, I think. I peeked in one day when Beakins was cleaning it. It's filled with all manner of strange gadgets, and Beakins informed me that Mr. Lamont is fond of boxing as well as using his gadgets. Very odd, I'd say."

Gadgets, boxing. Cathy began to smile. So *that* was what had awakened her that night! And she had thought all manner of diverse things. . . .

"What do you find so funny, Miss Cathy?"

Explaining how she had been awakened one morning at four o'clock, Cathy laughed when she added, "You can well imagine what must have been running through my mind as to the reason for all those odd, rhythmic sounds!"

"I daresay," Ida Mooney replied. "A gymnasium indeed. I wonder why he did not leave it as a bedroom. It used to be, you know."

"No, I didn't know. You, Miss Mooney, are a veritable fountain of information, and I confess to amazement and admiration!" Cathy said.

"Not only that, but it was *her* room," Miss Mooney said with a triumphant glance at Cathy.

"Her room?"

"Yes. The mother of the girls. And when whatever happened was over with, Mr. Lamont had the room turned into a gymnasium. Another mysterious event."

"Perhaps he just wanted to exercise," Cathy said in a sensible tone, though she wondered if it was true. *Her* room, and if she had been that important to Jesse . . . Had she? But what a thought to have. . . .

"Exercise—of course." Miss Mooney lifted a brow in a significant arch, then tucked the coverlet beneath the mattress to keep out drafts. "I shall relieve Pickworth now in his vigil over Jill. It's my turn. You get some rest, as you will surely need to be strong tomorrow."

"Yes. Yes, of course," Cathy murmured, only partially paying attention to Miss Mooney. Too many ideas swirled in her head now, vague images of a faceless woman who would abandon her children, a mysterious creature who had once lived in this house, and the watery form of a father who looked very much like Jesse Lamont.

Dreams dominated Cathy's restless slumber; they were wild dreams of terror and anxiety. She dreamed that her father crashed into Jesse's house, howling for his daughter and demanding that she be brought to him. Darcy was in the dream, and he had assisted Nathaniel Weston in the search for Cathy, until they had found and taken her from the house. Powerless to resist, Cathy had kicked and screamed, but it had seemed as if she were underwater, her kicks slow and futile, her screams soundless. Finally she had awakened, jerking upright and shivering.

The fire in the grate had died to nothing but gray ashes and slowly winking red eyes, sullen eyes that gazed somberly at her in the pitch-dark of the night. Somewhere a clock sounded a sonorous tone, the quarter hour, she supposed, and she pulled the coverlet up to her chin. It was much too cold, and she wondered if Miss Mooney was still with Jill. Perhaps she should check on them.

Sticking her feet from beneath the quilted coverlet, Cathy shivered again. An icy chill crept up her spine and lodged in her shoulder muscles, making them quiver as she reached for her warm fleece robe. It was not to be found in the dark. Cathy's searching hands did find a warm shawl, however, and in her haste she threw it around her shoulders. Even after pulling it around her so that it enveloped her in a warm swath, she was still cold. Padding across the carpeted floor, Cathy fumbled blindly for the doorknob, then pulled open her door and stepped into the hall.

She was at the opposite end of the L-shaped hall from the nursery, a fact Miss Mooney had remarked upon as odd. But Miss Mooney's room was next to the nursery, and the other spare room was kept closed. The stairwell was in the center of the hallway, and Cathy's hand slid along the highly polished railing as she passed. The hall lights in the sconces were burning low and one of them had gone out, leaving the hallway gloomier than usual.

Perhaps that was why she saw the shaft of light, coming from beneath the study door downstairs, something that would not normally have been noticed. Her heart began to race, and she realized that Jesse must be home. No one else ever went into his study.

Cathy's bare feet made no noise on the stairs as she slipped quietly down them, one hand skimming the banister and the other holding the shawl around her. As she reached the bottom she noticed that the study door was open a crack, and she put out one hand and pushed it. It swung silently, and she took several steps inside.

Fully expecting to see Jesse Lamont, Cathy was stunned by what she saw. A shambles met her eyes. A dim lamp burned on the desk, and from that wavering light she could see the over-turned chairs, emptied desk drawers, a storm of papers tossed carelessly about, and the books pulled from the shelves and dumped on the floor.

"Wha—?" Cathy began, stepping farther into the room.

A shadow shifted from the blackness, catching her attention so that she half turned. For a moment it didn't quite register, so attuned was her mind to the notion that Jesse had returned. Then reality struck her full force when the dark shadow surged forward menacingly.

Garbed from hooded head to soft-clad feet in black, the shadow lunged at Cathy, giving her no time to scream before a hand clamped over her open mouth. One hand was covered by a leather glove, but the other, the hand that covered her mouth, was bare. Cathy tasted the salt of sweat and her own blood as her lips pressed painfully against her teeth, and she also tasted fear. It rose in her throat, almost choking her as the powerfully built assailant forced her back against him. Her warm shawl slipped to the floor as she was held in a viselike grip and lifted slowly from the floor so that her bare feet swung free.

Kicking and squirming in desperation, Cathy could feel the coiled muscles in his arms tighten, cutting off her breath as his arm hooked around her neck.

"Be still!" a muffled voice growled in her ear. "Be still or I might hurt you. . . ."

Dimly sensing that only surrender would satisfy the intruder, Cathy sagged against him and was still.

"If I release you," the voice said through layers of cloth, "will you be silent and not scream?"

Cathy nodded, almost weeping with relief when the smothering hand was lifted from her nose and mouth. Gasping for breath, sucking in sweet gulps of air, she felt his grip loosen slightly.

"Please let me go," she pleaded shakily, and the fingers cutting into her arms tightened for an instant.

"I cannot."

"Then you intend to murder me?" she shot back in a trembling voice.

There was a muttered curse as the masked intruder held her against him, her back still pressed to his chest so that she could not get a glimpse of his face. A thousand thoughts raced through Cathy's mind, matching the tempo of her pounding heart as she sought an avenue of escape. If she screamed, he would kill her before anyone heard. If she attempted flight, he would very likely stop her before she'd made it to the door. If she attempted reasoning, he might listen.

"Listen to me," she began in a calm, reasoning tone, "I promise you that if you release me, I will not make a sound for five minutes. That should give you time to flee undetected. I have not seen your face and cannot identify you, so you would be free. Believe me—"

"Shut up!" the voice snapped, but his grip loosened even more.

Hope surged in Cathy, and she decided to press home her slight advantage. "I know you must be a decent man, perhaps down on your luck and forced into robbery as a means of supporting your family. I sympathize with you, I truly do, and I would never . . ."

Hollow laughter filtered through the black hood over his head, and Cathy became rigid with fear. What could she have said to amuse the criminal? Perhaps he was mad, and had escaped from some asylum for the criminally insane. She half turned in his grasp, uncertain what to do, and saw a flash of light glitter from a ring on his bare hand. It was an odd design, but that was all she had time to notice.

There was a blur as the ringed hand shot forward, and Cathy's head snapped back. Lights exploded in front of her eyes and there was a loud roaring in her ears before she descended down into a dark, velvety tunnel where there was nothing but a black void.

Cathy never felt the intruder place her gently on the floor, nor did she hear the sigh of frustration that whispered into the room, followed by, "So sorry, Miss Weston."

Chapter 11

*D*arkness swept on soft wings, blurred with pain and a sharp white light, piercing, cutting into Cathy's dreams. She moaned, and her eyelids fluttered briefly.

"Will she be all right?" someone asked in an anxious tone—Miss Mooney, Cathy thought, but wasn't sure. Nothing was certain in this cottony half world of dreams and pain. Only the pain was real, sharp with a razor's edge, cutting across her forehead in seething slices.

"Yes," another voice was saying, drifting into her sphere of sound, receding like ocean waves. ". . . all right . . . with rest . . . nasty blow . . . appalling thing to have happened to her . . . anyone know how?"

There was a click, a blank space. Then Cathy heard the voice again, this time recognizing it as that of Dr. Alexander. She wondered vaguely why he was there, and if Jill had gotten worse during the night. That thought brought the sharp memory of what had happened—how she had risen from her bed to check on the child, and seen the light in the study downstairs.

She must have cried out, for someone was pressing a cold rag over her forehead, talking to her in a soothing tone and telling her to rest, not to worry, that the intruder had gone and she was safe. The intruder. Yes, she remembered it all now, remembered going down the stairs thinking that Jesse had returned, but finding a stranger, an evil stranger who had debated about killing her. She'd known that, had been coldly, icily frightened of it, and she wanted to retreat now into the safer world of darkness.

"Cathy," someone insisted, "Cathy, you're quite safe now. No one will hurt you. Can you hear me, Cathy?"

She nodded, still not opening her eyes, still clinging to the cobwebs of shadows that somehow seemed safer. Light would bring reality.

"Miss Cathy?" a voice quavered, fear tinging the words with a hurting quality that would not let her rest. "Miss Cathy, please talk to me!"

Moaning, Cathy sighed and finally opened her eyes. She had to. Miss Mooney could not be frightened this way. It was too cruel. She licked dry parched lips with the tip of her tongue, and the world reeled as she tried to bring it into focus.

"Miss Mooney?"

A thin, cold hand squeezed Cathy's tightly, and Miss Mooney stroked back damp tendrils of hair from Cathy's forehead. "Yes, Miss Cathy, dear sweet Cathy—it is I."

A faint smile flickered for a moment on Cathy's lips as she tried valiantly to put on a brave face, but the effort caused a spasm of pain and she shuddered. "I . . . I feel as if I have been run over by a beer wagon," Cathy muttered with a long shuddering breath. "Wh-what time is it?"

"Nine in the morning. You've been asleep for several hours, Miss Cathy." Another squeeze of her hand, then: "How do you feel?"

"Wretched," was the moaning reply. Indignation filled her weak voice as she added, "He hit me!"

"We know, we know," Miss Mooney soothed. "But you'll be just fine."

Wincing against the effort to speak, Cathy asked, "How are the children? Jill? Is she—"

"They're all just fine, too, Miss Cathy. Jill's fever broke and she's now more worried about you than sick."

"Good," Cathy murmured with another sigh, and her eyelids drifted down again.

"Miss Cathy . . . Miss Cathy, did you see who it was who hit you? Did you know the intruder?" Miss Mooney asked, and Cathy's head rolled on the pillow.

"No . . . yes . . . I mean, I did see, but I didn't . . ."

"Leave her alone," a stern voice commanded, and Cathy's eyes snapped open. It was Jesse. She would recognize his voice anywhere, and her heart began to pound.

Silhouetted against the light from a lamp, Jesse stood with his hands clasped behind him and a brooding expression on his face. The drapes were closed against the harsh light from outside, and Cathy tried to see him better in the dim light afforded by the lamp. Even that effort caused her pain, so that he reached out to still her fretful movements with a gentle hand.

"Lie still, Cathy."

"Jesse . . ."

A bleak smile curved the harsh lines of his mouth as Jesse Lamont gazed down at Cathy's bruised face. A large purple mark marred the smooth perfection of her jaw and cheek and he winced at the sight of it.

Cathy, sweet Cathy—why you? It should not have been. . . .

Jesse's fingers coiled around her flailing hands and held them. This served to quiet her, and Cathy looked up into his eyes. Warmth glowed in the dark depths, more warmth than she had ever seen before, and a hint of another emotion. She smiled weakly, and Jesse's smile was genuine and warm.

"You'll be fine, Cathy," he said, then turned to the physician. "Isn't that correct, Dr. Alexander?"

"Eh? Harrumph! Of course the girl will be fine! I said so, didn't I? It was just a hard knock to the jaw, Mr. Lamont, as I said, nothing meant to do serious damage."

133

"Then you don't think the intruder meant to kill her?"

"No, he didn't," Cathy said before the physician could answer. "I know he didn't."

"And how do you know that?" Jesse turned to ask.

"Because it would have been so easy to do so," she replied simply. "I think he meant only to knock me out so he could escape without being seen or heard. I had surprised him, you see, by coming downstairs at all."

"Why did you go downstairs, Cathy?" Jesse asked in a puzzled tone. "If there was something you needed, all you had to do was ring for a servant, and—"

"But I had been awakened by a dream, and then because I was worried about Jill, I decided to check on her. Once in the hallway, I noticed the light coming from under your study door, and decided to . . . well, to investigate."

Jesse looked faintly amused, as if he had guessed why she'd crept downstairs to his study in the dead of night. "Why ever would you do that?"

Cathy's chin lifted, causing her a small amount of pain as she answered, "I thought you were home, and that you should know about Jill's illness."

"Ah," was all he said in reply.

Removing her hand from his, Cathy began to pluck idly at the coverlet draped over her. "I saw him . . ."

Jesse's features sharpened with interest. "You *saw* him? Well, who was it?"

"I meant, I saw *him*—you know, the intruder. He wore a disguise, of course. Black covered him from head to toe, with a dark hood shrouding his face, and his voice all low and muffled. . . ."

"Did you recognize the voice?" Jesse interrupted.

She shook her head. "No, not really. It was so low and muffled, as I said, and I was so frightened, that if it had been my *father* I would not have known it!" She paused, then added thoughtfully, "Though I do recall a ring he wore on his hand . . . an odd piece of jewelry that caught my eye just before everything went dark."

"Dammit!" Jesse swore softly, turning away so that Cathy would not see the sudden self-reproach in his eyes.

"But it's not your fault, Jesse," she murmured to his back, her expression bewildered.

"Now, now, Mr. Lamont," Dr. Alexander put in, "do not blame yourself. This was something entirely unforeseen. How could you have known? There has been a rash of burglaries in London lately."

Jesse merely shot the physician a cynical glance. He shoved his hands deep into his trousers pockets and shook his head, his gaze returning to Cathy. She struggled to sit up in spite of Miss Mooney's immediate protests.

"No, I don't think the man really meant to hurt me," she said slowly. "Truly I don't. He seemed more . . . dismayed than anything else."

Miss Mooney succeeded in forcing Cathy back down on the bed, her voice stern as she demanded, "Just how could you know such a thing, Miss Cathy?"

"Oh, I couldn't *know* it as much as I sensed it. Of course, I was so terrified at the time that it didn't occur to me, but now that I've thought about it . . ."

"You've decided he was just a harmless prankster, is that it?" Jesse asked dryly.

Cathy glared at him. "No, that is not it at all!"

"Then what is it? The intruder broke into my office, made a shambles of it, and, worst of all, seriously injured you, Cathy. You could have been killed."

The strain in his voice penetrated Cathy's confused mind, and she recognized the sincere worry in his eyes. He was truly worried about her—Jesse Lamont cared enough to worry about her!

"Off with all of you," Miss Mooney was saying then, and her

firm voice brooked no refusals. "Miss Cathy needs her rest. There will be time aplenty later for all your interminable questions and theories."

"I'll be back later, Cathy," Jesse promised as he withdrew under Miss Mooney's martial eye. "You rest."

"Jesse," she called after him, "I . . . I'm glad you're back."

His smile remained fixed in her mind for some time after her room was emptied. Only Miss Mooney remained behind to watch over her, and Cathy realized how the past few minutes had tired her. Slumping wearily against her pillows, she closed her eyes again, secure in the knowledge that with Jesse Lamont home, nothing could happen to her.

"Dreadfully sorry, old boy," Lord Bothmourne said to Jesse with a lifted brow.

Jesse shrugged. "It's nothing for you to concern yourself with, Johnny. You could have done little even had you learned that a man would be sent to snoop in my office."

Lord Bothmourne nodded, his gaze surveying the wreckage of Jesse's office. "Perhaps not, but I could have tried."

"And if you'd failed?" Jesse asked, perching on the edge of his desk and looking around the study. "It might have given the man warning, and then matters could have been worse."

"Worse? It was terribly nasty of him to have attacked Miss Weston," the duke said. "An utterly despicable thing to do!"

"Agreed. But I've a hunch he was after the notebooks, Johnny. If he'd found them, I shudder to think what might have happened to Miss Weston then."

"True enough, old boy. If she'd noticed . . . well, we can only imagine what might have happened and be grateful that it did not."

Jesse's wandering gaze was snared by a bright piece of cloth on the floor, half hidden beneath a jumble of books and torn papers. Bending, he lifted it, and the faint scent of lavender wafted to his nostrils. Cathy. This had to be Cathy's shawl, for it smelled like her, all fresh and soft. It must have been dropped in the struggle.

Stuffing the shawl into an emptied desk drawer, Jesse heard Lord Bothmourne say, "It won't be the notebooks next time, Jesse. It may be *you* he comes after. . . ."

"I'll make a more formidable opponent than Miss Weston did," Jesse observed tartly, and the duke frowned.

"None of that nonsense. This is a nasty business we are involved in, my boy. With this damnable war going on, the Prussians are willing to risk anything. The stakes are high—too high. They need France's indifference, and they know that *you* are the vital link." His expression was somber as he added, "Perhaps it would be safer to send Miss Weston and your nieces to the country until something definite has been established. Our messy intruder may not be as congenial the next time. You must consider the safety of your family."

"Dammit! That's just what I've been doing!" Jesse said, standing and pacing angrily around the piles of books and broken objects. A smashed globe of the world spun crazily across the floor at the touch of his foot, and he watched its erratic progress with a grim smile. Thus was the pace of the world as he knew it, lurching and wobbling along with no clear direction in mind.

"Jesse," Lord Bothmourne soothed, "surely you can see that it would be best—"

"But that's what's so wrong! It wouldn't be best, can't you see that? Look, I cannot send the girls to my country house because I can't protect them there. *Caroline wants them.* You know her capabilities, John. Pickworth—who is as good a watchdog as I could have—insists that he saw her lurking around the corner of this house a few weeks ago. No," Jesse said, shaking his head, "they must stay with me. Caroline won't come here when she knows I'm here. After her recent bit of viciousness, I'm quite certain that she is frightened of me."

"Apparently not frightened enough, or it wouldn't have happened," Lord Bothmourne said dryly. "And you can't be too sure of that. Only think—did you expect Caroline to attend the charity ball that evening? But she did. Caroline is capable of all manner of things, Jesse, even murder."

Jesse's mouth tightened. Murder. Such a compact, efficient little word for such a complicated, messy act. "You still think Caroline killed William, don't you?"

Lord Bothmourne's shoulders lifted in a brief shrug. "It stands to reason. And I've never hidden my thoughts on that matter, Jesse."

"Oh, no, you've been plain enough, John. I, however, am still not completely convinced. To give the devil her due, the local Italians saw the boat disappear in a thick haze. A storm was brewing, and when it struck, the waves overwhelmed him, that's all. . . ."

"Rubbish!" the duke said rudely. "You repeat the same story all the time, just like a bloody parrot! Who are you trying to convince with that thin tale? Certainly not anyone with a modicum of intelligence."

Jesse rounded on him with a fierce glitter in his eyes, but the duke stood his ground. "Look, Jesse," he said more gently, "Wills was an excellent sailor. I don't give a damn for what the Italians may have said. You watched the boat from the lighthouse. Can you honestly think differently? Wills made no effort to reef the sails under threat of the squall. What does that tell you? The man was an experienced sailor, old boy! That boat went down under full sail, we all know that. It was no doubt rammed by a felucca, though that hasn't been proven either. And my last point—Caroline knew where William was that day, knew he was sailing to Genoa. Have you ever learned of her whereabouts that particular day? No, you haven't," he answered for Jesse. "I don't have to be a genius to know for myself what happened, Jesse."

Deep grooves bracketed Jesse's taut lips, and his hands clenched into fists at his sides. "Dammit! I cannot believe that Caroline was involved in her own husband's death!"

"No, you *refuse* to believe it. There's a world of difference in the two words." Lord Bothmourne placed a hand on Jesse's shoulder. "You know the truth, old boy, whether you want to believe it or not. Why else would you have the children? Blind love is folly, my friend. Do not hold to it too tightly."

Jesse's glance was savage. "I know Caroline, and I know she's many things," he ground out, "but I also know she did not kill my brother!"

" 'But love is blind, and lovers cannot see the pretty follies that themselves commit,' " Bothmourne quoted.

Stiffening, Jesse said, "I do not love her—not anymore."

"Are you so sure? At what point in time did you stop? It has always been Caroline with you, Jesse, even before she ran off with your brother, lo, those many years ago."

"Don't get poetical on me!" Jesse snapped.

"You bring it out in me," Lord Bothmourne said calmly. "Look, Jesse, for years you've been tied up in this thing. Caroline is deeply involved. She tried to kill you! You know she's dangerous. I cannot understand why you did not leave her in prison or somewhere where she's no threat to you or the children."

"It was *because* of the children, Johnny. She didn't try to kill me for political reasons, you know that. It was because of my rejection of her, not because of Russia."

"No one can know that for certain."

"I do!" Jesse shot back. "I swore an oath to it. Do you recall that? I *swore* that she was only distraught because of our personal conflicts."

Sighing with frustration, Lord Bothmourne shook his head. "You have a formidable task to accomplish, Jesse. I know you can be trusted to complete it successfully, but you must remember—someone broke into this study last night and hurt Miss Weston, an innocent party. Can you promise it won't happen again? I think not. Stop feeling guilty about Caroline's sorry plight and think of those around you who may suffer needlessly." Bothmourne swept his hat from the cluttered desk and moved toward the study door. "Think about it, Jesse," he said again.

But Jesse remained stubbornly silent while the duke left the house. He heard the closing of the front door, saw Bothmourne step into his carriage, and heard the rumble of his voice as he gave his coachman directions. Bothmourne was a good friend to have. So why couldn't he bend in his convictions? Why couldn't John see that Caroline could not have done those things he claimed?

Cathy could have been killed. . . .

The words echoed in his head, over and over again. Lord Bothmourne was right. This was getting dangerous. Jesse could not yet believe that Caroline was responsible for any of those reprehensible acts. No, she may have acted impulsively the night of the charity ball, but she had loved William. Caroline would not deliberately murder him.

And Caroline had sworn always to love Jesse . . . another quiet voice whispered, leaving him sitting amid the ruins of his office in a haze of indecision.

Chapter 12

When Cathy opened her eyes later that afternoon, she was surprised to find Jesse on a chair beside her bed. He smiled at her, and she smiled back.

"Hello, sleepyhead," he said.

"Hello yourself."

"Care to chat for a while?"

"Perhaps . . ."

"How about some tea first?" he suggested, and Cathy gave a wary nod of her head, pleasantly surprised when there was no pain.

"Excellent idea," she answered with a smile.

Tea was served, and the conversation ranged from Cathy's childhood in New York to her ambitions with Miss Nightingale. They discussed her father, favorite places she had visited, even beloved pets she'd had as a child—but nothing was mentioned about the previous evening. In a short time, Jesse Lamont knew a great deal about Cathy, but she still knew very little about him. Dozens of questions popped into her mind, questions about Jesse that she wanted to have answered.

What's your favorite color? Your favorite dish? Do you like cigars after a meal? What about your childhood? Did you have any special fears? Likes? Dislikes? Have you ever been in love? . . .

But how could she ask that last question? And did it really

matter? After all, she had been in love, and Darcy had broken her heart. Now she was in danger of its happening all over again. She was too drawn to this enigmatic man who was gazing at her with such a thoughtful expression, and she recalled the first time he had gazed at her. It had not been a thoughtful stare, nor a stare that a man would bend upon a decent woman, but rather a wicked, lustful gaze that had stirred some deep emotion inside her. Yet when he had fallen at her feet that night, she had been attracted to him.

Perhaps she had somehow confused the desire to nurse a wounded man with the desire to love him. . . .

The following morning Cathy was propped against her pillows having her breakfast on a tray, when it occurred to her that she did not know how Jill was doing. Was the child still ill, or had she recovered? She immediately decided to investigate, Miss Mooney's objections notwithstanding.

Garbed in her customary brown serge day dress with a pretty lace collar, she promptly went to the nursery. Leigh and Erin greeted her at the door, tumbling over themselves like puppies and peppering her with questions.

"They said you were sick."

"Are you well now?"

"Did Uncle Jesse nurse you?"

"What's that big purple flower on your face?"

Laughing, Cathy knelt beside the two girls. "Wait a minute and let me catch my breath! First and most important, let me ask this—where's our Jill?"

"Here I am," a weak, pleased voice called, and Cathy turned to see Jill waving at her from the huge stuffed chair before the fire. "The doctor said I must rest."

"Then so you must," Cathy said, rising and urging Leigh and Erin ahead of her. She gazed down at Jill's thin, pointed face, noting the more healthy color. "It seems to be doing you some good. You look quite refreshed."

"So do you," Jill replied with an impish smile, and Cathy laughed.

"Tease! I suppose you're referring to my new decoration?"

"It's a pip," Jill said in an admiring tone. "How'd you get it?"

"By stumbling into something I shouldn't have in the dark," Cathy replied, and Jill nodded wisely.

"I heard Beakins and Jasper talking when they thought I was asleep."

"Then you know that it's nothing at all to worry Leigh and Erin with," Cathy put in briskly. Jill gazed up at her for a long moment, then nodded again. "Good," Cathy said. Then she added, "Does anyone know how a bruise is formed?"

The girls eagerly vied to be the first to answer, and Cathy took the opportunity to teach them about certain functions of the body and its natural defenses. It was an interesting lesson, made more so by the vivid example on Cathy's jaw.

French lessons were followed by reading from a classic, then lunch, after which Cathy suggested a brief period of rest. The girls happily agreed, and Cathy went downstairs.

Loud voices could be heard as she descended the staircase, and she paused on the bottom step. Perhaps she was intruding again and should return to her quarters, or even luncheon with Miss Mooney. But then any further indecision was banished from her mind as a man emerged from the study into the hallway. He looked up at her, and Cathy's chest constricted.

A loud roaring buzzed in her ears, drowning out the murmur of voices in the background as she stared at Darcy Sheridan.

No, not Darcy! Here? Darcy in London—he must be Father's surprise . . . Father . . .

"Darcy," she croaked at the same time as he exclaimed with pleasure.

"Cathy! Dearest Cathy!"

Staring at him in a dazed fashion, Cathy clung tightly to the banister and did not move. Her knuckles were white as she gripped the smooth oak railing, her eyes locked on Darcy's face. How could she have forgotten him so completely, forgotten the way his eyes glistened that certain way when he smiled, and how his hair fell across his forehead in a silky spill so that he was continually tossing back his head in that silly, affected manner? But she had, and now he was here and all those memories flooded back in a rush of mixed emotions.

And to make matters even worse, a tall, burly figure stepped up behind Darcy Sheridan to look at the slender girl frozen on the stairs. His bearded face with the long bushy side whiskers was just as she remembered it, just as overbearing, just as stern. Nathaniel Weston.

"Daughter!" he boomed, pushing past Darcy to approach Cathy. She stood like a stone statue, rooted to the bottom stair, watching her father's swooping approach with an apprehensive gaze. He resembled a gigantic bird of prey with his arms opened wide like huge wings, his hooked nose forming a beak over the voracious mouth that kept repeating her name, over and over. "Dearest Cathy . . ." Then his arms folded around her, smothering her in the voluminous folds of his sleeved cloak.

A great dark feeling of suffocation enveloped Cathy as her father held her tightly—too tightly as always. Though she struggled to loosen his grip it only tightened further, until she felt as if she must get free or perish. With a desperate gasp, she wrenched free of him, hurling herself down the last step to stand in the hallway, poised for flight.

"Cathy!" Nathaniel Weston bellowed, reaching out for her, and she turned blindly away.

Jesse Lamont chose that moment to step into the hallway and rake the visitors with a questioning gaze. His eyes narrowed as they rested on Darcy Sheridan for a moment, then flicked to the elder Weston.

Sheridan was staring coldly at Lamont, his icy gaze filled with hostility. Pinpoint lights of fury danced in his blue eyes when Jesse turned away in obvious contempt, and Darcy took one step forward.

But Jesse's attention had been diverted to Weston, who had managed to snare Cathy by one arm and turn her around to face him. "Dearest Cathy," Weston began, then gasped. "What is the meaning of this?" he demanded, grasping her chin in one hand and holding her face up to the light. "You have been struck!"

"Please, Father—"

"Do not deny it!" Weston roared, and his grip tightened so painfully on her jaw that Cathy flinched. Her gaze darted to Jesse in appeal, and he took immediate action.

Noting the exchange of glances between his daughter and Lamont—who had deceitfully harbored his child without replying to any of the Bow Street Runners he had employed to discover her whereabouts—Nathaniel Weston's suspicions were immediately aroused. He strongly resisted Jesse's calm request that he release Cathy at once.

"I shall not! What is the meaning of this? Are you the party responsible for this disfiguring mark on her face? Why, the girl is probably scarred for life, and—"

"*Mr. Weston!*" Jesse cut in so coldly that even Weston spluttered to a halt to gape at him. "You are hurting her with your tight grip. I *insist* that you release her at once! After you have done so, we shall retire to my study, where you will receive any and all explanations you seem to require. If not . . ."

Other possible actions were left to Weston's imagination. Sensing that he would not fare well in this contest of wills, Weston decided to bide his time and not antagonize the man who was housing Cathy. There would be time later to bring charges before the authorities if there had been any criminal actions, and Nathaniel Weston had no doubt that he was a man of consequence and would be heard. He always was.

Jesse was standing in the open doorway of his study, beckoning with one arm for them to enter, and Weston reluctantly released Cathy and ushered her ahead of him. Feeling much like a chastised child again, Cathy slipped quietly into the study, her eyes downcast. She moved to the nearest barrier between herself and Nathaniel Weston, a large wing chair that stood opposite Jesse's desk. Stepping behind it, she gripped the back with both hands, then gave a start of surprise. Her shawl—the one she had been wearing the night before last—was draped carefully across the back, a bright splash of color against the drab olive material of the chair.

Cathy's head jerked up to find Jesse, her eyes curious as she fingered the soft wool of the shawl. He met her gaze steadily, and it was as if only the two of them were in the study.

"Odd, what one finds in one's private sanctuary, isn't it?" Jesse murmured with a slight smile, then seated himself behind his desk and turned his attention to Weston. Forming a steeple with his fingers, Jesse contemplated Cathy's father and reputed fiancé with a long and considering stare. Sheridan had seated himself in one wing chair, while Weston occupied the other. Both men regarded Lamont with expressions normally reserved for a particularly repugnant felon.

"Now explain to me, sir," Weston began in a harsh tone, "why it is that my daughter is not only in your home, but has obviously suffered abuse at your hands!"

"Is this a formal accusation, Mr. Weston? No? How intelligent of you. First, let us discuss your daughter's residence in my home. She is in my employ as a governess for my three nieces and nurse to one of them, and she is accompanied by a suitable companion of your own choosing, may I point out. Furthermore," he continued, overriding Weston's sputter of protests, "she is of age and has chosen to be here. Need there be more said?"

"I should think so!" Darcy Sheridan blurted, rising to his feet and quivering with indignation. He pointed a shaking finger at Cathy. "Explain her physical abuse, if you can!"

"I certainly can, but I shall leave that up to Miss Weston. You will, I trust, believe her version of how she came by that unfortunate—but not permanent—mark on her face?"

Jesse's implied rebuke of Weston's earlier announcement of Cathy's permanent disfigurement made the older man's face flush a deep crimson. He glared at Lamont.

After a quick glance of appreciation at Jesse, Cathy stepped quickly into the breach. It was a rare opportunity to see her father so deftly handled, and suddenly she felt as if she could cope with his overbearing demands. Was that because Jesse was there?

"I was attacked by an intruder the night before last, Father," Cathy said swiftly, marveling at the mottled purple flush staining her parent's cheeks. "He had broken into the house, and I surprised him pillaging Mr. Lamont's study."

"Good God!" Weston and Sheridan chorused.

Then her father rose, looming over Cathy as she remained behind his chair. "All the more reason for you not to remain in this house!" Weston said firmly. "You shall come with me."

When he reached out for her, Cathy flinched away from him, her chin jutting out stubbornly as she said, "No, I will not, Father."

Recoiling as if he had been slapped, Nathaniel Weston stared hard at his daughter. "What do you mean, *no?*"

Summoning all her courage, Cathy glanced at Jesse for moral support, and was glad to see his encouraging nod.

"I think, Miss Weston," Jesse said, rising from his chair, "that I will leave you alone to discuss any decision you may make with your father. Should you need anything, just ring."

He's telling me he won't be far away if I need him.

"Thank you, Mr. Lamont," Cathy said aloud. When the study door had closed behind Jesse, she tilted her chin up and

147

met her father's steely gaze. Behind him, Darcy Sheridan was fuming, pacing about the study floor and muttering dire predictions.

"That man is insufferable! Mind, no one could be serious about staying in such a house with him unless they were quite mad!" he was saying in such awful tones that Cathy was tempted to laugh.

She didn't. Merely glancing at her former fiancé, she said, "Quite insufferable, I agree."

Halting in his pacing, Darcy glared at her. "You're thinking of staying here, aren't you?" he accused.

"And if I am?"

"Cathy, you are not capable of making such a decision," her father was saying sternly.

Darcy interrupted him, snapping, "Why do you think I came here, Cathy? Surely you know that I accompanied your father because . . . because I have changed my mind. There is to be no wedding with Patsy."

Cathy held up her hands. "Please, Darcy, don't say anymore."

"But Cathy!" Weston began, and she shook her head.

"No, Father. I wish you had not come. I wish both of you had remained in New York." She took a deep breath, then blurted, "Why did you insist upon searching for me? Could you not see that I did not wish to be found? Couldn't you guess when I left my hotel with no forwarding address that I did not want . . ." Stumbling to a halt lest she say too much, Cathy ended calmly, "I have made up my mind. I will stay here."

"But Darcy is here!" Weston exploded in disbelief. "I brought him with me to set things right! Can't you see that?" Surging forward, he grabbed her tightly by the upper arms before she could avoid it, and he gave her a rough shake as one would shake a rag doll.

"Mr. Weston . . . Mr. Weston," Darcy intervened, noting the rise of the man's color and how livid his complexion had grown. "Mr. Weston, please allow me to speak with Cathy." Deftly positioning himself at her side, Darcy wedged between them, noting that Cathy flashed her father an angry glance as she rubbed at her bruised arms. "Cathy, your father and I understand why you felt it necessary to run from us, to avoid us as you have. Truly we do. I did you a great injustice once, by promising love and loyalty, then abandoning you as I did. It was wrong. Now I've come to marry you."

"But Darcy, don't you see? None of that matters now," Cathy said softly. "None of it! That is not the reason I am here, or intend to remain here. I have faith in myself now, and know that I can do something with my life."

The rest of her words died unspoken as Cathy saw the raw anger and disbelief in Darcy's face, the rejection that he felt. She knew that feeling and knew it well. He would not listen to her now, might never listen.

"No, you don't really mean any of this," he was saying firmly. "You're only upset now because of your recent injury and the shock of our arrival. Tomorrow things will—"

"No! Don't you understand *anything*? Tomorrow will not be a bit different! I will feel this way tomorrow and the day after, and the day after that. . . ."

"Will you feel this way when you find yourself cut off without a penny?" Nathaniel Weston inquired nastily. His face was thunderous, his tone sharp and bitter.

"I have my own funds," she shot back after a first, startled hesitation.

"We shall see how far they get you, miss! And I may very well demand that your *employer* release you of any further obligation. How will that sit with you? Then you shall be totally without funds."

"Do you think Mr. Lamont a puppet to bow when you pull the right strings, Father? I don't. He will not heed your commands, but even if he should, I would not return to New York with you. I should simply find another position, then another, if necessary."

Her stubborn chin and the militant light in her eyes gave Nathaniel Weston pause. He recognized the firmness in her voice as a faint echo of his own, and was surprised at his sudden surge of pride. It seemed that Cathy had more of her father in her than he'd thought. But that was not enough. He demanded and expected strict obedience, and she would come to him. He would see to it.

Drawing himself up to his full height, Weston intoned, "I shall not give up until you are on the ship with me. I shall do my utmost to give Mr. Lamont excellent cause to dismiss you summarily."

"It will do you no good," Cathy said. "He hired a nurse and governess, and he will show me the door only if I fail to perform my duties."

"If he is a friend of yours, as he claims," Darcy said, "he will see the trouble he is causing by supporting your ridiculous position!"

"Ridicu——! I refuse to bandy words with you anymore today, Mr. Sheridan. Please be so good as to leave at once." Cathy glared at him so icily that Darcy took an involuntary step backward.

"Very well, daughter," Weston said. "We shall be at the hotel when you change your mind. Or if you simply wish to continue this absurd discussion, I shall be happy to give you the courtesy of listening."

"How novel a notion, Father! It would certainly be the first time you did so."

Only after they had gone did Cathy relax, sagging against the wingback chair and burying her face in her arms. It had been a draining interview, the most unpleasant she could recall in some time. And she knew her father would not surrender so easily. There would be more confrontations.

"So, are you an independent female now, Cathy?" a soft voice inquired, and her head snapped up to see Jesse grinning at her.

"Of a sort!" she shot back. "If my employer will see fit to keep me employed, that is!"

"How astute of you to know that," he marveled.

"Yes, isn't it? There are individuals who would call it survival instinct, I suppose."

Reaching out, Jesse tucked a stray tendril of her hair behind her ear, a tender gesture that was not lost on her, but immediately negated by his following comment. "I was rather rooting for the lions for an instant."

"The lions?"

"As in Daniel and the lion's den?"

"And you wanted them to tear me to pieces?" she demanded incredulously, her dark eyes flashing.

"Oh, no, nothing like that. I just felt rather sorry for such a pitiable lot of lions."

Her anger ebbed. "Oh. I thought them rather formidable at moments."

"To be sure, but to walk among lions unscathed is a taming of sorts, my dear. Changing their opinions would not have meant a triumph. Clinging to your *own* in the face of such bare-fanged adversity was the ultimate victory."

Awed by his summation, Cathy just stared at him for a moment. Admiration gleamed in Jesse's eyes as he gazed at her with approval, and she basked in the glow. As he spoke to her at length, using words such as *constancy* and *respect*, she gazed at him silently, watching his lips move and hearing his voice as if it came from a great distance. She was only vaguely aware of what

Jesse was saying, only dimly cognizant that they were alone in the study with bright light streaming in through opened drapes that revealed a fresh blanket of snow in the garden. Her entire being quivered with the certainty that she had, inexplicably, fallen in love with Jesse Lamont.

Chapter 13

During the next two days Jesse remained home and working in his study. Awed by her new discovery, and somewhat shy with this new emotion, Cathy was still able to admit privately that she liked having him so close. Even the redoubtable Miss Mooney was heard to remark that Jesse Lamont had altered for the better since they had come to his home, no doubt due to her own proper habits and rules.

Of course, Jesse had not changed at all, but Miss Mooney could never admit that she might be a bit taken with his persuasive charm. He used it when he chose, and he chose to do so a great deal with the elderly companion. It was a source of great amusement to Cathy to see Jesse behaving so solicitously to "Ironclad Ida," sending up hot toddies at bedtime, inquiring about certain domestic difficulties that could not be solved without her mature advice, complimenting her exquisite needlework. Several times Cathy found herself wishing that *she* was the recipient of such extravagant gestures.

But instead she received a message from her father. Nathaniel Weston sent a short, terse note requesting—rather, commanding—her attendance at lunch the following Saturday. At first tempted to refuse out of hand, Cathy decided to accept the "invitation." She would force her father to see the futility of his actions, and end any harassment.

Though grateful for Jesse's earlier support in her stance against her father's demands, Cathy now hesitated to enlist his aid again. After all, he was so very busy lately. The previous day had been spent with Lord Bothmourne closeted in Jesse's study with few allowed to interrupt. Only the arrival of several different visitors—all expected—had disturbed the two men. One of the visitors had been Lord Clarendon, the eminent politician and one of the most powerful men in Parliament. Cathy caught only a glimpse of him as he crossed the foyer and rapped softly on the study door, obviously a prearranged signal, for she could hear the soft scramble inside the study and the duke's exclamation of "Lord Clarendon!" before the door swung open.

Continuing on her way across the foyer and into the hallway leading to the rear of the first floor, Cathy's brow was knitted in contemplation. Strange goings-on were around her, and she wondered if she should not ignore anything she saw or heard. Matters of state were afoot, she was certain, and a small thrill ran through her body at being even remotely connected.

Not so Ida Mooney, who was disgruntled by the disruption of the smooth-running household.

"Ridiculous, all those men traipsing through the clean foyer and hall with their dirty feet! Why, poor Melinda has had to clean those floors three times this morning already!" Miss Mooney declared with some annoyance, slanting Cathy a severe glance as if it were her fault.

"Well, I still think it rather exciting," Cathy said. She had searched for Miss Mooney in the back sitting room that was used by the servants, and instead had found her in the butler's pantry from which the meals were served after leaving the kitchen. The tiny room was directly across from the dining room, at the front of the kitchen. Four wide steps led down into the kitchen, and an array of tempting smells wafted up them to the pantry. "Whatever are you doing in here, Miss Mooney?" Cathy wanted to know.

"Polishing the silver soup tureen," Miss Mooney answered. "I spotted some nasty smudges on it earlier."

"Can't one of the servants take care of that?"

"Of course, but as they are all busy preparing any and all manner of dishes in case His Royal Highness wishes to serve a meal, I decided to take care of it myself." Miss Mooney gave a flourish of her polishing rag to the bright surface of the ornate tureen, then smiled at her reflection. "See? It is already done."

"By 'Royal Highness,' I presume you mean Mr. Lamont?"

"You presume correctly. Oh . . . I almost forgot to give you this," Miss Mooney said, and reached into the pocket of the starched apron covering her tiny frame. She produced a thick envelope of vellum that looked as if it had seen much better times. "A letter from your mentor . . ."

"Miss Nightingale!" Cathy cried with pleasure, almost snatching the envelope from Miss Mooney in her haste. She tore it open and leaned back against the tall cabinets to read.

"Well?" Miss Mooney said after a few moments of silence. "What does she have to say?"

Swiftly scanning the cramped writing that scrawled across the pages, Cathy said slowly, "It seems that Nicholas the First—the czar of Russia—is fairly pleading for a conflict. Hundreds and hundreds of men lie injured in the Scutari hospital, wounded while trying to keep the Black Sea trade route free. She also says that Mary Stanley and some other untrained nurses are said to be on their way to the war's front, and that it was utterly ridiculous for any more nurses to come. Oh, the poor dear—Miss Nightingale says that she is living in a room with *forty* people, and the size of the room accommodates only *three!* How absolutely dreadful for her!" Cathy lowered the pages to stare unhappily at Miss Mooney.

"Aren't you glad you didn't go?" Miss Mooney asked briskly. "Only think how much more of a burden you might have been."

"Thank you, Miss Mooney!" Cathy snapped.

"Oh, I didn't mean it that way, my dear. I meant only that your inexperience would have reduced you to being no more than a charwoman by this time. After all, what could you do but clean linen and wrap bandages?"

"You're right, of course," Cathy said with a long sigh. "If only I had begun my training earlier, I could be so useful to Miss Nightingale!"

"But you didn't," Miss Mooney pointed out. "And you are useful here."

"That's true," Cathy murmured, thinking of the girls and Jesse. She was helping, and in a way she was even helping with the war effort. After all, Jesse was involved in politics, and she was quite certain that he and Lord Bothmourne and Lord Clarendon were desperately searching for a way to end the conflict. A word here, a phrase there, and she had intuitively discerned their mission. Of course, common sense decreed that all those in Parliament would be doing the same.

Cathy was still thinking about the hardships being suffered in Scutari while she ascended the steps to the nursery. Deep in thought, she pushed open the doors to find Ned Mahoney hard at work before his huge canvas. The girls were still perched primly on the edges of their chairs, holding hand-painted fans and wearing their Christmas gowns and stilted smiles.

Ned turned to smile at her, putting down his paintbrush as he said, "Hello!"

"Hello, Ned," she returned in a distracted tone, flashing him an abstract smile as she crossed the room.

"Lost in a fog?" he inquired, signaling to the girls that they could relax.

Cathy turned, changing direction to approach Ned. A troubled expression creased her face. "Yes, I suppose I am."

"Need a torch to find your way?" Ned teased.

Pausing before the unfinished painting, Cathy sighed. "I certainly do—do you have one?"

"Several!" Wiping off his paintbrush, Ned gave her a thoughtful gaze. "Personal problems? Or would you like to share the burden?"

"Oh, it's just that I've been so worried about the conflict, and with Miss Nightingale over there . . ."

"I suppose you've heard the most recent bad news, then. About Balaclava?"

Cathy's eyes grew round, and her voice was a hoarse whisper. "No."

"It's disastrous. It seems that—"

"Wait, Ned," she said, turning to the girls, who were listening intently. "Run along to Miss Mooney, girls, and she will help you remove your dresses. I believe that there is a bread pudding waiting upon you, too."

Smiling, the children ran gleefully from the nursery to find Miss Mooney, and Cathy turned back to Ned. "I didn't want them to hear this."

"Sorry. I didn't think."

"No matter. Do go on, Ned."

"On November 14 there was a devastating storm that wrecked more than a dozen ships in the Balaclava harbor. They were laden with winter supplies. The storm swept away the tents that sheltered the besieging army on the heights above Sebastopol, then proceeded to make an impassable mire out of the six-mile track that was the sole link between the camp and the base." Ned paused, then continued. "They are now marooned, with the worst Crimean winter in recent memory raging around them. It is reported that shiploads of cholera cases are pouring in from Varna, but there is no shelter for them, nor medical supplies or attention. The reports are that they are cold and starving."

"Dear God!" Cathy whispered, sick at heart.

"Yes. It would seem hopeless, wouldn't it? Perhaps the poor devils should just be sent home instead of dying off in a strange country—"

"Sent home! Without victory? Unthinkable!" Cathy said, earning a smile from Ned.

"You're right, of course. It's just that I feel so blasted dreadful about the loss of life."

"No more so than I, but such is war. If only their suffering could be eased!"

"Perhaps it can if the great heads of state will come to a decision," Ned returned. Then he asked, "Was that Lord John Bothmourne I saw earlier in the foyer?"

"Why, yes. Do you know him?"

"Only by sight. I've never been introduced, but I have had him pointed out to me by several acquaintances who are quite struck with his philosophies."

"Oh, really? And who are they?" Cathy asked idly, stepping back to gaze critically at the partially completed portrait.

"Disraeli was one of them. Do you know who he is?" Ned teased.

"Disraeli! My, such company you keep, Neddy! You should not spent so much time with the conservatives. Derby and his people are determined to regain control of the government, you know."

"So I've heard. You don't think Derby will succeed?"

"I don't know that much about politics, really, but I'm more inclined toward Palmerston."

"Palmerston!" Ned ejaculated. "I do believe you've been listening to Jesse Lamont for far too long, Cathy!"

"And I didn't realize that an artist would become so involved in political discussions, Ned," she returned with an impish smile.

"We are not a feather-brained lot, you know, appearances to the contrary. The next thing I hear will be your proclaiming Fox Maule as chancellor of the Exchequer!"

"Ah, an excellent choice," Cathy approved. "I shall certainly suggest it to Lord Bothmourne upon our next meeting. He *is* Sidney Herbert's right-hand man, you know."

"Good God, you've been mesmerized by these men, Cathy! Do let me seek help for you," Ned begged with a smile.

"Perhaps we should just eliminate any discussion of politics from our future conversations," she shot back.

"Another excellent notion," Ned said. "I've never involved myself very deeply anyway, and I suppose that the reason I am even remotely interested now is because of Benjamin Disraeli. He's an artist at heart, you know. Such men are needed in a formal government, especially in these turbulent times."

"Do you recall the party for Bulwer-Lytton?" Cathy asked suddenly. "Disraeli was there, and Lytton's wife, Rosina, made one of her disruptive appearances."

"Ah, yes, I do recall that particular night! A simply horrid affair, what with the rowdy Rosina flaying poor Lytton with her vicious tongue. I cannot understand why any host or hostess would include the woman at an affair with her estranged husband."

"Because it inevitably creates diversion in the form of vulgar entertainment," Cathy answered promptly. "It's much less expensive than jugglers and acrobats."

"Or bear baiting?" a deep voice inquired, causing both Ned and Cathy to turn around. Ned's mouth curved in a grimace.

"Oh. It's you, Lamont."

"Yes, it certainly is," Jesse agreed in an affable tone. "Disappointed?"

"Of course. I was enjoying Cathy's company until now."

"Sorry, old boy. You were doomed to disappointment." An eyebrow lifted in inquiry. "Is that the portrait for which I am paying so handsomely?"

"It is," Ned replied. "And well worth every shilling, I might add."

"You might, but *I* shall reserve opinion until it is completed," Jesse retorted.

"Oh, Jesse, how bad of you," Cathy reproved. "Ned is an excellent artist."

Ned grinned, enjoying the riposte Jesse was serving. "He knows that. He only denigrates my work to spark an argument. Correct, old boy?"

"Correct, Ned. I enjoy a good sparring now and again." Turning to Cathy, Jesse's gaze lingered on her lovely face. The bruise had faded slightly, lightening from the deep purple to a lavender spiked with shades of yellow, almost like a pansy. "You look much better, my dear," he said.

"Better than what?"

Jesse smiled. "Better than Ned."

"Perfection, indeed," Ned put in, his eyes moving to Cathy's face as she gazed back at Jesse with a soft smile.

Catching Ned's dark glance from the corner of his eye, Jesse suddenly knew the artist was enamored of Cathy. It was obvious in the way he looked at her, his gaze resting on her face.

"You were discussing Rosina earlier?" Jesse said then, deftly turning the conversation back to a safer topic. "I hear that she is mad as a hatter."

"Or more," Cathy agreed. "I recall meeting her the same night I met Ned. It was such a bizarre evening, and dear Neddy saved me from complete hysteria!"

"How wonderful for both of you," Jesse drawled, raking them with a sarcastic gaze. "And now you're the best of chums, right?"

"Right," Ned said, amusement curling his mouth at Jesse's obvious ire. Cathy gave them both a faintly startled glance.

"Oh, really," she began, then gave a light laugh. "I do claim Ned as a friend, but not Rosina or any of Derby's ilk! Actually, Jesse, I was just telling Ned that Palmerston may form a government after Christmas, but he doesn't seem to believe me. Do you suppose he's one of Derby's *spies?*" she teased.

Cathy's attempt at lighthearted humor fell flat. Both men gave her narrowed glances and dark scowls, and her gaiety shriveled immediately.

"Really!" she exclaimed with an exasperated stamp of her foot. "You two are such solemn fire-eaters! I was only attempting to inject some humor into your dour lives, and would appreciate any assistance you churlish gentlemen could give me."

Ned was the first to recover his composure. "Of course you would, Cathy. Shall I recite verses for you?"

Her answer was cold. "No, thank you for offering."

"My pleasure."

"I understand you received a letter from Miss Nightingale," Jesse said after a moment of uncomfortable silence.

"My, news does travel fast in this household, doesn't it?" Cathy observed tartly. "Yes, I did. Would you care to hear what she has to say?"

"Actually, I would. I am vitally interested in her perspective on the conditions there."

"I have it right here," Cathy began, reaching for the letter in her pocket, but Jesse stopped her with an outstretched hand.

"No, later, please. After dinner, perhaps." He flicked a glance at the clock on the wall, then murmured a farewell to them and pivoted on his heel, striding swiftly across the schoolroom to the doors.

As the doors closed behind him, Ned turned to Cathy. "An odd duck at times, wouldn't you say?"

"No, I find him quite astute."

"Yes . . . I say, I do wish you hadn't said you thought I was a spy, Cathy, dear."

She stared blankly at him. "Why? It was only a jest, for heaven's sake, Ned!"

"I know that, and *you* know that, but I get the impression that Lamont isn't at all certain about that!"

"Poppycock!"

"Perhaps, but he did seem rather cool after that comment, didn't you think?"

"If you want to know what I think, Ned, I think you worry too much about what Mr. Lamont may think. He is not an infallible weather vane of politics, you know!"

Arching a brow, Ned replied, "Perhaps not, but he *is* reputed to be a government spy."

"How ridiculous!" Cathy sputtered.

Ned smiled. "Is it? I think not. His brother, William, was a spy, and he was assassinated."

"Assassina——I understood that he drowned in a sailing accident off the coast of Italy. Why, even his wife was present at the time."

"But not on the boat," Ned pointed out. "William was quite alone when he was murdered."

Shuddering, Cathy shook her head weakly, refusing to believe such a wild tale. "That's not possible . . ."

"Oh, but it is. Jesse was there, too, though not on the boat, of course. He was on land, watching from a lighthouse." Ned's mouth twisted cynically. "Too absorbed with his brother's wife to notice his brother's death, I suppose."

Cathy's heart lurched. "I beg your pardon?"

Ned bent a questioning glance on Cathy's pale face. "Ah, I see you didn't know," he murmured.

Her hand rose to her throat. "Didn't know what?"

"About Caroline. Jesse was in love with her, the story goes. You see, he was once affianced to dear Caroline, and then he was sent to Russia for a time. While he was gone, William married Caroline, making for very bad blood between the brothers. The conflict eventually cooled, they say, but there are those who prefer to believe that Jesse's revenge for William's perfidy was the cause of the 'accident.' " Ned gave his paintbrush a vigorous cleaning with a rag, watching Cathy from one corner of his eye while he worked. She was quite pale, and it was obvious from her widened eyes that she had never heard the story.

"I . . . I . . . find that hard to believe," Cathy said finally.

"So did quite a few people, I understand." Pausing in the cleaning of his brush, Ned said more sympathetically, "If it's any consolation, both brothers were said to be spies, and both had been responsible for the deaths of others."

"I refuse to believe that," Cathy stated flatly.

"Dreamer. Would you refuse to believe ill of me if you heard it, sweet Cathy?"

"Probably."

"Then I feel exonerated for being the bearer of bad tidings. I only meant that you should know both sides of the coin."

She nodded. "Yes, I should."

"And now you know why I worry so about Lamont's believing I may be a spy for Derby," Ned went on. "Utterly ludicrous, of course, but if he should think I pose some threat . . ."

"Don't be silly. He thinks nothing of the sort. He has never paid the least attention to any of my idle remarks, and I do not think he will begin now. It was a jest, Ned, only a jest. If I had known any of this, I would never have said it, but I didn't. There is nothing to worry about."

Ned smiled. "You're right. I suppose I do worry too much, but you know how it is when one makes his living by reputation alone. If Lamont were to become dissatisfied with me for any reason, I may get very few portrait commissions in the future."

"I do not think he would be so petty. He may name you a radical, but hardly a disappointing artist!"

"So you favor my work?" Ned asked, turning back to gaze at the portrait. It had been sketched in: the girls stared out in shades of gray and white, with only the flesh tones added.

"It will be a remarkable likeness," Cathy said, stepping closer. She added thoughtfully, "I had never realized how strong a family resemblance there is between Jill and her uncle. Leigh and Erin must look more like their mother, Caroline."

Ned gave her a strange look, but remained silent. When Cathy turned to face him with a serious expression, he knew what her question would be.

"Ned, where is Caroline now?"

Shrugging, he said, "In London, I hear. Haven't heard too much about her. When she was married to William they always lived abroad." Placing his clean paintbrush on the easel, Ned asked carefully, "Do I detect a too keen interest in the lady? Jealousy, perhaps?"

"Jealousy!"

Another lift of his broad shoulders, then: "Do you have an . . . affection . . . for your employer, Cathy? Tell me!" he insisted when she would have turned away without answering. "I must know! Tell me I am mistaken—that you do not care about Jesse Lamont. You must know how I feel about you, Cathy, must know that I have cared about you since the first time we met at that deuced awkward ball. I've not tried to hide my feelings." His hand flashed out to grip her by the arms when she would have backed away, and his tone was urgent. "You haven't resisted my feelings before! Is it because of Lamont? He's a cold man, Cathy, a loner. He's never married, and has broken more female hearts than even I care to enumerate! Oh, I understand his fascination for you, but please don't lose your heart to him. I know him! He'll break you, crush you with his cruelty . . . all his life he has plotted and schemed; he's a manipulator, Cathy, a man who can twist events and people to shape the mold he wishes to fit. Can't you see that? Can't you see that even poor Caroline only turned to William out of desperation and loneliness?"

"I can't see any of that," Cathy said dully, pulling away and pressing her hands over her eyes. "Please, Ned, say no more."

"Listen, Cathy . . . I know you're upset, but let me beg a way to make amends for my hasty words," Ned said. "I have tickets to the opera, and I had meant to ask you earlier if you would go with me. Please say you will."

"Oh Ned, I don't—"

"Don't refuse yet! Just think about it and give me your answer later. Please," he added when she seemed about to shake her head, and Cathy paused.

Her heart ached, and she smarted from the sting of the revelations about Jesse. So he was in love with another woman—his brother's wife—and he'd been suspected of even murdering his own brother to get her back. . . .

Oh, Jesse! How could you be so faithless? So reckless? How could you be so cruel when I thought you were so gentle . . . when you kissed me so tenderly? I need you, love you. . . .

Jerking away from the direction of her thoughts, Cathy managed a smile. "I shall be delighted to go with you to the opera, Ned."

"Do you mean it?"

"Of course. It should be a lovely evening."

Ned grinned. "It certainly shall," he said. "I shall do my utmost to see that it is the best evening you've ever spent."

And when Cathy moved away from him toward the door, Ned watched her with a curious expression on his handsome face. She was so lovely, so tempting. He fully intended to walk away with the most precious victory of all. . . .

The contest is not over, Mr. Lamont—not yet.

Chapter 14

Saturday morning. Luncheon with her father loomed ahead of Cathy like a grim specter, but she braved the coming conflict with the courage of a true soldier, leaving the house in plenty of time to arrive at the hotel by noon.

Jesse watched from his study window, staring out the glass panes frosted with remnants of snow and wondering if Cathy would be able to withstand her father's stringent demands. He hoped so, for her sake. And for his own.

"Dammit!" Jesse swore under his breath. How could he have known how drawn to her he would be? But he was. Only once before had he been so attached to a woman for longer than one night, and that occasion had ended in disaster. He could not— would not—allow himself to be so vulnerable again.

Clenching his fist against the icy windowpane, Jesse pressed his cheek to the wooden frame. Cathy. His mouth drew into a taut line as he dwelled upon their relationship, defining and outlining every little detail. Nothing had happened between them that could be misconstrued as a lasting commitment. There had been no binding vows, would be no regrets. Or would there?

After knowing each other for only a few months, Jesse was startled to discover how attached he had become to Cathy, how he enjoyed the sight of her in her freshly laundered dress with her hair pulled back into that neat, prim little net she wore; he liked the way she smiled, openly and freely, not that practiced little grimace that so many women affected because of bad teeth or because some idiot had told them it wasn't genteel to smile so widely; and he liked the way her eyes sparkled when she was amused, those dark eyes which glowed so beautifully. Yes, there was no doubt that Cathy Weston was a most lovely, most desirable woman. Perhaps that was why his eyes lingered on her when they shouldn't, why his attention strayed to her again and again when he should be thinking of other things. And, worst of all, Jesse could not drive from his mind the memory of her lips opening beneath his searching mouth. To forget her kiss would be an exercise in futility.

A loud knock on the study door reverberated through the room, pulling Jesse away from his ruminations and giving him an irritated frown.

"Yes?" he called.

The door swung open and Pickworth entered. "There is a message from Lord Clarendon, sir. The delivery boy said it is urgent."

"Bring it to me," Jesse said at once, turning away from the window and crossing the room to meet Pickworth halfway. He tore open the envelope his servant held out, absently signaling for Pickworth to remain when he would have left. "It has happened at last," he remarked, looking up from the missive after a moment.

"Then you shall be leaving at once, sir."

"No, tomorrow morning."

"Very good, sir. I shall make the preparations. Will you be gone any length of time?"

"A month, maybe more," was the answer. Stepping to the fire burning in the grate, Jesse fed the note into the flames, watching as it was consumed. He stared at the flicker of hungry tongues lapping at the paper, turning it first brown, then black, crumpling it into nothing but fine ashes.

Love was like that, just as fiery and consuming, until it left a man the consistency of ashes.

Turning abruptly, he said to Pickworth, "Prepare my evening garments, please. I am attending the opera."

"During your absence, sir?" Pickworth asked in confusion.

"No, tonight."

"Tonight. Very good, sir. The white kid gloves, gibus hat, and diamond studs?"

"Naturally."

"Superfine or Saxony?"

"Superfine—it doesn't matter, Pickworth! Lady Waitley will not care a fig what material I choose, or probably even if I choose to wear none at all."

"I understand, sir," Pickworth politely lied. Clearing his throat, he said, "I was under the impression you had . . . er . . . canceled those plans, sir."

"Your impression was inaccurate, it seems," Jesse fixed him with a firm gaze. "Tonight of all nights, I must be away from this house!"

It would not have occurred to Jesse that Cathy might be having exactly the same thoughts. But she was. As she and Miss Mooney entered the hotel they once called home, she thought about Jesse, and how he would never return her deeper feelings. Ned had been right about that, and she had been so foolish as to believe otherwise. Of course, any such illusions were destroyed now in the light of what she had learned about Jesse Lamont. Men like Jesse never changed.

It would be so much easier to leave London and return to New York with her father, to give in and marry Darcy Sheridan. Yet she couldn't bring herself to do such a thing. It would be a denial of all she had tried to do, of all that she wanted.

Approaching the front desk of the hotel, Cathy dragged her thoughts back to the present, to the very real task now facing her.

"Courage," Miss Mooney murmured as Cathy took a deep breath and paused at the polished front desk.

A fixed smile curved her mouth, and she nodded. "Mr. Nathaniel Weston's room, please," Cathy said to the desk clerk.

"Why, Miss Weston, how nice to see you again," the desk clerk said, looking up from the row of keys he was placing in order. "It's been some time since you were here."

"Yes, it has, Theodore. Do you know if Mr. Weston is in?"

"Oh, I'm certain he is expecting you," the clerk assured her.

"Please take him up the message that I will be awaiting him in the front sitting room."

"Of course, of course, Miss Weston," Theodore said with a bob of his head. "I shall be delighted to do so."

"And will you ask him to come down alone?" she added.

"Certainly."

Cathy and Miss Mooney waited in the elaborately furnished sitting room with its horsehair-stuffed couches and fringed lamps. Round tables had been set in every conceivable spot, and a forest of potted plants bloomed in profusion.

"Rather stuffy," Miss Mooney remarked, seating herself on the edge of a red-velvet chair.

"Indeed," Cathy murmured in reply, pacing the carpet and wondering if she should not escape while there was yet time. *Courage, little coward, courage,* she scolded herself silently.

Nathaniel Weston arrived downstairs in a very short time, greeting Miss Mooney quite coldly and asking to speak to his daughter alone.

"Of course," Miss Mooney sniffed, her disdain at least equal to Weston's. "I can tell when I'm not wanted."

"You're so rude, Father," Cathy said when Miss Mooney had

moved to another chair. "It would have been just as simple for us to choose another spot."

"I did not ask you here to quibble about where your companion sits," Weston interrupted, his dark eyes burning into Cathy.

"I know that." Taking a deep breath, Cathy said without preamble, "I would like to put an end to your constant badgering of me, Father."

His brows rose fiercely. "Badgering? You call it badgering for me to want my only child to return to her home, where she is so greatly loved and well cared for? I call it common sense!"

Staring up at her father, Cathy found it difficult to assimilate this cold, overbearing man with the father she had idolized as a child. How she loved him; how she hated him—feelings so intense Cathy had the fleeting thought she must be deranged. It had always been like that between them, a love-hate relationship linking father and daughter in such a potent, volatile situation that she had often felt as if she were drowning in the tide of Nathaniel Weston's forceful personality.

But now she had somehow found the courage and strength to face him, to ask for respect and room to breathe. It was both exhilarating and frightening at the same time.

Nathaniel Weston, gazing down at his daughter's lovely, mutinous face, slowly began to realize that this was no longer the obedient, brokenhearted young woman who had left New York more than a year before. This Cathy was strong, and a small part of him rejoiced in her newfound strength. But he needed her. He could not lose her now. So when she stated her intention of remaining in London, Weston's heart hardened against her rebellion.

"Father," Cathy said calmly, "I have only come today in order to tell you of my intention of remaining in London. I will not be leaving. I've given the matter a great deal of consideration, and have decided that I will stay until next summer, perhaps longer."

"Cathy—no!"

Lifting one long-boned hand in a restraining gesture, she said firmly, "There's no need to argue. The point is moot. I have taken a position that I fully intend to honor, Father."

"You won't even give me the opportunity to speak?" Weston began dangerously, his jaw tightening. "You are my daughter and must obey my commands!" A brief glance around the lobby had the effect of lowering his voice, and he added more quietly, "I detest discussing such private matters in the lobby of a public establishment. It's common and vulgar, and I resent being put in this position. You have wounded me beyond all description, Cathy. I abhor this notion that a daughter of mine would be reduced to serving three common offspring of an even more common man. It is a disgrace, a shame that I shall never outlive. Our relationship has degenerated to chagrin and humiliation. I cannot—*will not*—let you do this." He gave his head a shake.

"You cannot stop me."

Weston's large, capable hands slowly clenched into tight balls. "But I shall!"

"I am of age," was the calm reminder.

"I shall disown you, Cathy. You shall not be allowed to do this to me without suffering the pain and agony you seem so determined that I shall endure!" Nathaniel Weston lifted one arm and pointed dramatically toward the hotel door. "If you pass through that portal today, I shall forget that I ever had a daughter. For as long as I live, I shall never speak of you—or to you—again. You will be disinherited from my estate and from my mind. Do you understand? Do you comprehend what I am saying to you, Cathy? I swear an oath to it—leave me now and you will be leaving me forever!"

Cathy shivered at his words and the fanatical light in his eyes. "Father, you cannot mean what you say. Money is one thing, but to put me completely out of your life as if I had never existed—how can you even contemplate such a thing?"

Stone-faced and silent, Nathaniel Weston gazed blankly at his daughter, as if she were already a stranger. Not a muscle moved in his face, no flicker of a lash to betray any emotion.

Shivering again, Cathy's eyes filled with tears. She had expected anger, yes; resistance, yes; but not this, *never* this. How could she ever find the strength to walk away and leave her father behind forever?

"Please, Father, don't make me choose between you and life. You cannot know what you ask."

"I ask obedience from my daughter."

Tears rolled slowly down her cheeks, and Cathy's throat tightened unbearably. He was determined to destroy her hopes for an independent life, determined to break her spirit and bend her to conform to his mode of thought. Pain slowly strengthened into anger. *How could she let him destroy her?*

Stiffening, she met his dark gaze, her hazel eyes refusing to turn away. "Father, you must reconsider what you are saying to me. It is not right for you—"

"Nonsense!" he said coldly. "There is only one decision you must make—that of putting aside this position. It is a scandalous and vile relationship with a provincial man, and I—"

"Stop it!" Cathy interrupted in a low hiss. She stood, trembling, filled with the certainty of a new and horrible revelation. Her father's last words had set vibrating a responsive chord within her, the knowledge that he would never let her love another man. He had chosen and promoted Darcy Sheridan only because he knew that he could control the younger man. If she was so foolish as to yield now, the rest of her life would be spent as a mindless puppet with her father and Darcy Sheridan tugging at the strings. Her spine straightened. "I am leaving, Father. You know where you may reach me if your feelings should ever alter."

Weston's arm snaked out and he grasped her by the elbow when she would have turned away. "I shall never reverse my stand," he grated through bloodless lips. "Leave now, and you are forever banished from my mind and heart."

Cathy struggled against the tears that once more pricked at the back of her eyes. It was difficult to accept the fact that her father could be so cold and cruel. But she had no choice. There was an entire world waiting on her, a world where she might have a chance of finding life and love. There was nothing she could say, no words that would express the wrenching decision he had thrust upon her. Pulling away, she turned and walked from the hotel lobby with her head held high and her shoulders back.

Miss Mooney rose to follow her charge, pausing when she recognized Darcy Sheridan descending the lobby stairs at a run. The young man reached Cathy, his fingers touching her arm and turning her around to face him, his tone bewildered and anxious.

"Cathy!" he said. "What has happened?"

"Father has disowned me," she said in a much cooler tone than the raging inferno of emotion inside would have revealed.

"Then . . . then you aren't coming back to New York with us?"

A faint smile tugged at the corners of her lips. "No. I am not."

"But Cathy . . . what about us?"

"Marry your Patsy and be happy, Darcy. You and I would never have been happy together."

"Cathy . . ."

She touched him lightly on the arm, and her voice was vaguely sympathetic. "It's for the best, Darcy. Trust me. Patsy will make you sublimely happy. I never could have done so. In the end, we would have detested each other." Standing on her toes, Cathy pressed a light kiss to his cheek. "Good-bye, Darcy. Be happy."

It was only when she reached the privacy and safety of the

waiting carriage that she allowed more tears to flow, and Miss Mooney was there to comfort her. She held Cathy in the loose clasp of her arms, stroking back the thick waves of hair and murmuring disjointed, soothing phrases.

"You are packed, sir."

Jesse looked up to see Pickworth standing in the study doorway. He was vaguely surprised to realize that he had half expected to see Cathy come rushing through the door at any moment, not Pickworth's rangy form looming like a demi-god in his doorway.

"Thank you, Pickworth. Did you send round the messages to John and Lord Clarendon?"

"Yes, sir."

"Very good." A lengthy sigh during which Jesse wondered when Cathy would return, a glance toward the darkening sky outside his windows, and then he said, "I suppose I should go up and tell the girls that I may not be back in time for Christmas." Another sigh, then the observation that he despised having to leave them at such a time. "But I must be in France for the next month. It is crucial, Pickworth."

"There is no necessity for an explanation, sir."

"I realize that. Perhaps I am only trying to justify it to myself, Pickworth." Jesse's smile was wry and faintly self-reproachful. "You cannot imagine how I dislike leaving Miss Weston and the girls alone during the Christmas season, especially after what happened earlier."

"But there is no reason to reproach yourself, sir. And I am certain that the assailant will not return. After all, he only came for one particular item, and he will now know that you would not dare leave it in the house again during your absence."

"True, Pickworth, true. Whoever our mysterious intruder is, he's not stupid. Careless, perhaps, but not stupid. I know that he is out there somewhere, lurking and watching, plotting like a fiend. I hate it. It nauseates me. Before, all the other times, it was easier. There was only myself to think of then. Now all that is different."

"I shall watch over them, sir," came the grave reply.

Relaxing his stiff posture, Jesse turned toward his faithful servant. "Yes, I know you will." His hard mouth quivered with the trace of a smile. "And remember that Mrs. Lamont is not to come near the house, Pickworth. It is imperative that she not be allowed near here."

"I fully understand, sir."

"I know you do, Pickworth, I know," came the weary reply. Jesse passed a broad hand over his eyes, then glanced at the mantel clock. Five-thirty. Where was Cathy? What had happened between father and daughter that could have delayed her for so long? It could very well be that she had decided to return to New York with her father, in spite of all her protestations to the contrary. Perhaps it would be for the best. He should be grateful that he was going to the opera and would not see her again before he left for France. A man in his position should not become too attached to . . . but enough of that.

"Pickworth, are my evening clothes ready?"

"Yes, sir. Shall I draw you a bath?"

"By all means. I shall be leaving early. Lady Waitley would appreciate a small supper before the opera."

Chapter 15

Cathy turned slowly in front of the walnut-bordered cheval mirror in one corner, gazing at her reflection. She wore a new gown, an absolutely beautiful new gown. The neck was a low scoop, with the bodice trimmed in layers of blond lace. Long pagoda sleeves drooped from the shoulders to dip gracefully over her arms. And on this night, Miss Mooney had finally persuaded Cathy to wear the cage crinoline. The dome-shaped undergarment made the rose-colored moiré and multiple flounces swell wide in a generous bell shape.

"I shall never be able to walk in it," Cathy pronounced gloomily.

"It's not walking that concerns me. It's how you will manage to sit," Miss Mooney said with a wry smile. "But Miss Cathy, you shall just have to remember that all the young ladies wear them now. It's the latest rage."

"Be that as it may, Miss Mooney, I am not certain I shall wear it." Cathy took several experimental steps in the gown, her movements clumsy and completely lacking in grace. "No, this definitely will not do. Do unfasten the buttons and laces, Miss Mooney."

"Won't you even try?"

"No. I feel utterly ridiculous in one of these."

Sighing, Miss Mooney moved to unfasten the back of Cathy's dress, observing, "But the skirt bells out so nicely."

"Damn the skirt, Miss Mooney! I think a few more petticoats and some extra starch will do the trick. I refuse to confine myself in this steel cage!"

Cathy turned with an irritable swish to face her old nurse. After eyeing Cathy's rebellious face and the determined set of her softly rounded chin, Miss Mooney said, "Very well, though I must protest your language. If you insist, I will gather more petticoats."

"I insist."

Within a remarkably short space of time, Cathy was attired in the much more comfortable froth of petticoats. Though not held out quite as far, the skirt flounces still had enough bounce to satisfy all but the most critical eye. Thin strands of lustrous pearls adorned her neck and hair, and should draw the eye away from any lack of volume in her skirts, she decided, leaning close to the mirror to inspect her image.

"Did you find the cape for me?" she asked distractedly. "I cannot recall where I must have put it."

Strolling to the tall wardrobe against the far wall, Miss Mooney grumbled to herself, but loud enough for Cathy to be certain to hear, "I don't know why you are trying to please that Mr. Mahoney. He's no gentleman either. Why . . . I've heard the most appalling things about young *artists.*" Pausing at the wardrobe doors and flinging them wide, she flipped rapidly through the assortment of gowns and mantles until she found the burnous mantle Cathy desired. "Did you know that some of them paint portraits of females wearing nothing more than what God saw fit to send them into the world with?" she demanded, turning back to Cathy.

A smile curved her mouth as Cathy reached out for the mantle. "Do you mean that the models are *nude,* Miss Mooney?" she asked in such an innocent tone that her old nurse narrowed her eyes in suspicion. "I am shocked beyond belief."

"I mean exactly that," was the tight answer.

"Well, I am quite positive Neddy would never do anything so appalling. As long as I have known him, he has been the very soul of propriety."

"I daresay." Miss Mooney thrust the mantle into Cathy's hands. Her gaze flicked dispassionately over her charge's face and gown, and she noted silently that Edward Mahoney was a very fortunate man to be escorting Cathy to the opera that evening. She had thought—quite wrongly, it seemed—that Cathy might be too upset over the morning's events to keep her promise to Mahoney. Hesitantly, she said, "I hope the evening removes any unpleasant memories for you."

Cathy gave her a bright smile and chirped gaily, "We must try and enjoy ourselves, Miss Mooney! Aren't you the least bit excited about going to the opera? Everyone who is anyone will be there, all in their best attire. It will be simply fabulous." Her smile dimmed only slightly as she added in the same lilting tone, "We must be happy—tonight of all nights!"

Recognizing her valiant attempt at gaiety, Miss Mooney smiled. Behind the mask of conviviality lurked shadows of anxiety and sadness, only briefly reflected in the liquid brown of Cathy's eyes. Nathaniel Weston had deeply injured his daughter, and yet she was doing her best to keep up appearances. Miss Mooney's mouth tightened grimly. Well, it was her duty to help the child. No father should abandon his daughter as Mr. Weston had done.

"We shall have a perfectly splendid evening, Miss Cathy. Give me just a moment to fetch my cape from my room, and I will be ready."

As the door shut behind her, Cathy's smile faded. Except for the day on which her mother had died, this had been the most dreadful day in her memory. In a way, it was as if the same debilitating thing had happened again. But this time, her parent had left by choice instead of an act of God. She had been abandoned.

A chill sliced through her as Cathy thought of all the beloved people in her life. Somehow, they had all been taken from her. Her mother, her father, and, of course, Darcy. All had abandoned her in some fashion.

Dropping her face into the cup of her palms, Cathy thought of Jesse. She loved him, yet feared loving him at the same time. How could she take such a risk again? Life was so fragile, a delicate gift that should never be abused, and love was just as fragile.

The opera house was filled to overflowing when Miss Mooney and Cathy arrived with Edward Mahoney. They were immediately assailed by familiar voices greeting Cathy.

"Miss Weston? Is that you?"

Another gay voice. "Cathy . . . I thought you had left dear old England."

Still another and another. "Miss Weston, how utterly delightful to see you again."

"What a pleasure to see you, Miss Weston."

On and on, happy, laughing voices responding to Cathy Weston's return to social life.

"You'd think I'd been away for years," Cathy murmured to Miss Mooney at the beginning of the intermission. "I never realized I knew so many people in London."

"It has been months since your . . . absence . . . an entire season," Ned put in. "Did you see Fran as we walked in?"

Nodding, Cathy said, "Was he with Lady Cowper?"

Ned laughed. "Yes. And did you see Sarah's aunt?"

"Yes."

"I believe you have been supplanted in his affections, dearest Cathy."

"You shouldn't tease, Neddy. Sarah Cowper has always been in love with Fran. They make a charming couple."

"Touché, and . . ." Ned's voice lowered as he lifted Cathy's gloved hand to his lips. "And so do we, sweet Cathy."

Miss Mooney's mouth pinched into a disapproving frown when Cathy merely smiled at Mahoney as if he were a naughty boy. Cathy, of course, was oblivious to her companion. She was much too absorbed in Ned's light kiss upon her hand and his flowery compliments. Her voice was dreamy as she commented, "It is so nice to be out and about again. The opera is delightful." Then, finally slanting Miss Mooney an inquiring glance, she added, "You've been so quiet this evening! Aren't you enjoying the opera?"

Forbearing to utter the tart reply on the tip of her tongue, Miss Mooney contented herself with, "I'm getting too old for these late-night affairs, I'm afraid. My delicate constitution requires that I return by nine."

"Perhaps a glass of punch or ratafia might help?" Ned suggested, politely concerned.

"No, thank you, Mr. Mahoney."

"Then some for you, Miss Weston?" Ned asked, turning once more to Cathy. "They have excellent champagne here."

Noting Cathy's hesitation, Miss Mooney immediately suggested that they both go to fetch refreshment. "I should like a glass of water," she added.

"Certainly," Cathy said at once. "Are you certain you do not mind being left alone for a few minutes?"

"Of course not. You two run along. The intermission will be over soon enough. You don't want to miss the beginning."

"Would you care to come with us, perhaps? We could—"

"No, no, I'll just wait here." Miss Mooney smiled and waved them off, then turned back to her perusal of the stage and rich, swagging curtains.

Cathy and Ned strolled down the long, carpeted corridor to

the wide sweep of stairs that led to the ground floor. The corridors were alight with bright faces and colorful gowns of satin, crepe, silk, and moire. Her fingers rested lightly on the arm of Ned's silk evening jacket.

"I think I should have champagne instead of punch," she remarked after a moment, slanting Ned a bright smile. "I have reason to celebrate tonight!"

His hand closed over the fingers on his arm, and his returning smile was warm. "You do? A celebration of life . . . or, perhaps . . . the company you are keeping?"

She laughed. "Well, that, too, but something else—I am a free and independent woman as of today. And London is now my permanent home."

"What good news, Cathy!" Grinning from ear to ear, Ned's blue eyes sparkled. "We should hasten to the champagne bowl, then! One glass will surely not be enough!"

Glancing toward the long line pressing close to the linen-draped refreshment table, Cathy shook her head. "I do not think we will get even one glass! Look at the crowd."

"Wait here," he said, "so that your gown doesn't get crushed. I will bring you *two* glasses, lovely Cathy!"

She was smiling when Ned moved away from her, watching him disappear among the throng of people. Ned, dear Ned, with his cheerful smile and sunny disposition. He demanded nothing of her but the leave to give her his affection, and she felt a sudden swell of appreciation. How absolutely soothing it was not to have to deal with a tumult of emotions when she had been so buffeted lately.

Cathy let her gaze drift across the familiar faces in the assembly, her mind also drifting in a pleasant haze, so that she was suddenly shocked at seeing an especially familiar face. He was laughing, his dark eyes glittering and his rugged features creased with amusement as he gazed at the woman clinging to his arm.

She was staring back at him in equal fascination, her head tilted coquettishly to one side.

She was beautiful, Cathy noticed with a rush of anxiety. Thick golden curls were tousled in an artfully arranged coiffure, and she had that flawless English complexion that so often eluded women, set off to perfection by the rich green silk gown she wore. To her dismay, Cathy suddenly felt uncomfortable and out of place. If only she'd known that Jesse Lamont would be attending the opera this evening with *another woman,* she would have feigned illness or given some other excuse not to attend.

Jesse was still laughing at some comment when he turned and his dark eyes chanced to meet Cathy's steady gaze. *Cathy.* His smile abruptly disappeared, and his dark, winged brow lifted in surprise. She was staring at him with huge, liquid eyes that expressed only too well her dismay and pain at seeing him with someone else.

Damn! Damn the luck! Jesse thought savagely. To meet her here, and when he was with . . . but she certainly wasn't with her father, he thought in the next instant. Perhaps it would be worth his time to find out with whom she was attending the opera.

Unable to continue gazing at him, Cathy looked away, hoping the feelings in her heart had not shown in her eyes. It had been such a shock, and she was not as good at hiding her feelings as she had once been. What was he doing here? Was he wondering if she . . . ? But then, with a sense of rising panic, she saw that Jesse had moved from his position and was striding toward her. He was approaching with a loose, easy stride, the fluid grace that she had always admired. It was difficult to keep her composure when he paused in front of her, his brow lifting in a quixotic gesture.

"Cathy? Whatever are you doing here?"

"Why . . . enjoying the opera," was her thick reply, delivered in a voice thankfully devoid of emotion. Unfortunately for her, none of Jesse's emotions showed on his face, either. His features were carefully schooled into polite attention and a rather distant curiosity.

"Of course," he replied smoothly. "I only meant, how did you arrive? Not alone, I trust."

"Oh, no. I am accompanied by Ned and—"

"Edward Mahoney?" he cut in so quickly she had no time to add Miss Mooney to the list. "How droll!"

Incensed at his amused, disbelieving posture and obvious assumption that she had no right to choose her own company, Cathy stiffened in anger.

"You said my Saturday's were free, Mr. Lamont," she reminded him. "Mr. Mahoney invited me to join him at the opera, and I responded with delight. Do you find that difficult to accept?"

"Accept?" Again the lifted brow and slight curl of his lips into a condescending smile. "My, no, not at all. Why should I? After all, I did say that you were free to do as you pleased on Saturdays, did I not?" Jesse glanced leisurely around the crowded hall. "And just where is our Mr. Mahoney?"

"He has gone to fetch champagne."

"Ah, champagne. An excellent notion." Though he was smiling benignly, Jesse's thoughts were anything but that. He was suddenly fiercely jealous that she should have attended the opera with a notorious rake such as Edward Mahoney. And he could not understand why. The artist was with Cathy tonight, and tomorrow—when Jesse had gone—she would be alone once more. Unless Mahoney decided to pursue his suit. The thought was galling.

"Yes," Cathy was saying, dragging his attention back to the conversation, "champagne is a delightful idea. And you? Are you not going to provide your . . . lady . . . with refreshment?"

His dark brow lifted even higher, a feat Cathy had not thought possible. "Are you presuming to scold me for not being attentive?" Jesse inquired with such icy politeness that she knew she had transgressed. "I hardly think a governess for my nieces should take it upon herself to also scold her employer," he added.

"A thousand apologies," Cathy said stiffly, smarting from his rebuke. "I had no intention of sounding as if I was doing so. If you must know, I was merely trying to think of a neutral topic of conversation," she said so sincerely that he believed her at once. His facial features relaxed slightly, and a reasonable facsimile of a smile flickered for a moment on his mouth.

"I see. My apologies, then. There are times when I am too defensive, I suspect. This is obviously one of them."

They stood for a moment while the crowd milled around them, and it was as if the vast, crowded room had suddenly grown smaller and less crowded. Their eyes met, and for an instant all hostilities ceased. Instead of barbed comments and cautious glances, they smiled at each other with genuine friendliness and a spark of an even deeper emotion. It was all Cathy could do not to blurt out a revealing comment that would tell him all too clearly how she felt. And when Jesse asked gently how things had gone with her father, she fought against the overwhelming urge to fling herself into the strong comfort of his arms.

"I looked for you when I arrived home, but you had already gone for the evening," she said. There was a short pause during which Jesse searched her eyes for a clue to what had happened. His expression was so concerned that Cathy felt a surge of love for him that she hoped did not show. "Father is returning to America without me," she said softly, so softly he had to lean close to hear.

She could feel him brush against her, smell the familiar scent of his shaving cologne and the faint whisper of tobacco and brandy that she usually associated with Jesse. It evoked a sudden memory of his lips upon hers, and she flushed.

A slow grin squared his mouth as Jesse reached out for her hand. "I am very pleased to hear that," he said in a low, husky voice. "Very pleased."

Their entwined fingers tightened briefly. Oblivious to the gazes from curious passersby, Cathy shivered. For a brief—horrified, yet breathless—moment, she thought he was going to kiss her. Then his grip relaxed and he took a step back and away from her, his voice normal and once more politely distant as he noted Mr. Mahoney's return.

"Here comes your escort with your champagne, Miss Weston. I trust I shall see you later?"

Forcing a nod and deep breath to fill her starving lungs with much-needed air, Cathy smiled. "Of course."

Ned Mahoney slid a shrewd glance from one to the other as he held out a goblet of champagne. "Good evening, Lamont . . . and Lady Waitley."

Only then did Cathy notice that Jesse's companion had approached and was standing only a foot away, her mouth pinched into a tight frown. She tossed her golden curls, an affected gesture that Cathy suspected she performed only for effect and not a desire to remove the dangling curls from her eyes.

"Hello, Mr. Mahoney," Lady Waitley replied silkily, her mouth now pursing in a provocative pout. "So nice to see you again. I understand from Jesse—Mr. Lamont—that you are doing a portrait of his nieces."

Ned could not hold back a smile. "Yes, I am."

"How delightful," came the purring reply. "And is this your companion? She's absolutely charming, Neddy!"

Ned grinned openly now. "Yes, I certainly agree. Lady Waitley, I should like to present Miss Catherine Weston. She is Lamont's governess."

The china-blue eyes hardened with sudden suspicion, but the

smooth voice never altered. "Governess? How nice. Jesse, you rascal, you never told me you had hired such a lovely young woman to look after your nieces!" Her laugh trilled into the air. "I can see why, of course, you devious devil! You knew I would be *consumed* with jealousy at the notion!"

Her light, teasing voice provoked a mischievous smile from Jesse. "Of course, Marthe. But now that you know all . . . well, what am I to do?"

Tensing at this affectionate banter between them, Cathy could not help but wonder just how good a friend Lady Waitley was to Jesse. Her throat ached at the thought, but she could not allow other than a bright smile to curve her mouth as she wondered silently if this woman, too, would make an attempt on Jesse's life. He seemed to cultivate deep, violent emotions from his women. . . .

"It's very nice to meet you, Lady Waitley," Cathy said aloud. "I would like to linger and chat, but Miss Mooney—my companion—is waiting for her ratafia, and I hate to keep her waiting. If you will both excuse us, please?"

"Miss Mooney is with you?" Jesse asked in obvious surprise.

"Oh, yes. She's never been to the opera, and we left her alone while we came to fetch champagne. She must be wondering why we have taken so long."

For some reason, it made Jesse Lamont feel a great deal better to know that Ida Mooney had accompanied Cathy and Ned to the opera. He wasn't certain why it made such a difference, but it did, and he didn't care to explore the reasons for that too closely. Not now.

". . . and we've already kept her out much too late," Cathy was saying when he returned his attention to her. "I'm afraid the evening has not been as pleasant for her as I'd hoped."

"Then you must return and make amends," Jesse said, with a polite bow. "It has been pleasant seeing you this evening, Miss Weston. Mahoney."

"And you also," Ned returned smoothly. "My best regards to you, Lady Waitley." Offering his arm to Cathy, Mahoney tucked her fingers into the crook of his elbow and swung her away in a graceful circle.

Watching Jesse Lamont's face, Marthe Waitley commented with a wry twist of her lips, "Such a sweet girl. I do believe that you are quite smitten with your little governess, Jesse."

His face hardened, and his eyes were cold and flinty, a fact that did not perturb Lady Waitley in the least. "I do not know what you are talking about, Marthe."

She laughed. "I wonder . . . I just wonder!"

Dark eyes narrowed on her oval face. "What do you mean by that?" he demanded abruptly.

"Only that I never thought to see you in love," was the soft, serious reply, shocking Lamont into silence. He turned to watch as Cathy ascended the stairs on Ned Mahoney's arm.

Am I in love with Cathy? No, I can't be. It's too late for me, too late for love. . . .

Chapter 16

*T*he house was pitch black when Jesse arrived home. The front door creaked slightly as he pushed it open and entered the dark, silent entry hall. Nothing stirred; only the tall case clock ticked in muted welcome. In just a few hours he would be leaving his home and sailing across the choppy waters of the Channel to France.

Shutting the door behind him, Jesse wondered darkly what this trip would bring. Success, perhaps? Could England somehow persuade Napoleon III to enter the war on a grander scale? Prussia would not stop its assault on Turkey unless France and England joined forces to stop them.

His heels clicked across the floor as he crossed the hall and paused at his study door. Raking a spread hand through his dark hair, he sighed heavily. There was so much to do and so little time, but he could not think clearly. He had drunk too freely of champagne when he should have kept his mind clear. Ridiculous, really, when one considered that he was certainly old enough to know better. But when he had seen Cathy standing there in the opera house with her lovely face and large, appealing gaze, staring at him as if he . . . as if . . . no, in that direction lay confusion and a sleepless night, he decided firmly, turning away from his study door.

Jesse took the stairs two at a time. Then he walked softly down the hall and around the corner. The house was sleeping. All were in bed. Even Pickworth had learned not to wait up on his master, so there would be no one awake.

But when Jesse stepped down the carpeted hallway and paused in front of his bedchamber, he saw the thin sliver of yellow light edging Cathy's door. It laced the edges in a silent invitation, and he hesitated.

She was awake. Just beyond the heavy oak door Cathy lay awake, perhaps reading a book or writing a letter. Was that what she was doing? Or was she lying awake thinking of him?

Turning swiftly away at the thoughts *that* provoked, Jesse bumped into the small lamp table in the hallway. It bumped against the wall, and he steadied it with one hand before reaching for his door latch. There was a creaking sound, and a square of light suddenly flooded the hallway.

"Jesse?" came the soft whisper, as he had somehow known it would. He turned.

She stood framed in the open doorway, her slender form silhouetted by the light behind her, dark hair draping in luxuriant ropes over her shoulders to frame the soft thrust of her breasts in the thin nightdress. He swallowed the sudden lump in his throat, and wished savagely that he had not drunk so much champagne and she had not opened her door to stand there so temptingly.

"Yes. What do you want?" he asked more harshly than he intended. There was the soft hiss of a quickly indrawn breath, and he regretted the fact that he must have hurt her feelings. "It's late," he added more softly.

"I know. That . . . that's why I was worried about you."

"About me?" He took a step closer, knowing he shouldn't, but unable to stop himself. The warm woman smell of her wafted across the short space separating them, the smell of lavender and lace and satins and silks. Jesse damned himself for his too vivid imagination. "Why would you be worried about me?" he demanded then.

She stepped back, her bare feet sinking into the thick carpet with a soft whisper of sound. "I can see that you've had a bit too much to drink," she said with a little catch in her voice. "Perhaps I'd better—"

"Yes," he snapped out, "perhaps you'd *better!*"

Cathy swung the door to close it, but Jesse's hand was there to stop it, pushing against it with a quick shove.

"Go to bed," she whispered, staring at him with wide, dark eyes. "We can talk tomorrow."

"Why? Why not now? You waited up for me, didn't you?" he asked. "We'll talk now, Cathy, love, dearest Cathy, Cathy, my sweet. . . ."

Panic thickened her voice as she tried to close the door against him. "You're drunk!"

"Drunk? Drunk?" he echoed, wishing with a snap of frustration that he was either more or less drunk. "Of course I'm drunk!"

"Go to bed, please!" she shot back at him, gazing at his tight face with confusion and rising alarm.

"Come with me, sweet Cathy," he whispered back so invitingly and huskily that she was stunned into silence. "I'll go to bed when you come with me . . ."

Her heart pounded beneath the curve of her ribs so loudly that it sounded like thunder in her ears, and Cathy gazed at him in frightened fascination. This was a Jesse she had never seen, a Jesse with desire plainly written on his features, as if etched there by a master hand. He waited for her answer, his dark brow lifted and his lips quirked in a tempting smile, a smile that promised more than she had ever dreamed it might, and Cathy briefly closed her eyes. When she opened them, she said simply, "No."

"No? Only 'no'? Can't you qualify that terse reply?" he mocked lightly, leaning one broad shoulder against the door-jamb and gazing at her with cool deliberation.

She shook her head, marveling at the fact that his expression of desire never waned, only sharpened even in the light of their calm conversation. "No, I cannot add more than that," she said with only the barest quiver in her voice.

His voice was soft, a silky caress in the dim light of her bedroom as he said, "But Cathy, we need each other. We're both emotional cripples, you and I. Can't you see that? We deserve each other, can comfort each other's aching soul . . ." He lifted a supplicating hand, and Cathy trembled with reaction.

In spite of her longing to yield to emotion and desire and melt into his embrace, she resisted, shaking her head again and stepping back. "No. No, I . . . I . . . can't. You don't mean any of this, Jesse. You're only drunk on wine or champagne, and will regret this tomorrow."

"Will I?" he demanded roughly, surging forward to pull her quickly into his arms. "I don't think so," he murmured as his lips descended on hers with bruising force. Moaning a faint protest that she didn't realize she'd voiced, Cathy was pressed against the hard length of his body, her thin nightdress offering little protection against the warmth of his hands on her hips and back. She could feel his fingers splayed across her hips as he urged her even closer, his mouth hungrily searing a path from her half-parted lips to the vulnerable arch of her throat. He tasted, teased, nibbled at her sensitive skin with a feverish desire that he hadn't known he possessed.

Clinging to him like a wilting vine, Cathy felt her will to resist drain away. In its place was a rising tide of passion to match the fire of Jesse, pulsing through her veins in a rush of tingling sparks. She clung to him, kissing him with fevered urgency, until finally she wrenched away with a gasp. Her breath was ragged as she gulped in a breath of night-frosted air, and her wide eyes regarded Jesse Lamont with longing.

There was a hand's breadth between them, and Jesse bridged the gulf with a single step, sweeping Cathy from her feet and into the warm embrace. There was the gentle slap of the bedroom door closing behind them. Then he was moving toward the wide, curtained bed against the far wall.

To Cathy it was the longest walk she had yet endured, and she trembled in his grasp. He lowered her gently to the feather mattress, and she felt it dip beneath their combined weight. Then his arms were gone, leaving her shivering and cold. Meeting her steady gaze, Jesse shrugged out of his coat and let it fall unheeded to the floor.

Her lips formed the word "Jesse," but he ignored her as he began to unbutton his shirt. Cathy's long lashes dipped over her eyes, then fluttered upward to watch as he smiled at her.

"Oh, Jesse," she murmured then, audibly, a soft sigh of sound in the still night air. Her heart raced with emotion and reaction, a steady thud-a-thud that should have rattled her rib cage, and she was certain he must have noticed it when his hands moved to touch her lightly.

One palm gently cupped a heavy breast, while the other slid slowly beneath the lacy hem of her nightdress. Cathy could not stifle the sudden moan that escaped her when his fingers slipped over her bare leg. She shifted beneath his hands, wanting him to touch her where no man had ever touched her before. Her body ached for his touch, the soft stroke of his fingers and the press of his hand, the feel of his lips on her skin in light, feathery kisses that radiated an intense longing from the pit of her stomach to her quivering nerve endings.

Arching against him, her hand tangled in the dark sweep of his hair, holding his head against the swell of her breasts as he kissed her. Cathy writhed, her breath coming in short pants, twisting beneath Jesse and longing for a release from the fire he was building inside her.

"Jesse . . . Jesse, don't stop," she said hoarsely when he paused. "Don't stop kissing me . . ."

"I won't, love," he promised, lifting his head to gaze at her. There was a fire kindled in his dark eyes, a smoldering passion that sparked a flame within Cathy. She caught her breath, mesmerized by his desire, by the yearning of her own heart and body.

Time moved in a slow wheel of motion, of the awareness that Jesse was pulling her gown over her head and the feel of cool night air whisking over her bared body. She lay in his arms, a warm statue of ivory flesh and perfection.

As Jesse gazed at her, his eyes roamed over her gleaming pale skin, the hollows and curves that tempted and tantalized, and his hands sought out the mystery that was Cathy.

"My God," he murmured huskily, "you are even more lovely than I had dreamed."

"Am I, Jesse?" she whispered in the heated haze that surrounded them. Her voice seemed to come from far away, slow, sensual, drifting across the short space between them. "Am I? Did you really dream of me?"

His magical movements made her rib cage expand with the heated rush of air she drew in, and she held it so long Jesse looked up into her passion-dilated eyes.

"Yes, Cathy. I dreamed of you more times than I should admit." There was a brief pause during which he paid rapt attention to the hollow of her flat stomach, his mouth searing and tasting, his tongue flicking against the tiny indentation in the middle. Then he looked up at her again. "I shall always dream of you . . . like this . . . your sweet body in my arms and the taste of you on my lips . . . honey . . . pure honey, all sweetness . . ." His voice trailed off again as he lavished kisses on her pale, writhing body.

Cathy, Cathy, he thought, *how I need you. . . .*

Her whisper floated through the love mist, and Jesse paused to look up. "Jesse, I love you."

Love. The word struck him as forcibly as a hammer. *Love.* There were echoes in that word, dark echoes, and he winced. Caroline's pathetic voice haunted him, whispering with dark triumph, *What about me, Jesse? I love you, love you, love you . . .*

Wrenching away from Cathy, Jesse sat back, his expression as tormented as his thoughts, the echoes of Caroline assaulting him. Images sliced through his memory. A pistol. Pain. Florence Nightingale. Lord Clarendon. John. Edward Mahoney. Jill crying. And all the time the pain, the burning piercing of pain that he'd thought had ended it all.

He didn't see Cathy's bewildered face framed by dark hair and pressed against the pillows; instead, he saw John Bothmourne shaking a warning finger at him, whispering, *It will not be the notebooks next time—it will be you he comes after. . . .*

"No!" Jesse said aloud, shaking his head to clear it of the unwanted ghosts. "No," he added more softly.

"Jesse?"

Cathy's voice, tentative and confused, reached him through his fog of memories, and he smiled down at her. She was so lovely, so . . . forbidden.

Rising from the bed, Jesse stood swaying for a moment, the effects of the champagne and brandy weighing heavily on him. He lifted his hand, the words he needed to say filling his head but refusing to be uttered, and he gave a long sigh. He was only vaguely aware of the flush staining Cathy's cheeks, of her movement to draw the coverlet across her pale, naked body, but he could do or say nothing to ease the thoughts that must be running through her head. Perhaps it was best this way, he thought in some confusion. Turning, he stumbled toward her door, only dimly conscious that Cathy had sat up in the bed and was staring at him with wide dark eyes, the coverlet pulled up to cover her breasts.

Stunned, Cathy gazed at Jesse's retreating back, watching numbly as he pulled open the door and stepped from the room. The door's faint click as it swung shut behind him sounded as loud as a rifle shot to her. Hot tears coursed down her cheeks, and a shudder racked her slender body.

He's leaving me . . . just like all the rest. . . .

She couldn't sleep. It eluded her, always remaining out of reach as she tossed and turned in her lonely bed. Jesse had been there. Then he'd gone without a single word of farewell or explanation. Why? Why, why, why? He'd almost made love to her, almost . . . *almost.*

Punching a depression into her feather pillow with her fist, Cathy rested her cheek in the cooler spot with a sigh. *Almost* was such a weak word. It lacked the strength of words such as *completed, finished, concluded, finalized, fulfilled.* She turned onto her back and stared up at the dark ceiling. No explanation, no apologies, no regrets. There had been nothing but silence. And it was the silence that sounded the loudest in her beleaguered brain.

Cathy turned over on her stomach, pressing her face against the pillow. How could she stay here now? How could she live in the same house with a man who had taken her further than any man had ever done? He'd humiliated and abandoned her. Rejected her. No, she couldn't stay. She would resign her post immediately.

When the first faint rays of sunlight pressed through the cracks in the draperies, Cathy was already dressed and ready for the day. Her fingers had fumbled maddeningly with the buttons, but had finally worked them into the holes.

Miss Mooney had knocked twice, as was her custom, then entered Cathy's bedchamber to find her struggling with the last button. Her brow lifted inquiringly. "My dear, you have them all in the wrong holes. Do let me assist you."

Cathy stood quietly while Miss Mooney quickly and efficiently reworked the buttons into the proper holes. She felt Miss Mooney's curious gaze on her, so she wasn't surprised when her companion observed, "My, my, you are in a tizzy this morning. I haven't seen you so rattled since we first came to England."

"I'm sure," Cathy murmured. Then, because it seemed as if Miss Mooney expected a bit more explanation, she added lamely, "It must be because of my interview with Father yesterday."

"Perhaps," was the noncommittal reply. "There. All done, and in the proper slots." She gave Cathy's shoulder a pat. "I do hope you are in a better frame of mind when you greet the children this morning. You are quite likely to give them a fit of horrors if you appear so rattle-brained."

A slight smile curved Cathy's mouth as she turned to Miss Mooney. "I think they are more stout-hearted than that! I doubt if my long face would do more than give them a temporary rash."

But a close inspection of her appearance in the long cheval mirror made Cathy wish she had a vast supply of paint to cover the circles beneath her eyes. Even her wealth of hair seemed lackluster and straggly. Cathy gave it a perfunctory brushing and tied it back with a ribbon. Appearances no longer mattered. She had an interview with Jesse Lamont that superceded everything.

Pausing at the bottom of the stairs with one hand resting on the newel post, Cathy could hear the laughter of the children at their morning meal in the dining room. She straightened her skirts and her spine, and had taken several steps toward the doors when Pickworth appeared at the opening to the servants' stairs.

"Miss Weston, I was about to fetch you," he said.

She turned. "Yes?"

Holding out a small, square fold of paper, Pickworth said, "I have a note here from Mr. Lamont."

"He's gone?"

"Yes, Miss Weston."

A tiny frown etched her brows together as Cathy reached out and took the note. Her hand shook slightly, and the tremor was immediately noticed by Pickworth.

"Are you well, Miss Weston?"

"Yes . . . yes, I am fine, Pickworth. Would you please see that the girls begin their studies as soon as they have breakfasted? I must retire to my room for my own studies this morning."

"Certainly, Miss Weston," Pickworth replied with a slight frown of concern. "I shall be happy to do so."

Slowly retracing her steps back up the stairs, Cathy stared down at the pale square of paper with apprehension. He was already gone. Jesse had left early, and she had not heard him. He must have taken great pains to be quiet.

Once in the privacy of her bedchamber, Cathy unfolded the note. Her eyes scanned the neat penmanship with growing dismay.

Dear Cathy,

I must be away and do not know when I shall return. Perhaps by Christmas . . . at least I hope so. I trust that you will care for the girls. I leave them entirely in your safe hands.

Yours affectionately,
Jesse

Crumpling the paper in both hands, Cathy stared sightlessly at the wallpaper. Gone for a month—perhaps more! And not a single word about the night before. How could she leave now, leaving the girls untended for so long? She was forced to stay, at least until Jesse's return. The children needed her, and somehow she felt as though she needed them also.

Chapter 17

December 20 loomed on the calendar, five days until Christmas. The household residing at number 8 Devonshire Terrace was haunted by thoughts of Jesse's return. When? There had been only one letter from him since his departure.

A week after Jesse's early morning leave-taking, Cathy had learned where he had gone. Lord Bothmourne informed her that Jesse was in France. To add to this sketchy information, she received a letter from Miss Nightingale, detailing the seriousness of the situation abroad.

Miss Nightingale had written:

> Of 54,000 soldiers, some 40,000 have died of wounds, frostbite, fever, dysentery, and cholera. Each day hundreds of wounded men are brought into the hospital at Scutari, where there are not enough beds. There are no towels, soap, mops for cleaning. Men are dying every day from just plain filth.

War was terrible, and Cathy felt a twinge of guilt for wanting Jesse back when he was in France trying to help bring an end to the struggle.

"Can't I go, Miss Weston?" a childish treble asked, and Cathy turned from her musings to see Jill at her side.

The thin-faced girl had filled out a bit in the past weeks, and her complexion did not seem as sallow as it had when Cathy had first arrived. There had been improvements in her attitude as well, for Jill had grown more congenial toward her governess. Smiling, Cathy reached out to stroke back a stray curl that had escaped Jill's hair ribbon.

"I'm sorry, Jill, but there is snow on the ground. Dr. Alexander said you should not take a chance on catching cold." Kneeling beside the child in a rustle of soft wool material, Cathy added, "But I shall bring you a nice surprise as a consolation. Would you like that?"

"Would you, Miss Weston? I should like that very much!"

Cathy smoothed out a wrinkle in Jill's pinafore. "Yes, I shall bring back something grand for such a brave girl!"

Smiling brightly now, Jill nodded. "Then I shall wait without complaining." Her voice lowered conspiratorially, and she glanced over her shoulder at the row of stockings hanging from the nursery mantel. "Would you do me a favor, Miss Weston?"

"Of course, Jill, if I can. What is it?" Cathy had seen Jill's glance toward the fireplace and dangling stockings, and knew what it would be.

There was a muted clink of coins as Jill withdrew a small velvet pouch from the pocket of her pinafore. She held it out. "I would like to purchase gifts for Leigh and Erin. I have seven shillings in here, and it is all I have saved."

Cathy held out her hand, and Jill placed the pouch in her palm. "Of course I shall, Jill. And would you also like for me to purchase your uncle a small gift? Leigh and Erin intend to do so."

A tight frown puckered the child's smooth brow, and for a moment she resembled the angry child Cathy had first confronted. She hesitated, staring at Jill's mutinous face, then decided that the time had come for a discussion.

"Come here, Jill. Let's sit down on your bed for a moment so that we can talk without tiring you."

Cathy led her away from the wide nursery window and back to her bed, and helped Jill onto the tautly stretched sheets and neatly quilted coverlet.

"Jill, darling," she began carefully, "why do you feel such resentment toward your uncle? I know that he loves you, and only wants what is best for you—"

"No, he doesn't!" the child shot back, the dark eyes that were so much like Jesse's glinting with furious sparks. "He doesn't want what's best for me at all, or he wouldn't have . . . wouldn't have . . ."

"Wouldn't have what, darling?" Cathy asked, taking Jill's hand between her palms.

"Wouldn't have taken me away from my mother!" Jill blurted. Her face was contorted with pain, bewilderment, and anger, and Cathy's heart went out to the child.

"Oh, darling," she said softly, "it's not quite like that at all. I understand that it has been hard on you to be parted from your mother, but perhaps your uncle did what he thought best for you. I am certain that Jesse did not mean to hurt you." There was a brief pause. Then Cathy added, "Perhaps your mother is ill, or in a position where she could not care for you—"

"My mother loves me!" came the defiant, frightened cry.

Curling her arms around Jill's thin shoulders, Cathy did her best to comfort her. "I am certain she loves you, Jill. There can be no question of *that*. But, ofttimes, we must be parted from those we love in spite of what we want. You must not hate your uncle for doing what he thinks is best for you."

Jill's thin shoulders began to shake. "But he took me away, and he won't even allow her to come . . . come and visit me!"

Drawing the girl into her arms, Cathy smoothed back the hair from Jill's forehead and wiped away the hot flow of tears from her cheeks. "There, there. Don't cry, little one. I am certain that if we talk to your uncle we can arrange matters for a visit. Your mother loves you, and your uncle does, too. Surely between them we can make arrangements for a special Christmas visit. Would you like that?"

Pulling away, Jill gazed up at Cathy with wary hope. "Do you really think we might?"

Cathy nodded. "We can try, my darling. It's Christmastime. Who would refuse?"

A smile broke through her tears, and Jill suggested, "If you ask him, I know Uncle Jesse won't refuse! I just know he won't!"

Taken aback, Cathy managed an answering smile. "Have you ever asked to see your mother before, Jill?"

For a moment the child just looked down at her fingers, twisting in the coverlet. Then she said in a small voice, "Yes, many times. But Uncle Jesse always had a reason for her not being able to visit. One time, I saw Mother at the park. She came to me. Oh, Miss Weston, she looked so unhappy. She begged that she be allowed to come here and live with Uncle Jesse and us, but he . . . he refused, and sent her away!"

"Do you mean that your mother came here—to this house?"

"Yes. I was supposed to be asleep, but I never slept well, you know. Anyway, I heard them arguing, so I went down the back stairs the servants use so that I might hear them better." Jill's head drooped, and her thin hands briefly covered her face, muffling her next words. "Mother was crying, and Uncle Jesse . . . Uncle Jesse told her never to come here again. It was so awful, and Mother cried so pitifully that I shall never forget it!"

Cathy hugged her close. "Don't cry, Jill. You know how foolish adults can be at times when pride has been damaged, or some other slight suffered. Perhaps if we approach your uncle properly, he will reconsider his position on the subject. Children should be allowed to see their parents, especially at Christmas."

Jill peeped at Cathy through her fingers. "Do you promise to try?"

"I promise, Jill. Now, let us get our mind on something less disturbing. Weren't you reading a fable?"

Cathy placed the book of fables in Jill's hands and smoothed back her hair, then smiled. "And Jill, perhaps if we try to make amends, you should purchase a small gift for your uncle. Rather like a peace offering."

"And a gift for my mother?"

"If you like."

Jill smiled. "I should like to buy her a painted fan. She always liked those."

"That is a lovely idea." Tucking the coverlet firmly around Jill's narrow body, Cathy nodded, "I had better hurry. Miss Mooney and your sisters will be wondering what is keeping me so long."

"You'll come straightaway to my room when you return?"

"I promise, Jill. Rest now, so you will feel up to the Christmas festivities we have planned."

Cathy found Leigh and Erin, along with Miss Mooney, waiting impatiently in the entry hall. The girls' hands were tucked into fat ermine muffs, and their fur-trimmed bonnets were tied snugly beneath their chins. Red-gold curls bounced as they leaped in excitement, and dark-fringed lashes framed green eyes glowing with anticipation.

"Oh, do hurry, Miss Weston!" Leigh begged. "I've been ever so impatient waiting on you!"

Laughing, Cathy teased, "I thought you had changed your minds."

"Oh, no!" came the chorus of voices, and Leigh and Erin stared at her in giggling horror.

"All right, then," Cathy said with a mock sigh as she reached for her warm cloak and bonnet. "I suppose we shall go after all."

Capering about the hall like a pair of frisky puppies, the two girls were more of a hindrance than a help as they tried to hurry Cathy into her warm winter garments. At last they were ready and Cathy opened the front door. A blast of cold air swept in, carrying with it the hint of Christmas in the air.

In spite of the blanket of snow that frosted rooftops, fences, lampposts, and trees, the streets were bustling with people. The warm carriage heated with a brazier of coals rolled to a crunching halt in the snow.

"Is this the shop, Miss Weston?" Leigh asked, excitement threading her voice. Her nose was pressed against the window glass.

"Yes, this is it!" was the cheerful reply.

The small group descended from the carriage into the slick street, and Cathy cautioned them to watch for patches of ice beneath their feet. Breath frost steamed in front of them in small clouds, and the girls laughed merrily. Horses' hooves clopped in a muffled clatter on the street, and even the rumble of wagon wheels had a muted sound as drays, carriages, and smartly appointed vehicles wheeled through the streets. Someone had tied tiny bells to their horse's harness, and the merry tinkle blended with the cry of vendors.

"Hot chestnuts!"

"Fresh mutton pies! Two a'penny!"

"Hot cross buns! Try my hot cross buns!"

Pedestrians hustled along the crowded streets in heavy overcoats and tall beaver hats that made perfect targets for mischievous boys throwing snowballs.

"Pernicious brat!" snarled a gentleman who was the target of such a prank. He dusted the snow from his fallen hat and lifted a fist into the air in baleful warning, then went on his way.

Cathy gave a gasp of laughter, smothering it with her wool mittens as the man stalked past, and the girls giggled merrily.

Cathy was still laughing when the next snowball struck her squarely in the middle of her back, splattering snow over her shoulders and her new shallow bonnet.

"Good heavens!" Miss Mooney exclaimed.

Cathy wasted no time on expletives. Scooping up a handful of snow from the cobbled stones of the pavement, she lobbed it gracefully at the young assailant, who was peeping around the edge of a stone wall to watch. It hit its mark, catching him by surprise and striking him directly on top of his head. Leigh and Erin went into gales of laughter, Miss Mooney elicited a shocked reproach, and the target gave a whoop of startled laughter.

"Hooray!" Leigh and Erin chorused between giggles.

"A direct hit, Miss Weston!" cried Erin.

Cathy dusted her mittens free of snow, then gave the girls a wink of conspiracy. "I always had a good arm, even when I was a young girl playing stickball."

"Good heavens!" Miss Mooney said again, faintly, as if she were shocked. But the ghost of a smile curved her thin lips, though she did her best to hide it.

"Capital shot!" came an approving male voice, and Cathy turned in surprise.

"Why, Ned! I didn't expect to see you," she said.

"After seeing your expertise with a snowball, perhaps I should be grateful," was the laughing reply. Ned Mahoney bowed slightly from the waist, and Cathy noted the gentleman at his side.

"Oh, I would not throw one at you, Ned," she hastened to add. "Especially since it has been a while since we have seen you. It has been dreadfully dull since you finished the painting, you know."

"Has it? I confess that I am delighted to hear it." He turned to the man at his side and explained, "I just completed a portrait of these young ladies for their uncle. It was a delightful interlude, and I am quite sorry it is over. May I present Miss Catherine Weston to you? Cathy, this is Mr. Wilkie Collins."

Mr. Collins bowed gravely. "A delightful toss, Miss Weston. You have quite a good aim."

Laughing, she said, "Thank you, Mr. Collins! I do believe I have met you before . . . or do I just recall your name for some reason?"

"Perhaps. My father paints portraits. I have only recently returned from Italy."

"And are you also an artist?"

"Oh, no, not like Ned or my father. I fancied the law for a while, but lately have been drawn to journalism."

"Ah, that is it! Of course! You are a friend of Charles Dickens's, and I have seen your name in his publication, *Household News*. It has also been in *Punch,* am I correct? You are a man of varied interests," Cathy observed.

"Speaking of which," Ned interrupted, "I have an invitation I should like to extend to you, Cathy."

"An invitation?" she echoed.

"Yes, to a reading by Charles Dickens. Do you recall meeting Mr. Dickens at the home of Miss Coutts, Cathy? He is giving a reading of his *Carol* tonight, and another reading on the twenty-third. I would like to ask you and Miss Mooney to accompany me. Wilkie and I are going to Sherborne this evening for the reading arranged by Macready, but I thought that on the twenty-third, you and Miss Mooney could attend."

"Well," Cathy began, and after an exchange of glances with Miss Mooney, ended, "I am not sure I should leave the children, Ned. With Mr. Lamont away and its being so close to Christmas, it might not be wise."

When his face fell and he appeared crestfallen by her answer, Cathy relented and said with a laugh, "Oh, give me a day or two to arrange matters. I shall send a note around, giving you my answer."

He brightened immediately. "Splendid! I know you shall enjoy it, Cathy. You've never heard a reading by Dickens, have you?"

"No, I haven't."

"They are all the rage now, and quite impressive," Wilkie Collins interjected. "And you must come to see a play I am helping prepare for Twelfth Night, Miss Weston. It will be held at Tavistock House, and is going to be great fun. Perhaps you and Miss Mooney could arrange to attend?"

"Wilkie helped adapt the play from Planche," Ned said with a laugh. "He is determined that all of London shall see it!"

"Well, I *am* impressed!" Cathy said. "What is the name of your play, Mr. Collins?"

"Fortunio and His Seven Gifted Servants," was the prompt answer.

"It sounds delightful. As Twelfth Night is so far away, the sixth of January seeming like months instead of only weeks, I shall not commit myself now. Let it suffice that I will do my best to join you at Tavistock House with Miss Mooney."

"I shall have to be satisfied with that, Miss Weston, though I shall greatly anticipate your attendance," Collins answered.

"And I anticipate viewing your play," Cathy replied. "Now, however, I must get these restless young ladies out of this brisk air. We have Christmas shopping to do."

"Until later," Ned said with an air of grave promise. "I shall count the hours!"

"Incorrigible tease," Cathy observed as he and Mr. Collins took their leave. She turned back to the impatiently waiting children, ignoring Miss Mooney's caustic observation as to Mr. Mahoney's credentials. "Now, on to the shops, young ladies! I can see the shopkeepers anxiously awaiting our arrival!"

Miss Mooney sniffed. "Humph! They are more likely greedily counting their gold than awaiting the arrival of penurious patrons such as we!"

"Oh, no," Erin assured her solemnly. "I have tenpence in my pocket!"

"Tenpence . . . oh, yes. I see. Then onward!" Miss Mooney exclaimed with a dramatic gesture. "To the shops!"

Chapter 18

As promised, when they arrived back at the house well laden with boxes and packages, Cathy went straightaway to the nursery to recount the day's events to Jill. Leigh and Erin enthusiastically described the sights and smells of the day, until Jill could almost see the wicked boy with the snowball, and smell the tantalizing fragrance of hot roasted chestnuts.

"How wonderful!" she said with a sigh, clapping her hands together. "And did you see the funny monkey with the organ grinder?"

"Yes, and he was such a cunning little thing!" Erin said with a sticky smile. She was busily sucking on a stick of hard candy that smelled strongly of lemon. "The monkey wore a fur cap and little coat of wool, and he held out his tiny little paw— why, Jill, it looked just like a human's hand!"

"Only black," Leigh added. "And there was fresh fruit right off a ship, Jill, and this huge goose hanging in the butcher's window! And in one shop window, there was the tiniest mechanical toy that when wound up could clap cymbals together and make a tinny noise. Oh, if only you could have gone!"

Relaxing back against her plumped-up pillows, Jill gazed wistfully at her sisters. "Yes," she said, "if only I wasn't so ill all the time!"

"You'll be well one day, darling," Cathy said as she sat on the edge of the bed and took Jill's thin, pale hand between her own. "Then you can go anywhere you like!"

"Truly?"

"Truly," Cathy promised. Her heart ached for this child who was so confined, and she offered up a silent prayer that she could keep her promise.

During the following days as Christmas drew near, Jill seemed to gather more strength. She felt so much better and had such a rosy color to her cheeks that Cathy and Miss Mooney felt no reluctance in leaving the girls in Pickworth's reliable hands on the evening of the twenty-third. Jesse was still not home for the holiday, and in spite of this, Cathy attended Dickens's reading of *A Christmas Carol* with Ned Mahoney. The room was crowded with familiar faces; among them was Lord John Bothmourne. All proceeds from the sale of tickets for the evening went to his favorite charity, and he graciously expressed his gratitude.

In the carriage on the way home to Devonshire Terrace, Cathy had the disloyal thought that Jesse would never have thought of such a kind act. He dwelled more in the realities of his own life than the misfortunes of others. Even Ned, sitting beside her, would not have considered such a kindness, she thought, gazing out the frosted coach window at the lamplit street. But even knowing that, Cathy could not help the surge of emotions that Jesse Lamont awakened in her, the reaction just the thought of him provoked. Was she destroying her only hope for happiness by her feelings for a man such as Lamont, a man who had rejected her under the most intimate of circumstances? Cathy writhed inwardly at that painful memory, and turned her attention back to Ned's enthused recital of Dickens's writings.

With the arrival of Christmas Eve, Cathy found she was considering resignation tempered with the amendment that she would wait until a suitable replacement had been found. Her gravest concern was Jill.

The child was terribly unhappy, and her brief return to good health seemed to have reversed in the past two days. Jill was growing weaker and weaker. Because of her growing attachment for the child, it was difficult for Cathy to accept the inevitable. It was quite probable that Jill would not live to be an adult. With this certainty in mind, Cathy determined that before she left Jesse's employ, she would convince him to allow a vist from the child's mother. It was singularly cruel of Jesse to keep the child from her mother under such circumstances.

In spite of this hanging over her head like a Damoclean sword—a metaphor she considered most appropriate—Cathy did her best to put on a cheerful countenance. She decorated the nursery with Christmas trappings, much to the delight of all three girls.

"Isn't that the most beautiful tree ever!" Jill exclaimed in rapt delight, clapping her hands together. A huge fir tree had been placed in one corner of the nursery and trimmed with bright red bows of satin and velvet. Because of the danger of fire, no candles were used on the tree branches. The girls had spent the better part of the morning fashioning angels from heavy paper. They had painted them, pasted on bits of delicate moss for hair, and strung white yarn through to hang the ornaments. Cathy had fashioned ornaments from fruit and nuts, enclosing them in squares of chenille net and attaching them to the branches with slender lengths of red satin ribbon.

"A magnificent tree!" Pickworth proclaimed it.

"Beautiful!" Miss Mooney said decisively.

"Much better than the tree in the foyer," the footman said.

The downstairs maids crowded into the nursery doorway to view the tree, and all pronounced it the best ever done. The three girls preened at their talent, and insisted upon showing it to any visitors who chanced by.

After lunch, Lord Bothmourne arrived in a gust of cold air and fresh snow, bearing gifts for Cathy and Miss Mooney as well as the three girls. These were delivered with a bluster of good cheer and the admonishment that the girls must be good or Father Christmas would leave them only switches and ashes in their stockings. This last produced giggles from the girls, who ran and put their gifts beneath the drooping branches of the nursery tree.

When Ned Mahoney arrived as promised, he also had an armful of gifts for the girls, as well as a small box for Cathy.

"Open it now," he urged, but she shook her head.

"No, Ned! Oh, you shouldn't have! I have nothing for you," she said regretfully.

"No matter. You aren't supposed to," he answered with a smile. "Cathy, you are very dear to me. I wanted you to have something that would always remind you of me."

"As if I could ever forget," she replied softly, a smile curving her mouth. Playfully lifting the small box to her ear, she gave it a light shake. "Give me a hint as to the contents," she teased.

"Open it! I implore you!"

"But it's not yet Christmas!"

"Oh, you torment me, sweet Cathy! Open it!" Drawing her into a corner away from the others, he said more softly, "Please open it now. I want to see your face."

"Oh . . . very well," she relented. Her gracefully tapered fingers gently picked at the shiny paper wrapping it until Ned threatened to tear it off for her, and she laughingly uncovered a small velvet-covered box. Flicking an uncertain glance up at him, she pried open the lid to reveal a small brooch resting on a bed of satin. Cathy drew in a deep breath of surprise at the obvious expense of the gift. "Oh, Ned! Why, it's . . . it's much too expensive a gift for you to be giving me!"

"Nonsense! Do you like it?" he demanded.

Staring down at the small breastpin fashioned of gold filigree and surrounded by lustrous pearls and glittering diamond chips, Cathy knew it must have cost Ned a small fortune. How could he ever have afforded such a present?

Impatient under her hesitation and silence, Ned demanded again, "Well? Do you like it?"

"Oh, Ned, of course I do! It's lovely!"

Taking her hand in his, he kissed her fingertips, then her slender wrist. "Cathy," he muttered against her pale skin, "You know that I adore you!"

Shrinking away from his fervent declaration, Cathy had the thought that he was far too infatuated with her when she didn't return that emotion. That would never do. She regarded Ned as a friend, but this . . . this gift was a present of intimacy, a gift given between lovers, not friends.

Placing the box gently in his palm and closing his fingers around it, Cathy said softly, "I cannot accept such a handsome gift, Ned. Really I can't. It's too . . . too intimate a gift."

Recoiling, Ned gazed at her in affront. "I insist," he said stiffly. "We are friends, and I want you to have this brooch. Please do not refuse me this."

Cathy gazed helplessly at him. "But I can't, Ned! This is a gift between lovers, and we are only friends."

"But we could be more!" he said in an impassioned voice. "Much more! Oh, Cathy—"

"Ned!" she said, drawing away from him, knowing what he was about to say. Outside the wide windows, Christmas carols were being sung by groups in the street, and the muffled jingle of bells rang cheerily. Cathy pressed close to the cold panes of window glass as Ned drew close enough that his breath whispered warmly across her cheek.

"But I love you, Cathy!" he said urgently.

She turned away, pressing her cheek close to the chill window glass. Matters were so confused now. If only she could fall in love with Ned, perhaps things would be simpler. But she couldn't. Her heart had no simple rules. Her heart belonged to another man, and she couldn't change that for any practical reason. It wouldn't be fair to Ned not to tell him, to allow him to think she might love him or change her mind. Strengthening her resolve to set matters right, Cathy straightened to turn away from the window and tell Ned the truth.

Then the sound of carriage wheels rolling to a halt in front of the house drew her attention, and she watched in silence as a man descended to the snowy street. Cathy's fingers curled against the wooden window frame. Her breath caught and her chest grew tight. She'd recognize that tall frame and elegant bearing anywhere. It was Jesse.

Cathy, sweet Cathy. She'd been constantly on his mind the entire trip, and Jesse was thinking of her now as he bade the hired hack to wait and strode impatiently up the walk to the front door. The memory of their last night together lingered in his mind as freshly as if it had been only an hour before. He could still taste the honeyed sweetness of her lips, could feel the press of her silken skin under the heel of his hand and the satiny weight of her breast in his palm. Her ghost had haunted him in the dark press of the night, had lurked just beneath the surface of his every thought until he had thought he would explode with the impatience to be home again.

And now, the sight of his front door and the cheerful gleam of lights in the snow-frosted windows cheered him more than he'd thought possible. He could almost smell the familiar scent of Christmas that would assault him when he opened the door —the rich smell of roasting goose, a plum pudding hidden in the pantry, the mincemeat pies that cook would place in the pie cupboard, the sharp scent of the fir tree that would be standing in the entry hall, the air of secrecy and laughter that would curl in dark corners and wait with a special scent all its own. Jesse tugged sharply at the doorpull and swung open the door.

He was immediately engulfed by the sights, sounds, and smells he'd just envisioned, and a smile curled his lips as he lowered his heavy leather satchel to the floor. Running footsteps sounded on the stairs, and he turned with a bright smile, expecting to see the girls or Cathy tripping down the steps to greet him. The smile faded as he saw Ned Mahoney right behind Cathy.

"Jesse!" she was exclaiming, her face alight with pleasure as she moved forward with outstretched hands.

But Ned reached past her to grasp Jesse's hand. "Hello, Lamont! You made it for Christmas, I see."

"Yes."

"Mr. Lamont!" came a pleased exclamation from behind him, and Jesse turned to greet Pickworth instead of voicing his dark thoughts. That damned artist was there—there in his house, with his Cathy! "Mr. Lamont!" Pickworth said again, this time more reserved. "We are so glad you made it home for Christmas Eve, sir. We weren't sure you would."

"Miss Christmas Eve with my nieces?" Jesse mocked lightly. "I wouldn't dare! They'd have my head, Pickworth!"

"And so they should, sir," Pickworth replied as he helped Jesse off with his heavy coat and took his hat. "May I take your bag upstairs, sir?"

"Please. And there's a man waiting outside with the rest of my baggage, Pickworth." Turning back to Cathy, Jesse managed a careless smile with just the right amount of gaiety and pleasure. "And a Christmas welcome to you, Miss Weston!"

"Miss Weston? Whatever happened to 'Cathy'?" she teased with only a trace of nervousness in her eyes. Jesse reached out to take her hands in greeting, and as she extended them again she remembered the little velvet jeweler's box still in her palm. She hesitated, and Jesse arched a dark brow at her.

"Unwilling to take my hand, Cathy? Oh. What is that?" he

asked, spying the small velvet box and feeling a cold lump settle in the middle of his chest. The iciness he was feeling transferred to his tone, and Cathy felt its chill.

"N-n-nothing! I mean . . . a gift, a lovely gift from Ned."

"From Ned?" Jesse's brow arched even higher, giving him a Satanic appearance that put Ned Mahoney on his guard and gave Cathy an attack of nerves. "May I see it? I do hope I have not duplicated your gift," he added sarcastically, reaching out to take the small box from her numb fingers.

There was a brief, heavy silence when he flipped open the lid and looked at the expensive brooch resting on its bed of satin. Jesse wrestled with the surge of jealousy that ripped through him, and thought of the simple painted fan he had brought Cathy from Paris. He'd thought it an appropriate gift, but this . . . this brooch made his gift look cheap and tawdry. The lid snapped shut, and he said in a stiff, clipped tone as he handed it back, "A lovely gift."

Flushing, Cathy said, "I told Ned that it was much too expensive a gift to exchange between friends, but he . . . he did not think it too extravagant."

"I'm certain he thinks you worth it, dear Cathy," Jesse said smoothly. His smile was distant and practiced as he turned away from her.

Cathy listened in numb acceptance as Jesse asked Pickworth to draw his bath and see to the baggage. When he turned back to her she had managed to compose herself so that she seemed as aloof as he, and listened with polite attention as he bade her a happy holiday.

"And is my present finished, Mr. Mahoney?" Jesse ended. "I find myself quite anxious to see it."

"Already hanging over the mantel in your bedroom, Mr. Lamont," Ned replied. "I saw to the placing of it myself, as you had ordered."

"Excellent. I must refresh myself after traveling nonstop since before dawn this morning. Perhaps I will see you later."

Cathy followed Jesse the few steps to the staircase and gazed up at him with an imploring expression in her wide, dark eyes. "Welcome home, Jesse," she said so softly that he had to turn back to hear her. There was a fleeting glimpse of something in his eyes as he stared at her, but it was so quickly hidden that she wasn't certain she'd seen it. "Jill, Leigh, and Erin worked hard to decorate the house for your return, Jesse. They especially want this to be a festive Christmas."

Jesse's gaze shifted to the hanging mistletoe and holly he could see wreathed in bunches and tied with gay ribbons, and his expression softened. "I can see that all of you must have worked very hard," he said, his gaze returning to Cathy's upturned face. "I shall look in on the girls before I take my bath."

"I'll tell them . . ."

"No need. I shall see them soon."

Turning away, Jesse climbed the stairs with quick steps and disappeared around the corner of the landing. As Cathy stood gazing up the stairs after him, Ned Mahoney came to her side. His voice was soft in her ear, almost a whisper.

"I can see that you care for him, Cathy. But it is a mistake."

Starting, she turned. "What do you—never mind. Please, Ned, let's not speak of Jesse."

Ned's broad hands cupped her shoulders and held her firmly in his grasp. "But someone *must* tell you, dear Cathy!" he snapped.

She tried to pull away, managing to retreat to a dimly lit corner of the entry hall before he caught her. Ned turned her around to face him. "Ned! Don't!" she pleaded.

But Mahoney did not heed her plea. Instead, he pulled her roughly into his arms, his mouth descending over her lips in a bruising, forceful kiss. It was not a light, gentle kiss between friends, but the urgent demand of a lover. Astonished by his unprecedented action, Cathy did not struggle but remained as limp as a rag doll in his embrace. Realizing her lack of participation, Ned released her at last, drawing back to gaze down at her in frustration.

Staring over his shoulder, Cathy did not utter a sound. Her eyes were wide and dark, mirroring her inner anguish, and Ned turned to see Jesse Lamont standing at the top of the stairs watching them.

Lying alone across her bed—the bed Jesse had once shared, however briefly, with her—Cathy cried deep, silent tears. She cried because she was miserable and it was nearly Christmas and she was alone. She even cried for her father. Sobs tore at her for the undecided future, for the possibility that she might have to leave Jesse and the children. And she cried for the expression in Jesse's eyes when he had seen her clasped in Ned Mahoney's embrace.

A shudder quivered through her slender body, and she pressed her face into her pillow. Her drapes were still open, and the night sky had cleared, so that the light from a bright moon flooded into her room in square patches of silvery shimmer. When Cathy turned her tear-streaked face back to stare out the window, she saw the crystal-clear night and glitter of stars pinpricking the dark velvet sky. Sighing, she rose from the bed, straightened the coverlet and her skirts, and went downstairs.

Why was it that on this night of all nights the world seemed so different? There was an aura of magic and mystery that filled the air, waited in corners and perched on rooftops, an aura of expectation. A smile touched the corners of her mouth as Cathy noted the expressions on the girls' faces at the dinner table.

Oh, to be an innocent little child again, to view the world through such naïve eyes and to wait for Christmas morning with such intense expectation! The three girls had filed into the dining room with barely suppressed smiles on their faces, even Jill, who had a bright, healthy flush on her thin cheeks. Jesse was inordinately pleased at the perfection of their table manners, and he complimented the girls with such grave assurance that they were delighted. He conversed with them on topics Cathy would never have dreamed of, talking of angels in the heavens and stars in the sky, explaining about the miracle of the three Magi, and the even greater miracle of the Christ child. And he discussed presents with them, to their delight. Even though he spared no more than a cursory greeting for Cathy, Jesse appeared devoted to the girls and she was satisfied. For the time being.

Once the evening meal was ended and the courtesies had been performed, Cathy and Miss Mooney ushered the girls upstairs to the nursery. Warm woolen nightdresses were donned, their hair brushed, faces washed, prayers said, and they were tucked under their mounds of quilts to sleep. Cathy saw that they were too excited to rest, and agreed to read them a story. She chose a tale by Dickens, *Cricket on the Hearth.* The girls snuggled beneath the quilts with wide, attentive eyes, and Cathy began to read.

By the time she reached the chapter on "Chirp the Third," she glanced up to find all three girls sleeping. Even Miss Mooney was dozing in her straight-backed chair. A smile slanted her mouth as Cathy quietly closed the book.

Reaching over, she gave Miss Mooney a gentle shake. "Go to bed, Miss Mooney."

Her eyes snapped open and she blinked owlishly at Cathy. "Bed? Oh. Oh, yes, of course." There was a brief, befuddled pause. Then she whispered, "Shall I comb out your hair for you?"

"No, not tonight. I think I can manage. I have some last-minute gift-wrapping to do, and there is something to check in the kitchen. I'll do it."

Rising with the slow motions of an aged person, Miss

Mooney flashed a grateful smile in Cathy's direction. "My bones aren't as agile as they used to be. They're no respecter of time or place, ignoring the fact that tomorrow is Christmas Day," she grumbled as she made her way out the nursery door and down the hall to her room.

Cathy smiled reflectively as she put more coal in the grate for the girls. They would wake early and it needed to be warm for them, especially for Jill, who seemed to take a chill easier these days in spite of her improved coloring. The chunks of coal spilled into the grate with a rattling thunk, and Cathy pushed them deeper into the iron basket with the huge scoop. The warmth from the fire flushed her skin and pinked her cheeks, and the coal dust darkened her hands. After quietly brushing off the coal dust, Cathy rose from the hearth and straightened her skirts, then took up a candle and let herself out the door. Next was the kitchen; then her tasks for the day would be done.

She had to remind Annie, the cook, to add some American dishes to the traditional English feast—at the request of the three girls, who longed to try them. There would be a rich gravy, mashed potatoes, glazed carrots, fruit salad, and a special fudge cake made from Miss Mooney's own recipe that she usually guarded like a hawk. Tomorrow, however, was special. The sideboard would be groaning with food.

Cathy's mind was lingering over the promise of luscious fudge cake as she descended the stairs, so that when she met Jesse exiting the dining room she was startled. The candlestick quivered in her grasp, the flame shimmering.

"Oh! I . . . I hadn't expected anyone else to still be up . . . Other than the servants, that is."

Again the lift of that dark brow in the supercilious gesture she had grown to dislike excessively. Her mouth tightened in irritation as Jesse murmured, "I daresay. Then what are you doing up at this late hour?"

"Seeing to last-minute details. I must leave Annie a note and recipe for the menu tomorrow."

"Annie has forgotten how to cook in my brief absence?" he inquired with such icy politeness and obvious disbelief that Cathy bridled.

"No, don't be ridiculous! It's for a special dessert the girls want to try. An *American* dessert."

"Ah, how refreshing. Americanizing my good English girls, Miss Weston?"

Keeping her temper with an effort, Cathy answered, "No, just allowing them to try different things, *Mr. Lamont.*"

A faint hint of a smile pressed at the corners of his mouth, but did not succeed. He stared down at her, his eyes dark and enigmatic, his features carefully schooled so that he revealed none of his thoughts.

How much he had missed her! He longed to tell her, but the sharp memory of Ned Mahoney holding her, kissing her, pricked at him with the sharp talons of jealousy, and he could not. Women. Were they all frivolous, erratic creatures without conscience? He'd thought Cathy different, but apparently she was not. She had lain in his arms, spoken to him of love, then flitted away to embrace Ned Mahoney. He had not missed the implications of Ned's expensive gift to her. Jesse's hands curled into fists as the overwhelming mockery of his feelings taunted him.

"Damn you!" he whispered, disgust vibrating in the tenor of his voice. "Damn you, Cathy!"

Stunned by his vehemence and passion, she gave her head a slight shake of confusion. "What . . . what do you mean?"

"I mean damn you and all faithless women!" he snarled at her before he caught himself, straightened, and pivoted on his heel to stalk away.

Cathy stared after him for a moment, unable to comprehend what was happening. She could see that Jesse was pushed beyond endurance, but she did not know what had precipitated this outburst. *Faithless women* . . . Oh, no, he wasn't going to get away without an explanation! Her mouth tightened in determination, and she rallied immediately. Cathy Weston stomped across the hall in pursuit of Jesse.

Chapter 19

Cathy's feet skimmed the stairs as she flew up them behind Jesse. The flame of her candle guttered and went out, plunging them into darkness as she reached him. Her fingers curled around his arm, halting him, her eyes adjusting slowly to the absence of light. Jesse was just a dark form, a shadow against the dim light filtering down from the upstairs landing.

"What did you mean by that?" she demanded.

"Mean by what?" he shot back, shaking her hand from his arm. She could feel his gaze resting on her, trying to pierce the gloom with contempt, and shriveled from it. There was a muffled sound of disgust before he turned away from her and continued up the stairs with a slow, measured tread.

For the space of a heartbeat Cathy stared after him, dazed by his coldness and indifference. Then anger resurfaced to give her the impetus she needed to pursue him, and she took the steps two at a time. How dare he treat her like this! How dare he shame and humiliate her without a reason!

When Jesse turned the corner of the corridor leading to his room, Cathy caught up with him. Once more grabbing him by his sleeve, she whirled him around to face her. The snuffed candle dropped from her grasp and rolled unheeded across the carpeted floor, coming to a rest against the baseboard on the far wall. Tension vibrated between them, crackled in the air, and in the light of the lamp burning on the hall table Cathy could see the naked fury in his eyes.

Forced to a halt, Jesse gazed down grimly at her. There was anger in her eyes as well, a deep, soul-searing anger and pain that misted over her beautiful dark-brown eyes. He flinched from it, from the pain he recognized.

Jerking her into his arms, he demanded gratingly, "Are you a fool?"

Shaking the hair from her eyes, Cathy shot back, "God, yes! I must be a fool to brave your anger! I must be a fool to suffer your abuse."

His fingers tightened painfully on her upper arms, and his scowl deepened. His face was only inches from hers, and the tension in the small space between them shimmered with intensity. His emotions were stretched as tautly as a bowstring, and he kept control with an effort as he ground out, "*My* abuse? It is fickle-hearted woman who heaps abuse on a man and puts us all to shame."

Recoiling from the cold, hard words that fell like lead between them, Cathy refused to allow him to see how he'd hurt her. Her voice was equally as cold and indifferent as she demanded, "How can you put the blame on all women for the actions of a few? You are a fool, Jesse Lamont, too blind to see that you speak with hurt pride instead of truth."

"And what would you know of truth?" Jesse spat back at her, his fingers digging even deeper. "You are a spoiled, pampered lady, with the harsh realities of life held at bay by your adoring parent! You think you are free and independent, but in truth you are only a foolish girl with rosy ideals and little notion of how harsh life can be!"

Staring up at him with fire in her eyes, Cathy had the brief thought his words could cut deeper than any she had ever heard before. Her chin lifted as she said quietly, "You can hurt me with your anger, Jesse, but only because I allow you to do so.

I'm not afraid to hurt, because I'm not afraid to care like you are. You—for all your fine, brave words—are a coward. You're afraid to care because you've been hurt in the past. Well, you're not the only one who's ever been hurt!" Her fingers coiled into a fist, pressing against his chest as she punctuated her words with soft thumps. Breathlessly, struggling against the hot tears welling behind her eyes, she panted, "I've been hurt, and I'm hurting now, but that doesn't make me an emotional cripple. I . . . can . . . love . . . again!"

"So I noticed when you were in Mahoney's arms," he shot back with such bitterness that Cathy flinched.

"Is that what this is all about?" Cathy stifled a sob. "Oh, Jesse! You saw me in Ned's arms, yes, but he was the instigator of that embrace, not I. Ned kissed me, but I did not kiss him back. I don't love Ned, I love *you*, Jesse."

He wanted to believe her—God, how he wanted to believe her—but there was some small, mocking part of him that refused to accept it. It was too dangerous to believe in someone else. Jesse's arms fell to his sides, and he gazed at her with a distant expression clouding his dark eyes.

"Go to bed, Cathy," he said tonelessly, moving wearily past her as if she had ceased to exist for him.

But Cathy had no intention of letting him go that easily, and in her desperation she flung down the gauntlet for him to retrieve.

"I'll go to bed, Jesse—if you come with me," she said softly, boldly, hardly daring to breathe when he paused with his back to her.

Turning slowly back to face her in the dim light of the hall lamp, Jesse's expression was a mixture of disbelief, anger, and surprise. His rugged features hardened, but his hoarse voice betrayed his emotion. "You jest poorly, my dear."

"This is no jest, Jesse Lamont."

He took several steps closer, his eyes scanning her face. There was a coiled tension in him that transferred to Cathy, and she waited with bated breath while he regarded her first with suspicion, then with acceptance.

"Do you realize what you are saying?" he asked at last.

Cathy nodded. "Yes, Jesse—I realize only too well."

"Why, Cathy? Why like this?"

"Why?" A tremulous smile touched her lips, and Cathy reached out to lay her hand upon his arm. "Let's take all our pain to bed, Jesse, all the hurt and pride, the spent tears—all the anger of unrequited love. Let's take it to bed with us, and love it to death. Let's burn away our sorrow with desire. . . ."

A heavy silence fell between them, a silence rife with unspoken words and the echo of those just said, and then Jesse was pulling Cathy into his arms, holding her tightly against him, his arms circling her, his mouth smothering her lips with his passion. The hunger of love ached in his soul. No woman had ever spoken to him as she had just done.

Cathy responded, wrapping her arms tightly around his neck, kissing him back with a wild, sweet yearning. This was her time, her moment with Jesse. All the shame of that last night together when he had left her feeling rejected and abandoned, vanished in her desire to be his, truly his.

With her lips fastened to his and her senses swirling, she was only vaguely aware that Jesse was lifting her into his arms and carrying her across the threshold of his bedroom. Nothing mattered but the man and the moment.

His foot kicked the door closed with a resounding click and they were alone in his lamp-lit room. Jesse's mouth lifted from its plunder of her parted lips, and he set her gently on her feet, feeling as awkward as a schoolboy and wondering what to do next. This was no simple seduction. Cathy was a woman he admired, a woman he cared for deeply.

Sensing his anxiety and hesitation, Cathy was touched. That the self-assured Jesse Lamont should be hesitant was a testimony to his deeper feelings for her. Smiling shyly, she began to unfasten the buttons of her spencer. The short jacket had thankfully few buttons, and she let it fall to the floor in a heap. Turning around, Cathy presented Jesse with her back.

"Please help me unfasten my gown, Jesse."

Yielding to the gentle seduction of her soft voice. Jesse unfastened the buttons with clumsy fingers. As it fell away from her in graceful folds, he began to shrug out of his own coat, watching as Cathy stepped out of the dress and laid it aside. Clad only in her thin chemise and petticoat, Cathy turned back to face him.

Her breath quickened, growing as rapid as the wild beat of her heart beneath her breasts at the look of admiration in Jesse's gaze. He was looking at her with hungry longing, a smile curling his lips.

Crossing the short space between them in one long stride, Jesse cupped her face in his palms and stared deeply into her eyes. Nothing was said for a long moment, and his hand moved to cradle the back of her head, his fingers loosening the heavy braids. As they fell in a silken rush, he spread the long strands with his fingers, murmuring, "I love your hair."

Cathy helped him finger-comb her hair, letting the chestnut waves drape over her shoulders. It framed her face in soft, fine tendrils, curling wantonly around the lace edging her chemise. Jesse's finger traced the path her hair had taken, gently exploring the creamy expanse of silken skin above the top of her chemise.

"You are so beautiful, Cathy," he said huskily.

Trembling under his admiring gaze and the touch of his hand, Cathy felt a rush of pleasure at his words. Her hands shook slightly as she reached to undo the laces, but Jesse stopped her.

"Let me."

A slow smile curved her mouth as she obliged.

Jesse slowly untied the laces, holding back the urge to rush, to take her in his arms and crush her against him. It took all his resolve not to hurry what should be slow. Slowly, surely, he untied the laces of her chemise and pushed the material aside, baring her small, perfect breasts. He was silent in deep appreciation of the beauty of her body, for the tiny waist and gentle curve of her hips, the long, slender thighs outlined beneath the thin petticoats. Jesse undid the ties of her petticoats and let them fall in a rustle of cotton to the floor at her feet, and Cathy stood unclothed before him. Soft lamplight gave her body a pearly, ethereal glow, highlighting her ripe curves and shaded, mysterious hollows. His throat grew tight and his breath short, and when Cathy instinctively made a move to cross her arms over her chest he stopped her.

"No, love. There is no reason to hide such a beautiful body . . . especially not from me."

Shivering with reaction and desire, Cathy watched as Jesse quickly divested himself of his clothes, his jacket, his vest, shirt, and trousers, until he stood as naked as she. She looked away, suddenly more shy than curious, unable to look at him.

He came to her, and she felt his rigid desire pressed against her stomach as he pulled her close. His lips were against her cheek as he murmured, "Where is all your fire of a few minutes ago, sweet Cathy? Have I frightened it away?"

As Jesse buried his face in the soft curve of her neck and shoulder, Cathy felt the tiny nip of his teeth against her skin, and shivered. He was pressed so firmly and fiercely against her that she could feel the growing heat of his passion. Lifting her arms, she circled his neck and drew him even closer. Her body instinctively arched against the hard angles and planes of his masculine frame, straining against him with a fervent desire to match his.

"The fire?" she murmured against his shoulder. "It's still there, Jesse, burning inside me, filling my entire being."

Jesse's response was a hungry, soul-searing kiss. His mouth covered her lips, plundering, drawing away her breath and pillaging the honeyed sweetness of her mouth. Blazing fires burned out of control, and his splayed hands moved in a heated caress over the supple curves of her back to her slim hips, gathering the ripe, creamy cup of her buttocks into his palms and lifting Cathy against him.

There was a coiling ache deep within the pit of her stomach, and Cathy moaned softly with pleasure and a mysterious longing. She needed him, needed him to ease that swelling ache inside her; only Jesse could give her that sweet release.

"Love me, Jesse, please," she said into the curve of his neck and shoulder. There was no shyness in her words now, they were bold and blurred with desire as she pressed against him.

Lifting her into his embrace, Jesse placed her gently on the high poster bed, shoving aside the bed-curtains with an impatient motion. He lay down beside her, his hands roaming her slender body with reverence and awe.

"Shall I play awhile, love, or shall I just burn with love for you?"

Gazing up at him, at the dark eyes and beloved features that had haunted her since first meeting him, Cathy whispered, "We aren't playing, Jesse. Burn away our pain with love."

There were no more words. Nothing needed to be said. Jesse shifted his body to lie across Cathy's, his arms on each side of her, holding her. She welcomed him with an open embrace, her arms circling his neck and her lips grazing his jaw, chin, and the firm contour of his lips before moving down the column of his throat to his broad, muscled chest. There was a faint musky taste and smell, exhilarating and heady, filling her senses with the essence of Jesse.

Tilting back her head, their eyes locked. Jesse moved between her slender thighs, entering her that first tiny bit with a firm, warm thrust that made her gasp. She arched, her eyes widening as he poised at her velvet entrance. Jesse's gaze never left her face, his eyes lingering on her as he moved ever so slowly, thrusting carefully until that barrier of innocence was gently pushed aside. Tensing, Cathy cried out beneath him, her breath coming in short pants as her fingers dug into the smooth flesh of his back. A whimper escaped her, and Jesse paused to stare down anxiously at her.

But she smiled at him with encouragement and love in her shining, wet eyes, and he smiled back. Closing his eyes, he gave himself up to the sweep of passion as he moved deeper and deeper inside her. He was lost in her, lost in the heat of her body wrapped tightly around his own. He moved and Cathy spontaneously moved with him. The tempo of their passion increased in steady waves.

Cathy clung to him, kissing whatever part of his body her searching lips could reach. She was as lost to the world as he was, and it seemed so far away and dreamy. Only Jesse was real, only his hard male body and her surging desire.

Jesse moved harder, faster, and Cathy thought she would die from the pleasure of it, die if he didn't touch her in some way she didn't quite understand yet. Rapture waited just beyond her reach, and she strained toward it with an ever-increasing urgency. Clinging tightly to him, she murmured against his sweat-slick shoulder, "Love me more, Jesse," not even realizing what she meant.

"Like this?" was the soft reply, and Cathy moaned with pleasure.

"Yes . . . Jesse . . . yes, like that!" The last word was only a whisper of sound, a sigh that was lost in the pleasure sounds of their lovemaking.

Moving together, pleasure and desire burned away any residue of anger, lost love, and pain. In one swift movement, the world faded completely, and both Jesse and Cathy were enveloped in a haze of satisfaction.

Afterward, lying exhausted and replete, they nestled closely in each other's arms. Their faces almost touched, cheek to cheek, mouth to mouth. Cathy's long lashes dipped briefly, and she wondered distractedly how it was that a man should possess such long, curling eyelashes. They fringed his dark, liquid eyes, occasionally shuttering them against her, but when his lids lifted she could see the love lights burning in their depths. With the silence that only lovers could understand, they spoke to each other of love and devotion. Their hearts spoke the language of love, and two souls were forever mated.

Chapter 20

*I*t was Christmas morning, and Cathy awoke, stretching luxuriously, feeling contented and lazy. She was ensconced in the wide bed with Jesse, nestled close to him, the sound of his heartbeat echoing in her ears, the warmth of his lean body against her. The long night hours had been spent in the silken web of love, kissing, touching, exploring new ways to please each other. Cathy hadn't realized the possibilities, the splendor of such a union. There had never been any intimacy with Darcy, no sharing of the souls and bodies, and she now knew that she'd only been living a lie when she thought she loved him. *This* was love, this wild, sweeping emotion that flooded through her now.

Loving Jesse was a unique emotion, something she had never dreamed existed like this. She could never leave him now, not now when he was such an integral part of her, as necessary as an arm or leg. To be apart from him would be too much like dying.

Lifting her cheek from atop his broad chest, she gazed up at his sleeping face, her eyes skimming over his rugged features. They were etched with the mark of the years, and somehow, instead of detracting from his looks, the tiny lines at the corners of his eyes and bracketing his mouth only added to his air of recklessness and assurance.

Sighing, her breath stirred the curling wisps of hair on his chest as she wondered if he couldn't stop the dangerous life he led. He'd served his country long and faithfully for the past twenty years. England had been his mistress for so long, and Cathy wondered if it was possible for her to replace such a mistress in his life and heart. She nuzzled closer, her arms tightening around him.

"Hello, beautiful," Jesse whispered in her ear, smiling when she glanced up at him in surprise.

Her lips curved in a welcome smile. "Good morning, Jesse, and merry Christmas."

His arms tightened. "Merry Christmas to you, Cathy," he murmured, rubbing his nose against hers.

She shifted quickly, and Jesse's lips were captured by her mouth in a long, tender kiss.

When their lips finally parted, Jesse rested his forehead against hers and asked, "Do you suppose I could have an early present from you?"

Bewildered, Cathy just stared at him for a moment, but when his hand shifted from her shoulder to her hip, then slid down over the curve of her spine to cup her close, she laughed. "Do you mean you haven't had enough of me yet?"

"Never," he vowed solemnly, and his grip tightened.

Aware of the shafts of gray light filtering through the closed drapes and the muffled rumblings belowstairs, Cathy said softly, "What if Pickworth comes in?"

"I'll behead him." Jesse nipped lightly at her neck, and his tongue flicked against the throbbing hollow in her throat.

"You can't do that!"

"Fine." His mouth trailed kisses along her collarbone to the valley between her bare breasts, and Cathy moaned. "I'll hang him instead," Jesse said against the warm flesh of her breast as his palm cradled it gently. "Happy now?"

"Oh, Jesse!" Her fingers tangled in his hair and she arched her back, pressing closer to the delicious tease of his tongue on her breast.

"I take it that means yes," he murmured, sliding lower in the bed and lavishing hot kisses over her rib cage to the small indentation of her navel.

Sighing, Cathy yielded up any attempt at coherency. She was lost in the magic of Jesse and his kisses, lost in a swirl of desire. Reveling in his touch, his gentle exploration of the hollows and secrets of her body, she could think of nothing but the moment. Nothing else existed for her, and she murmured a soft "I love you." When Jesse paused she opened her weighted eyelids to stare at him.

"What is it?" she murmured throatily. "Jesse?"

He was staring at her, his dark eyes shadowed. "It's nothing, love . . . nothing at all."

"But it is," she said, realizing that his stillness was strained and awkward. He pulled away, sitting up with the coverlet draped over his broad shoulders, and his movements were uncertain.

"Perhaps you're right, Cathy. Perhaps I should worry about Pickworth finding you here like this. It wouldn't do to leave you open to gossip . . . not from Pickworth, perhaps, but the downstairs maids would surely get wind of it sooner or later, as well as Miss Mooney."

Disappointment etched Cathy's face into a frown, but she recognized the sense in what he was saying. She had been only too willing to be swept along by passion and forget the proprieties. It wasn't that which disturbed her, however, but the underlying current in Jesse's voice. He wasn't telling the complete truth—there was more to his wanting her to leave than what he was saying, but she didn't know what.

Shrugging away her doubts, Cathy slipped from the bed and scooped up her clothing. She felt Jesse's eyes on her, and was self-conscious as she slipped into her petticoats and chemise.

Jesse hid a frown at Cathy's obvious discomfort, hating himself for being devious, yet caught between his own fears and his love for her. He didn't care a fig for Pickworth or Miss Mooney's shocked sensibilities, nor did he care if the downstairs maids gossiped their silly little heads off. He didn't care if the entire world knew that he'd spent the night with Catherine Weston—but he did care that he would have to hurt her. That bothered him more than the rest.

He couldn't commit himself to her. Not now. Not when there were still so many doubts to contend with, to overcome. Those were very real obstacles between him and Cathy, and he had to banish them from his life forever before he could offer her his untarnished love.

Jesse blinked as Cathy turned to him, her own doubts mirrored in her expressive face. "Jesse," she was saying in a trembling voice, "don't send me away with a lie between us. I can't leave without knowing where we stand with each other. I can see that you're troubled, that you're uncertain, and I . . . I want to help."

Helpless to voice his doubts, Jesse could only shake his head. "I'm sorry, Cathy."

She stood firm. "That won't suffice, Jesse. Not this time. An apology answers no questions, soothes no fears. I don't ask for magic, only answers." The mattress dipped with her slight weight as she sat on the edge of the bed and reached out to him. "I love you, Jesse Lamont, all of you—from the top of your head to the bottoms of your feet. I love the good, the bad, the indifferent, and I want to share your feelings and your life."

Wincing, Jesse threw back the coverlet and surged from the bed, turning his back to her. He pulled the linen sheet from the bed and wrapped it around his lean middle, stalking across the room with it trailing behind. "There's no need to discuss this now, Cathy," he said flatly. "It's Christmas morning. We need to be getting ready."

The clock on the mantel struck the half hour, startling Cathy, and she glanced at it. Half past five. The household would soon be stirring—all those who hadn't been up for an hour already. Miss Mooney had probably already been to Cathy's room looking for her. She rose slowly from the bed as Jesse swung open the doors to his wardrobe.

When she stood behind him she said softly, "There will always be some excuse, Jesse, some clear, concise reason for never discussing our intimate emotions. I won't let it be that way. Run from me, Jesse, as fast as you can, but be assured that I will follow!"

Turning to face her, seeing the resolute determination in her clear, steady gaze, Jesse felt concerned. How could he make her understand? And how could he tell her that he loved her when he had once sworn never to utter those words again to a woman? Stiffening, he said, "Let it go, Cathy."

"No."

Tormented, torn between love and anxiety, he said more harshly than he intended, "You can't understand! I care for you a great deal, but I can never let myself love you! Now do you understand? Never!"

Speaking past the glut of tears clogging her throat, Cathy said, "Why, Jesse? Why do you refuse to allow happiness into your life?"

"Happiness?" He gave a short, bitter laugh. "What is happiness? I can be happy for a moment, a second, a fleeting instant, but not for long. Can either of us sustain happiness? I don't think so." He shook his head and turned away. "Love is just a word, Cathy, a word. It doesn't endure."

Her voice, tear-choked and thick, came to him from over his shoulder. "But I would never stop loving you . . . never."

His back stiffened, and his voice was a low growl. "I have heard that song before! First from my mother—that was before she ran off and left us, you understand. She decided to flee to

Holland with a stranger rather than stay with the husband and sons she 'loved'! Yes, love! I was ten years old then, and didn't understand that love was only a word. I never saw my mother again. . . ."

His voice drifted into silence, and Cathy's heart ached for the pain he must have suffered then and was still suffering. "Oh, Jesse," she said softly, "you are still that lost, abandoned little boy, aren't you? Your mother was only one woman. You can't hold us all accountable for her actions."

Jerking around, Jesse yanked Cathy into his arms, his eyes fierce and dark. "Look at me, Cathy! You were right when you once said I am the walking wounded. See the scars I still carry from wounds that will never heal? I cannot offer you peace or love. I loved once—and it was my undoing. She was my heart, my soul. I would have died for her, and I almost did." His mouth twisted briefly. "Yet she was fickle, as are—" Relaxing his painful grip on her arms, he said, "An inconstant heart, my father was fond of saying. He was right. She married my brother, and took him to her bed. Was that enough for her? No, no, it wasn't. She was miserable, and punished me for her misery. William was also made to suffer for her perfidy as she bedded every available man within reach! And her children? Ah . . ."

Cathy swallowed the lump in her throat. "Caroline?"

"Ah, so you have heard of her! Well, who has not?"

Taking a faltering step back, Cathy braced herself against the wall as Jesse continued, speaking as if he were alone, his expression sneering and filled with bitterness. "Caroline. Beautiful. Intelligent. Fiery. And I loved her, ah, yes, fool that I was! I don't know if I've ever stopped wanting her, for whatever reasons. It's impossible for her to live here with her children, of course. I couldn't bear to have her under my roof, to see her in the morning, or at the table. I tried once. Did you know that, Cathy?" he asked, and Cathy realized that he was speaking to her. She shook her head numbly. Jesse's lips curved in a grim caricature of a smile. "Ah, yes, I tried once. I ended up in her bed, in the bed of my brother's wife."

Putting her hands over her ears, Cathy shook her head, tears streaking her cheeks at his pain and torment. "No! No, I don't want to hear any more!"

Jesse gazed curiously at her. "Don't you? Neither do I. My brother died knowing that I had slept with his wife. I would like to forget that, too. I can never wash away that sin." His hands clenched into impotent fists at his sides, and he sucked in a deep, steadying breath. "So you can see, dear Cathy," he said in a calm, reasonable tone, as if he were discussing the choosing of drapery material, "why it is that I cannot give you my heart. I don't possess one to give. That is the gist of it all. There is nothing in me that can sustain a relationship, nothing at all. And even if there was, I am afraid to take a chance. I've been unfair to you, and I apologize. Forgive me."

"Forgive you?" she choked, gasping with the effort to speak. "*Forgive* you? For what—loving me? You can't ignore what happened between us, Jesse! It's there, even if you don't want to admit it."

He made an impatient gesture with his hands, as if to dismiss her words. "I can't let it be."

"But you can't change it!" She took a deep breath to steady her voice. "It's not something you can control. Love is a feeling; passion is a feeling. It is there between you and me, Jesse. You feel it. I feel it. It cannot be denied. It won't go away just because you refuse to recognize it."

"Yes, it will," he said adamantly. "And if it doesn't, then you will have to go."

Stunned by the cold finality of his words, Cathy held tightly to her control.

"So you intend to pack me off, just like that, because I won't be a quiet, submissive mistress who doesn't expect commitment?

Is that it, Jesse?" Her eyes flashed dark fire at him as she added softly, "Damn you, Jesse! It won't be that easy. I have commitments to the children, and they need me. I also have Miss Mooney, who depends on my wages for subsistence. I cannot walk out of here without employment just because you find our situation inconvenient or annoying!"

"I didn't mean—"

"It is obvious what you meant!"

Jesse gazed at her for a long moment. Her face was flushed with anger, and he could see the tiny marks of his passion on her throat, the telltale bruises he had put there with his mouth. Inwardly cringing, he had the desperate wish that he could love her as he should, but he could not bring himself to trust in anyone yet. He was the worst kind of a cad and coward for yielding to his own passion and hurting this beautiful, courageous girl who dared face him with love when he rejected her.

"Cathy . . . you may stay," he said finally. "But this . . . this passion between us shall not happen again. You and I were not meant to be, and I only hope that you understand."

"I will never understand."

Turning away, his shoulders slumped forward. "I have nothing else to say now. Go—go before someone finds you here."

Cathy grasped the door latch and turned it, then shot at Jesse, "I feel sorry for you, more sorry than I do for my father! He never learned to truly love, only possess. But you—I know that you love me, and to love as we do and then throw it all away is a tragedy."

There was the soft hiss of the door swinging shut, then a click, and Jesse was alone in his room, alone with his ghosts and dark thoughts. Drawing back his hand, he swung his fist against the heavy oak door, smashing his knuckles and still not feeling the pain. There was so much pain inside him that he could feel nothing else. . . .

Chapter 21

The next several weeks passed in a haze of long days. First came the final days of December. Then January drifted by in a blur of stifled emotions and pain. Cathy felt at times as if she were a player in some hazy performance. Jesse was there. She was there. But the love and tenderness between them had disappeared, leaving her empty, a shell of her former self. If she hadn't experienced it, she would never have believed that a man could be so cold and aloof after being so warm and loving.

Jesse Lamont lived up to his infamous reputation of indifference. He behaved toward Cathy with distant courtesy as he did the other servants in his house. When they spoke to each other there was no hint of the intimacy they had shared, of the night spent in passion and love. At times, it seemed as if it had all been an illusion.

Illusions were still haunting her when she descended the stairs for breakfast one morning late in January. She was lost in thought, so that at first she didn't hear the loud voices coming from the study. As she reached the bottom step of the stairway she emerged from her fog of contemplation, hearing Jesse's voice lift in anger.

"Damn! They are all bloody fools!"

"Calm down," a masculine voice soothed. "It really means nothing. There will be an investigation, and some good will come of it. Something has to be done. We can't go on like we are now. Too many men are dying. . . ."

Cathy recognized Lord Bothmourne's baritone, and she stepped into the entry hall and closer to the study. Her brow was furrowed, and she recalled the terrible implications of Miss Nightingale's last letter. So much horror had been crammed into that neat scrawl filling the pages, telling of the lack of supplies, men dying of the smallest wound due to filth, and cholera raging through the camp. Pausing at the partly open door to the study, Cathy shamelessly listened to the conversation within.

Moving across the room to the french doors, Jesse raked a hand through his hair and gazed out at the garden. "But for Aberdeen to have resigned, and a new government formed! I never really thought it would come to this," he said, frustration thickening his voice. He stared at the stone fountain filled with snow. One lone bird was perched among the ice and snow, and Jesse had a sudden sympathy with that tiny creature alone in a stark cold environment. That was how he'd felt lately, since . . .

"You knew that there was a possibility of Aberdeen's resigning," Bothmourne pointed out in a reasonable tone. "With Roebuck's speech in the House of Commons, what did you expect? Palmerston is a good man. He'll turn the tide."

Pivoting on his heel, Jesse strode back to his desk and snatched up a sheaf of printed papers. "Here, look at this. This is Cathy's. *Household Words.* Take a look at it, John."

Arching a brow, Bothmourne picked up the serial and scanned the pages, only half listening to Jesse's comments.

"That's who the people read now, John! Dickens has written a parody, *The Thousand and One Humbugs.* Abbadeen has been strangled and replaced by Parmarstoon! Can you conceive of such a thing? There won't be any more respect for Palmerston than there is for Aberdeen."

Bothmourne folded the serial and tossed it back to Jesse's

desk. "Give it a chance, Jesse. If more supplies reach Turkey, things will turn around, and Palmerston has promised to form a commission of inquiry into the affairs of the war. *The Times* had been a bit kinder than our literary friend. Dickens is more worried about domestic affairs than foreign, surely you know that. He knows that for every shilling spent on defense, another shilling is taken away from the poor. You can't blame him, but there's no need for such alarm. Clarendon is still in, and that serves our purpose. Your trip to France was successful. Napoleon has offered more, and sooner. Look back to what you have assisted in bringing to England. Even the Swiss have promised troops, fifteen thousand Piedmontese. Allied contingents are higher than ever. Soon this madness will end, I assure you."

"Sebastopol . . ."

"Yes, Sebastopol will tell the tale, my friend. And there's the trouble. You have friends there, and now you plan its destruction. But it is the decisive battle. I only wish that someone besides Canrober was in charge."

Jesse sighed heavily. "I recommended Pellissier to the emperor, but who knows? Right now all I can think about is that *damned cable!* It will help end this damnable fiasco that the czar has put us all in. It's difficult to believe that one simple cable could be at the center of so much intrigue, isn't it?"

Bothmourne gave a short laugh. "You mean *you* are in the center of the intrigue, my friend!"

A cold chill shivered down Cathy's spine, and she inched closer to the partially open door. Jesse? In the middle of some sort of conspiracy?

Jesse was frowning, his fist bunching as he slammed it into his open palm. "They will try again, and soon, I think! Time is running out, John."

"Then move your information to the office."

"What good will that do? If they think they can find out the smallest detail concerning the laying of that cable, they will plunder whatever is necessary. No, they'll be back here, and moving my records won't change that."

"But you must secure them, Jesse!"

"Oh, I have, John, I have." Satisfaction threaded Jesse's voice as he added, "They are in a much safer place than before. Even if they manage to break into the house, it will not matter. I moved them from my office to my room. Someplace quite out of the ordinary, but simple enough to confuse them."

Moving closer to Jesse, Lord Bothmourne lowered his voice. "This brings William to mind, Jesse. I have news. The investigation is over. Caroline was not implicated."

Jesse sucked in a deep breath, then released it in a soft exhalation of air. "Damn! I'm glad of that." He shuffled through the papers on his desk, then moved toward the walnut table against the wall. "I feel in need of a drink, even as early as it is!"

"I still feel that the conclusion was wrong," Bothmourne commented idly, watching Jesse from the corner of his eye.

Shaking his head, Jesse turned back, the empty glass clutched tightly in his hand. "When are you going to stop, Johnny? This thing has been a source of contention between us for too long now."

"I want the truth, Jesse. You want to believe what is easy for you."

Jerking away from the table, Jesse slammed his glass down to its surface with a loud crack. Cathy gasped and moved quickly away from the door when she saw his approach. Seconds later it slammed shut in her face, and she was unable to hear the rest of his words.

"Caroline is the mother of those three delightful girls upstairs," came the sharp, angry retort. "Can you really hope that they would be happier knowing that their own mother was somehow involved in their father's death?"

Bothmourne's voice was deprecating and gentle at the same time. "That's a poor excuse, Jesse, and not even an honest one.

Of course I don't want the children to feel that their mother is connected with their father's death!" Leaning forward, he added with glowering intensity, "But I do believe that William was murdered, and you know it! He was my friend, Jesse." Straightening, Bothmourne let the pause lengthen, then said softly, "And somehow Caroline set him up. I know. You know. And nothing, not lies, not excuses, will ever cover up the truth. Your obsession for Caroline destroys your sense of reasoning, my friend. You look at her and see one thing, but the world views her in a different light."

"She is the mother of—"

"Dammit, man! She's twisted! Caroline will ultimately destroy herself, and if you continue to allow it, she will take you with her—to hell and back!"

"Enough!" Jesse said sharply. He stalked back to the walnut table and splashed a liberal amount of brandy into the glass he'd set down.

Bothmourne watched and lifted his brow. "Before breakfast, Jesse? I take it your *wound* is still kicking up a fuss?"

"Your sarcasm ill becomes you, Bothmourne," Jesse muttered, taking a healthy swig of brandy.

Reaching for the coat he had hastily draped over the back of the chair, Bothmourne murmured, "And drowning your sorrows ill becomes you, Lamont!"

When Jesse turned back to gaze curiously at him, Lord Bothmourne just shrugged.

Shutting the dining room door behind her, Cathy leaned against it and thought of what she'd overheard. It wasn't that she'd *meant* to eavesdrop so blatantly, but the conversation had been too engrossing to ignore. If Jesse was in danger, didn't she have a right to know? All Cathy's instincts warned her that the intruder she had so briefly and violently encountered had been after Jesse's "notebook" instead of silver or gold. Just what was in that notebook? And how did that affect Jesse?

She was still mulling over the dilemma after she'd eaten a light breakfast and gone to the nursery to begin the girls' morning lessons. Sunlight streamed in through the nursery windows in bright patches, highlighting their shining hair and scrubbed faces, and she forced her attention to the more mundane world of geography and grammar.

It was almost noon when Miss Mooney appeared at the door of the nursery with a letter in her hand. When Cathy gazed curiously at her she held it out, saying, "This came for you."

Cathy reached out hesitantly for it, then turned to the girls and told them to go wash for their noon meal. As they scrambled up from their desks, she glanced down at the envelope. An unschooled scrawl slanted across the outside of the envelope. "Why, it's a note from Ned," she murmured, and Miss Mooney sniffed indignantly.

"I thought you had decided not to see him again, Miss Cathy!"

"No, I didn't say that at all. If I recall correctly, I just told you that I thought it would be best to limit my social life for a time. At least until summer . . ." Cathy's voice trailed off as she unsealed the envelope and unfolded the paper to read.

Miss Mooney's skeptical gaze rested on Cathy's downbent head. "From the manner in which you've been moping about the house, looking for all the world like a stray kitten, I thought perhaps Mr. Mahoney must have offended you in some way. Or, perhaps . . . was it Mr. Lamont?" she shot home with such unerring accuracy that Cathy's head jerked up.

"Whatever gave you that notion?"

Sniffing again, Miss Mooney gave her a severe glance. "There is no need in trying to fool me, my dear! I have known you long enough to recognize when you are troubled, as you are now. I strongly suspect Mr. Lamont is behind your distraction of late."

When Cathy just stared at her without speaking, Miss Mooney continued. "What happened between you two is none of my affair, I know, but I think that we are close enough for you to be able to confide in me. I can see your suffering, and from what I can tell, Mr. Lamont is also suffering. No," she said when Cathy opened her mouth to protest. "I have noted the way he stares at you like a lovesick calf! Those dark eyes of his give away his intense feelings. He's in love with you, Miss Cathy."

Tears suddenly spurted from her eyes and Cathy looked down at her folded hands crumpling Ned's letter in her lap. "Miss Mooney, please. You mustn't say such things. It is really too . . . more than I can bear."

Staring at her with sympathy, Miss Mooney could see that she had correctly analyzed the situation. It was obvious to anyone who cared to look that Cathy and Jesse were in love with each other. And it was also obvious that something or someone was interfering.

"Are you concerned about Mr. Mahoney's feelings for you, Miss Cathy?" she asked carefully.

Cathy shook her head. "No. Ned is terribly sweet, and he writes of his devotion to me. He also asks to see me again, but that is impossible, of course. How can I, when I feel as I do about . . . I mean, I enjoy Ned's company, and he *does* take my mind off any problems, but I cannot encourage his feelings toward me. It's similar to the situation with Fran, if you'll recall. I had to stop seeing him to make him understand that there was no chance of a marriage between us."

"I understand, but you must get out of this house at times, Cathy, dear. For the past month I have watched you drive yourself into an emotional frenzy. Whatever has happened will eventually work itself out, but you cannot continue shutting yourself away from the world." There was a brief pause. Then Miss Mooney continued. "Mind, I'm not saying that I actually *like* Ned Mahoney, but he's a nice enough young man when all is said and done. I suppose I'm just being a foolish old woman, but there are times when I suspect Mr. Mahoney is secretly laughing at us."

Surprised, Cathy looked up at her. "Why would you say a thing like that?"

Miss Mooney shrugged. "I don't know. I just feel that way at times. Silly of me, I know, but there you have it."

Cathy rose and stepped closer to her, begging in an earnest tone, "Pray, speak your mind, Miss Mooney! I have respect for your opinion, as you must know, and would like to know why you would think such a thing of Ned Mahoney. He has never been anything but kind and considerate to me, and I have always thought him most sincere."

After another brief hesitation, Miss Mooney said slowly, "I have noticed the way he looks at Mr. Lamont. It's been evident to me that he regards him with contempt."

"Contempt? Perhaps it is because he knows of my . . . feelings for Mr. Lamont. He possibly sees Jesse as a rival for my affections."

"That could very well be true," Miss Mooney admitted after a moment's thought. She managed a smile. "Yes, I am sure that it must be that. Mr. Mahoney would obviously be threatened by your relationship with Mr. Lamont, and the proximity of your living arrangements must be anathema to him." Turning away, Miss Mooney asked over her shoulder, "And what will you write Mr. Mahoney, my dear?"

"Why . . . I haven't thought . . . perhaps I shall tell him that I intend to take the children for a walk in the park the first clear Saturday," she said with sudden decision. "He may meet us if he wishes, and we can talk then. Ned will be satisfied, I will be with you and the children, and he must appreciate the subtlety of my situation."

Miss Mooney inclined her head. "Very good, Miss Cathy."

Green eyes flashed with fiery sparks. Long lashes briefly shuttered the expectance lurking in the wide depths of Caroline Lamont's gaze as she glanced up from her writing to stare at her apartment door. It had been a long day of waiting, and now the moment had arrived.

When the door opened Caroline rose from the ladder-back chair and smiled brightly. Swooping across the room in a rush, she flung herself into the man's arms. "Darling! I thought you would never come!"

They embraced, lips meeting in an urgent kiss, and his strong, broad hands slid up and down the curve of her spine. "I've been longing for this," he murmured against her soft cheek when their lips finally parted.

Caroline smiled seductively. "Just for this?"

A slight laugh drifted across the short space separating them as he shook his head. "You have a voracious appetite, my love!"

"But only for you."

His gaze narrowed. "How I wish that were true, dear Caroline," was the dry comment as he released her from his embrace.

Caroline followed him the few short steps into the apartment. "You know that I love only you!" she protested.

"Do I?" He shook his head, commenting, "If that is true, why did you attempt to kill Lamont?"

"Because I hate him!"

"Are you so certain of that, my sweet?" he mocked. "Perhaps your heart still pines for his attentions."

Scurrying forward to fling herself into his arms again, Caroline pressed close. "I love you, darling. What can I do to convince you of my love?"

His arms folded around her, crushing her to him. "I could

tear out your heart for ever loving him," he replied roughly. "I love you, and want you more than anything." His mouth explored the clean arch of her throat with fiery kisses that made Caroline moan and go limp in his arms.

"Oh . . . darling . . ."

Pushing her away with a sudden movement, he stood back. "I almost forgot—I have a present for you, Caroline."

Her eyes glowed with delight as he pulled a small black velvet box from his coat pocket and held it out in the palm of his hand. "Open it now," he said huskily.

"Darling! How sweet and thoughtful of you!"

"It's a very special gift," he said as she took the box and opened it with fingers trembling from excitement. "It's a ring that has been in my family for years. My mother and father had matching rings just like this." Peeling off his glove, he held out his hand for her to see the ring glittering on his finger. It was an intricately wrought crest in an unusual shape, and the ring in the box matched it. "See? Now you will have one to match mine, Caroline. It is a symbol of our mutual affection."

Gasping with delight, Caroline took the ring from the box and held out her hand. He slipped the ring onto her finger, then kissed the tips of her fingers with slow, lingering motions.

"I want you to wear it always, my darling," he said in a voice husky with emotion.

"Oh, I will, love, I will!" Her green eyes glowed with satisfaction. "Such an unusual family crest—English?"

"German," was the soft reply as he pulled her into his arms and smothered her next words with his heated kiss.

Chapter 22

*I*t was a crisp Saturday morning that seemed to bring with it the promise of springtime—a welcome change for the middle of February. Cathy sat on the edge of the boudoir chair in front of her dressing table, braiding long strands of chestnut hair into neat plaits. It was the day she had promised to take the girls on an outing to the park.

Earlier she had gone into the garden to ensure that the weather would not be too cool, and had chanced to see Jesse working in his study. The french doors had been open to allow in a refreshing breeze, and she'd had a wide view of his study. It had been a quick glimpse, as Cathy had not dared draw his attention to her, and she had ducked back inside in almost the same motion.

Her nimble fingers worked the tied braid into a loose coil on the back of her neck. Then she covered it with a wisp of chenille netting. A final inspection in the mirror, and she was through, rising from the small chair to turn away, her thoughts lingering on the reflection. The face was the same, but the person behind that cool, emotionless mask did not seem the same. Had she changed so drastically? There were times she felt like only a wooden puppet with a master pulling at the strings to force her through the daily routines.

How long can I go on like this? . . .

As Cathy reached out for her reticule, her gaze fell upon the small painted fan Jesse had given her for Christmas. It lay propped against a powder box, a constant reminder of the ice in his gaze when he'd given it to her, his remote, aloof expression as he had placed the gift in her shaking palm with such a formal smile. Absently tracing the painted pattern on the fan with a fingertip, Cathy struggled against the hot spurt of tears behind her closed lids.

"Are you ready, Miss Weston?" a small voice called out at her door, and Cathy quickly dashed away her tears with one hand.

"Yes, Jill, I am ready," she called out. "You may come in."

Her door was immediately opened and Jill burst in with excitement dancing in her dark eyes, making her small, pale face more animated than Cathy had ever seen it. The curve of her lips and glow in her face was so infectious that Cathy could not help smiling back.

"Are you excited about going to the park, Jill?"

The dark head bobbed. "Oh, yes! I have not been out of the house since a month before Christmas, and I am quite sure that I shall have the bestest time!"

"Best time," Cathy corrected automatically. Her hand fell to the top of Jill's neatly combed hair, and she said, "Let us go, then!"

"I am ready. . . . Is this yours, Miss Weston?" Jill asked, her gaze falling on the painted fan. "Didn't you get that for Christmas?"

"Yes. Yes, I did, Jill. And it is quite lovely, I think."

Jill nodded in agreement. "Oh, yes, it is. My mother always loved fans like these. She used to get one every year at Christmas, you know, or for her birthday. They all had lovely pictures painted on them, rather like this one."

Tensing, Cathy's thoughts flew to the memory of Jesse's giving her the fan, and suddenly she realized that it must have been Jesse who had always given Caroline a painted fan. Old habits died hard, it seemed, she thought with a bitter twist of her mouth. Painted fans were so easy to give as gifts, and she could picture him as he presented the lovely Caroline with a different fan at each occasion. . . .

"Are you all right, Miss Weston?" came the small voice, and Cathy started, blinking and looking down at Jill's worried face. "I mean . . . you aren't ill, are you?"

"No, no, Jill, I am fine! I was just . . . just thinking of something that happened a long time ago, that's all."

Jill's relief was evident. "Oh. Well, Leigh and Erin are ready and waiting for us downstairs."

"Let me get my cloak, for the wind is still a bit brisk."

"Miss Mooney has had cook prepare the *nicest* picnic basket for us, Miss Weston!" the child chattered, putting her hand confidingly in Cathy's as they left the bedroom.

Cathy smiled down at her. Jill's cheeks bloomed, and her eyes sparkled with such delight and energy that it was hard to remain morose under such circumstances. It was the most animated she'd been since Jesse had grudgingly allowed the girls to exchange gifts with their mother during the holidays, an exchange that had been allowed under the most stringent of circumstances, coming on Boxing Day when the servants had received their gifts from their employer. Jesse had had the girls leave their presents with Beakins, who had, in turn, brought them the gifts from their mother. A most unusual manner in which to exchange gifts, in Cathy's opinion. Jesse's abiding mistrust sparked deep curiosity in her, and more than once she had wondered about Caroline Lamont.

Who was she?

Many carriages rolled through the park, taking advantage of the springlike weather. Pedestrians strolled along in their finery, while several fashionable ladies, wearing fine new bonnets and enjoying the rare sunshine, walked their dogs on velvet leashes.

The three Lamont girls capered about Cathy and Miss Mooney with all the pent-up energy of children who had been kept inside all winter, their bonnets soon askew and their cloaks unbuttoned, so that Miss Mooney was moved to scold them soundly for being rambunctious.

"It just isn't seemly for well-bred young ladies to leap about so!" she lectured, but behind her pale eyes lurked such a sympathetic twinkle that they were not a bit abashed by her remonstration.

"Yes, Miss Mooney!" they chorused obediently, and their bright smiles never dimmed.

"Here, Miss Cathy," Miss Mooney suggested several minutes later. "I will stay at this nice spot and see to the laying out of the picnic, while you take these wild young things for a nice, long, *exhausting* walk!"

"Excellent suggestion!" Cathy approved with a laugh. "Come along, girls."

They had not gone more than a few yards when they were hailed by Ned Mahoney. His light hair was ruffled by the breeze, and his normal sunny face rivaled the brightness of the day as he trotted up to where they waited.

"I saw you from across the park," he said, pointing, "and was afraid you would go too far before I could catch up!"

Cathy smiled back at him, enjoying the feel of the wind and sun on her face. "Oh, you could have caught us easily," she teased. "You seem quite athletic for a mere artist, Mr. Mahoney!"

Ned made an elaborate show of flexing his muscles, making the three girls laugh gleefully, and Erin took great care to flex her own thin arms.

"Shall I show you how fast I can run?" she demanded, putting her hands on her hips and staring up at Mahoney.

"Can you?" he asked. "By all means!"

"Not too far ahead of us!" Cathy called as all three girls began to sprint toward a thicket of trees.

She walked beside Ned in a leisurely manner, her full skirts swinging with the playful tug of the wind, the warm sun beaming down.

"They're lovely children," Ned commented. His gaze sliced down at Cathy's averted face.

"Yes," she agreed, "they are. I shall miss them."

Ned's gaze grew sharp at her quickly halted sentence. "I take it you're thinking of leaving your position?" he asked quickly, his brow lifting in surprise when she gave a reluctant nod of her head.

"Yes . . . yes, I am, though I hadn't meant to mention it to anyone just yet." There was a moment of brief silence, and her throat ached at the thought of leaving the sweet children she had grown to care about. Cathy turned to look up at him, her brow furrowed. "Please, Ned, don't say anything to anyone. I haven't even confided my decision in Miss Mooney yet."

His fair head inclined slightly. "Of course. I am honored that you feel such confidence in me, Cathy. But may I ask why are you contemplating such a precipitate action? I thought you were quite satisfied at Lamont's."

"Oh, I am satisfied with my position, and I adore the girls, but . . ." Her voice drifted to a stumbling halt, and she paused on the path to gaze up at Ned. "He's difficult, you know, and I worry about the girls' relationship—or lack of it—with their mother. It is a situation I feel cannot go on, and I am helpless to change it."

And I cannot bear to be so near to Jesse and not be with him, her aching heart cried silently.

"Lamont must have good reasons to keep their mother away," Ned was saying with a frown. "I understand that she was implicated in her husband's death. Perhaps that is why he will not allow her in the house. There are . . . other, more complex reasons I have heard . . . unsavory things . . ."

Cathy's delicate brow knit into a frown over her shadowed eyes. "Unsavory things? What unsavory things?"

"Well, there is—"

"Miss Weston!" a childish treble called breathlessly, "Mr. Mahoney! Do hurry! Miss Mooney is calling that lunch is ready for us!"

Turning, Cathy saw Erin race toward them, her cheeks pink from the wind and her bonnet bouncing against her back by the ribbons tied around her neck. Leigh and Jill were not far behind, and Ned Mahoney leaned close to whisper that he would tell her later, so that Cathy was forced to wait.

The term "unsavory things" kept echoing in her mind, so that she did little justice to the cold chicken, fruit, deviled eggs, bread pudding, and array of cheeses Miss Mooney had put into the picnic basket. Everyone else, including the carriage driver, who had his own tin pail of food from the same basket, did a great deal of damage to the repast. And afterward, when the lunch things had been repacked into the wicker basket and stowed beneath the seat of the carriage for the trip back to Devonshire Terrace, Ned bade Cathy a courteous farewell and took his leave without explaining his titillating remark. *Unsavory things* floated in Cathy's mind with burgeoning implications.

As the carriage rocked along the cobblestone streets and Jill leaned wearily against her side, Cathy thought again of Caroline Lamont. She seemed to be at the root of the troubles in Jesse's home, both the cause and—perhaps, with the right actions—the cure. A new idea was sprouting in Cathy's mind, an idea that had been nourished by Ned's remarks in the park. If Caroline was at the root of their troubles, then she should be exorcised. There was no other way to help Jesse, she decided.

The carriage finally lurched to a halt in front of 8 Devonshire

Terrace, and Miss Mooney helped the three tired, happy children down from the high vehicle.

"Aren't you coming, Miss Cathy?" she asked in some surprise when Cathy remained seated.

"No. I have some errands to run, Miss Mooney. I shall return soon."

"Errands that need to be done now?"

Cathy was firm. "Yes, and I would appreciate it if you would settle the girls down for a rest. They will need it after their unaccustomed exercise."

Miss Mooney's eyes narrowed. "Miss Cathy, you are up to something. I can feel it."

"I'll be back soon," was the firm reply.

Pinching her lips together, Miss Mooney snapped, "And what time shall I expect you?"

"I don't know."

Stiffening, Miss Mooney said, "As you will." Then she turned and stalked up the shallow steps to the front door.

Sighing, Cathy gave the driver Ned's address. Her heart was thumping wildly, and her throat was dry as she considered and reconsidered what she would say. There had to be a solution to all this, there just had to be!

But when the carriage arrived at Ned Mahoney's address, she was surprised to be told by his landlord that he was not in. She stood uncertainly on the front walk for several moments, wondering if she should wait—after all, he must have walked home from the park and would take longer—or if she should go back to the Lamont house.

Cathy had turned back to the carriage in dejection when she saw a familiar feminine figure strolling along the walk toward her. Riveted to the spot, Cathy recognized the tilt of that red head, the graceful, alluring walk, and the pale face. All that was missing was the pistol. . . .

Cathy stood with one hand on the carriage, hesitating. Then, as the figure swept past, she decided. "Wait here, Cummings," she told the bland-faced driver, who kept his opinions of the afternoon's activities to himself. "I'll be back in a moment!"

"Very well, miss."

Scurrying behind the woman at a distance of several yards, Cathy matched her pace to the mysterious female's. It had to be the same woman who had shot Jesse. She could never forget that face, nor the red hair and curvaceous figure, and she knew before she was even close enough to see them that the woman's eyes would be a bright, startling, green. . . .

The woman turned a corner and passed from sight, and Cathy quickened her pace. She pushed through crowded walks in determined pursuit, her eyes and mind concentrated on that straight-backed figure with the gracefully swaying skirts. Several times her quarry paused to peruse the display in a shop window, or to speak to a passing acquaintance. Feeling very much like a villain in a tragedy, Cathy would pause and pretend to admire a shop display, or rummage through her reticule as if looking for a lost object until the woman had moved on again.

It wasn't really too great a surprise when Cathy turned a corner to find the woman stopped and waiting for her.

"Why are you following me?" came the interested query, and Cathy could not speak. The mystery woman's voice was soft and cultured, faintly interested, as if she were asking the time or directions. It took a moment for Cathy to regain her voice.

Tilting back her head, she faced her and said boldly, "I recognized you from the shooting."

A delicate brow arched in surprise, and she didn't pretend not to know what Cathy was talking about. "You were there?"

Cathy nodded. "Yes, I was there. I saw the pistol and tried to warn him."

"I see." There was a brief pause, and then she shrugged and gave a little laugh. "I was rather *preoccupied* that night, and am afraid I noticed nothing else. I didn't see or hear anyone but

. . . him. I was almost mad that night." Her voice faded into silence and her vivid green eyes darkened with memory. Then she managed a self-conscious smile. "Just who are you?" she demanded so suddenly that Cathy recoiled.

"Catherine Weston—a friend of Mr. Lamont's."

The green eyes narrowed, and her face took on a hard cast. "Really? And just how close a friend, if I may be so bold as to ask?"

"I am the governess to his nieces." Cathy's composure was slowly returning as she spoke, and she took the opportunity to regard the woman in the harsh light of day. She could see now that she wasn't as young as she'd first thought, nor did she have that fresh appeal that came without the use of artifice and paint. Her glow came from a lightly, skillfully applied rouge, and her lips were barely brushed with paint so that they shone a bright pink. The large, striking emerald eyes were darkened with kohl around the fringes, and even her brows were penciled.

As Cathy was making her assessment, the woman's expression slowly changed from haughty and aloof to vulnerable, and she asked softly, "So you take care of my little girls?" It was a question that shocked Cathy.

"Take care of . . . ?" Cathy's voice lapsed into silence as she realized that she was speaking to Caroline Lamont. Of course! She had been the one to shoot Jesse—Caroline, the mother of his nieces, the woman he loved to distraction, and now this specter that had haunted her since meeting Jesse Lamont stood before Cathy in the flesh. Somehow, she was more fragile and vulnerable than Cathy had thought she would be, having visualized a mysterious woman of great strength, determination, and with evil stamped upon her features. So this was Caroline Lamont. . . .

"I didn't realize," Cathy said after a moment, "that you were Mrs. Lamont."

A flicker of a smile ghosted Caroline's lips. "I am. And how are my daughters?"

"They are well and contented."

Her answer was soft and sincere. "I am grateful for your excellent care of them. . . ." There was a short space of time in which Cathy thought she would say something else, ask, perhaps, about her daughters or even Jesse, but then Caroline demanded abruptly, "Why are you following me?"

"I didn't realize your identity when I began following you. When I recognized you from the shooting, I became curious, and wanted to . . . to find out more." A quick smile curved her mouth as Cathy added, "I have heard so much about you from your children."

This seemed to please her. "They do ask about me, then? I was afraid that Jesse had turned them completely against me, and after Christmas . . ." The smile faded. "I shouldn't have said that. I am sure that you feel a certain loyalty to your employer, but it's just that . . . that I *miss* my girls so very much!"

Cathy's heart wrenched with sympathy, and she thought of Jill's deep disappointment at not being able to see her mother. Would a child love her mother so if she knew her mother was was evil? It didn't seem likely. And would Erin and Leigh speak so kindly of a woman who had abused them? No, that was hardly likely either. For Jesse to keep a child as ill as Jill from her mother seemed unusually harsh and unnatural, and Cathy had her doubts about the wisdom of such a decision. Perhaps it was only that he was unable to cope with the loss of Caroline's love, and found it too hard to bear seeing her or even hearing her name. It was entirely possible, for hadn't she felt the same sense of loss and pain in the past weeks?

Impulsively Cathy said, "I wish that you could see your daughters, if only for a little while."

Caroline took an eager step closer. "Do you think it possible?

Would Jesse consent? Has he had a . . . a change of heart, perhaps?"

Regretfully, Cathy shook her head. "No, he has not changed in his refusal."

Caroline's disappointment was obvious, and she fumbled in her reticule for a handkerchief to dab at the spurt of tears in her eyes. "I . . . I see. I had thought . . . but he will never allow me to see them, never! I should never have let him take them from me, but I thought that if he did, things might work out. . . ."

With a pang, Cathy realized that the poor, deluded woman had thought to win back Jesse's love by giving him her children. Instead, he seemed to be using them to punish her. What a horrible fate, and for her to be a party to it was deplorable! Jesse must be terribly uncertain of his feelings for Caroline to take such drastic measures to ensure that he did not have to encounter her in any way, and that knowledge alone tore at Cathy's heart.

Cupping Caroline's elbow in her palm, Cathy steered her toward an alcove in the stone wall, where there was a bench beneath a bare-limbed tree. "Here," she said softly, "sit down. You look so distraught."

"Oh, I am!" Caroline admitted, sniffing and patting her cheeks with the linen handkerchief. They sat down on the bench only a few feet from passing pedestrians. "I had thought we could be a . . . a happy family again, you see, after the tragedy and all. But it didn't work out that way. Jesse refused to see me again, and when he was so cold and determined to keep my children from me, why, I . . . I went *mad* with pain and anger! Do you understand how it was? Do you?"

"I think I can," was the aching answer.

Caroline's fingers began to crumple the handkerchief, and in her distress she gazed past Cathy as if viewing the scene again. "Jesse refused my letters imploring him to see me, and when I arrived at the house, the door was slammed in my face. It drove me to the brink of madness, and I had this pistol. I took it, and followed him, and then I . . . I . . ."

"Yes," Cathy said quickly, "I know the rest."

Caroline's gaze slowly returned to Cathy, and she composed herself with an effort. "Yes, I suppose you do. I hoped that I'd killed him, you know."

"To have so much bitterness must have been dreadful for you," Cathy murmured.

A faint smile twisted Caroline's mouth. "It was. But not quite as dreadful as what followed the shooting. After I regained my senses and realized what I'd done, I was horrified. But the C.I.D. had very little compassion for me when they took me before the magistrate. Our Metropolitan Police are not very gentle at times, and the Criminal Investigations Department can be quite badgering. They seemed to think I was involved in some sort of ridiculous conspiracy to kill Jesse, and kept haranguing me about Wills's death. It was so horrible!" Covering her face with her hands, Caroline shuddered, and Cathy's heart went out in sympathy toward her.

Perhaps it had only been a reaction to the pain of her rejection and loss of her children, perhaps it could be excused, if one could excuse the shooting of a human being. At any rate, it could be understood by a woman who was undergoing the pains of rejection and loss herself. While Cathy felt no compulsion to do harm to the man she loved, she could certainly understand how Caroline had been driven to such a mad, desperate act. Such an unstable woman, who had suffered the loss of her husband, then her lover, and finally her children . . . yes, it could be understood.

"How did you get out of police custody?" Cathy asked when it looked as if Caroline was more composed.

Caroline's green eyes softened, and her voice was a throaty murmur as she said, "Jesse. It was the only kind thing he had done for me in years, and he refused to press charges." A bitter smile pinched her lips as she added, "And John Bothmourne arranged the formalities with his usual precise finesse! Dear Lord Bothmourne! How he detests me, blames me for Wills's death! It must have galled him bitterly to be forced to arrange for my release from custody!" She slanted Cathy a thoughtful glance, then added, "You know, I've always had the notion that it was the other way round—that Bothmourne had some responsibility for Wills's . . . unusual . . . death. After all, Wills was on assignment for Bothmourne when we were in Italy. Only dear Lord Bothmourne knew that Wills was going out sailing that day. John, Jesse, and myself were so close. . . . Well, I certainly didn't murder my own husband! I had nothing to gain and everything to lose, as has been proven." Pausing, Caroline fixed Cathy with a steady gaze. "I have been running on about my problems, haven't I? I apologize, but you are the first woman to listen with such sympathy, and I suppose I just folded like wet sugar cake. No wonder you were chosen to care for my daughters."

"Oh, I am vitally interested," Cathy said. "It has been such a confusing tangle to me, and I confess I did not understand why Jesse was so . . . so adamant about refusing to allow you to see your daughters. This is helping me to understand."

"Yes, poor Jesse. He did not cope well with Wills's death. After all, he practically reared Wills, and would never have done anything to give him the slightest moment of unhappiness." Her mouth once more twisted in an unattractive expression of bitterness. "I should know that better than any."

"What do you mean?"

"Just that Jesse chose Wills over me long ago."

"Perhaps just loyalty, or—"

"No. Not just loyalty. But I do recognize that to Jesse Lamont, loyalty and commitment mean everything. Some men might die or kill for a woman, but for Jesse—those emotions are reserved for only England."

Cathy rose, unwilling to hear these things about Jesse, yet morbidly drawn to hear them. Was it all true? Did Jesse care only about state, and not about . . . about her? *Then why his consuming passion for Caroline?*

Knotting her fingers into gloved fists in the folds of her skirts, Cathy said distantly, "I'm not at all certain I should be listening to all this."

Caroline rose and faced her. "But you must be aware of what is happening in your household. And besides, I want you—someone—to understand my pain, my desolation at the separation from my children! I'm not a bad mother! I do love them, and this has torn out my heart so that at times I do not know if I can go on. . . ." Ending in a choking sob, Caroline turned so that her back was to the walk and her face hidden from curious passersby. "Please," came the small, muffled cry, "Please help me see my babies!"

Unhappily, hesitantly, Cathy asked, "But what can I do to help you? I've already said that he refuses to consider it at all."

Caroline half turned. "He will never permit it. But you may."

Cathy recoiled. "No. No, I couldn't do that. It would be disloyal, unfair, and—"

"And in the meantime my daughter could die without seeing her mother again!" was the impassioned reply.

Pressing home her advantage, Caroline said softly, "He need never know. I certainly would not tell, and even if only for a brief instant, a fleeting glimpse of those dear, beloved faces, it would be the answer to my prayers!"

"Well . . ."

"Oh, do not deny my children this favor!" Caroline said with such wistful pain that Cathy gave a long sigh and nod of her head.

"I will see what I can do," she promised, ignoring the vague stirrings of disquiet that pricked at her. "Where . . . where may I reach you?"

Fumbling in the folds of her velvet reticule, Caroline withdrew a small scrap of paper. "Here. This has my address on it. You may send me a message at any time, and I will come."

Taking the scrap of paper, Cathy held it tightly in her hand. "I will see what I can do," she repeated, turning and walking in the direction of her carriage. "I must go now, but I will send you a message with the time and place of a meeting." She paused and turned back to say, "But only this once, Mrs. Lamont. After this, I can never help you again. I am obligated to my employer and to the children."

"I understand," Caroline Lamont said, adding, "and bless you, Miss Weston!"

It was only later, while seated in her carriage and gazing out the small window at the passing scenery, that Cathy thought to look at the address she'd been given. Her brow crumpled in a frown. Oddly enough, it was the same building in which Ned Mahoney lived. Perhaps that was why Caroline Lamont had been on that particular street at that particular time. And fate had brought them together and now she was promised to a clandestine meeting. Cathy folded the scrap of paper and stuffed it into a corner of her reticule.

Chapter 23

*E*vents were moving even more swiftly than Cathy had first thought. In the week since the day in the park and her meeting with Caroline, Jill had grown worse. Dr. Alexander had been coming twice a day to check on her, and his expression was grave in spite of his assurances that it was only a mild setback. Jesse remained coldly indifferent to any of Cathy's attempts to talk to him, and she felt adrift in a sea of confusion.

There was no one she could confide in, no one she felt would listen with impartiality, especially Miss Mooney, on the subject of Caroline Lamont. And to broach the subject to Jesse would be sheer lunacy!

Lying alone in her bed before most of the house began to stir, Cathy listened to the rhythmic sounds of Jesse exercising in his gymnasium. She could hear the whack-a-whack of his hands pounding against the hanging leather bag in a steady staccato of punches, and if she closed her eyes she could visualize his lean, athletic body poised in a tense stance. Cathy tossed and turned, finally rolling to her stomach and pulling her feather pillow over her head to block out the sounds and memory. But it remained, a steady fusillade of muffled blows, drifting through the walls and a thousand goose feathers to assault her ears.

Surrendering, Cathy sat up in bed and swung her legs over the side, determination etched on her features. If he insisted upon keeping her awake, then a confrontation would be her next step. She had to talk to Jesse before she exploded with pent-up anxiety and frustration.

Dragging a dressing gown from across the chair where she had thrown it the night before, Cathy barely took the time to wrap it around her body and belt it. Hadn't Jesse Lamont seen her in much less than a nightdress and robe before, anyway? Why bother with modesty when he had bared much more than her body, when he had stripped her soul and left it bare and bleeding?

Dear God, such morbid thoughts, Cathy thought with a wry smile at her own foolishness.

The lamps on the hall walls were burning low, and Cathy did not bother to knock on the door of the gymnasium. She pushed it open and stood in the doorway of the brightly lit room, her eyes slowly adjusting to the light. Jesse's back was to her, his arms flexing as he punched at the hanging leather bag. He was unaware of her presence, and continued pounding furiously at the bag as if it were his enemy.

Shutting the door softly behind her, Cathy moved across the room to approach Jesse. Sweat was pouring down his face and body, and as she reached him he halted his furious blows, his breathing harsh and ragged. An expression of pain marred his rugged features, and one hand moved to clutch at his side. Cathy's brow furrowed as she recognized the faint scar barely visible beneath his loose clasp.

Jesse hadn't heard Cathy, and his thoughts were as tortured as his muscles and the screaming pain in his side, reminding him of his mistakes, so many mistakes. Another scar, another reminder of his foolishness.

Straightening, he tugged off the leather gloves he wore and tossed them carelessly to the floor. Lines of weariness etched his face, and he realized that he wasn't the young man he once was, the young man who could have gone twice as long pounding at the bag and still been as fresh as when he'd started. Now, at forty-two, the years had taken their toll on his endurance. The years and his injuries, he amended silently. Time was gaining on him, chipping away at his strength, and he spared only the briefest regret. With time should come wisdom.

Shrugging, the blood still pounded in his ears and his heart raced from his exertions, and he half turned, starting when he saw Cathy standing a mere foot away. Damn! Had his reflexes grown that slow?

"Cathy. I didn't hear you enter."

He was short, abrupt, the familiar cold mask sliding over his features to hide his thoughts, and she sighed. "Please, Jesse, don't be so cold. I don't deserve this, and you know it."

Struggling against the almost overwhelming desire to take her into his arms—to whisper how beautiful she was early in the morning with her hair all loose and curling wantonly about her face, to stroke the gentle curves he could see through the clinging material of her gown—Jesse took a deep, steadying breath. "Yes, you're right," he said softly. "I apologize."

She came close. "Don't apologize, Jesse. Just talk to me," she whispered in such a husky, warm tone that he briefly shut his eyes. "Share your pain with me." Cathy reached out to stroke lightly the zigzag of the scar on his side.

Turning swiftly, fiercely, Jesse snatched her close. His voice was a hoarse groan as he muttered, "Dammit! Share my pain? It's been hell not being able to hold you in my arms, to feel the softness of your skin beneath my hands and taste the sweetness of your lips."

Her reply was a warm whisper floating across his bare chest. "Then hold me close, Jesse, hold me close. . . ."

He needed no further urging. His mouth plundered her willing lips with a wild, fierce pain and urgency that she shared with him, and Cathy felt the surge of her heart beneath his touch. She melded into him, her need matching his, and when their lips finally parted they were both shaking and breathless.

"Damn you," Jesse muttered after a moment.

"I am damned—damned for loving you, Jesse."

This elicited an unwilling smile from him. "And I, you," he said with a sigh. Gazing down into her eyes, those deep, amber eyes that promised so much, held so many secrets in their depths, he thought Cathy the most beautiful woman he had ever seen. "You must leave," he said after a moment that shimmered with tension.

Shivering with reaction, she shook her head. "No. I can't. I won't. I must talk to you, and I will."

Pain throbbed in his voice as Jesse said, "I cannot bear much more of this, Cathy. Can't you understand? I feel as if . . . as if I am about to explode."

"Do you think you are the only one suffering?" Cathy couldn't help crying out. "Can't you see how I've suffered, too . . . and am suffering now?" Pulling away, she said in great agitation, "Do you think this situation easy for me? I live here with you, endure your coldness, your rejection, and yet I go on. What else can I do? You've been so self-absorbed that you can see no one else's pain but your own, Jesse Lamont! And that includes your nieces!"

There was a tense pause, and Jesse's lips thinned to a taut line. "What the deuce are you talking about?"

"Jill . . ."

"Are you holding me responsible for her illness?" he spat furiously.

"No—for her unhappiness!" Cathy spat back. She sucked in a deep breath and said, "Jill needs her mother, Jesse."

"Her mother! That harridan! Have you gone mad?" Jerking around, he stalked to where his robe hung limply over a chair back and snatched it up before he turned. "You don't know what you're talking about, Cathy," he continued in a calmer tone, "so stay out of this."

"I know more than you think I do. Pray tell, how am I to stay out of it when I am responsible for those young girls, too? Jesse, you must stop thinking only of yourself and your problems, your feelings for Caroline. Jill should be the primary concern here. She needs her mother, and the poor child has begged me to ask your permission for a visit with her."

Staring at Cathy, Jesse's incredulity slowly changed to an expression of pain. Jill had begged him for the same thing. But how could he explain to small children that he was afraid of what Caroline might do? She was capable of almost anything, and that would be difficult to explain without going into too much detail.

"Please, Jesse," Cathy was saying, her lovely face gazing up at him so sweetly that he found it difficult to deny her anything, "please let the girls see their mother. If only for a moment or two, that might satisfy them, might keep them from thinking that you are the villain in this."

"And if I agree?" he asked stiffly.

"Then I will not leave them for a moment, and if you like, you can be there to see that—"

"No! No, I don't want to be there."

"But you will consider a visit?"

Sighing heavily, Jesse turned away. "Yes," he said so softly and with such resignation that Cathy's heart lurched. "She can come."

It won't matter for long anyway, because I intend to send you all away. . . .

But he didn't voice that last thought, and Cathy was smiling so radiantly that Jesse felt an overwhelming sense of guilt. How could he be so devious?

"Jesse!" she blurted, flinging herself at him. "Thank you so much! You won't regret it, I promise."

"I already do," he said wryly, "but my heart is not so hard that I will let a child die without seeing her mother."

A chill shivered down Cathy's spine. "What do you mean?"

"You must know what I mean," he replied brokenly.

"That . . . that she's dying *now?* But Dr. Alexander has said nothing like that. He's been so optimistic!"

"Has he?" Grimacing, Jesse swung about and aimed a blow at the hanging bag, striking it with his bare fist. It swung wildly, and he muttered a harsh "damn!" as he clasped his bruised knuckles in his other hand.

Stunned, hardly believing what Jesse was saying, Cathy could only stare at him with wide eyes filled with pain and disillusionment. Surely not, surely Jill would recover soon. Hot tears traced wet paths over her cheeks as she whispered brokenly, "Oh, Jesse . . . this bitterness and hatred will destroy us all. We need to let it go, to make things right so that if . . . if it's true about Jill, she will not have her last days so unhappy. She'll have those she loves around her."

"And what about me, Cathy?" Jesse's voice was ragged. "What about me? Will I always have to do without those I love?"

Then somehow she was in his arms, her mouth clinging to his, her body melting beneath his touch. Passion surged in a white-hot flame, consuming them as they slowly lowered to the mat on the floor, their clothes seeming to disappear of their own accord so that bare flesh met bare flesh, chest to breast, thigh to thigh. Shivering under Jesse's touch, her heart aflame and her eyes closed with sweet ecstasy, Cathy took him inside her with wondrous delight, letting their passion sweep her away. There was only Jesse, only this moment, and nothing else mattered.

The meeting had been arranged, with a flurry of details and biting intensity, but the final arrangements had been made. Caroline Lamont was to arrive at 8 Devonshire Terrace promptly at ten o'clock the following Saturday.

The designated morning was the last Saturday in February. Cathy would remain with the children, and Pickworth was to be near at hand. The most unusual stipulation—in Cathy's opinion—was that John Bothmourne was to be present in the house during Caroline's visit.

Jesse had abruptly decided to leave before she arrived. His destination, as usual, was a mystery. His farewell was polite, but curt, and it was apparent that the entire affair caused him a great deal of apprehension. Cathy was caught between pleasure for the excited children, and anxiety that something—anything— would go wrong.

When Caroline arrived, Cathy took a deep breath and signaled to Pickworth that she would answer the door. Lord Bothmourne was in the study, as arranged, and Cathy took another deep breath and swung open the door.

Caroline Lamont stood framed in the open doorway, her face creased with excitement, and her eyes glittering. She smiled nervously.

"Thank you, Miss Weston. Thank you so much for this!"

"Of course. Do come in, Mrs. Lamont."

Cathy swung the door open all the way, forcing a smile. "I am so happy for the children, who are beside themselves at the prospect of seeing you." Lifting one hand to indicate the direction of the nursery, she said, "Would you like to follow me?"

"I remember the way," Caroline said with a quick twist of her lips. Her eyes darted toward the closed study door. "Is Jesse home?"

Cathy shook her head. "No. However, Lord Bothmourne is here, if you would care to see him."

"Certainly not!" was the somewhat startled answer. Then her painted lips curved into a scornful smile. "I should have known that Jesse would leave his faithful watchdog on guard."

Forestalling any possible trouble, Cathy said quickly, "You have only a very few minutes, and the girls are anxiously waiting. Do come with me."

Beams of sunlight spilled across the nursery floor as three little girls sat impatiently waiting with scrubbed faces and neatly combed hair. When the door to the nursery opened, Erin and Leigh jumped up, their shining countenances brightening. Jill, too ill to get up from her narrow bed, pushed to a sitting position and gave a gasp of delight as Caroline entered the room.

"Mother!" she cried out in a weak voice, lifting her thin arms toward her. Erin and Leigh flew across the room on skipping feet to fling themselves at their mother, who knelt down to receive their embraces with open arms.

"Hello, my darlings," she whispered, then held them at arm's length to look at them. "You look so well. And how is my Jill?" she added, rising to her feet and striding swiftly toward the bed.

Sunlight brightened the child's face, but there was no mistaking the too bright eyes and pallor beneath the excited glow. "Mama!" Jill whispered, and Cathy flinched from the tearful glitter in the child's eyes.

Leaning back against the wall beside the door, Cathy sucked in a deep breath, thinking how glad she was she had dared plead with Jesse for such a reunion. Jill was expressing more emotion than she had since Cathy's arrival, and her pinched face radiated with happiness.

But as Caroline perched on the edge of the bed and snatched Jill into her smothering embrace, Cathy heard her whisper fiercely, "I've come to take you away from that fiend, my precious baby!"

Shocked by what she heard, Cathy was immobilized. Had she heard correctly? Had Caroline just said that she had come to take Jill away? No, surely not. She must not mean it in that way, or . . . but Caroline was sweeping Jill from beneath the quilted coverlet and rising from the bed. Cathy took a step forward, hearing Caroline say in a low, tight voice that she could not bear to be separated from her children for another moment, another day.

"Mrs. Lamont," Cathy said, her brow furrowed and her heart racing with alarm, "please watch what you say. The girls might misinterpret your intentions. I would like for you to assure them that you only mean how much you miss them, and that you would like to be with them—"

"Oh, I'm certain you would!" Caroline spat without turning around. "It would suit you fine!"

Recoiling, Cathy realized that Caroline was hovering on the brink of losing complete control. She could see her hands quiver, and there was a vibrating tension that transferred itself to her even from several feet away.

Caroline jerked around to face Cathy, and her green eyes were glittering with a deranged light. A cold chill shot through Cathy, dragging along her spine with tickling fingers, stealing through her body to leave her limbs leaden and weighted. She could only watch for a moment as Caroline surged to her feet, almost dumping Jill on the floor as she grated, "Oh, I can see what you're thinking! It is only what I expected from a woman who lives in the same house with . . . with *him!* You are probably the devil's consort, and I will not leave my daughters here to face such evil!"

Jill's pale face peered anxiously up at her mother, and her thin hand plucked urgently at Caroline's skirts. "Mama, no," she said weakly, but Caroline was beyond listening.

Retreating, Cathy went immediately to the bell cord and gave it a firm yank—two strong pulls, as was the prearranged signal with Pickworth. Her heart sank as she realized how quickly the situation had deteriorated, and she made a brief, silent apology to the absent Jesse for doubting his instincts. Gathering her composure, Cathy's mind raced quickly, recalling

Bothmourne's cold, barely civil instructions as well as his caustic observation that Cathy was playing with fire by promoting a visit. But this was no time to dwell on the fact that he had been right, and Cathy set into motion the plan Bothmourne had briefly outlined should Caroline cause a scene. Little had she thought she would have to use it. . . .

Caroline was cooing to Jill, cradling the frightened child in her arms and saying, "You want to stay with Mama, don't you, sweetheart? You want to leave this big, nasty house and come and stay with your mother, don't you, baby?"

Jill's tiny voice whispered an unwilling assent, and her terrified gaze searched for and found Cathy's calm, comforting visage. "Yes, Mama . . ."

"Mrs. Lamont," Cathy interrupted softly, forcing a bright smile to her lips, "would you care to see a portrait of the girls? It was painted at Christmas by a well-known artist, Edward Mahoney, and is quite good."

Caroline's head snapped up. "A portrait by Mahoney? Are you certain?"

"Yes, of course I am. It required quite a few sittings, but he did an excellent likeness of your daughters. I am sure you would be pleased with it," Cathy assured her in a pleasant tone. Her smile never wavered, and she gestured toward the nursery door. "It is just down the hall. The girls can have their morning refreshments while I show it to you. Then perhaps we can join them for some tea and cakes."

Leigh and Erin were huddled near Jill's bed, looking like frightened rabbits, and they gave short nods as Cathy told them Pickworth would be bringing up a tray in just a few moments. Caroline's suddenly suspicious gaze shifted from the girls to Cathy.

"I don't know," she began, but Cathy quickly assured her that it would be no trouble.

"Of course, Mrs. Lamont, if you prefer not seeing Mr.

Mahoney's excellent artistic effort, I am sure that it is not necessary," Cathy added in a carefully casual voice.

That seemed to have the desired effect on Caroline, and she turned toward the door. "Very well. I will look at . . . Mr. Mahoney's . . . work, but then I wish to come back to the girls."

"Of course." Cathy held open the door.

Ida Mooney arrived as the door swung open, her hands twisting nervously as her glance darted from Cathy to Caroline, then back.

Cathy kept her face carefully blank as she greeted her. "Good morning, Miss Mooney."

"Good morning . . ."

"You do recall Mrs. Lamont, perhaps? She is visiting with the girls, and wishes to see the portrait Ned did of them."

"I see." Miss Mooney cleared her throat. "How nice. Is there anything I can do?"

"Why, yes. Please see that the girls have their morning refreshment while we look at the portrait."

Caroline Lamont had begun to relax visibly, and her smile was wide as she stepped out the nursery door. "Well, do let us look at this famous portrait, Miss Weston!"

Cathy preceded Caroline down the wide hall, crossing the short space toward the door leading to the servants' stairs. Her heart pounded as she nervously considered the fact that Caroline could at any moment recall that these were the steps leading to the back of the house, and thereby successfully avoid Lord Bothmourne's carefully arranged scheme. *How could he have so accurately predicted such a catastrophe?*

"It's just inside here," Cathy said over her shoulder, firmly grasping the door latch and praying that he would be there.

Her prayer was answered. As the door swung open Lord John Bothmourne leaped forward and grasped Caroline by her arms, swinging her around so that two of the footmen could seize her.

After a gasp of outrage and fury, Caroline was carried kicking and screaming down the back stairs, her voice drifting back with shrill accusations and imprecations. Cathy shuddered, unable to meet Lord Bothmourne's cynical gaze.

"I'll get you for this, Johnny!" Caroline screamed back at him, her voice echoing up the long, narrow corridor.

Cathy was shaking as she finally lifted her chin to look at Lord Bothmourne. "What will you do with her?"

"She's being put into a carriage and taken away," he answered coolly.

"And then?"

"I hardly think it necessary for you to know."

Smarting from his implied rebuke, Cathy felt the overpowering need to defend her actions. "I know this is my fault, but when I met her quite by accident and discovered her identity, I felt compelled to arrange this visit with her children. She seemed so . . . so sad, and sincere, and her plea was so heartrending."

"The woman is a consummate actress," Bothmourne said. His head tilted to one side and he regarded Cathy thoughtfully for a moment. "You look as if you could do with a glass of sherry or ratafia," he said in a softer tone.

Cathy gave him a brittle smile. "Brandy would be more to my liking at this moment!"

"Shall we repair to the study for a glass of brandy and some private conversation, then?" he suggested with the first genuine smile he had given her that day.

Once ensconced in the huge leather wing chair opposite Jesse's desk, and with a snifter of brandy cupped in her hand, Cathy began to relax slightly. Reaction had set in, and her hands were shaking badly as she lifted the brandy to her mouth.

"Caroline Lamont is demented," Bothmourne began without preamble. "She is totally unpredictable. When she was young and more stable, it was rather exciting to be in her company. You never knew what to expect. One moment she would be laughing and gay, the next angry, or even weeping and sulky. She was different, contradictory, tempestuous, and all the young gentlemen were a little mad for her, including myself at certain times when she was gay." He paused and gazed critically at the fine brandy in his snifter. "Yet it was Jesse who was totally obsessed with Caroline. This was twenty years ago, you understand. He and the vivacious Caroline were engaged several times, would quarrel and refuse to see each other, then fall madly in love again. It was, as you can imagine, a tempestuous relationship. Work always took precedence with Jesse, and this irritated frivolous Caroline to no end. Jesse was working in Russia when he learned that his younger brother had eloped with Caroline."

Cathy was silent, contemplating the shock it must have given Jesse. Finally she mumured the observation that it must have crushed him.

"You cannot imagine. The two people he loved most in the world had hurt and abandoned him. But, to give him his just due, William was madly in love with Caroline. In the end, she destroyed not only herself, but her husband, and would do so to Jesse."

"So much bitterness, so much pain," Cathy whispered, and took another sip of brandy, letting its warmth flow down her throat and soothe her frazzled nerves.

To her surprise Lord Bothmourne rounded the corner of the desk and came to where she sat, leaning close to confide, "Yes, there has been. And if not for you these past months, I think Jesse would have gone mad. You have been good for him, Miss Weston, good for the children, and good for this entire household. In spite of this recent . . . lapse from grace . . . you have shown remarkable empathy and care for him, and I want you to know how much I admire you for it."

"Why . . . thank you, my lord, I have certainly grown fond of the children, and I have a great deal of respect and admiration for Mr. Lamont."

"More than respect, I think," Bothmourne began, and was interrupted by a quick knock on the door and the abrupt entrance of Pickworth.

The old servant had a frantic, harried expression in his eyes, and his normally combed wisps of hair were standing on end, as if he had raked his fingers through it.

"My lord! Miss Weston! Oh, it is so dreadful! Please, you must come at once. It's Miss Jill . . ."

Chapter 24

*I*f Cathy had once thought that nothing worse could ever happen to her after Darcy's abandonment, she now discovered that she had been quite, quite wrong.

From the instant that Pickworth rushed into Jesse's study with his terrible pronouncement, she knew that her cozy little world was disintegrating. By the time she and Lord Bothmourne reached the nursery, it was apparent that the worst had happened. Jill was gravely ill. The physician was sent for immediately, and then a summons was penned to Jesse.

Cathy wrote the note herself, refusing Lord Bothmourne's kind offer to do so. She felt a grave responsibility, and found it terribly hard to pen the few words explaining the urgency of the situation. It was left to Bothmourne to get the message to Jesse at an undisclosed location.

When Dr. Alexander arrived, he was shown immediately to the nursery, while Cathy waited in agonizing moments of uncertainty. Leigh and Erin had been ushered into Miss Mooney's cheerful little room, and were being distracted with games and a reading of Dickens's latest serial, but Cathy was alone with her thoughts . . . and her feelings of guilt. Had she somehow precipitated the child's collapse by inviting Caroline into the home? It was not only possible, but probable.

Pacing the carpet in Jesse's study, Cathy pressed her palm to her brow in distraction. How could she have been so naïve, so foolish? Even good intentions could not excuse her stupidity. And Jesse—what would he say? What would he think? Would he berate her for being so foolish? Would this add to his already overflowing store of bitterness?

Cathy sank to the bleak comfort of a chair and put her head in her cupped palms. It had all happened so quickly, and she did not know how to explain it, and did not know if Jesse was close enough to come back to the house to see Jill and demand an explanation for what had transpired.

Then the sound of the front door slamming shut and Jesse's voice in the hallway alerted Cathy to his arrival and she rose from the chair. She reached the hallway at the same moment as he started up the stairs. Jesse halted and pivoted to stare at her.

"What happened?" was his quick, terse question.

Cathy shook her head helplessly. "I don't know. One moment it was all right . . . and the next . . . but go to see Jill now. The doctor is with her."

Nodding shortly, Jesse flew up the stairs, his overcoat flapping noisily around his knees. Cathy sagged against the newel post and covered her eyes with one hand. She gathered her strength for the coming ordeal, and slowly straightened to go up the stairs. She must be strong, must be there in case Jesse or Jill needed her.

But when she entered the darkened nursery her resolve weakened. Jesse was sitting on Jill's bed, still clad in his overcoat, holding the motionless child in his arms. His broad shoulders were shaking, and his face was contorted with grief.

Cathy's heart sank as her glance flew to the doctor's grave face and he gave a slight shake of his head. Jill was dead. Cathy's throat clogged with grief, and was so tight she could scarcely draw a breath. *No, no! Not that poor little girl who had known such a short, bleak life! Dear God, it couldn't be!*

Leaning against a chair back, hardly able to stand, Cathy felt her lips mouth words, but did not know what she said. She didn't know that hot tears were running down her cheeks and splashing on the bodice of her dress, nor was she aware of the fact that her knuckles were gripping the chair back so tightly they were scratched and bleeding. All she could see was Jesse, his rugged features naked with pain and grief, tears streaking his cheeks as he held the child next to his heart. There was a buzzing noise in the room that grew louder and louder, and then Cathy blinked as someone gently took her arm.

It was Lord Bothmourne, and his face was soft and gentle as he cupped Cathy's elbow in his palm and turned her around, guiding her toward the door.

"Come with me, Miss Weston," he said, and his voice sounded as if it came from far away.

Nodding in quiet confusion, Cathy was only vaguely aware that she was being led from the nursery and back down the stairs to Jesse's study. As Lord Bothmourne seated her in a chair, Cathy realized that she was whimpering. It was a surprise, hearing her sobs and pitiful little gasps, and she gazed up at Bothmourne in bewilderment.

"I know this is a tragic occurrence, Miss Weston, but you must be strong. You must gather your self-control and be strong for Jesse. He will need you." Bothmourne gave that a moment to sink in, then added in a pitying tone, "I greatly fear that Jesse will need you as the scapegoat for this tragedy. He won't be able to blame himself, you see, for he has rarely been able to do that. He must vent his anger or go mad, and I want you to be prepared for what I fear lies ahead. Do you understand any of what I am saying to you?"

Cathy nodded. "Yes. Poor Jill . . . oh, if only I had not been so foolish as to allow her to be upset! If only—"

"Those two words, my dear, are the most pitiful, useless words in the English language," Bothmourne said strongly. "I suggest you remove them from your vocabulary. They will do you no good, Jesse no good, and certainly not the poor child. Jill has been ill since her birth, and her time has simply come. That is all there is to it."

Even though Bothmourne's tone was cold and flat, it imparted a sense of strength to Cathy that allowed her to accept more easily what had happened. She nodded. "Perhaps you're right."

"There's no 'perhaps' to it. I *am* right. And I am also right when I tell you that Jesse will certainly ventilate some of his pain in your direction. Expect it. Be prepared for it, and let it roll over you without absorbing it. And don't let him convince you that you are at fault, for he knew how gravely ill the child has been." Bothmourne strode to the windows and stared out at the garden, his voice seeming to come from some spot deep within him as he said, "I feel that I must break a confidence here, in order that you will more completely understand the situation. Jill was Jesse's child."

Cathy reeled as if she had been struck a physical blow. Of course! Why hadn't she suspected? The eyes should have told her, the strong physical resemblance to Jesse . . . No wonder Jesse had been so tortured, so secretive.

"It is a well-kept secret," Bothmourne was continuing, "and I expect you will keep it so. The child was born after William's marriage to Caroline, and Jesse has always cursed himself with guilt for yielding that one time to the sin of temptation. He will now believe that Jill's death is retribution, of course." Bothmourne's knuckles rubbed idly against the windowpane, and his gaze was distant. "I suppose that is why he has so wantonly courted danger these past years, hoping somehow that he will be made to pay for taking his brother's wife. . . ."

When his voice trailed into silence, Cathy stood and placed her empty brandy snifter on the desk. "But I don't believe that for a moment," she said with quiet conviction, and Bothmourne turned back from the window to stare at her.

"Somehow I knew you wouldn't," he said with a slight smile. "Jesse's in love with you, you know," he added so casually that Cathy gasped.

"In love with me? But . . . but he has never said so, and has firmly stated that he could never fall in love with me."

Lord Bothmourne waved away her words as if they were inconsequential. "He lies to himself. It's a habit he cultivated at the same time he decided he was in love with Caroline. Dammit! Jesse never instigated their relationship but only surrendered to it, the idealistic idiot! It was Caroline who pursued him, who tempted him, who engineered events so smoothly. And it was Caroline who murdered William Lamont, even though I cannot prove it."

"How can you be sure of that?"

He shrugged. "I just know. If I could find one solid bit of information that would tie her to the crime, I think I could convince Jesse of her guilt. Then he would stop blaming himself for Caroline's sins, and go on with his life. Until he does that, he's doomed to misery and doubt."

Cathy was silent, considering the shocking details just related to her by the duke. There was so much to absorb that her mind could not deal with it all, and she shook her head in weary confusion. "I don't know . . . I don't know what to do. . . ."

"Do nothing for now. Jesse will try to push you out of his life, but you must be strong. With Jill's death, he will be beside himself, and if I know him, he will say cruel and cutting things to you in order to keep you and his feelings for you at bay. Keep that in mind, Miss Weston, when he's snarling and snapping at you like a deranged terrier."

Cathy smiled. "I will. And, my lord . . . thank you."

A weak smile passed across the duke's lips, and his eyes crinkled at the corners. "Not at all, Miss Weston, not at all!"

* * *

The house was quiet, with the specter of death lingering in dark shrouds over the inhabitants. Servants tiptoed through the corridors, and a black wreath adorned the front door in crepe streamers.

With no other outlet for her grief, Cathy sat down at her writing desk and wrote a reply to Miss Nightingale's most recent letter. Yet her thoughts wandered, and she was unable to concentrate for longer than a few minutes at a time.

Miss Mooney tapped softly at her door, and, grateful for the distraction and companionship, Cathy begged that she enter at once. Miss Mooney's eyes, behind her wire-rimmed spectacles, were red and watery, and the two women held each other wordlessly for a moment before breaking apart with a sniff.

"The burial arrangements have already been made," Miss Mooney said after gathering her composure. "Beakins told me about them."

Cathy nodded. Of course the servants would know such things before anyone else, so she wasn't surprised. "What are they?" she asked softly. Her heart ached at the thought of Jill's tiny body being placed into the cold maw of the grave, gone from sight forever.

"There's rather an interesting tale behind it if you would care to hear," Miss Mooney said, and Cathy grasped at any diversion.

"Of course."

"It seems that, according to Beakins, who heard it from Pickworth, who knows everything, Mr. Lamont bought some burial plots off Harrow Road in Kensal Green Cemetery some ten years ago. No, it was longer, because I believe he said the spot had come to his attention in 1841 by the way of Charles Dickens, who surrendered his own plot to his young brother-in-law, George Hogarth. The young man had no grave of his own, and Dickens generously gave it up upon Hogarth's death. He later wept publicly over losing such a fine spot, creating quite a stir at a party given by his friend, Miss Coutts." Miss Mooney smiled slightly at the mental image of such an occurrence, then continued. "It seems that Mr. Lamont was present at the occasion, and as he had long feared for Jill's health, he went to visit the cemetery. He was quite impressed with it, and purchased several plots not far from where George Hogarth, his grandmother, and his sister Mary were buried. Of course, everyone knows that Dickens simply adored his sister-in-law Mary, and was quite undone at her early death. She was only seventeen, you know, and her demise caused Dickens an enormous amount of grief. It is said that for several months after young Mary's death, Mr. Dickens could not write a single word, an almost unheard-of occurrence!"

"And that spurred Jesse to buy cemetery plots?" Cathy murmured with a slight frown. "I didn't know he could be so sentimental."

"I imagine it was simply because he liked the setting of Kensal Green," Miss Mooney said more practically, and Cathy smiled.

"I'm sure of it," she agreed.

Straightening the shade on a lamp, Miss Mooney remarked that Erin and Leigh were sleeping in her room that night. "I think they need a great deal of comforting," she added.

Recalling how Miss Mooney had been such a comfort to her when her mother had died, Cathy was grateful for the older woman's presence. "Has . . . has Jesse come out of the nursery yet?" she forced herself to ask, wincing at the thought of that proud, grieving man locking himself in the room with the cold body of his daughter.

Miss Mooney slowly shook her head. "No," she whispered. "And he won't open the door to allow anyone in with him. It is Lord Bothmourne who has made the funeral arrangements for Tuesday."

Sighing, Cathy's shoulders slumped forward. As much as she

wanted Jesse to emerge from the nursery, she dreaded the moment when he did. Would he look at her with hatred in his dark eyes? And could she bear to witness his pain without breaking down? Lord Bothmourne's warning still echoed in her mind, resounding over and over, and she shuddered thinking of the time when she would have to face Jesse once more.

"Shall I brush your hair for you?" Miss Mooney asked, sensing Cathy's distress. "It always soothes you when I do."

Cathy shook her head. "No, Leigh and Erin need you more tonight. I . . . I'll finish my letter to Miss Nightingale and go to bed. It's late."

"Good night, Cathy."

Hugging her, Cathy murmured a soft good-night and closed the door behind Miss Mooney. She undressed slowly, too distracted to finish the letter, and put away her writing materials. Facing her reflection in the mirror, she brushed out her long hair with slow, sure strokes, thinking of Jesse and the torment he was suffering. If only she could help, but there was nothing she could say that would ease his pain, nothing.

Cathy turned down her coverlet and slipped beneath the cool sheets of her bed, inhaling the faint scent of lavender. It was familiar and comforting, yet she could not relax. Finally, after an hour of tossing and turning, of the tormented distraction of her thoughts, she lit her bedside lamp and tried to read. Even that didn't seem to help, but Cathy at last yielded to the dry pricking of her heavy eyelids.

She hadn't realized she'd fallen asleep or that the book had fallen from her relaxed hand to the hooked rug beside the bed, and it was Jesse who bent to pick it up and close it, placing it gently on the nightstand. He gazed down at Cathy's sleeping face, his features haggard and drawn. His throat worked convulsively, and he gave a slight shake of his dark head. It was best— he had convinced himself of that—but it would be hard to return to this house knowing that Cathy was no longer there. He must tell her to leave. . . .

"Cathy," he said, almost as a whisper.

She stirred slightly in her sleep, her long lashes fluttering against her cheeks but not lifting, and Jesse said her name again, softly, but loud enough to penetrate her slumber.

"Cathy. Cathy, wake up."

The sweep of dark lashes fluttered like delicate, fragile butter-fly wings, lifting to reveal glowing, dark eyes. "Jesse?"

"Yes. Cathy, I must talk to you."

She sat up, rubbing the slumber from her eyes, gazing at him in sleepy gratitude that he was not looking at her with hatred or fire in his eyes. "What is it, Jesse? What can I do?"

Solemnly, with very little inflection at all in his flat, dull tone, he said, "I've come to a decision, Cathy. I've been thinking about it for a while, and now . . . well, now there is no longer a reason to put it off."

"Put what off, Jesse? What are you talking about?"

"I've made plans for the girls to travel to Paris."

Confused, Cathy echoed, "Paris?"

"Yes. I have friends there, a childless couple who would like to take them in and see to their education. They are influential people and would treat the girls well."

"But . . . Leigh and Erin are so young to be sent away!"

Shaking his head, Jesse sighed. "No, I have already made the arrangements, in any case."

"Then my position has been terminated," she said softly, gazing into his dark, liquid eyes, which lacked expression. He seemed so . . . defeated . . . so weary and lifeless.

Jesse nodded. "Yes. You must leave."

Flinching, Cathy swallowed the sudden lump in her throat. After all, this wasn't unexpected. . . .

"And as to our other . . . situation . . . I have thought about that also."

"Situation? *Situation?*" Cathy stared at him. "Are you referring to our *love* as a situation, as if it were a mere trifle?"

"No, no, I didn't mean it that way."

"Then say what you mean!" she snapped.

He stiffened. "Very well. I want you to leave, Cathy. I want you to go away because I can no longer bear the sight of you. I have arranged for you to receive your year's salary as compensation. That will allow you to find another position without undue stress. And, of course, I shall write you a letter of recommendation."

"Shall you?" Cathy spat, anger surging in her. "And what shall the letter say, Mr. Lamont? That I am a basically competent governess but one who is prone to falling in love with her employer? Or shall you be a bit more crude, perhaps!"

"Cathy!" Jesse recoiled as if she had struck him.

"Oh, don't *Cathy* me! Do you think by sending away everyone who cares anything about you that you will be guarded from any more hurt? Is that your solution, Jesse? No love, no pain?"

"You don't know what you're saying!" he ground out.

"And you don't know what you're doing!" she shot back.

They glared at each other for several long moments, and the tension between them crackled like tiny bolts of lightning. Even as she gazed at him with fire and anger, Cathy could see that he had somehow gotten grayer at the temples, that the silver flecks of hair had increased, and that the circles under his eyes were dark and his cheeks gaunt. *Oh, Jesse, what are you doing to yourself? To us?*

But she said nothing aloud, meeting his flinty gaze with one of her own, her dark eyes steely and hard. Jesse reached out for her, his fingers biting into her upper arms as he lifted her from the bed, pulling her up and giving her a swift shake hard enough to rattle her teeth.

"Maybe you're right," he growled, "maybe I've learned to

protect myself. Or maybe I've just decided to bury my child and leave this house forever, leave all of it behind and not risk any more pain because I've dared to love another human being! Can you blame me?"

Hot tears stung her eyes then, and Cathy put out a hand to stroke the side of his face, rubbing at the clenched muscles in his jaw, trying to smooth away the pain. Her voice broke as she murmured, "Don't do this, Jesse. We love you; Leigh and Erin need you. *I* need you."

In spite of his harsh, hurting grip, she strained toward him, her lips brushing lightly against his taut mouth, ignoring the pain he was inflicting with his iron fingers. Suppressing a groan, Jesse pushed her away from him.

"No!" he said harshly.

"Would you let Caroline destroy us all?" she whispered, catching herself on the edge of the bed. Her dark hair swirled around her face, curling around the curve of her throat, framing the thrust of her breasts in the thin nightdress she wore, and Jesse turned away.

"I could kill Caroline with my bare hands," he said with such vehemence that Cathy shivered at his intensity.

"She's not worth it."

"No, she's not." His voice was curt, abrupt, his words clipped. "The girls are leaving for Paris in a fortnight. I want you gone by then. See to it."

Defeated, Cathy collapsed onto the mattress. "Yes, I shall leave," she said softly, raw emotions thickening her voice. He nodded, and strode swiftly from the bedroom without looking back, without pausing to hear Cathy's added whisper: "I'll leave for now, but I will be back, Jesse Lamont!"

Chapter 25

*H*arrow Road in Kensal Green was lined with carriages that bright Tuesday morning. The last few days of March had faded into April, signaling the arrival of spring. A strong wind whipped across the rolling hills, making tall trees sway and the limbs undulate. Gazing out the carriage window, Cathy had the bleak thought that the trees were bent in a posture of mourning for the dead child passing by in the crepe-swathed litter. Grass spread in a fresh green carpet over the cemetery, and flowers had begun to thrust tender shoots from the ground.

Such a contradiction, the buds and bright green of the grass coming alive in a world dedicated to the dead . . .

Dark thoughts cluttered her mind, and she clung tightly to her self-control as she recalled a Bible verse she had not thought of in some time. *This day I am going the way of all the earth.* Appropriate words on this day, Cathy reflected sadly.

She shivered in the cool carriage, and thought of Jesse ahead in the black funeral coach with his two nieces. Was he thinking of the futility of his daughter's short life, or was he merely accepting what fate had delivered him? Jesse had never seemed especially introspective, being more prosaic about life, yet he had a sharp intelligence that must leave him wondering as to the reasons for all this. Perhaps a simpler man would have accepted it all with equanimity, knowing that death was a part of life, but Jesse had a more complex intellect. Hadn't she spent time in his library, perusing his books with appreciation and a faint sense of surprise?

There had been a diverse selection of volumes, from Shakespeare to the current works of Bulwer-Lytton, indicating that Jesse certainly possessed a philosophy regarding life and man. Cathy sensed that Jesse's convictions would be distinctly earthbound in origins, but no less intelligent for that.

Her hands clenched around the silk strings of her reticule as the carriage lurched to a halt, and she exchanged a long glance with Miss Mooney. It was time.

Cathy and Miss Mooney joined Erin and Leigh at the side of the black carriage where they'd ridden with their uncle, and Miss Mooney took Erin's small hand in her own. Cathy did likewise with Leigh, her gaze shifting to Jesse's cold, hard face. He held himself ever so stiffly, gazing straight ahead, ignoring any who attempted to speak to him. The only flicker of emotion he betrayed was when four men gathered to carry the tiny coffin bearing Jill. Then it seemed as if the muscle in his clenched jaw would leap from beneath the skin. Her heart ached for him, but he neither expected nor wanted her comfort, and Cathy did not offer it.

The pallbearers gently placed the casket on the raw earth beside the open grave, and Cathy averted her gaze from the dark, yawning hole. Her throat ached with unshed tears, and her fingers tightened around Leigh's small hand. The mourners—most of whom she did not know, recognizing only Lord Bothmourne as one of the pallbearers—gathered around the coffin.

The brisk wind whipped at full skirts and tugged at the black veils covering the women's faces, and the men held tightly to their hats to keep them from being blown away. Jesse was the only bare-headed man there, and his thick, dark hair was blown back from his eyes, leaving his forehead bare and his black eyes narrowed against the wind.

Cathy looked down at Leigh for a moment, and when she looked up again she was startled to see that Jesse intended to speak at Jill's funeral. He held a small book in his open palms, and the wind ruffled the pages so that he had to hold them down to read. Jesse cleared his throat several times, and his face was carefully blank as he began to read aloud.

> "I am the daughter of earth and water,
>   And the nursling of the sky;
> I pass through the pores of ocean and shores;
>   I change but I cannot die.
> For after the rain when never a stain
>   The pavilion of Heaven is bare,
> And the winds and sunbeams with their convex gleams
>   Build up the blue dome of air,
> I silently laugh at my own cenotaph,
>   And out of the caverns of rain,
> Like a child from the womb, like a ghost from the tomb,
>   I arise and unbuild it again."

He snapped the book shut, and the crackle of the pages was muffled by the worn covers. Jesse's voice had broken on the last word, and its faint echo seemed to linger in the air like a wounded bird, drifting over the mourners' heads.

A minister's voice began the age-old phrase of "ashes to ashes, dust to dust," his thin voice almost drowned out by the mournful keening of the wind through the bare tree limbs. He held an open Bible in his hands and read from it as the mourners listened.

Glancing at Jesse as he lifted the first fistful of dirt, Cathy watched as the small oak coffin was gently lowered into the grave by ropes. It disappeared with only a whisper of sound, and then the ropes were let go. Jesse took a faltering step forward, and he stood with the fistful of dirt held out over the grave. It was several moments before he could open his fingers and allow the fresh earth to fall atop the casket.

Cathy winced at the thud of dirt and pebbles rattling atop the oak, and forced herself forward to bend and take a palmful of dirt from the mound. All the mourners filed past the open grave, each one releasing a small amount of earth. Only Erin and Leigh stayed back, and they were the last to approach their sister's grave. Each held out a fist of rose petals, slowly releasing them to drift down into the grave. When Cathy glanced up, her throat raw from the ache of holding back a sob, she met Jesse's anguished gaze.

Dark eyes met and held hers, and there was a world of unspoken pain in their depths. "Thank you for being with me at this time," he said hoarsely, and she could only nod. Any attempt to speak would have brought forth the pent-up emotion of tears, and Cathy was afraid the dam would burst.

She said nothing as Jesse put an arm around each of the children's shoulders and turned them away from the grave and toward his carriage. She was glad he seemed to have grown closer to them in his grief, and hoped that somehow the love of his nieces could help soften the worst of his pain. After all, Erin and Leigh had loved Jill, too.

"It's time to go, Cathy," Miss Mooney was saying behind her, and Cathy turned gratefully.

"God bless you," she murmured, accepting the offer of Miss Mooney's arm. Tucking her hand in the crook of the older woman's arm, Cathy thought how much of a comfort she had been in the past days. If not for Miss Mooney's tireless efforts, and her care for the bewildered young girls, who had lost their half sister and playmate, it would have been a wretched situation. "Thank God I have you with me, Miss Mooney," Cathy said as they reached the carriage.

"Thank God we have each other," Miss Mooney replied with a meaningful glance in Jesse Lamont's direction.

There was no reply for that, nothing but a heartfelt surge of sympathy for a man who could not accept comforting.

"Did you notice that Mr. Mahoney was present at the service?" Miss Mooney inquired after they had rocked along Harrow Road for a quarter hour. Cathy's brow rose in faint surprise.

"No. No, I hadn't. I didn't really recognize anyone," she confessed. "I was too afraid to look closely at other faces, afraid if I saw tears I would break down. That would not have done Jes—any of us any good."

Ignoring Cathy's slip, Miss Mooney nodded. "I felt the same. Still, it was rather a surprise seeing him there. I never had the impression he was very fond of Mr. Lamont. Of you, yes, but not Mr. Lamont."

"He seemed fond of all three girls," Cathy replied absently, gazing out the carriage window at the passing scenery of thatched cottages and undulating hills.

Shifting on the uncomfortable carriage seat, Miss Mooney remarked, "I wonder how he found out about Jill's death. It was not common knowledge as far as I knew, but still, I suppose people talk. Had you seen him lately?"

Cathy shook her head, rolling it from side to side against the frayed velvet squabs. "No," she said wearily, "not since that day in the park. I received a note from him once, but it arrived the afternoon of . . . of Jill's death, and I promptly forgot it. Odd, I reread Miss Nightingale's letter, but simply forgot about Ned's."

"You didn't reply?"

"Oh, no. I think the letter is in my desk drawer, but with all that happened, I didn't remember it until just now."

"Perhaps he finally came to understand that you did not return his affections," Miss Mooney commented.

A slight smile touched the corners of her lips as Cathy nodded. "I suppose he finally realized that I could not return them, as well as the reason why."

Miss Mooney wisely forbore to respond to that remark, and said instead, "I find it rather a relief that he no longer haunts us. He was nice enough, I suppose, but in a peculiar sort of way."

"I always knew you didn't like him," Cathy said, "and just put it down to your innate dislike of the vagaries of an artistic temperament."

Snorting with disdain, Miss Mooney murmured a vague comment about how artistic temperaments ofttimes covered a multitude of sins, then fell silent. The carriage rocked along at a sedate pace as each woman gazed out the window, and finally Miss Mooney asked, "Are you thinking about the children— Erin and Leigh?"

Startled by the woman's perceptiveness, Cathy glanced up with wide dark eyes. "Why . . . yes! And I was thinking about Jes—Mr. Lamont, as well. Did you notice anything peculiar about his reactions today?"

"Peculiar? It's hard to define that term when you're speaking about a man who has just lost a young niece, but yes, I did notice a certain *reserve* about Mr. Lamont. And it was a bit odd that he read such an *unusual* poem instead of some verse from the Bible."

"Father Timothy read from the Bible," Cathy pointed out.

"Yes, that's true. Church of England, isn't he? I seem to recall his once visiting the house."

"It was Father Timothy who bore the news of Jill's death to Caroline Lamont at Lord Bothmourne's suggestion," Cathy said quietly.

Nodding, Miss Mooney observed, "I cannot imagine how difficult it must have been for even that poor, deranged woman to learn that her eldest child had died only a few moments after her abrupt and ignominious departure."

"I find it most awkward to feel even an instant's sympathy," Cathy said firmly. "I am much more concerned about Jesse Lamont and his apparent lack of emotion. He was far too composed at the funeral."

Reflecting, Miss Mooney gave a slow nod and said, "Yes, I think you are right, Cathy. He was. Perhaps that is why he took his nieces with him in his carriage. Perhaps he feels the need to be near them."

Shaking her head, Cathy frowned. "I don't know. Somehow I feel as if there's something else. Anger, grief, and deep depression would be a more normal reaction than this . . . this calm acceptance! He's too passive, and I always considered Jesse Lamont a man with fight in him."

"Are you forgetting that only a few months ago his own sister-in-law attacked him with a loaded pistol? He was seriously wounded, and now his niece died in his arms—no, I find his reaction normal enough," Miss Mooney disagreed.

Recalling that few knew of Jesse's true relationship to Jill, Cathy was silent for a moment. And she smiled when she heard Miss Mooney vigorously defend a man toward whom she had once harbored great disdain.

"Perhaps his depression is due to the severe crisis he has had to undergo in recent months," Miss Mooney was arguing. "The poor man! No wonder he is quiet! He is a gentleman and under a great deal of strain!"

"Enough!" Cathy begged. "I concede your valid points, Miss Mooney! But consider that I am just as concerned as you are," she added. "I am worried that there is an underlying reason for Jesse Lamont's placid demeanor. And . . ." She paused to regain her faltering composure, then continued softly. "And I only want what is best for him."

* * *

As their carriage lurched to a halt in front of the house at 8 Devonshire Terrace, Cathy was surprised to see Lord Bothmourne's carriage pull away. She had thought he might stay awhile to comfort Jesse, but apparently not. He would have noticed anything too different in Jesse's mood.

After descending from the carriage, Cathy turned to help Miss Mooney and was distracted by the sound of another carriage drawing to a halt behind theirs. Half turning to see who had come to visit on this, of all days, Cathy's eyes grew wide. Caroline Lamont stepped down from the carriage in a flurry of moiré skirts and silk petticoats.

Glancing at Miss Mooney, Cathy said tersely, "Please alert Pickworth that Mrs. Lamont is here. I shall try to detain her as long as possible."

Scurrying up the steps, Miss Mooney never glanced back as she shoved open the front door and disappeared into the house. Caroline had moved up the sidewalk, and Cathy now stepped in front of her.

"What do you want here?" she demanded shortly.

Caroline lifted a penciled brow. "I hardly think that is any of your concern!" she snapped.

But when she made another attempt to pass, Cathy again stepped in her path, saying, "Please, Mrs. Lamont. Now is not the best time to visit. Surely you understand that."

Flinging back her bright head, Caroline sneered, "Of course I do! That was my child who was buried today, and I was not even allowed to attend her funeral! Don't try to stop me from seeing Jesse Lamont, Miss Weston, for I intend to do so at once!"

After a brief hesitation, Cathy moved aside. Apart from a violent act of prevention, there was nothing she could do to stop Caroline from approaching the house. It would be up to Pickworth or Jesse now.

Sweeping past in triumph, Caroline rapped sharply on the front door, then pushed it open and stepped inside. Her backward glance was seething with malice, and Cathy was spurred to follow immediately.

Pickworth was barring Caroline's path, as Cathy had hoped, and as he inquired in his iciest tone just what she meant by coming in uninvited, Jesse stepped from his study to determine the cause of the furor in the entry hall. He stopped short at seeing Caroline with Cathy right behind her, his dark brow lowering over his black eyes in a tight frown.

"What is the meaning of this, Pickworth?"

The elderly servant began to explain that Mrs. Lamont had barged in without being admitted, but Caroline interrupted boldly. "I must see you at once, Jesse!"

"We have nothing to discuss," he said stiffly, and she surged forward.

"Oh, but I think we do! I shall not leave this house until I have said what I came to say, and if you attempt to have your servants remove me, I shall make things very, very difficult."

Her fixed, glassy glare was so intent that Jesse paused, then finally gave a curt nod of his head. "Very well," he consented. "I will give you five minutes of my time and no more. Ever."

Standing silently in the still-open doorway, Cathy could not speak as she watched Caroline precede Jesse into his study. Danger shrieked at her, making her scalp prickle and her throat tighten, but she was helpless to interfere. Surely Jesse would be wary of this woman, knowing her capabilities as he did. Cathy looked at Pickworth, who had such a strained expression on his face that she knew she must look the same.

"He'll be all right," she said softly, and the older man gave a reluctant shake of his head.

"I hope so," he said, "I hope so."

They both waited. Cathy closed the front door and paced small squares in the foyer while Pickworth stood by stiffly with his face blank and his hands trembling. Time dragged. Five minutes passed, then another five, and still no sound from the study. There was only the muffled murmur of voices that could be heard, but no specific words.

Another five minutes passed slowly. Then Cathy and Pickworth were startled to hear Caroline scream shrilly. "I should kill you!" came the fierce cry, followed by a bark of harsh male laughter.

Cathy and Pickworth surged toward the door just in time to hear Jesse's snarling reply that she had already killed him for all intents and purposes. As Cathy gripped the door latch with the intention of pushing it open, she heard a sharp, single shot tear through the sudden silence.

"Dear God!" Cathy shrieked, shoving at the door with all her strength. She could feel Pickworth beside her, and for one terrible moment she thought the door must be locked and that Jesse was lying dead inside with another bullet wound. Then the door gave way all at once, swinging open as Cathy pawed frantically at the latch, sending her surging through the opening with Pickworth close behind.

Instead of finding Jesse sprawled on the floor as she expected, Cathy's first glance was of the pistol lying on the floor near the desk. Her second horrified glance was of Jesse Lamont bending a struggling Caroline backward over his desk, his hands curled around her throat as he slowly strangled the life from her. Caroline was gasping and retching, making terrible gurgling sounds as she clawed at Jesse's fingers.

"Pickworth!" Cathy cried, stumbling toward the struggling pair. "Pickworth, do something!"

The elderly servant stood immobilized for a moment, but another scream from Cathy propelled him forward. Though thin, Pickworth was wiry, and he firmly grasped one of Jesse's arms with both hands, pleading that he stop.

Cathy grabbed at Jesse's other arm, panting as she tugged at it, her voice a half sob as she begged him to stop. "Dear God, Jesse, don't do this! Oh, please don't do this, Jesse!"

But Jesse's grip didn't slacken, and his face was as hard and cold as marble as he kept his grip on Caroline's throat. Cathy beat at him with her fist and he flinched, but still didn't let go, and she screamed in his ear, "Stop it, Jesse! If not for my love, for the love of the children who are left!"

A flicker of doubt quivered briefly in his eyes, and Caroline sagged back against the desk as he slowly released his grip. Deep purple marks already marred the smoothness of her throat, and Caroline gagged and choked as she tried painfully to suck in air.

"I wanted to kill her," Jesse said in a curiously flat tone, holding out his hands and gazing at them as if they belonged to someone else. "I wanted to choke the life from her lying, wicked body." He looked up at Cathy.

"But you didn't kill her, Jesse," she whispered. "She's still alive. Jesse, she's still alive."

His gaze focused on Cathy as if just noticing her, and then his hands flashed out to draw her into his embrace. He buried his face in her hair, holding her close, feeling her slender body next to his. *Can I ever let her go?*

Pickworth, who was half smiling at this tender exhibition from his employer, turned to Caroline and his smile faded. "I think you will live," he said coldly, helping her up from the desktop.

Caroline shot him a narrow glance, her hands cupping her bruised throat and massaging the tender flesh. She tried to speak but her voice was only a weak gasp, a harsh, guttural sound without form. Finally, with the aid of a glass of water—coldly and unsympathetically offered by Pickworth—she was able to make herself understood by gestures and hoarse whispers.

"I . . . want . . . to . . . go . . . home . . ."

"I'll fetch a carriage," Pickworth said immediately, glad that the woman would soon be out of the house. As he left the study, he bent and scooped up the forgotten pistol, placing it firmly in his coat pocket.

Jesse paid Caroline not the slightest bit of attention, seeming to have forgotten her existence. For the flame-haired woman who saw in his face her own loss as he held Cathy in his loving embrace, it was sheer torture. A broken sound emerged from between her dry lips, and Jesse finally lifted his head to look directly at the woman he had just tried to kill. There was no love in his eyes, no emotion beyond a faint glint of pity, and Caroline briefly closed her eyes. She'd lost her husband, her child, and she'd lost Jesse. It was painful, and it tore at her heart. Her shoulders slumped forward in defeat.

Recognizing this, Jesse put Cathy gently aside and moved toward Caroline. His voice was flat, remote, as if he were giving directions to a stranger as he said, "I do not love you, Caroline. I don't think I ever did. I was obsessed with you, perhaps, but not really in love. I do not ever want to have to see you again, not here in my house or in any part of the world. You gave me a child, and for that I am grateful, but now she is dead. Go, and do not ever come back, or I will not be responsible for what I may do. Do you understand that?"

Fearfully, with a new respect in her watery green eyes, Caroline nodded, still unable to speak. She backed away from Jesse and went through the study door, and Cathy could hear the rapid tapping of her footsteps in the entry hall, then the slamming of the front door.

When Jesse turned back to Cathy, she fell into his embrace, murmuring against his chest, "I thought she had shot you again."

He shrugged. "She didn't really want to kill me. She just wanted to control me, as she has always done with one ploy or another."

Releasing Cathy, Jesse moved to the sideboard and picked up the crystal decanter of brandy. He poured it into two glasses without bothering to ask Cathy if she wanted any, then turned to her and held out the glass.

"To the future," he said solemnly.

Cathy took the glass, circling it with her fingers, gazing deeply into his eyes. "Is there one—for us, I mean?"

Frowning, Jesse said softly, "I don't know. I do know that I don't want to send you or the girls away. . . ."

Chapter 26

Gazing at him with her heart in her eyes, Cathy asked cautiously, "What do you mean?"

Silence fell, and the clock on the mantel ticked loudly as the minutes passed. Finally Jesse set his glass of brandy down on the desk and moved to take Cathy's from her unresisting hand. "Perhaps I shouldn't have said that," he murmured quietly, then turned away.

Cathy watched as he went to the french doors looking out onto the garden and stood with his face close to the glass panes. It was growing green in the garden, and early irises and crocuses had already begun to thrust up from beneath the leafy mulch of the well-tended flower beds. A soft sigh slipped from Jesse as he regarded the grounds with sadness. So many new growing things, with winter behind and spring promising new life. On the way back from the cemetery he had seen new lambs frolicking in the fields, heard the bawling of calves, and seen the stiff-legged gait of newborn colts trotting beside their mothers. Life anew, but . . . for him? Could he begin again? Dare he love again?

Cathy stepped close, and he turned to face her. "Jesse, I know that you are torn between what you fear and what is true. I understand. I think you will be able to decide what you want if

I leave for a time. Stay with the girls, for they need you, but let me go so that you may see for yourself what you want."

After a moment's thoughtful reflection, Jesse nodded. "Yes, I think I need to spend some time with Erin and Leigh. It's a bit painful for me right now, seeing them run about when Jill—my child—is dead, but I shall cope with it the best I can."

Cathy put her hand on his sleeve. "I know about Jill. I also know that she loved you, Jesse."

His face contorted with pain and he whirled back around to stare outside. His voice was muffled as he said, "No, I don't think she ever understood—"

"You wrong her, Jesse. She did. She loved her mother, yes, but it was with the kind of love one has for an . . . an animal that has been injured, or is sick. I saw that in her face that day, Jesse. She felt protective of Caroline, felt that someone should care for her. You didn't need Jill, and her mother did."

Jesse's voice was a hoarse whisper. "Oh, but I did need her and didn't know it! Just like . . . just like I may need you, Cathy."

"We'll find that out, but now is too soon to think of such things. You need to rest, Jesse, and I think perhaps I do, too. The past months have been hectic for me."

Slowly turning back to face her, Jesse said, "You're so independent, Cathy . . . so strong . . ."

She certainly didn't feel strong at that moment, when she wanted to fling herself into his arms and cling to him, to beg him not to let her go, to taste the sweetness of his lips and feel the crisp strands of his dark hair beneath her exploring fingers. Cathy battled the urge to deny her words, instead resolving to allow Jesse to do just as she suggested. It would never work between them if he didn't *know* that he wanted her, needed her, as she needed him.

"Where will you go?" Jesse was asking, and Cathy gave herself a mental shake.

"Back to the hotel with Miss Mooney. It will be the only logical answer, of course."

"And your father?"

"I doubt that he will come for me again. He has disowned me, remember?" she said lightly, betraying none of the pain that casual comment caused.

"Dear Cathy, perhaps—"

"No, Jesse. I can take care of myself. You may find that your life is much simpler without me, you know. I cannot expect you to be responsible for me just because of what happened to us. That smacks of the burden Caroline put on you all these years, and I won't do that to you."

"I insist that you accept a year's salary as compensation for early departure from your position," Jesse stated firmly, but Cathy was already shaking her dark head, silky strands of hair loosened in her struggle with the door whipping about her face.

"No, Jesse," she said. "I won't accept a shilling more than I've earned. Don't do for me what you would not do for anyone else."

Reaching out, Jesse tucked a sable curl behind her left ear, dragging his finger across her cheek as he drew back. "But you'll have to find work again," he protested softly.

"Yes, and I shall."

"Perhaps I'm wrong to let you go."

Lifting one hand in protest, Cathy smiled. "I am not leaving just because of you, Jesse. I need to rest, to have some peace in my life for a time. I have to have order to enable myself to think clearly, and with a reasonable amount of sanity."

A small grin tugged at his mouth. "Are you hinting that I have driven you mad?"

A gurgle of laughter escaped Cathy. "Yes, in a way you have!"

"I'm sorry," he said without a trace of repentance in his laughing, dark eyes.

Cathy wrinkled her nose at him. Her tone was husky and warm as she said, "I'm not. I have no regrets as far as you're concerned, Jesse Lamont!"

Cathy rose early the next morning, filled with energy and determination. She made arrangements to move back to the hotel, went through her armoire and gave away clothes to the maids that she no longer needed, made a study plan for Erin and Leigh for the coming month so they would not fall behind in their studies, and cleaned out her dresser drawers, packing things neatly away in a large steamer trunk.

A glance at the clock told her it was well after noon, and she decided to go downstairs and check with Annie, the cook, to see if she could beg a tray. And she'd also promised to give her Miss Mooney's recipe for fudge cake for the girls. Miss Mooney had jealously guarded the recipe, and a subsequent attempt to duplicate the Christmas cake had ended in disaster. Annie, of course, had been quite put out with Miss Mooney, but no amount of pleading would budge the older lady; the secret recipe remained just that—secret. But now Miss Mooney had had a change of heart, and Cathy was to share the recipe with an anxious and eager Annie.

As she reached the landing, Cathy's footsteps slowed. She heard male voices, and recognized Jesse's raised in anger. She paused and peered around the corner post to see three strange gentlemen and Lord Bothmourne conversing with Jesse in the foyer.

"I was here all day except for a couple of hours in the afternoon!" Jesse was saying in a tight, angry voice.

"Where did you go?" one man inquired in a polite, but persistent voice.

Jesse almost snarled at him. "For a damned ride—alone!"

"Really, Inspector Marrow," Lord Bothmourne put in, "Mr.

Lamont had just buried his niece! It is perfectly natural that he should need some time alone. I protest your incivility!"

Patiently, as if he dealt with such resistance all the time, the man flicked a polite smile in the duke's direction and asked Jesse, "Did anyone go out with you? A coachman, perhaps?"

Bothmourne snorted irritably as Jesse shook his head and the inspector scribbled in a small notebook. "Well, of all the most absurd! . . ."

"Oh, leave them alone, John," Jesse said with a weary, careless wave of one hand. "They're only doing their jobs, and I really don't care at this point."

Cathy crept farther down the steps as Jesse pivoted and stalked to his study door, indicating that the men should follow. He left the door open after they had filed inside, and she couldn't resist drawing closer to hear. An inspector? Of what? For what? The step creaked under her foot and she paused, straining to hear.

A voice drifted from the study. "Was Mrs. Lamont at the funeral, Mr. Lamont?"

Slumped in the chair behind his desk, Jesse shook his head. "No."

Lieutenant Browne arched a brow in surprise. "She didn't even attend her own daughter's funeral? I find that most astonishing!"

"Be that as it may, she did not," Jesse retorted sharply. "She did come here yesterday afternoon, however. It is hard to absorb the fact that she is dead."

Cathy reeled, catching the banister to keep from tumbling down the last three stairs and ending in a heap on the foyer floor. *Dead? Caroline?*

Gathering her composure, Cathy strode boldly to the study door and entered, pausing just inside the room. Jesse stood and indicated her with one arm. "Gentlemen, this is Miss Weston, the children's governess."

A faintly skeptical, suspicious glint flared briefly in the inspector's eyes, then was gone. But not before Cathy saw and noted it. She stiffened, striding forward and saying, "Good afternoon, sirs. I overheard your conversation, and was moved to learn the details." Deciding boldness was the best policy in light of the inspector's inquiring gaze, she said, "How did Caroline die?"

Ignoring that question, Lieutenant Browne asked, "Were you present when Mrs. Lamont came to this house?"

"Leave Miss Weston out of this, for the love of God!" Jesse exploded.

"She might provide some useful information, Mr. Lamont," Inspector Marrow said quietly.

Jesse was quick to say, "I don't wish to have her involved, Inspector. Your inquiry can be made later."

"Ah, but it cannot. You see, I must insist that you and she and whoever else I think may help answer all and any of my questions. Caroline Lamont did not just die, Mr. Lamont, not in an accident, and not because of illness. She was murdered, sir."

"Murdered!" Cathy could not help gasping. "But who . . . how was she . . . oh, no!" she added when she saw the inspector's gaze shift back to Jesse.

"I'm afraid that I must inform you that you are under arrest for suspicion of murdering Mrs. Caroline Lamont," the inspector was saying to a taut-lipped Jesse.

Lord Bothmourne quickly stepped forward and put a quelling hand on Cathy's arm. The tension in his fingers warned her not to offer a protest, and she closed her open mouth with an effort. *Jesse—arrested for murder!*

"I say, Inspector," the duke was saying coolly, "this is most irregular! I must protest at your cavalier treatment of Mr. Lamont."

"I register your protest, Your Grace, and shall duly note it to the magistrate," Marrow said politely. "I must, however, do what I feel is best."

Unexpectedly recalling that she had once informed Ned Mahoney that Jesse was not a murderer, Cathy strangled the desire to laugh hysterically. This was so absurd! It could not be true, could not actually be happening while she stood by and did nothing!

"Take care of the children for me, John," Jesse was saying calmly as he lifted up his overcoat from the back of a chair. "And see to the household," he added with a meaningful glance in Cathy's direction.

"Never fear, Jesse, I shall see to all details. I mean to join you at C.I.D. headquarters in a short time."

Cathy shook her head. *Criminal Investigations Department.* It had such a final ring to it. She much preferred the more common title of Scotland Yard, called that for its offices in the buildings once occupied by Scottish royalty during visits to London. Somehow it sounded less threatening to her, less official.

Pickworth arrived with a distressed expression and tears welling in his eyes, and silently handed Jesse his hat. "To keep your head warm, sir," the old man said, and Jesse smiled.

"Thank you, Pickworth. I see that the household is as alert as ever," Jesse replied with a cocked brow.

"Yes, sir. We do manage to learn what is necessary," Pickworth replied with shaky dignity.

Cathy stood with Pickworth and the duke as Jesse was escorted from the house by the inspector and his two men. Her lips trembled, and she longed to run to Jesse and spirit him away from the officials who were putting him into their carriage.

"It will be all right," Bothmourne said, and she shook her head.

"I don't see how."

"It will."

True to his word, Lord Bothmourne lingered long enough to assure Cathy of his intentions to rescue Jesse. "And don't say anything to those bumbling idiots!" he added testily. "They do more harm than good most of the time. I cannot imagine their arresting Jesse like this, but there you have it."

"Your grace, I know Jesse did not kill Caroline! But yesterday—when she barged in and made a scene—he not only threatened her, he tried to strangle her!"

A frown marred his clear brow, and Bothmourne shook his head. "Devil of a fix! Well, don't fret over it. Jesse is innocent, and I shall see that he doesn't hang for it. I am certain that our dear Caroline had many unsavory friends who would have dearly loved to strangle her. All we have to do is discover which one."

Sighing, Cathy muttered, "I hope you're right."

"Of course I am. Now get some rest while I go down to Scotland Yard and argue with those doddering fools. It shan't take long. . . ."

Cathy watched from the open doorway while Bothmourne got into his own carriage and ordered his coachman to Scotland Yard. All her plans to leave on the morrow faded instantly, destroyed by these new developments. She would not leave while Jesse was in trouble. *In trouble*—it seemed a mild phrase for the truth of it. A devil of a fix, indeed, she mused.

Chapter 27

*I*t was a waking nightmare. The police arrived early the next morning and meticulously searched the house, looking for any clue that could possibly prove Jesse's guilt. They found none, and were gone by the time Cathy finally forced herself to go downstairs to the dining room for breakfast.

She sat numbly at the table, hearing echoes from earlier times when Jesse had also sat there, feeling a sense of disaster lurking in the corners. Pickworth had reluctantly placed the morning tabloids beside Cathy's untouched plate at her insistence, and she finally reached out and opened the top paper.

The headline screamed:

Revenge at last!
Woman shoots lover months earlier—
now found murdered!

Cathy shuddered. What a shocking display of exploitative journalism, she thought, and irritably snapped the paper closed again. Opening a more sedate tabloid, she read of how Caroline Lamont had been found strangled in her own lodgings, and that her dead husband's brother had been arrested for the crime. Even this subdued account hinted that it had been an act of passion for his brother's wife that had provoked Jesse.

"Miss Cathy," came Pickworth's soft, worried voice, "are you certain you should be reading such ridiculous accounts? After all, we *knew* Mrs. Lamont, and know that she was certainly not always such a . . . a *victim!* Why, she even came *here* with a pistol, and might very well have shot Mr. Lamont again if we had not intervened."

Looking up at his kind, strained face, which seemed to have gathered a host of new lines around the eyes and mouth, Cathy said softly, "It will be all right, Pickworth. By the way, what did you do with Caroline's pistol? The police did not mention finding it, you know."

A satisfied expression creased his face. "I hid it. I thought they might find it and use it as evidence against Mr. Lamont, so I kept it in my room. Shall I fetch it for you?"

"No! Oh, no, I don't need it." Cathy paused a moment, then said, "Since they have already searched Jesse's study, perhaps you should put it in his desk."

"Very good, Miss Cathy. And shall I have Annie prepare you something more to your taste? You've not eaten a bite of your morning repast."

Managing a faint smile, Cathy murmured, "I'm afraid I'm not very hungry this morning, Pickworth. I cannot think of a single thing that would be edible."

The elderly servant sighed. "I understand completely, Miss Cathy. Miss Mooney and the young ladies are not as hungry as usual, either. I brought back downstairs breakfast trays that were barely touched, though the little misses did eat their fresh fruit."

Smiling, Cathy said, "Erin and Leigh have always been partial to wild berries."

"Indeed they have, Miss Cathy."

"Pickworth?"

"Yes, Miss Cathy?"

"I should like for you to take around a note to Lord

Bothmourne, if you will. Do you mind? I mean, I want you to take it *personally*."

"I understand completely, Miss Cathy, and shall go and fetch my coat and the driver."

Rising from the table, Cathy hurried upstairs to fetch her writing paper. She penned a quick note to the duke, begging for information about Jesse. The apprehension and waiting were wearing at her nerves, fraying them into tatters, and she could not bear to wait much longer. Was he well? Was he frightened of the outcome of the investigation? None of those things could she write to Lord Bothmourne, of course, but Cathy thought of them as she sealed the small envelope and rose from her writing desk.

She found Pickworth in Jesse's study, and gave him the small square of vellum. "Deliver this into his hand only," she instructed. "I trust no other."

"Of course, Miss Cathy," Pickworth said, and shut Jesse's upper desk drawer before he placed the envelope into his coat pocket. Automatically straightening the blotter on the desk and rearranging the pens and ink bottles, Pickworth gave Cathy a solemn smile and promised to return immediately. "Shall I wait for an answer, Miss Cathy?"

"Yes, please," she replied. "I hope he will return with you, but if not, I would desire to know his reply."

"Very good, Miss Cathy. Beakins is below stairs if you should need anything before my return. Just pull the bell cord and he will come."

"Thank you, Pickworth."

Sitting alone in Jesse's study, Cathy contemplated the rich furnishings, rubbing with her fingertips at the tiny frown etched between her brow, hoping that Lord Bothmourne would return with Pickworth. Somehow it was comforting to sit in Jesse's study, gazing at the reminders of Jesse and visualizing him sitting behind the desk or pacing the floor, remembering his beloved face as he had gone to the butler's table and poured her a glass of brandy. Dear Jesse, how he loved his soothing bit of brandy! And it couldn't do her any harm, either, Cathy decided in that moment, rising decisively from the leather wing chair and crossing to the walnut table.

Brandy before ten—drunk again, she quoted silently with a smile, and lifted her half-filled glass to the unknown poet responsible for that line. The liquid burned a path down her throat, filling her nostrils with a rich aroma, soothing her frazzled nerves as it curled through her system. A remarkable remedy if taken in temperance, Cathy mused, and poured another half glass.

She ambled across the rich carpet and went to stand at the french doors looking out into the garden, her thoughts drifting. So many unanswered questions, so much to worry about with Jesse's future hanging in the balance.

Jesse. How would she survive without him? He consumed her every waking moment, filled her thoughts, his memory lurking in every corner of her brain. She could close her eyes and conjure up a visual image of Jesse, his dark eyes laughing, the tiny streaks that she thought so distinguished and handsome silvering his temples, adding distinction to an already handsome countenance. And if she let them, her thoughts would wander to the heated moments spent in his bed, with his strong, hard body close to hers, his broad shoulders and the muscled ridges of his flat belly and thighs . . . dear God, she had to stop thinking of him!

Swirling away from the french doors, Cathy went back to the butler's table and lifted the brandy decanter again before she paused. No, too much brandy would muddle her thoughts and leave her too confused to listen to Lord Bothmourne should he return with Pickworth. Slowly lowering the decanter back to the gleaming surface of the table, Cathy gave a long sigh.

The brass knocker on the front door gave a sharp rap, startling her from her thoughts, and Cathy half turned. It could not be Pickworth back so soon, and besides, he would just enter. Shuddering at the thought that it might be the police, she smoothed her skirts, tidied her hair, and strode from the study to the front door.

She swung it open to see Ned Mahoney on the front stoop, his fair hair neatly combed and his face gravely smiling. "Hello, Cathy."

"Hello, Ned. What . . . what a surprise. Do come in," she invited, holding open the door.

"Have the servants all left in a huff?" Ned inquired lightly as he entered the foyer. "I didn't expect for you to answer the door."

Cathy shut the door and indicated the parlor with a wave of her hand. "No, I was just the closest. Pickworth's out on an errand for me, and the others are all belowstairs right now and could not have heard the knock. Do come in and sit, Ned, and I shall ring for some tea."

"No, no tea, please. Just your company for a few minutes," Ned said quickly, preceding her into the parlor.

Cathy followed, offering to take Ned's coat and hat, but he shook his head. She nodded, and chose a chair next to the settee. The brandy was still warming her blood and leaving her relaxed, and Cathy gazed into the fire burning in the small hearth as Ned unbuttoned his overcoat and lowered his long body to the firm comfort of the settee.

"Ned, I would like to express my appreciation for your presence at little Jill's funeral," she said a moment later, turning back to him. He was relaxed and smiling, drawing off his riding gloves and tucking them into his pocket. Cathy added, "I did not see you, but Miss Mooney said you were there. I was too . . . too distressed to really notice anyone present."

"I understand," Ned said soothingly. "I would not have intruded on your grief, Cathy." There was a short pause. Then he said softly, "I read in the tabloids about Jesse being arrested for Caroline Lamont's murder. It seems as if death must come in threes, as I have always heard."

Cathy shuddered. "Threes? There have been only two—"

"But if Jesse is hanged, that will make three," Ned said softly.

Cathy surged to her feet. "Do not say that!" she spat furiously. "He will not hang! He did not kill Caroline!"

"Forgive me, Cathy," Ned said with an expression of dismay. "I did not mean to upset you!"

Clasping and unclasping her hands, Cathy began to pace the parlor floor. "Oh, perhaps you didn't, Ned, but that was an awful thing to say!"

Ned rose to his feet and reached out to take her hands between his, clasping them between his broad palms with a tender gesture. "I apologize. Perhaps I am just as upset as you are, and am saying the first thing that pops into my head." He gave her hands a squeeze, murmuring, "Forgive me?"

"Yes, of course, Ned, but please! Your ring is cutting into my hand," Cathy said, glancing down with a frown at their entwined fingers. Her face grew still, and she gazed at the silver ring on Ned's third finger, noting the unusual, intricate design. That ring—where had she seen it before? Certainly not on Ned's hand, because she had never noticed him wearing one. A quick recollection of a similar ring flashed through her mind, and she saw a dark shadowed face, a black mask, and a purring voice. . . .

Snatching her hands from his, Cathy jerked her head up to stare at Ned. He was watching her closely.

"Is there something the matter, Cathy?"

"No!" she said quickly, too quickly. "I . . . I drank some of Jesse's brandy, I'm afraid, and it has left me silly and imagining things."

"Imagining things? Like what things, Cathy?" came the silky question, and she shook her head.

"Silly things, things that could not be true . . . Oh, Ned! I feel as if I have become deranged with all that has happened these last months!" Cathy blurted, moving uneasily away from him. He was so still and stiff, staring at her with his pale, steady gaze, as if trying to penetrate the fog of her thoughts.

Then, suddenly holding out his hand, Ned said, "I never wear this ring, you know. It is a rather unusual piece, don't you think?"

Cathy nodded, her voice a whisper. "Yes. Yes, it is an unusual design. I don't think I've ever seen one like it."

"Haven't you?" Ned smiled and moved closer. "I think perhaps you have . . . once."

Cathy's heart was pounding furiously, and the blood that had so recently been warm in her veins was now cold and moving as sluggishly as ice water. She shook her head, trying not to believe that Ned Mahoney had been that masked intruder in Jesse's study, had been the man who had so brutally knocked her to the floor, had been the alleged spy who was searching for Jesse Lamont's documents. . . .

"It's all right, Cathy," Ned was saying in a silky tone that made her shiver, "I don't mind your knowing. You were bound to discover the truth sooner or later, you know. Perhaps I understood that without realizing it—hence, the decision to wear the ring today. I did wear it that night, you know."

Through stiff lips Cathy bluffed, "What night? I don't understand—"

"It won't work. You know. I see it in your face." Ned stepped closer. "I rarely wear the ring. It represents certain things I won't go into now, and I wear it only on . . . special occasions . . . like now. I came to finish it, my dear, and you are to help me."

"I . . . I don't know what you mean, Ned! Finish what? I really think I should—" Cathy had been moving away from him, closer to the bell cord dangling unobtrusively in a corner, but Ned anticipated her action.

"No, dear," he said, moving swiftly between Cathy and the cord, "I do not think we need tea or crumpets just now. I have other . . . delicacies in mind."

Jerking her close with iron-strong fingers cutting around her wrist, Ned held her body against his, his mocking lips only inches from hers, feeling her tremors as she shuddered against him. "Let me go!" she said feebly, and he shook his blond head.

"No, not yet, my sweet. I have duties to perform, and in spite of your lovely face and generous curves, I must attend to them first." He held her tightly against him so that she could not wrench away, and his voice was a warm whisper against her cheek as he said, "I knew you might put it all together one day, and I had to come and find out just what you knew. A stroke of luck finding you alone, but with Jesse out of the house at last, I knew I could see you."

Struggling against him, Cathy's mind was swiftly racing from possibility to possibility. "Why did you break into Jesse's study?" she asked after a moment. "If you work for the same government, there should be no reason for it."

"Precisely, my dear."

A long moment of silence descended, and with each tick of the ornate French clock on the mantel, Cathy grew more frightened. *Of course!*

"Did you plan my being here?" she asked when she could force the words past her frozen lips.

"Plan it? No, never that. Used our previous acquaintance, perhaps, but at first I was rather put out at your presence in Lamont's home."

"I see."

"Do you? How clever of you! But then, I always knew that beneath that fluffy exterior there lurked a rather fine mind." His grip tightened. "And now I have come to the rather sad conclusion that you will diminish my effectiveness in England if I allow you to go free. My affection for you cannot overshadow my goals, my dear. I am faced with a most perplexing problem —do I let you live when my own fate lies in your lovely little hands?"

Cathy swallowed the surge of panic rising in her throat and considered her options. To scream would only give him reason to be violent, and probably would do no good anyway since the servants were belowstairs and out of hearing. To struggle would be futile, for Ned's strength was wiry and firm. She must remain calm, for wit was her only hope.

"Death does come in threes, you know," she said lightly, and Ned laughed.

"Ever the wit, Cathy, dear! But it must be done without any of the blame being attached to me, as in Caroline's case."

Cathy shivered. "Caroline? Of course, you are the one who strangled her."

"Of course. I see my faith in your intelligence is not unfounded. The foolish woman, if only she had not been so wretchedly determined to pursue Jesse Lamont, everything could have been accomplished without a hitch. But she wasn't." Ned's voice had grown impatient, and he edged toward the still-open parlor door with Cathy clasped in front of him. "There are things I must do before I leave, and I should—"

"But how did you ever convince Caroline to fall in with your clever plans?" Cathy asked desperately, hoping Ned would be willing to boast of his genius and delay any action.

"Convince her? That idiot! She was so simple, so intent on having Jesse in her bed, that she was as malleable as potter's clay!" Ned laughed softly. "She didn't begin to cause me any trouble—excepting her inexpertise with a pistol, of course— until she discovered that I had painted a portrait of her children. I hadn't counted on that, you see. She had no idea that I knew you, or that I had ever been in this house. She had no idea of any of the truth, and probably never had an idea of her own in her entire life." His voice was contemptuous, filled with loathing, and Cathy shuddered inwardly as he continued. "It was all my doing, my plans, of course. I had to subtly convince her that by shooting Lamont she would remove any suspicion that might fall on her from her husband's death."

"William's death?"

"Yes. He had to be removed, you know. He wasn't as clever as Jesse, and he was inept. His bungling could have caused my government a great deal of inconvenience, and besides, William had no idea of the importance of the information he held. His very stupidity made him dangerous."

"And you caused his death by ramming William's boat with a felucca," Cathy said, recalling Bothmourne's words and his suspicion of Caroline. It hadn't been Caroline at all! It had been Ned—Ned all along! Poor misjudged Caroline, she had been a tool to gain his evil ends.

"Yes . . . yes, I did," Ned said, pleased by Cathy's perception. "Of course, Caroline had to arrange for William to be sailing that day in that particular area of the bay, and had to lure the hot-blooded Jesse from his brother's side. I imagine it wasn't too difficult for her. . . ."

Ignoring Ned's blatant attempt to irritate her with images of Caroline and Jesse, Cathy said casually, "No, I imagine not. I've heard that William loved to fish, and a word or two about a certain kind of fish in a certain secluded cove would do the trick."

Giving a sigh of admiration, Ned said, "I stand in awe of your deductive abilities, Miss Weston! I should have had you with me these past months, but your rather regrettable attachment to Mr. Lamont made that impossible, I'm afraid."

"I'm certain it did," Cathy answered primly, eyeing the bell cord and wondering if she could somehow escape from his grasp long enough to give it a good, sharp tug.

But then Ned was propelling her out the parlor door and into the entry hall, his grip firm and harsh as he edged her toward the study. "Shall we retire to Jesse's study, my dear? I have some explorations to do."

"You still haven't found what you need—the information you seek," Cathy observed. "Jesse must have hidden it very well."

"Perhaps so, but not so well that I cannot find it, given ample time and light," Mahoney returned coolly. "I was rather pressed for time and light the last time, if you will recall."

"Yes, I recall it very well. A scourge that visits most criminals who haunt houses at night, I believe."

"Your sarcasm is showing, Cathy," Ned chided gently, his fingers digging more harshly into her upper arms as he guided her across the foyer and into the study.

She relaxed into his grip, forcing herself to remain calm. "You won't find it here," she said, stalling for time.

"What do you mean?"

Cathy had never heard that note in Ned's voice, that hard inflection, and she had a sudden mental picture of him killing poor misguided Caroline with a cold, methodical ruthlessness— just as he would kill her when she served her purpose. Yes, Ned Mahoney must make an excellent spy for whatever government he served. . . .

"Just what I said. I heard Jesse talking to the duke—"

"Bothmourne! What a thorn in my side that insufferable man has been!" Ned said harshly. His fingers dug deeper. "I want to know what he said, Cathy."

"If you will only grip my arm less tightly, I can speak without pain," she said in a half gasp, agonized tears sparkling in her huge dark eyes. Ned obliged, loosening his grip just enough to allow her to speak without effort. "You must search in his bed-chamber, for that is where he has it hidden. I do not know the spot, but I am certain that as a reputable spy, you are well aware of the favorite hiding places of other spies," she said with only a trace of sarcasm.

Ned chuckled mirthlessly. "How caustic you can be when you wish, my dear! Very well—up the stairs we go."

But once in Jesse's Spartan bedroom, Ned frowned. It was clean and neat, bearing only general signs of its usual occupant. There were very few luxuries in the room, and not many ornaments to clutter the dresser or lamp tables.

After quietly and carefully locking the door behind him, Ned tied Cathy into a chair and began his swift search. He tore open drawers and pulled out everything in the armoire. The two framed portraits on the wall—one of them Ned's painting of the girls—were taken down and mercilessly torn apart. The French clock on the painted mantel was smashed and its works dissected. Clothes were inspected and pockets and linings ripped apart. The few books in the room were tossed onto the floor after a spurious glance through them, ruffling the pages to be certain there was no hidden compartment. Bed hangings were torn down and slashed with his pocketknife, and feather pillows were sliced open and the room littered with goose feathers. Even the mattress was hacked into ribbons. Ned at last looked up in frustration.

Cathy had remained quiet during this procedure, though wincing when Ned had slashed at the portrait of the girls. Looking away from the glitter of suppressed fury in his eyes, Cathy's glance focused on the litter at her feet. An open book lay almost touching her toes, its olive-green leather cover slashed apart by Ned's knife. No secret papers had been tucked inside, and he had carelessly tossed the volume aside. Now Cathy's focusing eyes grew large and round as she saw the neatly hand-printed words on pages carefully cut to fit inside the book. Her heart pounded, and she looked quickly away, hoping Ned had not noticed the direction of her gaze. Her toe pushed at the book, edging it beneath the table and out of his sight.

But Ned had noticed Cathy's sudden stiffening, the angle of her gaze, and the open book lying on the floor amid a heap of goose feathers and shredded silk bed hangings.

"What have we here?" he asked softly, crossing to where she sat tied in the boudoir chair. "Have I missed something?"

"I imagine you've missed a great deal in your misguided life," Cathy said sharply, "such as common decency and the possession of a conscience!"

"Tut, tut! Your wit is degenerating into banalities, my dear." A smile slanted his mouth as Ned stooped to pick up the book Cathy had tried to hide. "Well, well! I recall this particular volume quite well," he murmured, peering at the ruined cover. "Lamont always kept it near him for *sentimental* reasons, I presume. Ah! *The Anthology of 1829,* French edition."

"And how would you know that?" Cathy could not help asking.

He smiled. "Because, my dear Cathy, our lovely Caroline gave it to him. It is a volume of Shelley's poems, her personal favorite. Rather apropos that she gave her drowned husband's brother a volume of poetry written by a man who also drowned off the coast of Italy, don't you think? I always thought it had a certain delicious irony to it, but I'm not sure Jesse deduced the connection. Oh, don't let it distress you," he added at Cathy's repulsed expression, "I am certain that if Jesse had caught the connection he would have done the proper *moral* thing and tossed the book into the fire. Ah, but it is plain that he did not, for here we have my prize, right atop 'Julian and Maddalo.' "

Ned took his pocketknife and carefully sliced through the binder's glue holding in the inserted pages. He removed them with an expert flick of the blade, and perused the neat printing for several moments before looking up at Cathy again.

"And now that I have what I have needed for lo, these many weeks, my dear, I am confronted with a pretty problem indeed!"

"Oh, I promise not to tell anyone," Cathy said with weary sarcasm, and her effort at humor was richly received.

Laughing heartily, Ned shook his head. "I admire you immensely, Cathy Weston! Yes, more now than ever before!"

"But you obviously don't intend to let that admiration stand in the way of getting rid of me as a witness," Cathy said tartly, and he nodded.

"No, I'm afraid I don't, my dear. . . ."

Chapter 28

Only the intervention of Lords Bothmourne and Clarendon saved Jesse from being detained longer by Scotland Yard. It had been extremely difficult to convince Inspector Marrow of Jesse's respectable reputation, and Bothmourne had spent most of the night gathering proof of Jesse's service to the foreign ministry and his country.

"I still think it was the file on Caroline Lamont's involvement in William's death that did the trick," the duke said to Jesse as they rocked along the foggy London street in his ducal carriage. "Marrow softened only after considering how she was still a suspect in the death of her own husband."

Gazing idly out the window, lost in a mire of gloom and worry over the situation, Jesse dragged his attention back with an effort. "Perhaps," he agreed so dully that the duke lifted an inquiring brow.

"Dear me! Are we sunk in despair, Jesse? Good God, man, I got you out of there, didn't I?"

Jesse managed a smile. "Yes, you did, John, and I'm very grateful. Also very tired. I didn't sleep well in that musty cell."

"With the shadow of the hangman's noose drifting across your window?" Bothmourne mocked so pithily that Jesse had to laugh.

Rubbing at his eyes, Jesse said, "Yes, with that damnable shadow drifting across my cell window! I was damned worried that you might not be able to prove my innocence, John. After all, I *did* try to strangle Caroline earlier in the day, you know."

"Yes, I know." At Jesse's puzzled look, he explained, "Cathy told me. She was worried they would discover that fact somehow. Can't say that I blame you, of course, for I've longed to do that very thing for years, but your timing was execrable, Jesse."

"I agree," was the weary reply.

"How convenient." Bothmourne shifted on the carriage seat, his eyes piercing Jesse. "Who is your likely candidate for the murder of fair Caroline?"

Shrugging, Jesse said, "I haven't the vaguest notion."

Nodding sagely, Bothmourne frowned, his fingers tapping against his knee as he considered several possibilities. "I do," he said at last, but when pressed by Jesse to divulge his suspicion he shook his head. "No. Not now. I must have more proof, and with your latest tendency to explode into violence, I would not want you to be tested."

"I take it this is a person I know well," Jesse said mildly. He thought of Cathy, and how vehement she had been against Caroline, how she had refused to talk more of her that day. But Cathy would not commit such a crime. It was beyond her capabilities. Anger, yes, but not murder.

"Miss Weston is very much in love with you, you know," the duke said then, startling Jesse. "Perhaps after all this is over with, you might take that into consideration."

Wetting suddenly dry lips with the tip of his tongue, Jesse asked carefully, "What do you mean?"

Lord Bothmourne shrugged. "Nothing. Only that I am trying to change the subject, old boy. Ah, we are almost at your house."

* * *

Mahoney was descending the stairs with Cathy held in front of him, his hand covering her mouth to stifle any sound she might decide to make in a last attempt to alert help. The heavy ring on his hand cut into her tender lips, and blood oozed between his fingers, dripping down to stain Cathy's lace collar.

Though not struggling, Cathy just waited on the first opportunity to escape him. Her heart pounded fiercely and she could feel the adrenaline pulsing through her body in mounting spurts. She had to get free, had to warn Jesse or Bothmourne about the information Ned now held. It could cause the deaths of thousands of soldiers at Scutari if it fell into the wrong hands, and Mahoney had made it clear he intended to give it to his government. Jesse had worked for months to gather the information that would ensure the success of France and England's cooperation against the Russian czar.

Ned balanced on the second step from the bottom for a moment, holding Cathy against him. "I'm deciding on whether to exit through the french doors and garden, or to go out through the front door," he said softly.

Stiffening, Cathy prayed he would choose the front entrance. Perhaps someone would see her. Perhaps Beakins or Annie, or even Cummings the coachman would see her and sense that something was wrong.

But Ned chose to go out through the study, dragging Cathy with him. She had a moment's thought of Miss Mooney and the children upstairs taking a nap, and feared that she would very likely never see them again. Would they grieve her death? Would Jesse?

Ned stumbled over the carpet's edge in Jesse's study, and as his grip on her loosened she wrenched away from him. Fleeing across the study, she fumbled with the latch on the french doors, but, hearing Ned close behind, flung herself away. Cathy skirted Jesse's desk, wondering if she should bother to waste her breath

in a scream, seeing Ned's coldly intent face only a foot or two
away.

"I'll scream!" she spat, and he laughed.

"Go ahead. No one will hear you! I know very well how
thick these walls are, my dear. Servants belowstairs can't hear a
thing, only the bellpull." Ned's lips curled in a sneer as he
cajoled, "Come along, Cathy. It's useless to fight me, you know.
And no one will question your sudden absence. The police will
determine that the poor frightened governess must have fled the
house of a mad murderer, and will not bother to look for you."

"Miss Mooney will know. Jesse will know—"

"Ha! And who do you think will listen to Jesse? The inspector at Scotland Yard? No, I don't think so!"

Dodging Ned's sudden lunge, Cathy frantically felt on Jesse's
desktop for a letter opener, any sort of weapon to use against
him. As her fingers grazed the drawer pull she recalled
Pickworth's straightening the desk, shutting the top drawer as
she had brought him the message to take to Lord
Bothmourne. . . .

Cathy yanked open the desk drawer, and there lay the pistol
Caroline Lamont had brought to kill Jesse. Her fingers curled
around it, lifted the heavy weight, and pointed it directly at
Ned's chest.

"You may thank Pickworth and Caroline for this," she said
with a trembling note of triumph. Her hands quivered, and she
steadied them with an effort.

Ned had paused and straightened slowly, his eyes fixed on the
pistol as he mocked, "Both dead, my dear."

The pistol muzzle quivered. "What . . . what do you
mean?"

"I left your good and faithful Pickworth lying with a broken
head in a back gutter. Oh . . . and I also took the liberty of
removing your little note to Bothmourne. 'Poor Jesse . . . I

cannot bear to think of him in a cold cell,' " Ned mocked in a falsetto voice, quoting part of Cathy's words to Bothmourne.

Her lips grew taut, and she spared a moment's grief for the elderly servant who had been so ill treated. "You shall hang for your crimes against the government as well as against the innocent!" Cathy grated.

"Do you really think so?" Keeping a wary eye on the pistol, Ned made a slight movement, as if retrieving a handkerchief from his coat pocket. "No? A pity. I meant to shed a tear for my untimely demise. . . ."

With a sudden lurch he dove sideways, and the pistol fired in reflex action. Cathy hadn't known she would actually pull the trigger, and was faintly surprised to hear the loud report. As she recovered from the recoil of the heavy weapon, Ned lunged for her, his long arm whipping out to knock the pistol from her hands. It skittered across the carpet.

Both leaped for it at the same time, and only Cathy's grim determination kept Ned from reaching the weapon. He half turned, snarling at her to let go of his coat, but she hung on. Her fingers raked at Ned's arms, tore at his face, and left long, bloody scratches, but he shook her off, throwing her to the floor. His fist slammed against her head in a dazing blow, and the world spun in a kaleidoscope of light and shadow. Cathy blinked, trying to focus her eyes, vaguely aware that she was hanging on to consciousness by a slender thread.

A sob tore from Cathy's throat as Ned reached the pistol and turned around, bringing it up to level the cold muzzle directly at her. She lay on the floor, held up by one arm, her other arm crossing in front of her face in a futile effort to protect herself.

"Stupid doxy!" he snarled at her. "You've almost ruined it all! Now I must shoot you and leave your body here, and that is certain to raise more questions. Too bad your precious Jesse isn't here to take the blame for this, too."

But as he slowly thumbed back the hammer on the shiny

revolver a soft voice came from the doorway, "But he *is* here, Mahoney. . . ."

Then things happened so quickly that Cathy could never quite recall the sequence of events afterward. Mahoney pivoted, the pistol aiming for Jesse in the open door, a shot, and then a scream, followed by pandemonium in the house.

Servants appeared from everywhere, screaming, bellowing orders, and Cathy fainted.

"Shh! She's coming around now. . . ."

"There's blood on her face—is she—"

"No, only a cut or two. She's fine."

The voices drifted in and out of her head like whispers of wind, and Cathy finally lifted her heavy eyelids to gaze up. She saw Miss Mooney's anxious face, Lord Bothmourne's, and—most dear to her—Jesse's.

"You . . . you're not shot?" she whispered.

Smiling, he shook his head. "No, not even scratched like you are, thanks to Johnny."

"Johnny?"

Grinning, Bothmourne said, "I've been known to be a fair shot with a pistol, and just happened to have my little dueling pistol in my coat pocket. A habit of mine, lately, since all these *deaths*."

"And . . . and Ned?" Cathy murmured, half afraid to hear the reply.

Jesse's mouth slanted in a grimace. "Dead. John's an *excellent* shot, not fair."

"Oh." Cathy swallowed. Then she said faintly, "Ned was right."

"About what?" Jesse asked.

"Death does come in threes, it seems."

Jesse's grip on her hand tightened briefly, and, wincing at the throb in her head, Cathy tried to sit up. She realized she was still lying on the floor, though someone had put a pillow under her head and covered her with a light blanket.

Sniffing, Miss Mooney observed, "It seems that she will live after all. I shall go back upstairs to tell the girls that all is quiet down here. They are hiding in a cupboard and waiting for my return."

"Poor things," Cathy murmured as Jesse's arm curled behind her shoulders and held her upright. "I should go to them."

"No. Not now," Jesse said firmly. "Later, perhaps. Right now I intend to have Pickworth see that your room is made ready for you."

At the mention of Pickworth, Cathy recalled Ned's cruel explanation of his death. "He . . . he's dead, Jesse!"

Starting, Jesse stared down at her. "Dead?" he echoed.

She nodded, and hot tears began to flow. "Yes. Ned told me. He said he left him with a broken head in some alley or some such horrible thing."

"Well, bless me, but he tried!" a thin voice snapped irritably, and, half turning to see who spoke, Cathy recognized the elderly servant's bandaged face.

"Pickworth!"

"My old head is much harder than that snake gave me credit for," Pickworth said, adding, "I'm sorry for not delivering the note as you told me, Miss Cathy."

"That . . . that's quite all right, Pickworth," Cathy said with a faint gasp of amusement. The humor of the situation struck her then—that the old man would be concerned about not having completed his duty after having his skull almost bashed in—and she began to smile.

Suddenly, in spite of the horror of the past days, the torment and uncertainty that had haunted her, Cathy began to laugh—quietly at first, then with more energy. After a moment of startled silence in which everyone regarded her as if she had gone mad, the others joined in. Jesse's study rocked with gales of relieved laughter, and the servants, the duke, and Miss Mooney laughed the hardest of all.

It was while the others were all laughing in relief that Jesse and Cathy stole away for a few moments of privacy. Shuddering at the sight of Ned's blanket-covered body lying on the study floor, Cathy turned away.

"It's all right, love," Jesse murmured against her hair.

She drew back to look up at him. "Is it, Jesse? Is it all right?"

"More than you know," he vowed then, a smile curving the sensual line of his mouth. They were in the hall just outside the dining room, with the door to the servants' stairs behind them. Jesse pulled her into his arms, his fingers lightly grazing her bruises. Then his lips kissed each tiny mark. "I wish it had been I who had killed him for this," he said quietly, and Cathy shivered at his calm ferocity.

"It's enough that he's dead," she replied.

"Cathy—"

"Yes?"

"I love you."

The three soft words reverberated in her head for several heartbeats, until she realized that Jesse had gone stiff and must think she did not care.

"Oh, my darling! I love you, too! Oh, Jesse!"

His tensed muscles slowly relaxed, and then he was lifting her in his arms and swinging her around, throwing back his head and grinning his love and happiness. Then, setting her back on her feet with tender care, Jesse folded her in his embrace and kissed her with all his stored-up love and humility and tenderness.

It was a searing kiss, a deep kiss filled with his pain as well as his happiness, and Cathy responded with her whole heart. She clung to him with her arms around his neck, her eyes closed, oblivious to the world around them.

"Ahem!" came the insistent voice for the third time, finally penetrating the love haze surrounding Jesse and Cathy. Blinking in surprise, the lovers parted to see Miss Mooney standing in the doorway to the servants' stairs, her hands resting on her hips and her mouth pursed in a tight bud. "Well! If you two are going to do that sort of scandalous thing, you might as well get married!" she snapped.

"Miss Mooney," Jesse said with a grin, "that is exactly what we intend to do as soon as decently possible!"

Epilogue

Monday, April 16, 1855

*E*mperor Napoleon III and Empress Eugénie landed at Dover,
and were received by England's Prince Albert and escorted
to London. As the royal carriage drove though St. James's
Street, the emperor pointed out to his empress the small house in
King Street where he had lived during his poverty-stricken years
in exile.

When they arrived at Windsor Castle, Queen Victoria received them at the grand entrance while bands played the famous song written by Napoleon III's mother and adopted by the
French army as its national anthem.

Dinner was taken in the magnificent St. George's Hall, and
the conversation naturally turned to war. As the emperor related
to the queen the innumerable attempts that had been made to
assassinate him, the would-be murderers coming from England
across the Channel in droves, the queen made a gesture.

"We have here with us tonight," she began, "a couple who
have been instrumental in alleviating some of this problem at
great personal risk."

Across the room a page leaned forward to whisper into a
man's ear, and he slowly stood, his companion rising with him.

"May I introduce to the company Jesse Lamont and his lovely
bride, Catherine Weston Lamont," was the announcement, and
the room grew still and quiet.

With trembling legs, Cathy walked beside Jesse to approach the dais where Queen Victoria sat with Napoleon III. She dipped in a deep curtsy, recalling the endless instructions she had been given on court protocol. Somehow, in a daze, she heard the queen commending her and Jesse for halting what had turned out to be a massive conspiracy that would have seriously injured the war effort. Mahoney had been only one tentacle of a gigantic octopus of treachery and intrigue that included the severing of the cable that stretched across the Channel between England and France. Jesse had gathered the necessary data that would be used, giving times and places, and had managed to preserve it until it could be put into the proper hands.

"And how long have you been married, Mrs. Lamont?" the queen was asking politely, and Cathy gave a start of panic.

Clearing her throat, she rose from her curtsy and said, "Six weeks, Your Highness."

"Six weeks?" Queen Victoria gave a chuckle. "I've been married to my husband for fifteen years, my dear. I find it a state most delightful."

Cathy smiled shyly. "I am certain that I will also do so for the next fifteen years, Your Highness."

Fixing Jesse with a stern eye, the queen said, "See that your wife can say the same thing after fifteen years of marriage, Mr. Lamont!"

Bowing, Jesse said that he fully intended to do so. "And as long as we live," he added.

Cathy met his gaze with such adoring eyes that the rest of the evening paled by comparison.

Much, much later, alone in their wide bed, after Miss Mooney and the girls had heard for the final time the most minute details about their evening at court—during which time Jesse had been knighted for his supreme efforts—they relaxed in each other's arms.

"Happy?" Jesse murmured against Cathy's hair, letting his lips trail from her smooth brow to her soft mouth.

"Ecstatic," Cathy replied with a luxuriant sigh. "Should I call you 'Sir Husband' now?"

" 'Your Grace' would be nice," Jesse reflected with mock gravity, and Cathy rolled atop him to put her hands on each side of his face.

"How about," she began, kissing his eyebrows, his nose, his jawline, his ears, "calling you simply Sir Jesse?"

"That has a nice ring to it," he said huskily as she slid lower in the bed and began kissing the taut ridges of muscle banding his chest and stomach.

"Or," Cathy said against his flat stomach, "I could call you *love.*"

"Yes!" Jesse answered with a gasp, his hands tangling in her hair. "That is the most coveted title of all, my darling wife!"

And when he rolled over with her beneath him, his breath tangling in her dark hair and his eyes shining with his love, Cathy thought that only the knowledge of the new life growing in her could make either of them any happier. She had been blessed indeed, and none of the past sorrows could touch them now. Her world began and ended with Jesse.